SPARTANICA

Powers Molinar

To Barbara, Nathaniel, and Christine

They are the sun in my sky
and my inspiration every single day

Table of Contents

THE SURVIVORS OF SAPERTYS

BOOK ONE

SPARTANICA

Powers Molinar

ACKNOWLEDGEMENTS

Special thanks to my dedicated beta readers:

Barbara of the Order of Massa
Nathaniel of the Order of Massa
Christophe of the Order of Guiard
Brenda of the Order of Wilhelmson
Thomas of the Order of Guiard
Tobias of the Order of Cruz
Everett of the Order of Mitchell
Kelly of the Order of Brogdon

Their time and contributions to *Spartanica* were invaluable and greatly appreciated.

ONE

SURE, I'VE HAD
FREAKY DREAMS BEFORE

(TY)

My digital alarm clock insists it's 1:13 a.m. Seriously? How can it possibly be only 1:13 a.m.?

My name is Ty Mitchell, and I just had the longest, most vivid dream of my life and, according to the red digits glaring at me through the hushed darkness of my room, it lasted approximately five minutes. Don't get me wrong. I'm ecstatic it's over. I don't know how much more I could've taken. My heart's already beating at light speed (that's roughly 670,616,629 miles per hour), and my hands are shaking even more than when I got my whooping cough booster last month at the doctor's office. I utterly despise getting shots.

I mean, sure, I've had freaky dreams before. And I'm talking truly bizarre, like the one where our pet goldfish were sitting at the kitchen table, dealing cards, smoking cigars, and playing Go People. Or when I was on that out-of-control rollercoaster, doing loops and switchbacks and corkscrews while sitting next to this girl from my seventh-grade class, Emma Denzelton. I was screaming my head off, positive we

1

were about to fly off the tracks, when she very calmly tapped me on the shoulder and asked me to pass the butter. Why, you may ask, would I have butter on a rollercoaster? Beats me, but I did, and I passed it to her. So, anyway, I've had freaky dreams before, but I've always kind of known it was a dream, even while I was in it.

This one was different. It felt real. I totally thought I was really on this other world doing stuff. My brother, Marcus, was in it, and I have never once dreamed about him before. He's annoying enough during the day. I definitely don't need him in my head at night. Still, it wasn't just Marcus. There were the Atlantean kids and the Desrata. All that stuff.

But, gosh, come on. It had to be a dream. How else could I just end up back in bed five minutes after everything supposedly started . . . unless Professor Otherblood's hypotheses about using majinecity to curl time weren't really so crazy after all?

Desrata? Majinecity? Professor Otherblood? Confused yet? I am. You have no reason to believe me, but I'm really not a lunatic (at least I didn't used to be). Maybe, if I think through it all, something coherent will pop out. I'm usually very logical and calm (well, logical, at least), so hang with me.

Why, you may ask, would I remember exactly 1:08 a.m. as the time my dream started? First of all, I never wake up before 6:50 a.m. on a school day. Actually, I never wake up after 6:50 a.m., either. Ever since I was a kid, I've just told myself to wake up at exactly 6:50 a.m., and I have. That gives me just enough time to get ready to catch the school bus. So for me to wake up at any other time is just, quite honestly, peculiar. But there was this humming sound. That must be what woke me up. That, or the stench from the dirty socks Marcus left on the floor again. Imagine a lethal combination of toxic waste and two-day-old dead skunk. Got it yet? Marcus' socks are worse. Much worse.

So my clock read 1:08 a.m. when this humming noise woke me. I tried to ignore it and go back to sleep but it kept getting louder, so I climbed down from my loft bed to see where it was coming from. I stepped out of my room into the hallway, totally expecting to see Marcus and our Aunt Andi wondering about the same thing, but I was alone. I tiptoed slowly across the hallway and through the shadows, toward the nightlight at the top of the stairs. I should've gone back to bed right then. Maybe this whole strange episode never would've happened. Instead, I grabbed the handrail and gradually navigated down each step, peering into the darkness below for any hint of what might be waiting.

Near the bottom of the staircase, pictures on the walls started rattling as the noise generated a rumble strong enough for me to feel in my feet through the floor. Desperately yearning to stay close to my escape route back upstairs, I felt along the wall with my right hand through the kitchen entrance. I hooked my wrist around the corner as far as it would go and strained to flick the light switch on, but nothing happened. I tried it several more times in rapid succession but got zilch. The nightlight upstairs was still on, so I knew we had power. Why wouldn't the kitchen lights be working?

The hum gradually worked its way up into a ruckus loud enough to make my head hurt. I covered my ears with my hands, craned my neck over to the doorway, and peeked in, expecting more pitch black confusion but, instead, saw a rainbow of colors flitting across the hardwood floor from the left onto the refrigerator and cabinets on the other side of the room. A kaleidoscope of light beams was pulsating from under the basement door next to the oven.

Just when I thought my skull was going to split because of the ever-growing clamor, it stopped. Except for the ringing in my head, I was standing in perfect silence. Anyone with undamaged hearing, unlike me, probably could have heard a pin drop. The light show, to my amazement, continued to blaze and pulled me toward it like a magnet. I had to see what was doing this.

Opening the basement door, I was immediately engulfed in a blanket of bright colors that filled the room, forcing me to shield my eyes. Squinting just enough to see in front of me, I carefully lowered myself onto my stomach and slithered down the stairs far enough to see below the basement ceiling. The entire room was bathed in countless different-colored light beams, like thick, circular laser searchlights, swirling out of the "A" room door. The "A" room is where Aunt Andi stores and studies "A"rtifacts from her job. She's head archaeologist at the Sabrina Turner Institute for Civilization Studies in Chicago and brings home all kinds of ancient stuff to research.

I swung my legs around and slowly plodded down the stairs, still shielding my eyes but astonished by what I saw coming from the "A" room. As I cautiously stepped onto the basement floor, the light show stopped. All of it. All at once. Instantly, I was standing in our totally dark, totally silent basement, essentially blind and deaf, hoping to recover from the overwhelming sensory onslaught. That's when one of my worst fears ripped through me like a lightning bolt. I realized I was all alone, in the dark, in the basement. Have you ever been in your basement all by yourself when it's totally dark? It's like you're not even in your own house anymore and some psycho is lurking in the shadows, just waiting to kill you. I know there's no reason why anyone would be hiding in my basement, but, disoriented in the infinite darkness, the mere thought was utterly terrifying.

Finally summoning the courage to move, I used my hands and feet to shakily find the stairs again when the basement lights turned on. Yes! The motion detector switch must have seen me move! Sanity was returning to my world!

My overriding instinct was to double-time it up the stairs, but my outright curiosity demanded I at least peek around the corner into the "A" room, so I guardedly slinked over and inched my eyes along the wall until I could see in. Everything inside looked normal, so I walked in and saw a dozen or more roughly two-foot by two-foot copper-looking blocks hanging side-by-side in a single line on the walls around the room at eye level. They looked like big, rectangular pennies but were so shiny it was like they were glowing. Each block had inscriptions engraved all over, but the writing was oddly different from anything I remember Aunt Andi studying down here before. I reached out to touch one but yanked back suddenly because it was so cold. I don't mean cold like metal. It was cold like it had just come out of a freezer. I moved along the wall toward the back of the room, holding my hand an inch or so in front of each block along the way. They were all like giant ice cubes, yet I couldn't feel anything unless I was almost touching them.

"What are you doing?" I unexpectedly heard from behind.

Somebody screamed like a chicken. I realized it was me as I spun clumsily to find my brother in the "A" room doorway.

"Whoa!" he exclaimed, laughing so hard he could barely talk. "Sorry about that, little sister! I haven't heard such a manly scream down here since your birthday party!"

Marcus was referring to my thirteenth birthday party last month when a bunch of friends slept over in the basement. It was an awesome bash, but, somehow, our pet tarantula, Peter Parker, got out of its cage and crawled into a sleeping bag belonging to a neighbor kid, Joey Joe Slatter. When Joey Joe opened it to climb in, Peter Parker vaulted out and landed right on his leg. Joey Joe froze for a second, petrified by what he was looking at, shrieked at the top of his lungs, and ran upstairs. It took a while to get Peter back into his cage, but when Joey Joe finally came back down, the front of his pajamas were soaking wet. He tried to say it was because he spilled his root beer. Nobody bought it.

I quickly checked to make sure the front of my pajamas weren't wet before yelling back, "You are such a jerk. What are you doing here?"

"What am I doing here?" Marcus asked.

His face was red from laughing but he was finally settling down.

"I came to the kitchen for a drink of water and saw the light on," he said. "Why are you skulking around the basement in the middle of the night?"

"I'm not skulking," I insisted, still wigged out. "The humming noise. Are you telling me you didn't hear that incredibly loud humming noise? Stuff was rattling. The floor was vibrating. It was like a UFO abduction."

"No," Marcus snorted sarcastically. "No rattling. No vibrating. No UFOs. No little green men. I knew you'd snap one day. You've always been wound a little too tight."

"I didn't say I saw a UFO," I snapped back. "Can you listen for just once? I said things were rattling and vibrating like in a UFO movie. Seriously, you didn't hear anything?"

I was desperate for Marcus to corroborate at least some small part of the whole creepy episode. He finally got a clue and realized I was dead serious about the whole thing.

"I didn't hear any noise, dude," he said. "I'm going back to bed."

Just as he turned to leave, the hum started again. It was much softer but definitely the same sound as before. Marcus started to say something, but I raised my left hand to stop him.

"Wait!" I whispered. "Shh. Listen."

I hadn't noticed before, but in the center of the room a solid black, perfectly smooth and shiny crystal orb about the size of a large cantaloupe was sitting at waist level on a small, ornate wooden stand with four round legs. It was obviously the source of the hum, which was getting louder again with each passing second.

"Why is that bowling ball making noise?" Marcus asked, his eyes fixated on it.

"See!" I blurted, terrified out of my wits but ecstatic Marcus knew I wasn't losing my mind. "It was a million times louder before! We better go wake up Aunt Andi."

As the volume ramped back up, the orb's color gradually morphed to maroon, then red, and finally a brilliantly bright, pulsing crimson. In the blink of an eye, the array of light beams I'd seen before shot out from the orb and filled the room. The intensity bothered my eyes, but I squinted to see orange, blue, green, yellow, and red rays swirling everywhere like a multi-faceted spotlight saturating the room. As the hum once again reached an ear-blistering volume, the beams gradually blended until all the colors faded into a very bright white light that consumed everything. I buried my eyes in the creases of my elbows but peeked out a few seconds later to see nothing. Literally zippo! No orb. No table. No "A" room. No Marcus. No me! I could feel my fingers wiggling in front of my face but couldn't see them. There was nothing but raw emptiness.

"Marcus?" I yelled, hopelessly trying to be heard over the now rampaging scream that, I assumed, was still blaring from the orb. "MARCUS?" I hollered louder, this time unable to even hear myself!

Instantly, without so much a hint it would do so, the hum stopped, leaving nothing but unbridled silence in its wake. I called to Marcus again but still couldn't even hear my own voice. I could feel my mouth open and air rush past my vocal cords, but no sound came out. Powerless to communicate or do anything to understand what was going on around me, I just stood terrified and motionless in my own personal void, imagining this must be what birds experience when they fly through the middle of a big cloud. No sensation. No sound. Nothing. The hair on the back of my neck stood straight up and a chill shuddered through my soul as it dawned on me that I'd either been magically transformed into a red-bellied woodpecker, or I was dead.

TWO

THE ~~END~~ BEGINNING OF A
REALLY STRANGE DREAM
(MARCUS)

If my little brother, Ty, is anything, he's predictable. He always has an answer (not that he's always right) and will gladly be the first to explain how anything works, even when he's just heard of it for the first time. Our Aunt Andi says he's our "instant authority" on everything.

Don't get me wrong. Ty is really smart. Book smart, that is. He'll gladly recite the first two hundred digits of pi and explain how gravity works better than any teacher. But he can get on people's nerves (including mine), usually without realizing it.

Finding him staring at the wall in the "A" room all by himself in the middle of the night was totally not right. I should've known right away something was sideways because he was awake and it wasn't exactly 6:50 a.m. He's so proud because he doesn't use an alarm clock. Big deal. Everyone uses an alarm clock. If using an alarm clock wasn't normal, they wouldn't have been invented. Am I right?

But finding Ty was only the beginning. A really bright light shot out of this bowling ball in the "A" room, forcing me to cover my eyes. I opened them back up after a bit to find I was in total whiteness. It's like total darkness except everything's, well, I think you get it. It was beyond freaky. I couldn't even see myself! I started wondering whether it was real. After all, something that weird had to be a dream.

After straining my eyes forever to see anything other than nothing, I spotted what, at first, looked like a tiny dot a million miles away. I wasn't truly sure it was there until another, bigger dot appeared next to it. Then another, and another. Then a bunch more popped up one at a time and meshed together until the white was completely replaced by alternating shades of dark gray and black. Now I was sure it was a dream. After all, everything goes dark just before you wake up, right? And if it was just a dream, I'd be back in my bed, safe and sound, in just a few seconds. I kicked back to let the insanity of the past few minutes float away. As I stretched out my arms to get comfortable, my right fist hit something.

"Ow!" someone yelped.

"Ahhhh!" I screamed and jumped back, turning to see a pained expression on Ty's face staring back at me through the dimly lit shadows, his hand rubbing his side where I'd hit him.

"What was that for?" he blurted angrily.

"Ty?" I yelled as my heart jumped into my throat. "What are you doing in my dream?"

He ignored me, completely distracted as he tried to squint his way through the obscurity to find some clue as to where we were.

Something or someone suddenly jerked my left arm with so much force that I slid backward across the floor and through the air until my left hand smacked into a wall, trailed shortly and painfully by the rest of my body. I was hanging off the ground by my left wrist. Behind me, a thud, followed immediately by a not-so-manly whimper, confirmed the same fate had befallen Ty.

"Ow!" he blustered frantically. "My wrist!"

He fidgeted like a freshly caught bluegill at the end of a fishing pole.

"Oh, what the heck is going on?" he cried out. "Marcus, where are you?"

"I'm right here," I answered, trying to work myself free.

"Can you touch the ground?" he asked.

"No!" I replied, gritting my teeth and putting everything into trying to break free from my bondage. "I'm stuck, too! What's keeping us up here?"

"I don't know," Ty continued, getting more panicky with every word, "but I can't even see the ground! Ow, my watchband is digging into my skin! I think I'm bleeding!"

He suddenly gasped and stopped flailing.

"Dude, what if we're suspended over a bottomless pit?" Ty said. "If we break free, our bodies will fall into infinite nothingness forever."

His voice quivered in fear, but that wasn't really unusual.

A nervous laugh tried to work its way into my throat until I looked down. Ty was right. We could see exactly nothing beneath us. All we really knew was that we were both hanging off the ground with one arm each pinned over our heads against a wall. Now my only interest was to stay perfectly still so my own watchband wouldn't break. Not that I believed in Ty's bottomless pit theory, but . . . it's not like his overactive imagination is wrong every time.

"Okay," I tried to say in a very measured way, not moving a single muscle other than to speak. "So maybe we should stay real still and just hang here until we know what's under us."

"Uh, yeah," Ty replied, mimicking my delivery. "Real still."

So there we were. The Mitchell brothers, each of us hanging by the wrist in total silence, neither one wanting to push our luck and fall into the bottomless pit, if it was actually there. I kept expecting my eyes to adjust more to the darkness but could still only see dimly lit outlines. Then, in the distance, I thought I saw a miniscule light blink a few times. Staying perfectly still, I focused my eyes on the exact spot where I saw it and waited to see if it would happen again.

"Marcus," Ty whispered, trying to talk without moving his lips.

"Shh," I shot back quietly.

"No, Marcus, I really . . . ." Ty persisted.

"Shh," I repeated.

"Don't shush me!" he chastened with an annoyed tone, still trying not to move his lips, like doing so would trigger his arm to release. "I really, really, really . . . ."

"Shut up, Ty!" I whispered. "I think something moved over there."

Now I was doing the lip thing, too. The flashing light reappeared, but much closer this time, and it looked like there was more than one.

"Dude," I whispered, "I think something is over there, and it's moving this way."

Ty stiffened like a statue.

"But, but, but I don't see anything," he stammered, trying to convince himself nothing was there.

We hung in silence, hopeful the space around us would remain undisturbed, for what felt like an hour. I didn't see any more lights, and the only thing I could hear the whole time was my pulse pounding like a jackhammer in both ears.

Finally, convinced the threat, real or imaginary, had passed, I took a slow, deep breath and said, "Okay, I don't think anything's—"

Without warning, something big moved through the shadows directly in front of us, maybe twenty feet away. The sound of footsteps and a dozen or more of the tiny lights I'd seen before slowly advanced toward us. I barely made out the silhouette of a human head and shoulders through the dimness. Someone was coming at us and all we could do was dangle helplessly.

The commotion stopped and a woman's voice gently said, "Initiating scan."

A single, thin, blue laser beam shot up from where the woman was standing and stopped at the ceiling where it fanned out, in blinding fashion, three-hundred-sixty degrees and engulfed everything in front of us. Shielding my face with my right hand, I turned my head and, through the narrowest possible slit in my right eyelid, saw Ty hanging by his left wrist, also sheltering his vision.

The blue light vanished, leaving us in total silence and darkness again, right up until the woman's voice said, "Intruders detected. Weapons armed and locked on."

THREE

REMOTE SENTRY 113
(TY)

"Wait!" I screamed. "Don't shoot! Marcus, she's going to kill us!"

Again, she said, "Weapons armed and locked on."

"Aaaaah!" I shrieked, turning my head and covering as much of my face as possible with my free arm. "Please don't kill us!"

"Identify," she commanded.

Marcus and I looked at each other through the shadows, turned back at the thing, and both said, "What?"

"Identify," she repeated.

"Uh," my brother said hesitantly, sounding challenged to catch his breath, "I'm Marcus. This is Ty."

"Identification failure," she responded. "Weapons armed and locked on. Hands down."

"What?" we both said again, the hysteria in our voices reaching peak levels.

"Secondary identification measures are required," she said. "Failure to remove facial obstructions will result in severe negative personal consequences."

"Marcus, don't cover your face," I said, putting my arm down, hoping to keep us alive through sheer submissive obedience. "I think she wants to scan us again."

I barely finished my sentence before a blazing red light shot right into my eyes. Even jamming my eyelids shut did little to shield the intensity. "Ahh, it's so bright!" I protested. "My eyes! I'm going blind!"

After an eternity, the fireball finally turned off, enshrouding us in dark shadows again.

"Identification confirmed," the woman said.

"I can't, I can't see anything," I shrieked. "I'm blind! I'm blind!"

"You're not blind," Marcus implored. "Our eyes just need to adjust. Settle down!"

Although I couldn't see, it sounded like the woman turned and was leaving. Good riddance of a bad nightmare, if you ask me!

"Wait!" Marcus hollered. She stopped moving.

"What are you doing?" I blurted exasperatedly. "Do you want her to come back and arm weapons again?"

"Can you get us down?" Marcus asked.

"Yes," she replied.

"Oh, uh, okay," a surprised Marcus sputtered. "Then, uh, get us down."

She turned back around and came toward us until she was only a few feet away. A warm blue glow emanated from where she stood, accompanied by the sound of something charging up.

"Are you happy?" I shrieked. "She's arming weapons again! She's going to kill us!"

A pencil-thin blue line shot over my head, instantly freeing my arm. My body and mind were immediately overcome by a devastating sensation of endless descent. I screamed a scream as unending as the infinity into which I was tumbling. I had been freed from my vertical prison only to plummet into a vast pit of death, never to be seen again!

15

"Turn on the lights," I barely heard Marcus yell from far above as I hurtled into the abyss.

The woman said something in response, but she was too far away by now to be audible.

"You can stop yelling now!" Marcus screeched.

I did so, and as my eyes adjusted, it became painfully obvious I wasn't plunging to my death at the planet's core. I was, in fact, lying on the ground, in the fetal position, with Marcus four to five feet away, staring down at me, still hanging on the wall by his left wrist.

Overwhelmed by the need to explain, I said, "Well, it *felt* like I was falling. And you even said, you even said there could be a pit!"

He just kept looking down at me with that *you're such a schmo* look. I hate that look. He wouldn't have thought I was a schmo if there really was a pit there.

I quickly realized it would be pointless to try to defend myself, so I ignored the whole situation and sat up to get a better look around. We were in a large, dark, cave-like space, except that the floors were very shiny and smooth, like they were installed over the natural rock to create a flat surface. My watch was still stuck to the cave wall above and behind me with each half of the metal band completely flattened up against the wall. I didn't see any actual lights, yet a bright glow from all around us lit the room, which didn't make sense because the cave itself and the floor were both pitch black.

Marcus looked up at the woman and warily asked, "Can you please get me down, too?"

"By your command," she replied and turned toward him.

She was easily six feet tall and built like a human, which she obviously was not. While her voice was like a lady's, nothing else about her was feminine, most noticeably her completely bald head. She wore a black t-shirt and pants but no shoes. Her skin was smooth and light gray and her eyes had a haunting green glow around the edges. She reminded me more of an animated mannequin than a real person. Her lips moved very convincingly when she spoke, and she blinked her eyes often enough for me to notice, but the rest of her face was completely expressionless. It was like somebody tried to build a human replica but didn't quite finish the job.

She extended her right arm and pointed above Marcus' head. The same blue laser that had cut me down shot out from her index finger and neatly etched a path through his watchband, dropping him to the ground where he fell onto his right side, winced, and rubbed his wrist. Both halves of his severed watchband immediately flattened up against the wall, as mine had. The laser turned off and the woman gracefully moved her hand down to her side, her gaze still fixed on Marcus.

"Amazing," I uttered, stunned by a paralyzing combination of awe and extreme fear. "Marcus, who is she? What is she?"

"I don't know," he replied, gingerly rolling into a crouched position. "Maybe we should ask her, if you're done falling to the center of the Earth."

"Oh, shut up," I complained but got interrupted.

"I am Remote Sentry 113, assigned to perimeter defense," the woman announced.

I started relaxing a little. This thing actually had a name and didn't seem like she was there to kill us or take us prisoner.

While Marcus sat there, obviously terrified, I dug deep into my courage (which I always did . . . well, mostly) and asked, "What is this place? Where are we?"

"Insufficient authorization," the sentry responded.

Marcus and I looked at each other, puzzled.

"We're not authorized to know where we are?" I said.

17

"Insufficient authorization," the sentry reiterated.

"Okay," I said, "well, we're from Newkastel, Illinois, near Chicago. Can you help us get back there?"

"Location Newkastel, Illinois, not recognized," the sentry responded.

"Maybe, since it's some kind of security robot, it only knows about the inside of this place," Marcus guessed, shrugging his shoulders. "Let's have a look around."

Marcus stood up for the first time since being cut off the wall.

"Insufficient authorization," the sentry said. "Unauthorized movement within the complex is strictly prohibited during system lock."

"We can't look around?" I asked, confused by what she'd just said. "Are we supposed to just sit here forever?"

The sentry turned, tilted her head down, locked her creepy emerald gaze directly onto me, and said, "Unauthorized movement is strictly prohibited while the complex is in system lock. You may stay where you are or be escorted out."

"Okay," I answered very quickly and compliantly, my eyes wide open and my feet pushing me back against the wall as far as I could go.

Even though she sounded calm, she was seriously intimidating when she looked right at me. I just hoped she wouldn't come any closer.

"Where will we be if you take us out?" Marcus asked, prompting the sentry to finally look away from me toward him.

"You will be outside the complex," she replied.

"Uh, yeah, I could have figured that out for myself," Marcus continued with a slightly exasperated tone, his voice echoing into the surrounding spaces. "I mean where will we be? What is the nearest city? We are not from here. Can you please help us? Where can we go once we're outside the complex?"

The sentry took two quick steps toward him. Marcus flinched a little and swallowed hard, unsure whether the sentry was going to stop, which it did.

"You are leaving now," the sentry commanded and turned away. "Follow me."

"But where are we going?" I pleaded.

"Out," she insisted. "You will follow me. Now."

FOUR

OUTSIDE THE COMPLEX
(MARCUS)

I totally thought the sentry was going to rip my head off when she started walking towards me. But give me a break! We just wanted to know where we were, and all it could say was *Out*. Now we were walking behind this thing on our way to being booted into the street, or wherever. The room we were in was a lot larger than I first thought. As we moved across it, the lights behind us turned off just as more in front of us turned on. The newly visible part of the room was similar to where we'd just been except there were eight flat, red, rectangular panels, each about the size and thickness of a kitchen table, arranged in the shape of an octagon and hovering in the air around ten feet off the floor in the far left corner. I couldn't tell what was keeping them aloft, but, hanging there like that, they formed the outline of an oversized stop sign. Ty stared at it, too, until the lights went off as the sentry led us through a door out of the room.

Before the lights in front of us came on, Ty asked, "What were those big red floating panels?"

The lighting in front of us lit up and exposed a hallway, the walls of which were lined on both sides as far as we could see with more sentries identical to the one we were following. They stood perfectly erect, shoulder to shoulder, with their eyes closed and their arms at their sides. I gasped and jumped back, startled by their sudden presence. Ty screamed at the top of his lungs and turned to run. He instantly tripped over himself and landed at the feet of a couple hibernating sentries, both of which opened their eyes, bent over at the waist until their faces were only inches from Ty's, and simultaneously said, "Insufficient authorization."

Ty screamed again, rolled to the center of the hallway, and tried to stand up when Sentry 113 reached around and grabbed the front of his shirt near the collar, effortlessly lifted him off the ground, and continued walking in the direction she was originally taking us.

"You are leaving now," she said, still in a very measured, seemingly friendly tone. "Follow me."

The two sentries Ty had awoken straightened back up and closed their eyes. Not wanting to be left alone with this freak show, I hustled to keep up with 113, who was still suspending a flailing Ty off the floor in front of her while she walked.

"Let me down!" Ty demanded, squirming furiously, trying to loosen her grip.

"Do you agree to follow me under your own power?" the sentry asked without stopping.

"Yes, yes!" Ty replied. "Just put me down!"

The sentry stopped, softly lowered Ty to the floor, and said, "Follow me."

Instead of obeying, Ty turned to me and started to say something, but I put my finger to my lips to keep him quiet until we could get out of there. The sentry was obviously very strong, could shoot a blue laser out of her finger, and had lots of reinforcements if she wanted them. Making her angry wasn't going to help our situation.

We continued through a half dozen or more sections of alternately lit hallways, all of which were wallpapered with friends and family of 113. She stopped after a few minutes, and all the lights went out.

"Well, what are we—" Ty started to ask when a bright white light flashed in front of us. A cluster of large, overlapping two-dimensional rectangles materialized and hovered a few feet over our heads twenty or so feet in front of us.

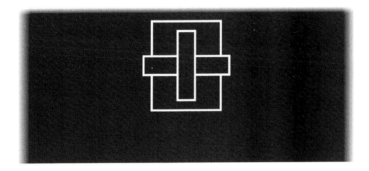

The floor immediately started trembling as the big rectangle in back slowly dropped down until its bottom was level with the floor, where it came to rest. The rumbling stopped as echoes faded into the vastness behind us.

"You will exit here," the sentry said.

The rectangles were still visible, but now there was a muted glow, only marginally brighter than the darkness around us, through a newly formed opening at the bottom.

"Repeat," the sentry emphasized. "You will exit here."

Neither Ty nor I moved. A few seconds later, it sounded like the sentry was walking away, her footsteps waning into the distance.

"Is she leaving?" Ty asked. "Hey, you can't just leave us here!"

Ty took off running after the sentry. A loud and painful-sounding *WHACK!* immediately rippled through the space we were in, followed by the collapse of something to the floor.

"Owwwww!" Ty howled through the darkness. "That wall wasn't there before! Ugh, I think I broke my nose! Oh, no, I'm bleeding again!"

I shuffled my feet slowly toward the sound of his fidgeting until my knee bumped into him, causing me to stumble to his other side.

"Ow!" he hollered again. "What are you doing? Don't kick me!"

"Jeez, I'm sorry!" I exclaimed, turning back and kneeling down next to him. "Just relax! I couldn't exactly see you."

I reached back and felt, at arm's length, the wall he must have run into.

"Can you stand up?" I asked.

"No!" he dramatized. "I think the upper lateral cartilage detached from the nasal bone. I'll never breathe correctly again. This is how sleep apnea starts! I need to see a doctor!"

"Oh, okay, fine," I said sarcastically. "Then let's just sit here in the dark forever until your nose heals."

Sometimes Ty's need to make a spectacle out of everything gets on my nerves, like right then. He started to say something when a sudden bump from behind knocked me on top of him again.

"Ugh, what is your problem?" Ty protested. "Get off of me, you clumsy dork!"

"Wait!" I insisted, clambering back onto my knees. "Something pushed me! What the heck?"

I reached and felt the wall I had felt before, but instead of being arm's length away, it was right next to us and moving closer!

"Dude, get up!" I said, shuffling myself backward. "The wall is coming! Get up!"

"The wall is what?" Ty responded. "Ow! What the heck?"

Ty had obviously discovered what I already knew and quickly slid himself along the floor until he ran into my shins.

"That wall is moving!" he said incredulously. "How can the wall move?"

I looked back and saw the new opening directly behind us.

"Wow!" I said. "The sentry really wants us out of here. The wall is pushing us right toward that opening."

"I'm not going out there!" Ty insisted. "Hey, let's stand off to the sides and see if it'll go around us. You go that way."

He stood up and pushed me to my right. We both probed around in the darkness.

"No good," I said. "There's nowhere to go."

I kept feeling around for a path, a door, a crevice, anything, any little spot to avoid the unstoppable, silent flat steamroller from nowhere.

"We have to go out the opening, Ty," I said. "It's our only choice. Come on, there's almost no room left!"

I stood next to the doorway but heard nothing back.

"Ty, come on!" I urged.

Finally, the outline of a human form roughly fitting Ty's size materialized from the other side of the opening. We both stepped through and out of the complex. A burst of fresh, cool air made it immediately obvious we were outdoors and not in another building. It was relatively dark but just bright enough to see the open space nearby. We were standing in sand with a high, rocky cliff wall fifteen or so feet in front of us. We turned back around to look at where we'd come out but saw nothing but another sheer rock cliff face. Not only was the exit from the complex gone, there was no hint of any kind of human-built structure. It was as if we just arrived in the sand from nowhere. I reached out and touched the rock, just to make sure my eyes weren't playing games. My hand met up with hard, rough stone.

"Did we just walk out of this rock?" I asked, exasperated.

"WHAT?" Ty bellowed in disbelief. "So are we supposed to believe all those sentries and the red octagon thing were a mirage?" He looked around the open space surrounding us and said, "So where the heck are we now?"

"Outside the complex," I answered before realizing how stupid I'd just sounded.

"Yes," Ty ranted, "I know that, Einstein! Thanks a lot for the in-depth analysis! Come on, you know what I mean! We're not exactly in Newkastel! How did we get *here* . . . wherever *here* is?"

"I have no idea," I said, suddenly feeling beaten and exhausted.

Looking down the narrow alley in which we were standing, I could see that the rock formation across from us ended not too far away. It looked brighter down there, like maybe there was a direct light source.

"Let's head this way," I said with a yawn, gesturing toward the light. "Maybe we'll see something that looks familiar."

We started walking.

"Do you remember standing in the 'A' room," Ty asked meekly, "when the orb started making noise and everything turned white?"

"You mean that bowling ball?" I asked, rubbing my eyes. "Yeah, I think. It's all kind of blurry."

"It's like, right at that moment," Ty pontificated as he focused straight ahead with his detective face all scrunched up, "our molecules were hurled through a wormhole all the way to Egypt or Saudi Arabia, or maybe even Wyoming."

"Maybe," I said. "Can we play *Where in the World Is Ty?* tomorrow, after we've gotten some sleep?"

As we reached the clearing, Ty turned to his left while I kept looking straight ahead, struggling to focus my weary eyes. Glancing up, I saw the moon, but it was really far away and looked somehow different. I wasn't an astronomer, but the light and dark areas somehow weren't the same as I remembered.

"Does the moon look different to you?" I asked but got no response. "Hey, does the—" I started to repeat, but as I turned to get my brother's attention, I saw why he hadn't responded.

He was also looking at a moon. A different moon. A moon covered with green and blue swirls, so big it filled the entire sky and so close I thought it was going to roll right over us. Overwhelmed by its enormity, I stumbled backward to the ground as my eyes followed it up and over my head.

After a moment of awestruck paralysis, Ty looked back at me, the color completely drained from his face, and said, "Dude, I don't think we're in Wyoming."

FIVE

HAMSTER BALLS WITH ATTITUDE
(TY)

"Tyyyyyy," Aunt Andi called out. "Tyyyyyy, time to get up, sleepy head. Bus comes in half an hour. Come on, get dressed, sweetie."

The smell and sizzle of bacon cooking on the stove were in the air. Mmmmm, bacon. My favorite, with the possible exception of . . . wait . . . could it be? Do I possibly smell chocolate crepes? Yes! Aunt Andi was making choco-crepes and bacon, and on a school day! After the nightmare with the sentries and the moons and all that, I felt like I just woke up in paradise!

Wait. She said the bus was coming in half an hour? The clock read 7:30. How could that be? I was going to have to hustle to avoid the ultimately lame embarrassment of being dropped off at school in front of the other kids by a parent, which was always good for a day's worth of sarcastic comments and maybe even a humiliating new nickname. One time, I missed three straight days of school because I was sick and got labeled "Ty-phoid fever boy" for a month. So, anyway, I really didn't want to be late.

Aunt Andi passed by my door in the hallway as I finished putting on my socks. I dashed downstairs, sat at the kitchen table, and happily started devouring my wonderful breakfast. Spreading powdered sugar on crepes was one of my favorite things to do. Every nanometer of crepe had to be covered so the entire top looked like a miniature floating iceberg. Then I'd roll it up and take a big bite . . . pure heaven.

There was a knock at the front door.

"I'll get it, Aunt Andi," I yelled and walked over but, when I looked out, no one was there.

Before I made it back to my feast, there was another knock at the door. I looked back, but still no one was there. As I stood, watching out the window, a third knock rang out with absolutely no one on the other side.

"Ty, get up," Aunt Andi said, still upstairs, "we have to go."

"I'm already downstairs!" I hollered in the general direction of her voice. "There's knocking but nobody's here."

"Ty," she cried out, except that she suddenly sounded like Marcus, "they're coming. Wake up!"

Something hit my left leg, and hard! An intense shooting pain momentarily reminded me of the time I bounced off the trampoline at Thomas Guiardson's birthday party and landed on the bar, except this was a million times worse!

I woke up screaming and clutching my leg to find I was rolling through tall grass and heavy brush while whoever had rammed into me tumbled a few feet away. When I finally stopped moving, I looked up, ready to scream in pain, when a hand clamped over my mouth from behind.

"Shh," a girl's voice said. "Be quiet."

I reached up to pull the hand away, but it didn't budge. All I could do was sit there on the ground, whimpering and rubbing my leg while tears welled up in my eyes. Looking to my right, I saw Marcus whispering loudly with some guy.

"Look, stay here and die or come with us," the other guy said. "I don't care, but we're leaving."

He turned and gestured to a few other kids to get going.

"If I take my hand away," the girl prompted from behind me, "do you promise to stay quiet?"

I nodded vigorously and the vise grip squeezing my head released. She stepped around in front of me and kneeled down.

"Are you okay?" she asked. "Can you walk?"

The night before, Marcus and I watched not just one but two moons move through the night sky before we found some taller grass to hide in and sleep. I managed to convince Marcus we shouldn't just lay down out in the open where animals or evil marauders could kidnap or kill us. Lots of good it did. Now my left femur was probably broken in ten places, not to mention all the tendon damage. It was going to take months to heal, followed by years of therapy.

"It hurts," I insisted, wincing on the ground from the agony of it all. "I think it's broken."

The girl felt around my leg, pushing pretty hard a couple of times.

"Ahhhhh!" I grimaced, struggling to be brave in the face of excruciating pain and danger. "Right there! Right there! That's where it's broken!"

The girl stood up and peered into the distance as if she was looking for something on the horizon.

"It's not broken," she said dismissively. "You'll be fine." She looked down and offered a hand to help me up. "Let's go," she said. "We need to leave before the Desrata get here."

I looked back and saw the rest of her group was already heading out.

"Anina, come on!" one of them whisper-yelled.

The girl standing by me looked up and waved her other hand. She looked back down at me with an expression of finality and said, "Last chance."

I grabbed her hand and pulled myself up. She immediately ran off toward her friends.

Marcus walked up from behind me and said, "I don't know who those kids are, but the guy I was talking to said something or somebody nasty will be coming through here in a minute. I really don't think we want to wait around to find out what they're running from."

Both of us scoped the direction from which the kids had come, looking for any movement. We stood at a boundary between rocky desert and the beginning of thick grassland that eventually turned into dense forest. The sand in the desert part was bright orange and looked like it went on forever. Some of the trees in the distant forest must have reached twenty stories into the sky, much higher than any I'd ever seen. The night before, it all looked and felt much smaller, more contained, probably because the huge moon dwarfed everything. The size of the open expanse around us made me feel really small, like a minnow in the ocean.

"That girl, Anina, called them Desrata," I muttered.

Something about that word gave me the willies and triggered my ever-present natural instinct to run away. Looking ahead again, we could only barely see the kids that had literally run into us or, at least, into me.

"I'm not waiting to find out what's chasing them," I finally insisted. "Let's go."

Marcus and I took off to catch up to the group. In the distance, we could see the very tops of a couple of buildings toward which the kids were heading. Running uphill in the sand is really hard but especially difficult when your leg might be broken, which I thought mine could still be, even though

Anina said it wasn't. Marcus jogged alongside me as the kids ahead of us disappeared over the far side of the small dune we were hustling up.

We finally had to slow down to catch our breath. As we climbed higher, the tops of more buildings rose up from the sand in the distance. At the top of the dune, it was obvious we weren't just looking at some buildings. We were looking at an entire city, or at least the destroyed remains of one. Not a single structure was standing. The entire place was leveled. Seeing a metropolis that big in that shape right in front of us was staggering. It reminded me of TV documentaries I'd seen about London during the Blitzkrieg or Nagasaki after the atom bomb at the end of World War II.

"What the heck happened here?" Marcus asked rhetorically.

Amongst the ruins were five super-tall curved towers spread evenly around the edges of the city. They were obviously damaged, like pencils jaggedly snapped in half, with each base still standing noticeably upright. The one closest to us was the shortest but still had to reach at least a hundred feet into the sky. The furthest tower was much taller, but even it had lost a portion of its top. While the towers were black, the other buildings in the city, or at least their remains, were all different colors. As with the towers, they were shiny and smooth looking, like a bathroom sink or a bathtub.

Getting beyond the freak-out of seeing all that destruction took a few seconds, but I finally looked down and saw the kids we were following.

"Hey," I pointed out, "there's Anina and the others!"

They were running directly at the city, near the shortest tower, and didn't look so far away anymore. At least we'd be running downhill to catch up to them. As Marcus and I took off again, the ground started vibrating. A slight tremble quickly ramped up into a menacing shudder.

"Earthquake?" Marcus asked with a confused expression.

As we looked back, the source of our shuddering feet appeared in the distance. Coming toward us very quickly were three really big hamster balls. You know, those clear, hollow plastic balls you put a hamster into so it can run around on its own, except these were easily twenty feet tall. Three of them were rolling across the desert floor right at us. They were still too far away to tell what was driving them, but I doubted it was hamsters. After all, the average hamster brain is only the size of half a sunflower seed, just like Marcus'.

"Come on," Marcus said and headed down the hill towards the city. "Let's go."

I honestly couldn't move. The hamster ball things were amazing. They were so fast I didn't want to look away.

"For those things to work," I muttered to myself, "there must be a stationary inner ball that doesn't rotate while the outer ball spins around it. How cool is that?"

The ground vibrations grew noticeably in magnitude as they approached, making it hard to stand in one place.

"Come on, Ty," Marcus screamed hysterically. "They're coming!"

I'd never heard Marcus sound like that. Scared. He nimbly scaled back up the hill, grabbed my shirt, and pulled me in the direction of the shortest tower at the edge of the ruins.

The ground rumbled so violently it became hard to run straight, but we finally made it into the city and hid behind a pile of rubble after climbing over what felt like endless debris. My entire body was shaking because, you know, I was exhausted, and not because I was scared or anything.

The pieces of mangled building we were hiding behind were completely white and very smooth. I couldn't tell where each piece had broken apart. There weren't any jagged edges or cracks on any of the pieces. They were more like hardened liquid, except they were as heavy and solid as concrete or steel.

We peeked around our makeshift fortification as the three hamster balls rolled up over the dune outside the city and stopped. Each one was almost perfectly transparent except that the sunlight bent as it passed through them, making everything behind look a little magnified and fuzzy, like looking through a glass of still water.

All was quiet for a few seconds until a loud click and the sound of rushing air broke the silence. A hatch or some kind of door on top of the middle hamster ball opened. Someone—or make that something—big . . . very big . . . popped up through the hatch and peered into the city. I couldn't see it clearly, but either its face was made of something shiny or it was wearing a shiny face shield.

It turned suddenly and looked right at me. I jerked back to avoid being seen, lost my footing, and fell on top of Marcus, who grabbed me so I wouldn't slide further.

"Marcus," I whispered, "it looked right at me!"

Marcus covered my mouth with his hand and put his finger to his lips to silently shush me. I gestured with my hands to let him know I was settled down and he let me go. Carefully moving to his other side, I saw an opening in the rocks where I could look out on the hamster balls again. The hatch on the middle one wasn't open anymore.

I turned to Marcus, shook my head, and mouthed, "I don't think it saw me!" with a thumbs-up and a nervously confident smile on my face.

A tremendously bright flash of light, like a lightning strike, suddenly filled the open space around us, followed immediately by a KABANG! that sent me flying through the air until I landed hard on my skull and left shoulder. Before I could even look up, another KABANG! littered white rubble down from above. I had no idea where Marcus was. I shielded my eyes to try to look around but felt my head powerlessly thud down against a rock as consciousness swiftly slipped away into numb oblivion.

SIX

YELLING-GIRL
(MARCUS)

"Get up!" somebody a million miles away yelled. "Can you hear me? GET UP!"

I opened my eyes to find I was on my back, laying at an angle on a very uneven, rocky surface. My ears were ringing and my head was pounding like a jackhammer.

"Run!" the same voice, a female voice, urged from somewhere.

I looked around to find the source of the yelling and saw a girl watching me from behind another debris pile fifty feet or so away, pointing at something on my other side.

"Over there," she yelled, "before they zero you! You'll be safe if you can just make it—"

KABANG!

Another tremendously loud detonation lifted my body off the ground and dropped me excruciatingly back down. The ringing in my ears made it impossible to hear anything else. I looked over to where the yelling-girl had pointed and saw a doorway a hundred feet away on the other side of a couple of debris piles.

I got to my knees, but the dizzying carnival ride inside my head made it hard to stand up, much less run.

"We have to move now," I somehow heard her say, "before they zero us!"

I looked back, and she was kneeling right next to me. I couldn't fathom how she had gotten to me so quickly.

"Can you move?" she asked. "We have to hurry!"

"I just, I just need a minute to—" I started to say when she threw me over her shoulder like a weightless sack of potatoes and ran toward the doorway.

Wait. Ty. Where was Ty? He was right next to me just a second ago.

"Where's my brother?" I objected in a woozy, dust-filled haze. "Where's Ty?"

Another earth-shattering *KABANG!* came from right behind us, and we flew like wounded birds through the doorway. The landing wasn't as rough as I expected, thanks to yelling-girl cushioning my fall. I quickly got to my hands and knees and looked down. Her eyes were closed and she wasn't moving.

"Hey, look," I grumbled, my world still twirling like a top, "you just saved my life, but I have to go get Ty. Can you hear me?"

She didn't respond.

I struggled to stand up, putting my right hand on a nearby wall for balance. The door we'd been blasted through was completely caved in. Where once was a passage to the outside now stood a solid pile of twisted building wreckage.

"Ty!" I bellowed. "Ty!"

The screaming made me even dizzier, and I fell sideways against the wall. I felt like I was going to pass out. I peeked over at yelling-girl, but she wasn't on the floor where we'd landed. Was I looking in the right place? All I knew was that I had to get Ty. That was my last clear thought before my eyes closed and I felt myself hit the floor.

SEVEN

THE LAST JORNO
(YELLING-GIRL)

It's been over eight annos since the last jorno of Spartanica. Eight annos I've been here by myself, surviving in the hollowed-out, collapsed residue of my home city. The city Father used to lead. The city we all used to love and talk about like a member of the family. Although it's been a very lonely eight annos, it's been mostly quiet. Sometimes so quiet my mind could do little more than try to remember the way things used to be. The people. My friends. The buildings. The life I used to have. How Mother and Father promised they'd come back for me. How they didn't. How nobody did.

But not today. Today had been chaos unlike anything since the last jorno. Draid blasts rocked me out of bed all the way down in my little personal fortress on level twelve in the coliseum building. I ran up to level one and headed out to scope around when I found a couple of boys around my age hiding behind one of countless exorbalis piles that litter our former capital.

Just as I saw them, another draid blast hit barely on the other side of where they were hiding. A bunch of exorbalis rolled on top of one kid, the skinny one, while the bigger one flew up in the air and dropped lifelessly back to the ground. I thought he was dead, but he started moving after a bit, obviously stunned. I got him inside the door to an old government building, one of the few that actually still vaguely resembled a structure, just as another blast hit squarely behind us and collapsed the entrance.

The kid I carried inside tried to get up but passed out on the floor. He was as safe there as he was going to be anywhere nearby, so I cleared a new door through the rubble and hustled over to where I saw his scrawny friend get hammered. I had to dig around for a minute or so just to find him. He was unconscious, too, but breathing, so I slung him over my shoulder and hustled back to the doorway, just hoping we could get there before we got zeroed.

We made it back in one piece, and I set the second kid down next to his friend. Now that they were safe, I had to get a look at who was draiding the gehanna out of my home. Cautiously sneaking back outside, I quickly headed around to the far left of where I found the boys, scaled a tall exorbalis pile, and scoped out beyond the city border into the arduszone but didn't see anything other than three large divots in the orange sand at the top of a hill. There weren't any more draid blasts either. Whoever or whatever was blasting Spartanica was gone.

I ran back to the boys, both of whom were still unconscious. I carried each one back outside and to a medica room on level six in the coliseum building and locked them in.

I was completely exhausted by the time I got the second kid, the bigger one, in there. My head felt like it was ready to split in two. I barely made it back to my bed on level twelve and collapsed. That is, if you'd call an old sunken mattress laying on a countertop a bed. I knew I should probably stand watch over those boys, but I was drained and knew they could never find me in my room. There was only one way in and no one was ever going to find it, unless I wanted them to. The room used to be where Mother would change out of her leadoje outfit after practice and reinigen before going home. Now it *was* my home, but only because I remembered Father saying once how this building had the thickest walls of any under the cupola.

I just needed a little sleep. Just a little sleep, and I'd grab my majrifle and go meet my new "friends."

EIGHT

OPEN THE DOOR!
(MARCUS)

"Ty!" I screamed as I woke and popped up into a sitting position. "Ty!" I yelled again in a panic, my eyes wide open and my heart pumping so hard it felt like it would burst through my rib cage.

"What, what, what?!" someone to my left blurted in a startled tone. "Why are you screaming? Ow, my head's killing me. My shoulder!"

I turned to see my brother lying on the bed next to mine.

"Ty!" I blurted with a huge smile on my face. "You're okay? You're okay!"

I'll never admit it out loud, but I felt tears in my eyes. What a relief.

"I'm fine!" Ty whispered, switching to irritation. "Can you PLEASE stop yelling?"

He stared at me out of the corners of his eyes, still resting his head on a pillow with his hands massaging his temples.

"Why are you crying?" Ty asked.

I lay back down and rubbed my eyes.

"I'm not crying," I insisted. "The lights are bright in here. The air is dry, too." I took a deep breath and finally said, "Dude, I thought you were dead."

"Well, I'm the one that should be crying," Ty whined. "I think I got hit on the head and shoulder with one of those big white rock things. I probably have an aneurism and need immediate attention. Oh, no, I think my blood pressure's dropping!"

That was when I knew Ty was just fine.

"Do aneurisms lead to excessive whining?" I mumbled sarcastically.

"So funny," Ty whimpered back. "Marcus?"

I stopped rubbing my eyes, looked up at the ceiling, and sighed.

"Yeah, I know," I answered. "Where are we?"

I sat up again and looked around. We were in a large rectangular room with four beds lined up on the same wall. Ty and I were on the middle two beds. Several examination tables and storage cabinets stood between the beds and the door. Everything was white. The room was very bright, but somehow it didn't bother my eyes. I didn't really see any lights. It was just like the complex. The lighting was just there without having a source.

I looked at Ty and said, "We gotta get outta here."

"Are you kidding?" he replied emphatically. "With this head wound? I should stay immobile for the next forty-eight hours, AT LEAST! Do you want me to develop a subdural hematoma?"

"Ty, think about it," I said. "Someone or something brought us here. Do you really want to wait around for whatever it is to come back? For all we know, we're being allowed to heal so we can be human sacrifices at some religious ceremony."

I was exaggerating, but it was only because the little voice in the back of my head insisted we leave that room ASAP.

It was immediately obvious by the worried look in Ty's eyes that he was seriously considering the whole *being a sacrifice* thing.

"No," he started. "No. Um. Okay. Let's go, but gingerly, so I can maintain an equilibrium. That's critical at this stage."

He got off the bed holding his hands out as if he needed them to stay balanced. He picked up the pace once he saw I wasn't waiting for him.

"Hey," he whispered loudly, "hold on!"

He caught up to me standing in front of the door with a blank look on my face.

"Where's the handle?" I asked, completely befuddled. "Do you see another door?"

We both turned and looked across the room from side to side. There was no other door.

"Well, isn't this just great?" I said. "A door with no handle."

I walked over and started looking through several medical cabinets and drawers.

"Maybe there's something useful in here," I said.

"Like what?" Ty asked.

"Something to pry open that door," I replied. "Or, even better, something to eat. I'm starving."

"You think there's food in here?" Ty said as he watched what I was doing over my shoulder. "Why would they keep food in here? This is like a doctor's office, not a restaurant."

"It doesn't hurt to look, does it?" I asked, still pilfering but finding nothing but medical supplies. "Aren't you hungry?"

"Yes," Ty whined back. "I'm so hungry I'm getting lightheaded. Or maybe that's my head wound. I'm not sure, but I really don't think we'll find any food in here."

Like a rocket counting down to liftoff, my patience with Ty was quickly ticking down to zero. My head and body hurt. I was confused, starving, and frustrated, and Ty just wasn't getting it. My brother, who could be so smart without even trying sometimes, was now like talking to a rock. I could feel my face turning red as I looked over at him.

"Then I guess we better find a way to OPEN THE DOOR!" I yelled.

"Whoa . . . ." was all Ty said in response, but he wasn't bewildered because of my sudden tirade. He was looking and pointing over my left shoulder. I turned to find the door wide open.

"When did that happen?" I asked, simultaneously moving quickly away from the exit, wondering who or what was about to walk into the room.

We crouched behind a table and peeked over the top at the gaping hole in the wall. A dimly lit hallway was bordered on the far side by a glistening black wall. We stayed put for a few seconds but nothing else happened.

"Okay," I said, standing up slowly with my eyes glued to the door. "Let's go have a look."

Ty didn't exactly volunteer to come with, so I pulled his shirt sleeve to get him going. As we poked our heads into the hallway, the lights immediately got brighter, but we didn't see anyone, so we stepped out. I turned slowly and peered back into the room we were just in. I looked up and found strange symbols engraved into the wall above the door.

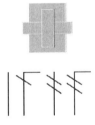

"Hey, look at that," I said. "Wonder what it means."

Ty turned, looked up, and squinted his eyes as he always did when he was really thinking hard about something.

"What does it mean?" he asked rhetorically, obviously getting a little freaked. "It means we're nowhere near home. That's what it means. Where the heck are we?"

"No idea, dude," I responded, "but we can't just sit around. We need to figure things out and find a way home."

"Yeah, I guess," Ty replied, shaking his head. "Those bottom characters look kind of like what I saw on the copper blocks hanging in the 'A' room. It feels like I've seen the top symbol, too, but I can't remember where."

Ty turned and walked up to the smooth, glass-like black wall on the other side of the hallway, and put his forehead right up against it, like he was trying to see through it to something on the other side.

"Okay, left or right?" I asked, giving Ty the choice as to which direction to go. I didn't think it was a complicated question, but then again, when it came to doing something with Ty, I'd been wrong before.

"Uh, my left or your left?" Ty asked, obviously still deep in thought about the black wall.

So, yeah, it was a complicated question, at least for Ty.

"Let's just go this way," I -finally said, nudging him to move to *my* left.

The corridor was straight and empty as far as we could see. The ceiling and wall on the right were tan. We passed another door on the right, but, just like with the medical room, it had no knob or visible way of opening. The top symbol above the door was the same as above the other door, but the bottom symbol was a little different.

"What is up with these doors with no knobs?" I asked. "How are we supposed to get in?"

From behind us came a girl's voice I vaguely recognized.

"Short answer?" she said. "You're not supposed to get in."

Ty and I both stiffened straight up like statues and froze.

"Now lay down on your stomachs," she ordered, "before I find out just how big of a hole this majrifle can put in the back of your heads."

NINE

WHO EXACTLY ARE YOU GUYS?

(YELLING-GIRL)

I did not expect to see those guys walking in the hallway. How did they get out of medica? I swear I sealed the door, and they couldn't possibly have the security access level to open it. I definitely needed to figure it out later. Still, I totally caught them by surprise! That was the most fun I'd had in annos.

"How did you get out of medica?" I demanded.

They both just stared silently at the floor.

"You mean that doctor's office?" the scrawny one finally said. "I, I, I, I don't know! The door just opened."

After all these annos alone, I was thinking it'd be really nice to have other people around. I'd gotten used to being alone all the time, but that didn't make it any easier. But still, for all I knew, these guys were just here to take or destroy everything.

"Sit up against the wall, very slowly," I commanded. "I'm Specialist Tech Com 3 certified with this majjy and can drop a pulse within four microns of any target, so don't try anything."

They just stared at me and slowly slid against the wall. I kept a few onons between us, just in case they got stupid and tried to rush me.

"Why are you here?" I asked.

The scrawny one, holding his hands above his head, said, "We just followed those other kids. You know. Anina and her friends. And then those—"

"Other kids?" I asked, looking around nervously. "What other kids? How many? Where did they go?"

"Uh, yeah," the bigger boy said. "We ran into a bunch of kids around our age outside the city."

The scrawny one started shaking his head.

"That's not true!" he said. "That's not true! We didn't run into them. *They* ran into *me* and it hurt . . . a lot! I can show you the bruise. It's huge!"

"Shut up!" I yelled and turned to the bigger kid. "How many?"

"I don't know," Marcus said. "Eight, maybe nine."

"That's just great," I said.

I felt like I was starting to lose it. I could handle these guys pretty easily, but now a gang of others were outside somewhere. All these people in my city made me nervous and trigger-happy. I took a deep, slow breath, like Mother used to tell me, and got centered.

"Okay," I said. "One thing at a time. Who are you? Where are you from? Why are you here?"

"I'm Marcus," the bigger kid said, "and this is my brother, Ty. You're the girl who pulled me inside when the bombs were going off, aren't you?"

"When the *whats* were going off?" I asked. "Boms? That's a strange word. You mean when the city was being draided from outside the cupola frame? Yes. I lugged both of you inside a building entrance so you wouldn't get buried in exorbalis debris."

"I don't remember any of that," Ty said with a puzzled look on his face.

"I'm not surprised," I replied, still spooked and looking around for the other visitors these guys mentioned. "I don't remember much when I'm unconscious, either."

I didn't get the feeling these guys were a real threat but still needed to know more about them.

"How many annos do you have?" I asked.

"How many what?" Ty questioned with his face all scrunched up, like I was speaking a different language.

"Zah . . . how many *annos* do you have?" I repeated. "You look to have twelve or thirteen."

Marcus jumped in immediately and said, "You're right, we both have thirteen annos. We're brothers."

"Brothers?" I asked. "Twins?"

How else could two brothers have the same number of annos?

"No, no, no!" Ty started, becoming visibly irritated. "That's what people say every time. Marcus was born in January. I was born in December of the same year."

January? December? I didn't understand what those words meant. The way these guys spoke was confusing.

"Uh, he means the same anno," Marcus added, looking nervously at his brother.

They were obviously hiding something. Everybody I'd ever known from Spartanica and Atlantis always spoke Atlantean. Some of these words were definitely from a different language.

"Where do you come from?" I said half-jokingly. "Lemuria?"

Lemuria was on the other side, the dark side, of the planet, even further away than Atlantis. I'd never known anyone from there.

"You're not outlanders, are you?" I asked. "You don't look like you live in the arduszone."

"Lemuria?" Marcus answered, shaking his head vigorously. "Outlanders? Oh, no. No way." He paused for a couple of seconds before looking back up at me. "Okay, look, we're not from here, wherever *here* is. Do you have any food? We haven't eaten in a while. If we can get something to eat, we'll tell you whatever you want to know."

TEN

PRIORITY ONE NOTIFICATION
(TY)

I couldn't ever remember being hungry in a dream before, but I was hungrier now than I'd ever been awake. Except for maybe the time Aunt Andi made liver when I was seven and she said I couldn't have anything else until it was gone. If you've ever been cursed enough to have to eat liver, you know how awful it is. Why would anyone want to eat an internal organ? Honestly, serving it should be considered cruel and unusual punishment. Anyways, I didn't eat it for dinner that night. Or for breakfast the next morning. I love my Aunt Andi very much, but I had to take a stand for kids everywhere that day. She obviously wasn't pleased with me, and it was still there when I came home from second grade for lunch. I was sooooo hungry but I could hardly even look at it.

Finally, after hours of begging him, Marcus agreed to eat it for me if I gave him my favorite toy race car, a candy-apple red 1985 McLaren F1 MP4/2B with white racing stripes and real-action steering. It was the coolest car ever, but I would've given anything to make that liver go away. So I went to my room and got the McLaren. My liver was gone before I even came back. I don't know how he ate it so fast, but I didn't care. Aunt Andi came home later, saw it was gone, and gave me ice cream. Remembering that whole scene now makes me think maybe Marcus really wasn't so bad after all.

So, this girl who was ready to put a hole in my head a while ago was now supposedly taking us to get some food. We walked forever to get wherever she was taking us. The hallways were very long and straight, and there were a lot of doors along the way, each with the same top symbol but different on the bottom. We took a couple left turns but the black wall stayed on our left the whole way.

"Why is this wall black and shiny but the other ones aren't?" I finally asked.

"Because it's not a wall," the girl said. "This is the level-six viewing deck for the leadoje tournament courts. You can't see them because the lights are off in there. Watch this." Speaking louder, she announced, "Recognize."

A man's voice from somewhere overhead responded, "Recognized."

Marcus and I both looked up, as if we expected to see some guy hinged in the ceiling looking down on us.

"Enable leadoje coliseum lighting," the girl continued.

White light flooded the black glass from behind to reveal a bunch (I mean thousands) of seats with a huge flat surface at the bottom. It reminded me of when we went to the Chicago Bears game at Soldier Field, except this place had a roof.

"Whoa," was all I could say. It took a lot to impress me, but this was quite remarkable.

"That's great, really," Marcus said as he started walking again in the same direction we'd been moving before we stopped, "you can tell us all about it while we eat."

"Disable leadoje coliseum lighting," the girl said, and the wall went totally dark again. We came to a door and took a couple flights of stairs up to another hallway that led to a room that looked like a cafeteria with tables and chairs.

"Grab a seat," the girl said. "I'll be right back." She disappeared through another door.

I was famished, but Marcus looked downright ill. His skin was growing more pale by the minute. He put his head down on the table, looking away from me.

"I sure hope she doesn't bring liver," I said with a smirk.

"Yeah, Knuckles isn't here to eat it this time," Marcus replied. "Although I'm so hungry I'd probably chow it down myself right now."

"Whaddaya mean?" I asked, suddenly suspicious. "You ate mine and yours that one time when I was in trouble."

Marcus turned toward me with a sinister smile on his face.

"You don't really think I ate that stuff, do you?" he said. "If ever toxic waste was put on a dinner plate, that was it."

"But I traded you the McLaren to eat it for me," I said, becoming more dismayed with every word. "That was my favorite car."

"No," Marcus replied. "You gave me that dumb car to make your liver go away, so I made it go away, just like I made mine go away."

I sat back in utter disbelief.

"First of all, it wasn't a dumb car," I insisted. "Second, Knuckles? You gave the liver to our dog? I could've done that myself and kept the McLaren."

"Yeah, but you didn't," Marcus replied. "Besides, we almost got busted, anyways. Even Knuckles wouldn't eat the second one. He took it outside and buried it. He finished covering up the hole just as Aunt Andi pulled in."

"But I loved that car," I complained, visualizing its sleek curves and racing tires in my mind.

"So did Joey Joe," Marcus said. "I traded it to him for his autographed picture of Michael Jordan a couple of weeks later."

"Really?" I retorted. "Well, let me tell you something about that picture—" I started to say before the girl came back and set down a couple of bowls of food on the table.

"Don't get used to this," she said. "Even if I decide you can stay here, you get your own food from now on."

Marcus sat up and immediately started eating.

"Thank you, thank you, thank you!" he said. "Mmmmmm. Yum. What is it? Wait, I don't even care."

"Quagga, carrots, asparagus, veet root, and ginger," the girl said. "All simulated, of course. It's my favorite. I call it the Bellana Bowl."

I had no idea what quagga was, but it sure smelled good. I put a little dab on my spoon and tasted it with the tip of my tongue. It was delicious. I took a big spoonful and saw that Marcus was already almost finished with his.

"Bellana Bowl?" Marcus asked with his mouth mostly full. "Is that your name? Bellana?"

"Yes," she responded. "If you want more, I'll show you where to get it."

I thought for a moment and asked, "What do you mean *simulated*? This isn't real food? It looks and tastes real."

"No," Bellana responded. "I wish it was real. I haven't had real food since . . . well . . . for a long time. But SMILEy does a pretty good job of keeping me fed."

"Smiley?" I asked, shoveling another big spoonful into my mouth. "Who is Smiley?"

Bellana glanced at me in disbelief and said, "SMILEy! Every facility has a SMILEy! Surely you have a SMILEy wherever you're from?"

If she was trying to make me feel dumb, she was succeeding.

"Oh, well, yeah, uh, of course," I stammered with a half-full mouth and an uncertain smile. "Ole Smiley boy. You bet!"

Marcus glared at me.

"No, we don't," he said, turning to Bellana. "What's a smiley?"

"You're serious?" she asked.

We both stared blankly right back at her.

"I'm beginning to think you guys *are* outlanders," Bellana said, "no offense."

"Don't worry," Marcus responded. "None taken."

"System Managed Integrated Living Environment," Bellana continued. "SMILEy. Some people call him SMILE, but I always liked SMILEy. He controls the lights, food, heat, water. Everything. And he responds to my commands. That's how I turned on the leadoje illumination and made your food. He really is my best friend."

A computer for a best friend, I thought. That's really sad.

An announcement came from overhead and said, "Priority one notification."

It was the same voice we heard before in the hallway.

"Fazah!" Bellana exclaimed. "Priority one? SMILEy's never reported a priority one before. I think it's a security warning."

She raised her head and responded in an unsure voice, "Priority one notification, proceed."

"Seven intruder life forms have entered the facility at location Zetta One," SMILEy responded.

"Zah!" Bellana gasped, almost hysterically. "That's right above here."

"Well, who else lives in the city?" I asked.

"No one!" Bellana responded. "I've been here by myself for annos."

"It must be those kids we saw before," Marcus said.

"Six hundred fifty square milles of wrecked city," Bellana asked suspiciously, "littered with tens of thousands of flattened buildings, and they just happen to walk into this one?"

If a mille is anything near the same as a mile, Spartanica was bigger than Chicago and New York together, which I didn't doubt for a minute. The place looked humungous from out in the desert.

"Well, I don't know," was all Marcus could muster in reply.

"Okay," Bellana said, obviously working to stay calm. "Regardless, we should go check it out before they get very far, right?"

While it sounded like a question, I think it was actually a request. The three of us hadn't known each other very long, but it felt like we kind of trusted each other already. Bellana was looking for a little backup.

"Can we get one of those things you had on before, when you said you were going to blow holes in the backs of our heads?" Marcus asked, pointing to his right forearm.

Bellana moved quickly back toward the door from where she had brought our food. Along the way, she turned and said, "Are you certified on a majrifle?"

Marcus and I both shook our head and stood up.

"Then they won't work for you," she finished. "Besides, you'd end up hurting yourself more than anyone else. Stay here. I'll be right back with mine."

She disappeared through the door.

Marcus looked over at me and said, "Great! What are we supposed to defend ourselves with? Nasty language?"

Bellana burst back into the room with the majrifle back on her right hand and forearm. It looked more like a tan, flexible plastic cast than a weapon. It fit like a long glove, but her fingers and thumb stuck out the end. There was no barrel like on a gun. If it had bullets, I couldn't see from where they'd shoot out.

"The Zetta One entrance is directly above here, three floors up on level one," Bellana said and looked toward the ceiling. "Recognize."

SMILEy responded, "Recognized."

"Locate intruder life forms," she commanded.

"Intruder life forms are on level one," SMILEy continued, "moving away from Zetta One along the inner perimeter toward Zetta Two. Correction. Intruder life forms have stopped between Zetta One and Zetta Two."

"Why does he say *life forms*?" Marcus asked. "Are we talking about humans or animals or what?"

"Identify species of intruder life forms," Bellana instructed.

"With ninety-two percent probability, intruder life form species is Homo sapiens," SMILEy responded.

"So, they're human," Bellana added.

"Affirmed," SMILEy replied. "Intruder life forms are most likely human."

"Don't you lock the doors to this place?" I blurted, stunned and a little distraught that anyone could apparently just stroll in.

"Don't yell at me!" Bellana exclaimed defensively. "There are only two entrances. I tried a hundred different ways to secure them but their locking mechanisms haven't worked since the last jorno. Besides, I haven't seen a single human anywhere for the past eight annos. Why now all of the sudden?"

"Update," SMILEy interrupted. "There are now six active humans in the facility."

"Which exit did the seventh human use to leave?" Bellana asked.

"The seventh human did not exit the building," SMILEy answered.

"Well, come on, SMILEy, how can that be?" Bellana frustratingly barked. "He didn't just disappear! Where did the seventh human go?"

"The seventh human's life measurements can no longer be detected," SMILEy responded. "With eighty-eight percent probability, the seventh human has expired."

The three of us looked at each other in horror.

"Somebody up there died?" I said, looking at Marcus as a chill ran down my spine. "What if it was one of those kids? We need to go up there *now!*"

Marcus looked at Bellana, gestured toward the hallway, and said, "Lead the way."

We ran out of the cafeteria and found the stairway. The symbol on the stairway door was like this:

It was similar to the symbols we'd seen over the other doors. Bellana had said the intruders were three floors *up* on level one. That meant we must have been on level four. The symbol on the stairway door had to mean *four*, like *fourth floor*. As we reached the next floor up, the symbol on this door was like this:

It had to mean *three*. And if the floor numbers got smaller on the way up, that meant most of this place was built underground. That huge stadium and all those rooms . . . it was all underground.

"Okay, hold it, hold it," Marcus insisted just before we reached level one; each of us took the opportunity to catch our breath. "We can't just go all Rambo through the door. We go quietly and slowly until we can see who's out there. I'll go first."

Bellana grabbed Marcus before he could take another step and said, "I have the rifle and I've memorized every inch of this place. I go first."

She had a good point and obviously wasn't backing down. Marcus nodded and stepped back. Personally, I didn't care who went first, as long as it wasn't me.

"The hallway between Zetta One and Zetta Two is around the corner to the right," Bellana explained. "Ready?"

We both nodded. I looked at Marcus and bravely said, "Um, I'll let you go second."

"Yeah," he whispered, "you're such a pal."

Bellana turned the handle (the stairway doors actually had normal handles) and slowly opened the door. Luckily, it didn't squeak. She poked her head into the hall, looked around, and gave us a thumbs-up to move forward with her. I stepped through after Marcus and left the door open in case we needed to retreat quickly. We hugged the wall, walking on our tippy toes toward another hallway just ahead. On the left was a door to the outside with the following symbols on it:

The ceiling and outside wall behind us were smashed in. Even the floor back there looked collapsed, but it was too far away to be sure. The part we were in wasn't damaged, but no lights were on. We could only see because of the light coming through the windows and doors from outside.

Bellana reached the corner and pointed as if we should expect to see the intruders around it. She leaned over to peek as Marcus and I stood perfectly still. She pulled her head back quickly, looked at us, and nodded to let us know there were, in fact, people there. She stuck her head out again to get a better look.

"Click, click," the stairway door reverberated behind us as it closed. What would normally have been an insignificant noise echoed endlessly through the silent hallway. Bellana immediately jerked her head back with a terrified look on her face.

"Run!" she whispered and took off.

We sprinted back to the stairway door. I got there first but couldn't get it open.

"Come on!" I uttered in desperation as I turned the handle both ways with no luck.

Bellana body slammed me out of the way and tried it. She turned the handle down as far as it would go and leaned on it with her whole body, but the door wouldn't budge.

At the end of the hall, some guy came running around the corner at us.

"Bellana, open the door!" I urged.

She grunted loudly until she was screaming. The latch popped and the door finally opened.

"Hey!" the guy coming at us blurted. "HEY!"

We piled through the door and closed it. The guy on the other side slammed into it. Even with the three of us leaning up against it, the door jutted open briefly before slamming shut again. Bellana reached over and torqued the handle back to a latched position.

"Can you help us?" we heard from the other side. "Please? We source from Atlantis. I am Kinnard of the

Order of Jahnha. We need help! Will you help us? Please!"

Bellana backed away and looked through a small window in the upper center of the door.

"Open it," she commanded.

"You know this guy?" Marcus asked.

"No," she replied. "But I know his Order. They are known to be of great respect and honor. Open the door!"

She grabbed me and Marcus at the same time and effortlessly pulled us toward her in spite of the fact we were putting everything we had into keeping the door closed.

She opened the door and said, "I am Bellana of the Order of Bellator. We will help you."

ELEVEN

THAT'S ANINA!
(BELLANA)

I remembered hearing about the Order of Jahnha but didn't know much. Father and the other leaders used to mention them in company with other favorable Orders from time to time. I didn't have any negative memories of them being discussed with the Order of Malus or Nocens, so I wasn't too worried. I recall overhearing Father saying the Malus and Nocens Orders were ruthless and vengeful, and that they were never to be trusted.

My biggest question? Jahnha was an Atlantean Order and Kinnard was maybe an anno or two older than me, at most. What was a kid from Atlantis doing here? It wasn't like Atlantis was just a couple oras away. It was practically on the other side of the planet. Why would he be so far from home?

I opened the stairway door, and an exhausted Kinnard bent over and put his hands on his knees. His long, stringy, dirty blonde hair hung down over his face. He was still wheezing heavily when he stood back up, exposing dark circles under his eyes that stood out against his pale skin. He started walking to his left, and pointed.

"My friends," he pleaded, "there . . . around the corner . . . please."

Marcus, Ty, and I followed him and found six more kids around our age or younger sitting against the outer wall. They were in terrible shape. They had long, greasy hair, like Kinnard's, and wore filthy, ragged clothes. Two younger boys did little more than look over at us. A third guy that looked around the same age and build as Kinnard was tending to a girl with blood all over her chest and midsection. He sat on one side, holding his hand over the injured girl's heart, while a couple of other girls sat and cried on the other side.

"Huh, that's Anina!" Ty gasped behind me, clearly shaken by her condition.

"What happened to her?" I asked.

The boy holding her looked up at us and said, "She was impaled in the chest by a shard of exorbalis during the draiding. It's still lodged between her ribs. Do you have functional medica facilities here?"

"Yes," I responded.

"You must take us there immediately," he insisted.

"Just a protoka, Nekitys," Kinnard contended, looking at the boy, trying to stand up straight again while still catching his breath. "We don't even know you."

"Do you want her to die?" Nekitys said very bluntly. "I have the knowledge to help her if we can get the proper equipment and supplies."

Kinnard stared up at him briefly and said, "Okay, but Arianas is going with you."

"What about me?" the girl who obviously hadn't been selected yelled hysterically.

"Yes, Iryni, you too," Kinnard said, gesturing with his left hand. "Get going."

Both girls immediately stood up. They had very fair skin with thick, wavy, but unkempt, ratty black hair that wound its way down to their waists. Arianas was taller and looked to be a little younger than me, maybe with eleven or twelve annos. Iryni couldn't have had more than ten annos.

Nekitys picked Anina up and said, "No. I must properly tend to her first, without distraction or interference."

Arianas and Iryni glanced expectantly at Kinnard for confirmation they were still going.

"She's dying," Nekitys added in a dry, emotionless tone.

"Ok," a defeated Kinnard finally said, sounding disgusted that he'd yielded to Nekitys against his better judgment. "Just go."

"What about us?" Arianas blurted, terrified she may never see Anina alive again.

Kinnard glanced at both girls and shook his head to signify they were to stay with the rest of us.

"You're going to let *him* just walk off somewhere with Anina?" Iryni yelled.

Kinnard scowled forebodingly at Nekitys and said, "So help me, Nekitys, you better know what you're doing."

Nekitys, unfazed by Kinnard's not-so-thinly veiled threat, turned to me and said, "Which way?"

I led him back toward the stairs with Anina cradled in his arms.

TWELVE

LUCKY BREAK
(MARCUS)

After taking a closer look, I recognized Kinnard as the guy in the desert who told me they were being chased by something. His hair was pulled back into a tight ponytail then, but was a ragged, twisted, filthy mop dangling down over his shoulders now.

"Is anybody else hurt?" I asked.

They all shook their heads.

"No," one of the girls answered, drying her eyes, "not really. We just need to rest for a bit."

"Do you have anything to eat?" one of the boys asked.

"No," Ty replied, "but we could try to get SMILEy to make something."

"SMILEy?" Kinnard asked hopefully. "Do you mean a SMILE? Is the SMILE in this building operational?"

"Uh-huh," both Ty and I responded.

Kinnard looked at the others and got several exuberant looks back.

"I think we're dreaming," he said. "We haven't seen a working SMILE since we were little kids. Let's go, guys."

Kinnard stood up slowly and extended his hands to a couple of kids on the ground. Ty and I did the same to help the others up.

"How are you called?" Kinnard asked.

"How am I called?" Ty said with a confused look and tone. He shrugged his shoulders and said, "People call me Ty."

"And I'm Marcus."

"Is there anybody else here?" Arianas asked.

"Uh," I stuttered, unsure of how to answer. Bellana said she'd been the only person here for eight annos, however long that was. Ty chimed in before I could finish my answer.

"You mean just in this building or the entire city?" he asked.

Kinnard glanced up, clearly rattled that Ty might have a different answer depending on what Arianas meant.

"Well," she said, "either one, I guess."

"No," Ty finally said, looking at me for confirmation. "There's no one else here but the three of us."

A modestly irritated Arianas said, "Why did you ask me what I meant if there's no difference?"

"Because he's Ty," I interjected, hoping to lighten the mood before Ty really started getting on people's nerves. "You'll get used to him after a while. Well, after a long while. Maybe."

Everyone smirked except my brother who just shook his head and looked away.

"Fazah," one of the boys gasped. "Three people in all of Spartanica and we just happen to walk into the building where you live. That's just amazing."

"Yeah," Kinnard replied with a blunt finality that hinted he was ready to move on. "Lucky break, I guess. But now that we're all best friends, let's go find that SMILE dispensary before I pass out from hunger."

"It's on level four, back this way," Ty said.

We all followed as he headed for the stairway. I stopped briefly and looked outside through the Zetta One doors. The universal wreckage was just as I'd remembered. Endless piles of debris of varying heights littered the landscape separated by incidental paths that aimlessly wound their way around.

Kinnard walked up next to me.

"You three are fortunate to have this place," he said. "Nothing we could find in Atlantis was even accessible, much less functional."

The top of the short, black curved tower near where we first came into the city was in the distance on my right. It looked to be at least a ten-minute walk. How had Bellana gotten me and Ty from way over there to this building and down to a room on the sixth floor? It wasn't like there were any pickup trucks or even wagons sitting around and she couldn't have carried us all that way.

"Yeah," I finally answered Kinnard, still pondering my little mystery. "Well, let's go eat."

THIRTEEN

SKYSCRAPERS?

(TY)

The Atlantean kids wolfed down their meals like they hadn't seen food in years, but they reeked so badly Ty and I couldn't eat with them, so we just hung out at the far end of the table. They weren't very talkative, anyway, and just wanted to sleep after they finished gorging themselves. Bellana came in just as they finished and announced Anina was going to be okay, but that Nekitys didn't want her to be disturbed for a day or two. After some brief chatter, we all followed Bellana to another, larger medical room with ten beds on level six. We left the Atlantean kids there and headed back to the cafeteria to eat, praying the air had freshened up while we were gone.

"How far down does this building go?" I asked as we ascended the stairs back to level four.

"Twenty-seven levels," Bellana explained, "but only levels three through eleven are usable. Everything below level eleven is wrecked."

"Why build so deep?" I continued. "Why not build taller buildings above ground? You know, like skyscrapers, maybe?"

"Skyscrapers?" Bellana asked quizzically. "What are those, weapons?"

She just stared at me, shaking her head cluelessly. I stared right back with equal disbelief as we reached the door to level four.

"If we built everything above ground," she continued, "we'd need a huge cupola to cover it all. We'd have to be at peak majstice every jorno just to keep it engaged."

I could swear we were speaking the same language but I had no idea what Bellana just said. The blank look on Marcus' face told me he didn't understand any more than I had.

We reached the cafeteria.

"I'm beat," Bellana announced. "Will you two be okay here if I go slumber for a while?"

"No worries," Marcus responded. "Do you mind if we look around, or do we have to stay in here?"

"You can walk around but stay in the building," she said. "With all the excitement lately, you never know what could be happening outside."

"I'm not going anywhere," I insisted, shaking my head. "This place is huge. What happens if we get lost? It could take forever to find us. We could get locked in a room again and starve long before anybody finds us!"

Bellana turned to Marcus, looking very weary, and asked, "Is he always like this?"

"Yes," Marcus said with a smirk.

I just looked away with an annoyed expression on my face.

"Actually, he has a point," Bellana said. "Wait here."

I looked at Marcus with an *I told you so* expression as Bellana headed out of the cafeteria. She returned moments later with what looked to be a couple of small aspirins in her hand.

"These are shadowcomms," she said. "We dissolve them in infants shortly after birth. Each one is unique and can be tracked by any SMILEy."

"Seriously?" I asked. "What do you mean *dissolve them?*"

"They get taped to your skin and dissolve into your bloodstream over ten jornos or so," Bellana answered as she handed one to each of us. "You can just keep yours in your pockets." She raised her head and said, "Recognize." SMILEy recognized her. "Assign shadowcomm 3z9x2b9x to subject Ty. Assign shadowcomm 3z9x2b9y to subject Marcus."

SMILEy replied, "Shadowcomm 3z9x2b9x has been assigned to unknown subject Ty. Shadowcomm 3z9x2b9y has been assigned to unknown subject Marcus."

"Confirm locations of Ty and Marcus," Bellana commanded.

"Subjects Ty and Marcus are on level four, in room one, the dining module," SMILEy answered.

"See?" Bellana said. "Ha! Now you can't hide." She turned to walk away and said, "Get yourself some food and I'll see you later." She gestured toward the back of the room and said, "There's a viewtop in the corner if you get really bored. Lots of good information in there. You might even learn something. Good rest."

70

FOURTEEN

SAPERTYS

(MARCUS)

Once Bellana was out of earshot, Ty turned to me, very excitedly, and said, "Dude, this place is so totally like *Star Trek*! I'm just waiting for someone to fire phasers and photon torpedoes!"

"Yeah, you're a regular Captain Kirk," I said as I headed toward the large, black, square table with three chairs per side to which Bellana had motioned. "What do you suppose a viewtop is?" I asked.

"No idea," Ty replied, sizing up the table suspiciously as he followed me over to it.

I walked around to the far side, pulled out a chair, and sat down. As soon as I did, the tabletop lit up and a semi-transparent, three-dimensional, rotating symbol that looked like the one we'd seen over all the doors magically appeared and floated in the air above the center of the table. Its sudden appearance startled Ty, sending him tripping backward over his own feet. He got back up and carefully reached out to touch the symbol, but his hand passed right through.

"There's nothing there," he said, sticking his other hand in. "It's a holographic projection. See? This place *is* just like *Star Trek*!"

"Why do we keep seeing this symbol everywhere?" I asked. "What the heck is it?"

"Answer," the SMILEy voice responded. "The symbol being displayed is the official logo of Spartanica, capital city of Sapertys."

The voice caught Ty off-guard, and he yanked his hands out of the symbol and stepped back.

"Capital city of *what*?" I asked.

"Answer," SMILEy said. "Capital city of this planet, commonly referred to as Sapertys. The name is derived from the ancient Atlantean word for *hope*."

The Spartanica symbol disappeared and was replaced by a semi-transparent, multi-colored, rotating globe.

"What?" Ty blurted. "We're on a planet called Sapertys?"

"Answer," SMILEy replied. "Yes. A three-dimensional representation of the planet Sapertys is currently being displayed."

An instant silence filled the room as Ty and I glared ominously at each other through the hovering depiction of a world blanketed by water from its north pole half way down to its equator where green, yellow, and brown hues delineated varying land topologies. While the top half of the sphere was illuminated, the bottom was strangely dark.

"What about Earth?" I asked. "How far away is Earth?"

"Answer," SMILEy said. "Reference 'Earth' not defined."

"What?" Ty said, truly confused. "What does *that* mean?"

"Answer. Among the eight hundred eight thousand sixty-five known solar systems, there is no planet called 'Earth.'"

Chills ran down my spine as Ty and I tried to process what SMILEy had just said.

"We're not on Earth anymore?" Ty asked, utterly devastated. "How could we not be on Earth?"

I reflected back on all the weird stuff that had happened in the past day and said, "Oh, man. Think about it, dude. The white light. The complex. All this freaky stuff. It all started in the 'A' room. Those copper blocks on the wall and the bowling ball that went berserk. Somehow . . . I don't know. Somehow we ended up here, on a different planet."

"A different planet?" Ty blurted, becoming visibly upset. "A different planet? Dude, SMILEy hasn't even heard of Earth. I could deal with being on a different planet." Ty paused before saying, "Well, not really, but . . . this isn't just a different planet, Marcus. It's a different reality! A parallel universe! How are we supposed to get home from a parallel universe?"

"How do I know?" I answered defensively.

Ty was yelling as if everything was my fault.

"You're supposed to be the genius!" I continued. "Do something, I don't know, genius-like! I mean, think about it for a minute! What's so special about *this* planet? Why did we end up here instead of somewhere else? If we can at least figure that out, maybe we can find a way to go back the same way we came."

"Okay!" Ty said, trying to calm down. "Jeez, don't get all torqued off! You might actually be on to something." He stared intently at the holographic planet rotating in front of us and said, "There must be a reason we landed *here*. Maybe we triggered some kind of doorway in the 'A' room, and this place was on the other side." Ty focused his gaze squarely on me through a green landform on the globe and said, "Marcus, we have to find the way home. We have to find that doorway!"

FIFTEEN

MAJINECITY
(TY)

I'd been lost before. Like when I was seven and wandered off while Aunt Andi was shopping for clothes at a department store. I couldn't find her, so I decided to check the ladies' dressing rooms. The first two were empty but not the third one. Only problem was it wasn't occupied by Aunt Andi. Let's just say I got a very scary surprise lesson in female anatomy from a very loud, very angry lady wearing shiny green underwear. Come to think of it, we hadn't been back to that store since.

But Marcus and I weren't lost at the mall. We couldn't go to security and wait for Aunt Andi. We were where no earthling had gone before. We were on a planet called Sapertys, in a destroyed city called Spartanica, with a bunch of refugee kids from Atlantis that stunk like last week's meatloaf and a warrior girl speaking a language that vaguely resembled English.

"Well," I said, "I'm guessing Bellana and the Atlantean kids have no clue about any of this. We need to learn as much as we can about this place and hope something useful pops up that helps us get home."

"Yeah, but where do we even start?" a dejected Marcus said.

"Right here, I guess," I said, pointing at the globe hologram.

Marcus and I stared at the globe for a bit, not quite sure what to ask, when Marcus said, "What did Bellana say when you asked her about skyscrapers? Something about a cupola?"

"Yeah, that's the word she used," I responded. "What the heck is a cupola?"

The globe disappeared and was replaced by an overhead image of the city. Spread evenly around the edges were six white columns that touched at the center. The image rotated into a three-dimensional view from the side, where we could plainly see that the white columns were actually tremendously tall, curved pillars that arched up over the city. A glowing red dome formed around the outside of the pillars. The image of the city at the bottom faded out, leaving only the pillars and the dome circling slowly in front of us.

"Answer," SMILEy responded. "A cupola is a majineically engaged, transparent protective field constructed to shield population centers and military facilities from external provocation."

"It's a shield?" I said excitedly. "Like a force field? They protect the city using a force field? No way! That is so ultimately cool!"

"We saw those towers when we came into the city, but they were black and broken," Marcus said, pointing at the image. "They were still pretty tall but nowhere close to touching at the top like those."

"That's why they don't build tall buildings," I rationalized. "They'd need a super-tall cupola to cover skyscrapers. That'd take a lot more power. What does *majineically* mean?"

"Answer," SMILEy responded. "Majineically is a verb modifier used to indicate that a device is engaged using majinecity."

"Okay," I said, getting a bit annoyed with the piecemeal answers. "What's majinecity?"

"Answer. Majinecity is the invisible field generated by the roiling of a planet's outer liquid irogen core. A planet's majinecity can be amplified by the coincidental orbits of natural satellites or a planet's non-circular orbit around one or more suns."

"That's magnetism!" I announced jubilantly. "What they call majinecity is magnetism. Just like at home. Earth has magnetic poles because liquid iron flows at the core. That's how a compass works. The arrow points to magnetic north."

"But SMILEy said this place has an *irogen* core," Marcus said.

"What is irogen?" I said.

"Answer," SMILEy replied. "Irogen is a material whose molecular structure is comprised of sixteen iron and two nitrogen atoms."

"So what's the difference between iron and irogen?" I said.

"Answer," SMILEy said. "Irogen generates a majineic field approximately one thousand seventeen times more powerful than iron."

"Are you even serious?" I blurted and looked at Marcus. "Do you know what this means? Do you have any idea what SMILEy just said?"

Marcus just stared at me, obviously getting annoyed with the whole discussion. I began to realize I was dancing around the answer just like SMILEy was doing to me.

"Okay," I finally said. "Sorry. This planet has a magnetic field, just like Earth, but it's over a thousand times more powerful. It explains our watches . . . in the complex. Remember?"

"Remember what, Ty?" Marcus responded, still waiting for the punch line.

"They were made of metal," I answered. "As soon as we landed here, the planet's super-magnetic field latched onto the metal in our watches and tried to yank us to the North Pole. That's how we were suspended on that wall. Magnetism was trying to pull our watches right through it. The magnetism here is so strong, they use it to power everything, like we use electricity. And they don't even have to generate it! They pull it right out of the air. Wow! This is heavy stuff."

"But that can't be," Marcus said. "What about the iron in our blood? Wouldn't the big magnet latch on to everybody and—"

"What are you guys doing?" a voice said from behind us, interrupting Marcus just when I was starting to be marginally impressed with his thought process.

We both looked up quickly to find Nekitys standing in the doorway. I had no idea how long he'd been standing there. Had he heard us talking about Earth?

"Oh, hey," Marcus responded. "Just, ya know, passing time. Uh, how's Anina?"

"She's going to be fine," Nekitys said. "There were several shards of exorbalis in her chest from the Desrata attack. One struck her brachiocephalic artery, just above her heart. She lost a significant quantity of blood, but the medica resources here are excellent."

Nekitys had very light-colored skin, similar to the others from Atlantis, except, based on what Kinnard had said, I wasn't sure he was from Atlantis.

"Oh, that's good to hear," I replied, desperate for a way to get on a subject other than what Marcus and I were doing. "How do you know Anina and the others?"

"I joined them while they were escaping from the Desrata detention fields," Nekitys answered. "I noticed them moving in the shadows. They saw me and asked me to go with them. Were you ever held in the fields?"

"No," Marcus responded, shaking his head and yawning.

I was feeling tired, too, but the stuff SMILEy was telling us was too interesting for me to care.

"It's a good thing you got away," Marcus added and looked at me. "You want to get some sleep?"

"I'm tired, but what I'd really like to do is—" I answered but shut up as soon as I saw the look on Marcus' face that told me it was time to go. "Well, sleep does actually sound really good."

We headed for the door.

As we passed, Nekitys said, "Good rest."

"Uh, yeah, thanks," Marcus said without turning around as he and I walked down the hallway.

"Yeah, see ya," I added.

Marcus and I made our way down to level six to find somewhere to sleep. I kept my mouth shut until the stairway door on level six closed behind us.

"Detention fields?" I railed. "Detention fields? Well, you know what that means."

"What?" Marcus asked.

"These guys are all escaped convicts!" I said, filling in the blanks for Marcus. "This is just great. Like we don't have enough problems? Now we have a bunch of serial killers living here with us. There's no way I'm going to sleep. That's probably exactly what they want us to do so they can sneak in and kill us."

"Ty—" Marcus tried to cut in, but I had to bring up something else.

"And that Nekitys," I continued. "There's something not right about that guy. He looks a little older than us, but he talks like a doctor. How does he know so much about human anatomy? They don't exactly teach arteries and veins in middle school. No way. He probably used to kill cats and dogs when he was younger and do autopsies in his basement. That's what serial killers do when they're kids, you know. And the way he stares. Psycho all the way."

Maybe I was just tired, but Nekitys just plain creeped me out.

"I know what you mean," Marcus said. "I get a bad vibe from him, too. But Kinnard and the others seem okay. And Nekitys did save Anina's life."

"Yeah, and what about that?" I pontificated. "Remember when SMILEy said one of the intruders was dead?"

Marcus stopped walking and said, "*Oh, yeah*, that's right."

I could tell his wheels were finally turning.

"But all SEVEN kids are alive, and Nekitys was holding Anina when we found them," I said.

"So, what, he brought her back to life?" Marcus replied. "SMILEy must've just been wrong or Anina's heart rate slowed way down because she lost so much blood. Where are we going to sleep?"

"I don't know," I said.

I wasn't done talking about freak-boy Nekitys, but I was about to drop from exhaustion.

"Anina's still in the room we were in before, and I'm *not* sleeping with those other kids!" I insisted.

"Why not?" Marcus said sarcastically. "Because they're serial killers?"

"Ha ha," I answered. "No. Because they stink."

Marcus stopped and nodded in agreement, like moving and thinking at the same time was a real challenge.

"Then I don't know where to go," Marcus replied. "I wish we could figure out how to open these knobless doors."

"You saw how Bellana did it," I said. "All she does is say the room number and then *open*. Watch this."

I walked over to the nearest door. Its bottom symbol looked like this:

"0619, open," I commanded.

To my amazement, it actually worked.

"No way," a dumbfounded Marcus said.

"Yeah, that's right," I announced, pointing both index fingers back at myself very proudly. "I am the man."

We looked inside and saw a couple of couches and chairs and a table in the back but not much else.

"Ty, I have to admit," Marcus announced, nodding his head and yawning again as he moved quickly into the room, "you are a genius. I call the couch on the left."

Yeah, he said I was a genius. I'd been saying that since we were little kids.

SIXTEEN

WHAT'S UP WITH THESE GUYS?
(BELLANA)

"How did you guys get in here?" I asked, startling Marcus and Ty awake.

"Huh, what?" Marcus mumbled incoherently. Ty put his head back down and buried himself under the blanket.

"Well, we needed somewhere to sleep, and these couches are the most comfortable thing I've ever laid on, so we just stayed here," Marcus said.

"And we didn't want to wake you up," Ty added from the muffled safety of his cocoon.

"I don't care," I blurted, frustrated by their answers. "How did you get the door open?"

"Ty just did like we saw you do," Marcus said.

Ty popped his head out and said, "It wasn't just me! Marcus did it, too! I didn't even want to come in here!"

"You are so lame!" Marcus yelled. "You're the one—"

"Shut up!" I hollered, just about at the end of my patience with these two blockheads. "Both of you! Just shut up!"

Ty sat up, his hair sticking out all over the place. I almost laughed, but this door issue wasn't funny.

"I don't care where you slept," I said. "How did you open the door?"

Ty and Marcus looked at each other, each hoping the other would answer.

"Well?" I finally prompted.

"Like I said," Marcus answered, "we called out the room number and said *open*, and it did. What's the big deal?"

"What's the big deal?" I replied angrily. "You walk into *my* building and start opening doors? *That's* the big deal. I'm the only one that should have the authority to open anything."

It was obvious Ty and Marcus didn't realize they'd done something I didn't want them to do. There was no point making it an even bigger deal.

"Anyway," I continued, "everybody's going for a reinigen and then to eat. I thought you should come with."

"Great idea," Marcus replied and jumped up. "I'm ready to eat again."

Ty threw his covers off and stood up as well.

"Okay," he said, rubbing his eyes. "Let's roll."

"Dude," Marcus said, "serious bed head alert."

Ty felt around his head, grimaced, and said, "Oh, yeah . . . scary."

He licked his hands and tried to tame his rebellious locks as we stepped into the hallway and met up with the Atlantean kids, except for Nekitys and Anina.

I took everybody down to level eleven to clean up, but Ty and Marcus didn't use the reinigens. They just stood in the back like statues the whole time while everybody else went through, as if neither boy had ever seen one before. Where the gehanna could these guys have grown up not to have seen a reinigen? I always figured each of the central cities had them.

Although they looked Spartanican, I started to think these guys might actually be all the way from Lemuria, on the dark side of the planet. And why not? If there were kids from Atlantis here, why not Lemuria?

We eventually made it back up to the level four dining module and got some food. As soon as we were all seated at the table, Kinnard stood up.

"Okay, just quickly," he said, pointing to each one of us as he said our names, "Bellana, Ty, and Marcus, this is Iryni, Naetth, Yra, and Arianas." Kinnard sat back down, looked at me, and said, "And you already know Anina and Nekitys. That's everybody."

"So you're all from Atlantis?" I asked.

"Born and bred," Kinnard answered, taking a big mouthful of food. "Except Nekitys. I don't know where he's from. He just sort of tagged along."

Kinnard grabbed a napkin and wiped some drool off his chin that dripped out while he was talking.

"What do you mean, *tagged along*?" I asked suspiciously.

Kinnard looked at the other kids. They glared back at him as if to emphasize he needed to keep his mouth shut.

"Nekitys saw us escaping from the Desrata detention fields," Kinnard said.

"Kinnard!" Arianas yelled as all the Atlantean kids became visibly upset.

Kinnard put his hand up to calm them down and said, "Do you really think these guys are best friends with the 'rats? Why haven't they turned us in? Why are they helping us?"

Kinnard glanced over at me again and then back at the Atlantean kids. "Bellana is of the Order of Bellator," he said.

An awkward silence filled the room as the other kids looked at me with an expression that said *Really?*

"Was your father . . . ." Naetth started to ask but paused.

"Guelphic Commander of Sapertys," I replied, finishing what he was hesitant to say. "Yep, that's him."

I looked down at the table and hoped my eyes wouldn't start tearing up. It was painful to think, much less talk, about Father and Mother without being sad and angry enough to get outwardly upset. I loved and missed my parents so much. I had so many happy memories, right up until they abandoned me here all alone. How was I supposed to forgive them for that? Even now, I was so proud these kids knew I was a Bellator, but, at the same time, I was so angry about being forgotten I didn't even want to admit my family name.

The room was completely silent again. I got the feeling the Atlantean kids had a million questions, not that I had a lot of answers.

Kinnard finally broke the ice and said, "So, anyways, the 'rats imprisoned us in the detention fields for over two annos; we were working twenty-hour jornos with barely adequate food and water to keep us strong enough to labor. It was pure gehanna on Sapertys. Sleeping on the cold ground. Watching other detainees die." He closed his eyes and shook his head. "We finally found a gap in their security and escaped one night. We kept moving until we got here."

"But what are all of you even doing on this side of the planet?" I finally asked, bewildered these guys were so far from home. "What are a bunch of Atlantean kids doing anywhere near here?"

"Atlantis was destroyed," Kinnard said, obviously trying to maintain his composure. "All at once. Everything. Everyone. It was all just gone. Seven, maybe eight, annos prior. We were all too young to understand what happened. Atlantis looks just like here, outside. It was flattened."

The other kids started to get emotional. One of the girls, Arianas, hid her face with a napkin.

"We left the shelter module our parents put us in once the food started running out," Kinnard continued, "but nobody was outside. Our home city was a big empty nothing. We found food and water and waited for three or four mensis, hoping our parents, or anybody, would come back, but nobody did. We thought things might be better here, so we packed up and started walking."

"You've been coming here," I said, "for eight annos? How did you do that? That's unbelievable."

"There were eight of us when we started," Kinnard explained. "We all made it almost all the way here. Then we got caught by the 'rats. I don't really want to talk anymore about that, but it took us two annos to get out of that gehanna hole. Two of us are still in the detention fields. At least we hope they're still there."

"If it's so terrible," Ty asked, "why would you hope they're still there?"

"Because," Kinnard paused, "if they're not there, they're dead."

Ty blushed, obviously feeling stupid for asking, but I had wondered the same.

"We're going back for them, right?" Naetth asked. "We can't leave Perditus and Kalahn there."

All the Atlantean kids looked at Kinnard in anticipation.

"I know we can't leave them there," Kinnard started, "but it's not like we have an army to go break them out. Especially with all the advanced armaments the 'rats have now." He turned back toward me and said, "When they first threw us in the fields, they were nothing more than fast-moving animals shooting arrows and throwing spears. But in the last anno or so, they changed. They started wearing uniforms and using advanced weapons and transports."

"I saw them walking with humans more than once," Naetth said.

"I never saw that," Kinnard shot back aggressively. "Did anyone else?"

The other kids shook their heads to indicate they hadn't.

"Where would the humans have come from?" Kinnard asked. "Not here, obviously."

"What about the outlander tribes?" I said. "They're all over the territories."

"Outlanders?" Kinnard smirked. "Seriously? We traveled with a few different outlander groups on the way here. They're little more than wandering tribes that traded with each other and had strange dancing rituals at night. They're not much more advanced than the 'rats. I doubt they could've helped."

"Well, I saw what I saw," Naetth said, shaking his head in disbelief as he looked away.

"The 'rat fields are only a three-jorno trip from here," Kinnard said. "Even less in one of their new sphaeras." He turned to me and asked, "They've never bothered you here?"

"Actually," I said, taking a deep breath, "a couple of annos prior, a bunch of animal-looking things came into the city. They totally surprised me, but I was able to stay away from them. I pulled a few heavy-duty draiders out of the armory and pounded them until they left."

Zah! I hadn't wanted to mention the armory! Mother always said *weapons and boys make a big noise.* Now the secret was out. Me and my big mouth!

Yra immediately seized on my slip.

"Your armory is intact?" he asked enthusiastically. "Ours was flattened. Hey, guys, we have weapons!"

I didn't respond, hoping the whole topic would somehow go away.

"So what?" Kinnard responded agitatedly. "Even with a full armory, we'd still be ten kids against the

Desrata kingdom. Let me know how that turns out for you."

Yra looked at the other kids in disbelief and then back at Kinnard.

"So we're not even going to try to save them?" Yra yelled, his face turning red.

He smacked his bowl so violently it flew across the room and against the far wall as he stormed out.

Kinnard sighed and said, "Perditus and Kalahn were like a big brother and sister to Yra."

We all sat in silence for a few minutes. The Atlantean kids looked at each other from time to time as if they wanted to say something but changed their minds.

Talking about when those animals came into the city reminded me of just how close I had come to being killed. The animals were strong, vicious, and lightning fast. They were almost on top of me before I even knew they were in the city. If they ever came back, I wasn't sure I'd be able to fight them off again alone. I needed help, and the only candidates to come along in the past couple of annos since the first attack were sitting in front of me. It'd be a huge risk trusting these guys with weapons, but Kinnard seemed like he had his head on straight, and being from the respected Order of Jahnha meant he was likely somebody I could trust.

"So, are you guys certified on maj weapons?" I finally asked. "Rifles, cutters, lofters, draiders?"

"Seriously?" Kinnard asked, surprised at the question. "Of course not. Those are military weapons. Even if Atlantis was still standing, I'd be too young to be a warrior."

"Well, same here," I replied, "but we have full virtual certification in SMILEy for all the weapons. I can enable access for everyone. Each one only takes a couple of settimas. If the Desrata are getting better armed like you say, they might just come back here again, especially if they think you're here. I could use some help defending this place."

Kinnard thought for a moment.

"Hmmm," he started, looking at the others, "a chance to blast Desrata warriors with real weapons? Who's up for a little training?"

SEVENTEEN

I DON'T KNOW HIM,
AND I DON'T TRUST HIM
(MARCUS)

The thought of learning to use the weapons Bellana talked about sounded really cool! Back home, Aunt Andi only let us shoot our BB guns. This sounded much more, I don't know, manly.

"The virtual warrior environment is in the armory building," Bellana explained. "We'll have to go over there to do the training sims. SMILEy controls that building, so we won't need to bring anything."

We finished eating and followed Bellana, who had put her majrifle back on, back up to the Zetta One doors. Yra joined us on the way without saying anything.

"Wait here," Bellana said. "I want to scout around before we go." She pointed out through the doors to the left and said, "See that tall pile of exorbalis over there? You can see everything from up there. It'll just take me a protoka. I'll be right back."

"You shouldn't go alone," Yra insisted, putting his hand up as if to volunteer. "I'll go with you."

Everyone else raised a hand except Ty, a fact immediately noticed by the rest of us.

"Well," Ty said, looking at the other kids and nodding vigorously, "someone should stay here in case you all get hurt out there and, uh, need help getting back."

Yra scowled at him and said, "You're just scared, galanod. Weenk, weenk, galanod, weenk weenk."

I knew Yra was making fun of Ty but had no idea how. Even name-calling here was bizarre.

"Uh, okay, whatever," Ty replied. "But I'm not scared! Okay, fine, let's go then! I'll even go first, come on!"

"No," Bellana abruptly interrupted. "You'll only slow me down. It'll just be a protoka. Stay here."

She opened the door and took off for the big pile.

Shortly after she left, Nekitys came walking up from behind us.

"Hey, hey!" Kinnard yelped as he moved aggressively toward Nekitys. "Who's with Anina? She's not alone, is she?"

"She wanted time to sleep," Nekitys replied, "so I let her be and came to let you know she's doing very well. Her wound is almost healed, and she's getting her strength back. When I didn't find anyone in the dining module, I started looking around."

"So you just left her alone?" Kinnard yelled, visibly angry.

"I'll go be with her," Arianas volunteered, looking at Nekitys and Kinnard for approval.

"That would be acceptable as long as you don't disturb her," Nekitys replied.

Kinnard kept his eyes glued to Nekitys, as if he was trying to find something suspicious in what Nekitys was saying, but couldn't. He finally turned around and backed off. With no one objecting, Arianas headed for the stairway.

"Are you going somewhere?" Nekitys asked me. "Where's Bellana?"

Kinnard spun back around and glared at Nekitys again.

Nekitys avoided his stare and said, "What? Did I say something wrong?"

The expressions on Nekitys' face always looked fabricated. It was as if he was consciously trying to coordinate the muscles on his face to make us believe he had real expressions. All it did was make him look twitchy, robotic, and creepy.

"I don't want him going with us," Kinnard said, shaking his head vehemently.

"Why not?" I asked.

"Because I don't know him, and I don't trust him," Kinnard yelled angrily.

"You don't know *me,* either!" I pointed out. "I didn't know any of you before yesterday. Isn't the point to be able to defend ourselves against those things that kept you locked up? Having one more certified weapons handler will be a big help."

"What if he's one of them, huh?" Kinnard asked. "Back in the fields, he always stayed to himself. He never talked to anyone. And he was always watching the rest of us. You'd look up and there he'd be, poking his nose around the corner. Just like when we escaped, he was just standing there, looking at us. We had to bring him along to make sure he didn't give us away." Kinnard looked at the Atlantean kids and said, "Remember how they would take Nekitys away for jornos at a time and then . . . poof . . . he'd just show up again? Whenever they took anyone else away, it was for good. It was permanent. No one ever came back . . . except Nekitys."

After more awkward silence, Nekitys said, "Okay, then. I'll stay here."

Kinnard stared at him and finally gasped, "Ugh, no you're not."

Kinnard was seriously getting on my nerves.

91

"But you just said . . . ." I chimed in, looking as confused as I felt.

"I know," Kinnard flung his hands forward from holding his head. "I know. Zah! I don't want him here alone, either."

Just then, Bellana returned.

"We're clear," she said, "let's go." She looked toward the rear of our little group and said, "Oh, hi, Nekitys. Are you coming to the armory with us?"

Everyone looked at Kinnard, who just rolled his eyes and pushed past Bellana standing in the outside doorway.

"Okay, then," Bellana muttered, caught off-guard by the tension she'd unexpectedly strolled into.

Nekitys stepped past me on his way outside. I backed up to give him plenty of space. The vibe I had about him had skyrocketed to the top of the weirdo scale, just above the kid in my tennis class that sang to himself in Russian and danced during matches. Ty's contorted expression told me he was thinking the same. Now I really wanted to learn how to use a majrifle. I never knew when it was going to come in handy.

EIGHTEEN

THE ARMORY
(TY)

So we *finally* headed off to the armory when Marcus walked over.

"You were right, dude," he whispered loud enough for me, but no one else, to hear. "Nekitys is definitely out there."

Based on what I'd just witnessed, I had to agree. Nekitys was a few cards short of a full deck.

"Yeah," I responded in the same manner, so no one else could hear, "but I think he's more the strange kind of weird, not the dangerous kind of weird."

"Seriously?" Marcus replied. "Dude, weird is weird, okay? There aren't, like, different categories."

"Do you really think he's dangerous?" I said. "I mean, do you really think he'd hurt one of us, or all of us? Like you said before, he saved Anina. SMILEy said she was dead and he saved her. How did he do that? He could've just let her die. And it doesn't sound like he's ever been violent. Even in Kinnard's stories, Nekitys never hurt anyone. So he's a bad guy because he keeps to himself and stares sometimes? I mean, heck, some people think *I'm* weird."

Marcus nodded his head and said, "Yeah, you're right about that."

"Shut up," I said, more annoyed that Marcus wasn't taking me seriously than anything else.

"No, no, dude," he attempted to clarify, shaking his head but with a mischievous grin, "I meant the part about Nekitys, not you."

I just looked away, like I always did when I knew it'd be a waste of my time to keep talking, which, with Marcus, was most of the time.

This little expedition to the armory was the first time I'd actually seen the city since we first got here. It was big, and I mean *as far as the eye can see* big. Whatever took this place down had to be unimaginably powerful. Oddly enough, now that I had time to examine things more closely, I didn't see any bomb craters or blast patterns. It looked more like pictures I'd seen after an earthquake than a warfare attack. But it sounded like whatever did this to Spartanica did the same to Atlantis. Could these cities have been demolished by some planet-wide natural catastrophe, like maybe a meteor strike?

Just as I thought I might be piecing the mystery of Spartanica's calamitous demise together, one glaring hole in my logic popped up and slapped me in the face.

"Where are the people?" I muttered, more to myself than anyone else. "Why aren't there any skeletons, or even individual bones? It's like no one even lived here."

We walked for half an hour more. Everybody stayed mostly silent the rest of the way. Bellana finally stopped and gestured toward another non-descript, light-brown pile of rock.

"This is it," she said sarcastically. "The great Spartanica Regional Defense Armory. Pretty impressive, huh?"

No one said a thing. The silence spoke volumes.

"Come on," she said, "I dug down and built a way in over here."

She walked to her right, but I didn't see anything that even resembled an entrance. She kneeled down and started heaving big chunks of rock off to the side.

"Can I get a hand?" she asked, pointing at the rubble around her. "Let's get all these out of the way."

The rocks looked heavy, but Bellana moved them so easily I thought their heft had to be an illusion, like the fake boulders used in movies.

"So, it's true," Kinnard said. "What I've heard about Guelphic Varkis descendants, like the Order of Bellator. I thought it was just a legend. Do you have the speed, too?"

Bellana didn't answer right away but kept heaving stones.

"I don't know," she finally said dismissively, "I guess so."

"The Guelphic what?" Marcus asked.

"Father used to tell me ancient stories about the founders of Spartanica," Kinnard started. "He said Spartanica was the first organized settlement, then village, and then city on Sapertys. Before that, all Sapertyns were outlanders, scattered around, living and roaming in tribes.

"The first leaders of Spartanica were called the Guelphic Varkis. They and their descendants were said to have super-human strength and speed and other physical and mental abilities that they used to protect the city. Father said Spartanica would've lost the Great Carlidian Wars if not for the powers of the Guelphic Varkis. Descendants are said to retain these gifts even now. Looks like at least that part of the story is actually true."

Everyone stared at Bellana in awe. She finally stopped working and stood up.

"*My* father never told me those stories," she said, looking around at all of us. "I've never heard of any of this. I just know these exorbalis blocks aren't going to move themselves, and umbra's only thirty protokas or so from descending." She pointed at the sun and said, "I don't really know what happens out here at night, and I don't want to find out. We should get inside and close this up before umbra arrives. Now, can I get a little help, please?"

Marcus and I and the others tried, in futility, to help move the debris. Bellana moved five for every one Marcus and I together managed to budge. The Atlantean kids weren't having any more luck than we were.

A tunnel started to emerge as each additional block was taken away. Once a couple of dozen blocks or so were tossed aside, an opening just wide enough to slide through opened up.

"That's enough," Bellana said. "I'll be right back."

She slid headfirst down the hole and disappeared. As daylight faded, the moons we'd seen before started to rematerialize overhead. The blue and green swirly one still filled most of the sky. I couldn't understand how it could be so close yet not visible during the day. It looked like we could throw a stone and hit it, or at least Bellana probably could. The other moon was nearer than before but still pretty far away.

Bellana climbed effortlessly back out of the tunnel.

"The illumination is on now," she said. "Let's get everyone inside and I'll close it up. The tunnel leads to the second-floor ceiling, so there'll be a bit of a drop at the end."

I wasn't going to argue with getting inside. My back and hands were killing me even though Marcus and I had only slid two blocks. I saw no reason to damage my body any more than it already was. After all, if I was going to become a magnetic weapons master, I needed to be in prime condition!

I kneeled down to get a better look in the tunnel. Marcus subtly reached out and pulled my arm back.

"Let the other girls go first," he muttered.

Naetth and Yra laughed out loud. Iryni was marginally kinder.

"Oh, ha, ha!" I objected. "Funny! I was just looking!"

One by one, first Iryni, then Naetth, Yra, Marcus, Nekitys, and Kinnard climbed down headfirst. I insisted on going last, except for Bellana, so no one would think I was afraid.

I started down the steep diagonal slope as soon as I couldn't see Marcus ahead of me anymore. The rocks were very hard and, oddly enough, very slippery. I inched myself down and got to where I could see light shining up. The tunnel got wider along the way, and I increasingly had trouble keeping my grip.

"All clear?" Bellana yelled from above.

It startled me, and before I could react, I was sliding out of control toward the exit. I yelled a little, you know, just to let everyone know I was coming.

"What's wrong?" Marcus hollered up the opening.

I kept trying to stop . . . and screaming.

"Ty, what's—" an unsuspecting Marcus started to say again as I shot through the ceiling hole like a penguin through the water and landed right on his head.

We both collapsed to the floor with a loud, painful thud.

"Ughhhhh," Marcus gasped as we struggled to recover from the unexpected impact. "What the heck, Ty!"

"I lost my grip when Bellana yelled!" I replied. "I'm sorry! I didn't mean to! Ugh, my stomach's killing me. Why do you have such a hard head?"

Marcus finally got his bearings and pushed me off him. I winced and tried to sit up. Bellana came sliding headfirst through the hole, gracefully flipped her legs around, and gently dropped to her feet like an Olympic gymnast.

"What happened?" she asked.

All the other kids were smiling at each other, trying not to giggle.

"Ty just . . . you know . . . dropped in," Yra said and started laughing.

Actually, they all started laughing.

"Shut up, you jerk," I yelled.

Marcus and I slowly got up and looked around. There was a lot more debris in this building than in the coliseum. The ceiling was collapsed in most places. The spot we dropped into was the only open area in sight.

"This way," Bellana directed. "Over this pile. The stairway door is on the other side. We need to go down to level twelve."

We all followed as Bellana crawled over the rubble toward where she'd pointed. I waited until the end and climbed after Nekitys. We must've crawled for ten minutes before reaching an opening near a stairway door where we all slid down to the floor. Bellana opened the door and led us down the stairs. Nekitys and I started talking and fell a little behind the others.

"The fields were pretty nasty, huh?" I asked.

"Yes," Nekitys replied. "The Desrata are merciless slave masters. They patrol the area around their settlement and capture anyone that wanders by and force them to work."

"What kind of work?" I asked.

"In the fields, detainees mostly plant, fertilize, weed, and harvest food, all by hand," Nekitys explained. "That's where I spent my time. We were never allowed to mingle with detainees from other areas."

"Is it true," I asked, "what Kinnard said, about you getting taken away?"

"I have no memory of being taken away," Nekitys responded. "I just remember working and surviving in the fields."

"How long were you there?" I asked.

"I don't know," Nekitys said. "As far as I can remember, I've always been there."

Whoa. Nekitys had been in the detention fields his whole life?

"You were born there?" I asked.

"I don't know," Nekitys responded. "I just don't remember being anywhere else, except for here, of course." He looked at me and asked, "Where are you from?"

My mind stopped cold. Where was I from? How was I going to answer that? Oh, uh, hey, I'm from Newkastel. You know, north of Chicago . . . on Earth.

"I'm from Spartanica," I said, without really thinking it through.

"No, you're not," he replied.

If my mind was cold before, it was frozen solid now.

"What do you mean?" I asked, failing miserably to sound genuinely confused.

"You look Spartanican," Nekitys answered, "but you have to follow Bellana everywhere. If you're from here, why don't you know where you're going? And if you're from Spartanica, why did we find you sleeping outside the city?"

Shoot. I had forgotten about Nekitys being with Anina and the others. I didn't actually remember seeing him out there.

"Well, the truth is," I finally said, "I don't really know where I'm from, either. I just don't remember anything before a few, uh, jornos ago, when we saw each other in the desert."

"I understand," Nekitys replied robotically. "I am, however, unfamiliar with the word *desert*. Do you mean when we came across you and Marcus in the arduszone, outside the city?"

Jeez, another Spartanican word I didn't know.

"Yes," I said, willing to say anything to end the conversation before we caught up to everyone else. "In the arduszone. Uh, what did I say?"

"You said *desert*," Nekitys responded in his creepy, expressionless way. "Strange word. Desert. It doesn't reference against any of the known languages."

The others were waiting for us on the level twelve landing. We finally caught up and stepped into the hallway. It looked a lot better than the one on level two. It was well lit, but the floor, walls, and ceiling were dark, shiny, and smooth. The lighting was actually more of a bright glow all around, which was odd because everything was so dark. Thinking back, it reminded me of the complex the sentry had kicked us out of.

"Wow," Yra said, quite impressed as he looked around, "this must be a command level. I saw a virtutour of the command level in Atlantis once, and it was just like this. I'll wager the Center of Command is nearby."

"It is," Bellana said. "We'll walk past it on the way to the warrior sims."

"So this is a military base or something?" Marcus asked.

Bellana pointed to a string of symbols etched into the wall above our heads.

⬛ ⊂1Λ0ΤΛ⅄1ƆΛ ⬛

ƆƎ⅄ΤƎ0 08 Ɔ0⅄⅄Λ⅄0

"Spartanica Center of Command," she said, "where our warrior leaders could see and control everything. I only found it by chance when I was exploring one time way back."

We followed Bellana down the hall past numerous closed doors. After a few seconds, the wall to our left was replaced with a full-length window through which we could see into a huge room that had control panels and big displays on the wall. The doors were a little further down and automatically opened as soon as Bellana got close to them. She stepped into the room. A very excited Yra followed behind her but bumped into something and fell backward to the floor.

"Hey, what the gehanna?" he blurted.

Bellana, with a confused look on her face, said, "What's the problem?"

She stepped out of the room and back in without incident.

"Come on already," she said.

Yra tried to put his hand through the doorway, but he couldn't push it any further than the door frame, even though nothing was visibly there to stop it. He tried two hands and leaned forward with no luck.

"It's like there's an invisible wall here," he said in a frustrated tone and tried putting his right shoulder into it.

"Wait," Bellana said, stepping back into the hallway without a problem. "Try again."

Yra complied but the same result. Kinnard and Naetth tried as well but did no better.

Bellana scrutinized the doorframe closely.

"There's a security field?" she said, stepping slowly back into the Command Center. "I must be the only one with access. Sorry about that. Didn't know."

"A security field?" Naetth asked. "Like a cupola over the door?"

"Yeah," Bellana responded. "I guess. I don't know why this module doesn't just have regular security like other doors."

"A security field obstruction can withstand significantly more blunt force impact than a standard security door," Nekitys announced, as if he was reciting it from a book. "Critical military installations are commonly protected using security field technology."

"And exactly how do *you* know that?" Kinnard asked suspiciously. "I thought *you* only ever lived in the fields."

"I did not say that," Nekitys said. "I said I only remember ever being in the fields."

Kinnard looked uncomfortably at the rest of us as if to say *you really think we can trust this guy?*

"Exactly when did the 'rats start teaching human military security protocols?" Kinnard spouted angrily, looking directly at Nekitys. "I must've missed class that day."

"Anybody more interested in running sims than arguing can follow me," Bellana announced and took off down the hall.

Nekitys turned and followed her, as did everyone else except me and Kinnard, who closely watched Nekitys walk away before moving on.

I stayed back on purpose. I needed a closer look at that security field. It was way too cool to just ignore. I put my hand out slowly to touch it, ready to pull back in case it hurt. I kept reaching and reaching, but my hand went right through. So did my arm. I slowly moved my entire body through the open door. Within seconds, I was standing in the Command Center, just like Bellana had, still waiting for something to zap me, but nothing happened.

I stepped back out to catch up to everybody before they got too far away, but looked up and saw Bellana, motionless, watching me from down the hall. I froze, and we stared at each other for a few eternal seconds. I wanted to say something in my defense, but I hadn't really done anything wrong. I mean, it wasn't my fault I could go through the security fields, was it?

Someone further down another hallway called out, and Bellana took off without saying a word. I headed out as well, desperately hoping she wouldn't make a big deal out of what she saw me do.

I found the others heading into a cavernous room as big as the gym at school. It had a dozen or so oversized mats on the floor, like when we did wrestling. I hated wrestling. I hoped we didn't have to do that as part of learning to use the weapons.

Above each mat was a white globe suspended from the ceiling. They were the first things I'd seen in Spartanica that actually looked like regular lights, except they and the poles they were hanging on were one solid, shiny piece.

Bellana set her majrifle on a bench, walked onto the nearest mat, and said, "Simulator, recognize."

A deep, booming, and, quite honestly, scary male voice echoed from above.

"Recognized," it announced. "Bellana of the Order of Bellator. Proceed."

Everyone looked up suddenly, a bit rattled. I knew it was only a computer, but I didn't want to make it angry.

"Activate warrior sim pad one," Bellana said.

A green laser light fired out of the white ball above Bellana's pad and fanned out into a big cube that surrounded the mat, including a green ceiling twenty feet or so above.

"This box is your sim area," Bellana said. "You tell the simulator which weapon you want to train on. You have to start with the majrifle. Once you've passed all the majrifle sims and get certified, you can train on a cutter. The rifle and cutter use the same appendage, but you'll only be able to access stuff you're certified on. Now, watch this."

She put her right arm and hand in the air.

"Majrifle, current model, stand-alone sim," she commanded.

From out of thin air, a majrifle, just like the one she'd been wearing, materialized on her arm.

"The key is to let the rifle do the work," Bellana said. "Don't try to force the pulse out with your body. Let it surge freely through the appendage. The more you try to muscle the pulse, the more it'll hurt and the less accurate your blasts will be. Watch."

Bellana pointed the rifle at the other side of her cube and fired several times. Semi-transparent balls shot through the air and exploded against the green wall on the other side.

"See, nice and easy," she said. "Deactivate sim pad one."

The rifle on her hand and the green cube surrounding her mat disappeared.

"What about the heavy artillery?" Kinnard asked. "You know, the lofters and the draiders?"

"Those are advanced sims," Bellana answered. "Like I said, you have to be certified on the rifle and cutter before you can access sims for draiders or lofters."

Kinnard nodded in approval, looked at Bellana, and said, "When do we start?"

NINETEEN

WARRIOR SIMS
(BELLANA)

Everybody's warrior enthusiasm cooled off when I told them they first had to watch two oras of introductory instruction about the majrifle and cutter appendage. To get certified, you had to understand how it worked, when to use it, and when not to use it. They could be tricky and sensitive until you got the hang of them. But that was why we had sims. You could do stuff in the sims you could never do in real life without losing an arm, or worse.

The rifle instruction would keep everybody busy while I set up access for them to use the sims. I debated whether or not to give Nekitys access. It was one thing to let him train, another to actually give him a weapon. He seemed harmless enough, but Kinnard had brought up some real questions that Nekitys didn't answer.

Deep down, to be honest, while it was fun having people around, it made me uncomfortable. At least I knew where the Atlanteans came from. I didn't really know anything about Ty and Marcus. They looked Spartanican, with the tan complexion, dark hair, and dark eyes, but where had they been the eight annos prior, and how did they survive the last jorno? They were definitely not from Atlantis. Atlanteans always had very fair skin. Their hair and eyes could sometimes be dark, but not their skin. That was why I'd wager Nekitys was from Atlantis. His skin was the lightest of them all.

"Bellana?" Marcus asked from behind me.

I jumped a little, startled by his sudden presence, and turned around.

"Sorry about that," he apologized.

"That's okay," I said. "Is the instruction done already?"

"No," he replied. "We're just taking a break. Something's been bothering me."

"Do you mean Ty or Yra?" I responded jokingly.

Marcus didn't laugh. He was very serious and looked right at me.

"What happened?" he asked.

"What happened to what?" I asked.

"To Spartanica," he said, "and Atlantis. What destroyed these cities? I've seen images of both places before, what do you call it, the last jorno, on a viewtop. They were beautiful. They were big. There were people." He paused for a moment and said, "What happened?"

This was a subject I didn't like to even think about, but I figured we'd have to cover it sooner or later. I'd buried it deep in my mind annos prior so I didn't have to deal with it. It snuck out every so often, late at night in the silent darkness when I couldn't sleep, but I'd stuff it back down into the outlands of my mind. I assumed Kinnard and the others did the same since no one had dared to bring it up.

I looked up at Marcus, half hoping he'd gone back to the instruction, but he hadn't. I felt an umbra descend over me, like the sun in my personal sky was setting.

"I don't know," I responded curtly. "One jorno I had a family, a city, a school, friends, a life. The next jorno it was all gone. I only had six annos when it happened. I remember bits and pieces . . . like everybody being very scared and running around. Mother and Father put me into the shelter. They said they were going back for others, but no one ever came."

He didn't need to know they *promised* to come back.

"You have no idea what happened?" he asked again. "Does Kinnard know anything about the attack on Atlantis?"

"We haven't exactly talked about it," I said.

Marcus nodded and looked down.

"Okay," he said and started walking away. "I get it."

He stopped with his back still toward me and said, "If it was me, I'd want to know who did this. I'd have to know. Whatever it takes. I'd find out."

He left the room.

That's what Father used to always say . . . *whatever it takes.* I could remember one night when Father stayed up late with me because I couldn't remember my division tables. I was frustrated and tired and wanted to quit. There he was, responsible for the lives of millions of people, yet he had time to help me with homework.

I could still hear him patiently saying, "We'll figure it out together, Belly Beans, whatever it takes."

I wished so much he was with me now. He'd know what to do.

I finished setting up everyone's access and headed back to the sim room.

"Okay," I asked, "who's first?"

"Me!" Yra yelled as he ran onto the mat with both hands over his head. "I'm first!"

Nobody objected.

"First you have to—" I started to say.

"I know!" he announced. "I know! Watch! Simulator, recognize."

"Recognized," the sim responded. "Yra of the Order of Kelleen. Proceed."

"Activate warrior sim pad one," Yra ordered.

The green laser light overhead activated and surrounded the sim mat, but two mats away from where Yra was standing.

"Oh," he said. "Which mat is this one?"

"Look down," I suggested.

The number of each pad was imprinted in font size two-hundred on the middle of the pad.

"Oh, yeah," Yra said. "Uh, activate warrior sim pad three."

The correct sim initiator activated, encasing Yra in its green hue.

"See," he said, looking over at the rest of us very confidently, "I got this."

"Terminate pad one simulation," I announced, and the sim box on pad one turned off.

"Majcutter, current model, stand-alone sim," Yra requested.

"Insufficient certification level," the sim responded.

"Aw," Yra complained, "those cutters look awesome. Okay, majrifle, current model, stand-alone sim."

"Yra, you have to—" Kinnard tried to say but was cut off.

"No receiving limb was detected," the sim replied. "Request ignored."

"If you don't raise your arm," I yelled, becoming visibly annoyed, "the sim doesn't know where to materialize the rifle. Did you even watch the instruction?"

"Sorry!" Yra replied sarcastically with a *what's the big deal* look on his face. "Fazah! Relax!"

He raised his left hand and repeated the majrifle request. It appeared where expected.

"Zah!" Yra exclaimed. "It feels like I'm actually wearing one. Naety, look at this thing!"

Yra walked around the sim pad, amazed at how the simulated rifle moved with him.

"Watch this," he said.

Standing in the middle of the mat, he aimed at a corner and fired. The kickback sent him spinning backwards through the air until he slammed into the opposite sim wall, landing on his head with a thud.

"Yra!" Iryni hollered.

"Terminate pad three simulation," I yelled.

The sim box and rifle disappeared, leaving just Yra collapsed on the floor, motionless.

Kinnard got to him first and knelt down. The rest of us quickly crowded around.

"Yra," Kinnard said, tapping his face gently. "Yra. Come on, wake up."

Yra's head moved a little and he slowly opened his eyes.

"Hey, hey!" Kinnard continued. "Are you okay?"

Yra sat up and looked around, noticeably dazed.

He finally focused on Kinnard, got a big smile on his face, and said, "That was so maxymus! Wow! I want to go again."

Everybody let out a collective sigh of relief as he jumped up, ready to go.

"No," I insisted. "You obviously didn't watch the instruction. You're going to kill yourself."

"What?" Yra objected, looking back and forth at me and Kinnard in utter disbelief. "So I have one little accident and now I can't get certified?"

Kinnard gave me a look that said *it was just one mistake . . . don't be so rigid.*

I took a deep breath and said, "Let's get everybody else on a sim pad and started. Then I'll come back, and you and I will work your sim together. And remember, everybody, the majrifle has four intensity settings . . . *stop, knock down, knock out,* and *kill*. Each step up from *stop* is more powerful and has more kickback than the previous level. Use the sim to figure out what you can handle. The default setting is *knock out*, which is what sent Yra on his little voyage through the air."

"Can we change it so the default is *stop*," Kinnard asked, "just to be safe?"

"We could," I responded, "but actual majrifles are defaulted to *knock out* so warriors don't have to change the setting when they're under attack. The idea is that you can kill someone after you knock them out, but you can't un-kill them. Adjusting the intensity setting is a really important part of the training."

Kinnard nodded in agreement and looked around.

"Everybody get that?" he announced, pointing at Yra. "Check your intensity setting first or you'll end up like this guy."

Everyone chuckled briefly as Yra sneered and rolled his eyes.

"Everybody take a mat and get your sim started," I said. "Once your rifle materializes, change your setting to *stop*, practice your footwork, and take a few shots. We'll maybe add in targets next time." I looked at Yra and said, "You just wait over there until I get everybody going."

He gave me a *you must be kidding look* but finally tromped over to some benches.

Kinnard stayed behind while the others dispersed.

"Nice work, warrior," he said with a smile.

It kind of caught me off guard.

"Oh, uh, thanks, but no," I said, smiling and shaking my head. "I'm just a kid. My father was the warrior."

"Then you're obviously your father's girl," he said as he backed away, looking at me until he finally turned.

I thought about that for a moment. Father's girl. Yeah, I guess you could say that.

TWENTY

HEAD OVER HEELS
(TY)

I'd heard of the saying *head over heels* before, but it usually meant being in love or something dumb like that. But in the sim room, *head over heels* described exactly what had happened to Yra. It was like in a movie when a motorcycle crashes into a car and the rider gets thrown *head over heels* through the air. Yra's feet spun around to where his head normally was and vice versa. I didn't think that could really happen except on a screen using computer-generated special effects. It wigged me out to see it happen right in front of me.

"I'm not shooting one of those things," I told Marcus. "You saw what happened to Yra. No way that's happening to me."

"Don't watch Yra," Marcus said. "He's a spaz . . . and an idiot. Did you see him staring into space the whole time the training video was running? I'm surprised he didn't blow himself up. Just do what the video and Bellana said."

We both looked back and saw Iryni flawlessly fire three straight pulses across one end of a sim wall. She made it look very easy.

"Maybe you should just let that little girl protect you while you paint your toenails?" Marcus said.

"I can do it!" I insisted. "Jeez, I was just saying!"

We practiced for quite a while. I started feeling pretty good about the whole majrifle thing. I got thrown on my butt a couple of times, but I didn't think anything was broken. I squeezed my fist once when I didn't mean to and got popped up in the air ten feet. Another time, I was off-balance and got blasted backward into the wall. I looked around but nobody saw me. In fact, I think everybody else got thrown around like a rag doll at least once. It looked like Bellana got Yra straightened out. At least I didn't see him go airborne again.

"Hey, everybody," Bellana announced, "that's enough. Your arms and backs are going to be sore, but that's normal. Terminate your sims."

We all did so and walked over to her. Kinnard was limping a little, and Marcus had a bloody nose. Iryni and I looked fine. Nekitys, well, just looked like Nekitys.

"You did really good, Ty," Iryni said with a smile.

I'm not accustomed to people giving me compliments, so I wasn't sure what to say. I glanced over at her, trying to hide my disbelief.

"Uh, me?" I said, pointing at myself. I must have looked like such a dope.

"Yeah," she said, "you were hitting a lot of targets."

"Oh, yeah, well, you know," I sputtered. "It, uh, was just luck, I guess."

Iryni smiled and nodded.

"Uh, my shoulder is killing me," Marcus moaned.

This day was getting better and better!

"Whiner," I blurted, looking over at Marcus and then back at Iryni with a smile.

Marcus gave me his death face, but I just stared back with a *how does it feel* look.

"That's why we should stop," Bellana said. "Warriors usually do hard physical training for three mensis before starting maj sims. Let's go eat and head back. The sun will be up in a bit."

"How can that be?" Marcus asked. "We haven't been here that long."

"We've been here over four oras," Bellana said. "Umbra only lasts around five."

"Five oras, five protokas, to be exact," Nekitys chimed in.

Everyone looked at him. He just stared unflinchingly at Bellana.

"Uh, thank you, Nekitys," Bellana said, nodding uncomfortably. "Now that we have that all straightened out, let's go."

TWENTY-ONE

GUELPHIC COMMANDER OF SAPERTYS
(MARCUS)

Bellana had to literally heave each one of us up through the exit hole in the second-level armory ceiling. It was humbling to be around a girl strong enough to lob me like a missile without even trying. She heaved Ty up so hard his head collided with the top of the tunnel. He held on inside, but his legs dangled down as he tried to use them to push against the air. After the usual drama, Bellana reached up and pushed his feet to get him going again.

We finally all made it outside, waited while Bellana closed up the tunnel, and started walking back to the coliseum. Kinnard was strangely quiet but looked like he was thinking hard about something. Then his gaze found Bellana.

"My father knew your father," he said. "Forticus of the Order of Bellator. Not well, but they spoke more than once at government convenings. I saw Forticus give a speech in Atlantis once, not long before the last jorno. I had six, maybe seven annos. I think the entire city was there to hear him. He said the *three sons of Sapertys* were really one people, one family, working together. He talked about how history showed that we had overcome threats through the ages and would always do so. The crowd cheered so loudly, even louder than at a Victor Cup final. Gehanna, he was more popular than Chancellor Lanticas, even in his home city."

"It was like that here, too," Bellana said. "Growing up with him was like a fairy tale most of the time."

"Yeah, a fairy tale that turned into a nightmare," Yra added, putting an immediate damper on the conversation.

Neither Bellana nor Kinnard spoke the rest of the way back. The only real chatter was between Iryni and Ty. They blabbered the entire way about how they were the smallest among the group and would be the best choices to go on secret missions because they could sneak around more easily than the rest of us. Ty asked Iryni if she'd ever seen *Star Wars*. That was brilliant. He obviously got talking and forgot where he was. Iryni, of course, said *no,* and Ty, realizing his slip a little too late, just changed the subject.

Once we got back to the coliseum, the Atlantean kids went to check on Anina and Arianas. Bellana said she needed our help with something and led us to a chamber on level three that looked like a dressing room. There were mirrors on the wall on one side with swivel chairs spread evenly in front of them, like in a barber shop. Each chair had a gray, hollow, shiny dome above it that looked like a big hair dryer. The wall on the other side was covered with one large full-length mirror.

"Have a seat," Bellana said as the door closed behind us.

Ty and I sat next to each other. Bellana collapsed into a chair across from us, looking wiped out.

"Where are you guys from?" she asked.

Ty and I just looked at each other, wondering what to say.

"You show up from nowhere," Bellana continued. "You look Spartanican but speak a language I only partially understand. You can access secure doors and pass through security fields, but you only have level ten access. You need to help me understand, and we're not leaving this room until I get the truth."

I turned, looked at her, and said, "You wouldn't believe us if we told you."

"No more games," she said, growing visibly impatient and frustrated. "Where?"

What else could I do? If I lied and she found out later, she'd be angry and would never trust us again.

"We're from Newkastel, Illinois, north of Chicago," I finally said.

"Yes," Ty added, nodding his head, quite hopeful Bellana was taking this all in. "On the planet Earth. Have you heard of it?"

Bellana waited so long to reply I thought she'd fallen asleep.

"So, if I'm getting this right," she said very sarcastically, "you're from a different planet?"

"Yes, yes, that's it!" Ty pronounced and looked at me excitedly. "I think she's really getting it."

"Bellana," I explained, "I know this all sounds nuts. But we somehow wound up outside the city in a building that looks a lot like the command center on the inside, but a rock cliff wall on the outside. A remote sentry kicked us out, and we ended up sleeping in some tall grass until we met Kinnard and the others, but only because they were running from the 'rats and stumbled into us."

Ty was nodding his head faster with my every word.

"We followed them here and then you saved us," I continued. "We live with our Aunt Andi in a house on Woodbine Circle in Newkastel, Illinois, United States of America, Earth . . . and we have no idea how we got here."

Bellana sighed in disbelief. I couldn't blame her obvious skepticism.

"What do you want?" she asked. "The weapons? The city? Why are you here?"

"I just want to go home," Ty whimpered.

I had to agree.

"Then go," she said, gesturing toward the door. "No one's keeping you here."

"Go where?" Ty said. "We don't know how to get home! We don't even know how to get back into the complex!"

Bellana just sat with her head back and her eyes closed.

"The complex?" she said. "So, if I'm to believe all of this, you don't know how you got here. You don't know how to get home. I don't think you're looking to take anything or hurt anybody. And if you were, you'd probably be able to do it eventually, anyway. I can't protect everything all the time. You can call this home if you want. It looks like you already have access to everything. And when you remember where you're really from or just decide you want to tell me, let me know. I'm going to stay right here for a while. I'll see you later. Good rest."

She passed out right in front of us.

Ty and I left the room. Personally, I wanted to get some sleep, too. We got ten steps or so down the hall when I stopped.

"Hang on," I told Ty and started walking back to the dressing room. "What did she mean we could pass through security fields?" I reached the door and said, "Room 0323, open."

The door opened but Bellana wasn't inside. Ty walked in behind me.

"This is the room we were in, right?" I asked, knowing full well it was.

"Yes, 0323," Ty confirmed.

118

"Where is she?" I asked. "She couldn't have left here after us, could she?"

"No way," Ty answered. "We weren't that far away. We would have heard her leave. She just disappeared, dude."

I looked around one more time and said, "Looks like we're not the only ones with a secret or two."

Ty and I went back to 0619 to crash. Somebody had made up our couches with sheets and blankets and gave us each a pillow. There was a handwritten note on Ty's couch that said *Sleep tight. Stay warm. Gotta hit more targets tomorrow* followed by a smiley (not a SMILEy) face and an "I."

"Oh, well," Ty stammered, trying to act normal but failing miserably, "that, uh, that was, you know, nice of Iryni."

"Yes," I said, "indeed, it is. Very nice. I think little Ty-fry has a girly friend."

"No," he responded defensively. "She's just really nice. See, she made your bed, too."

"Yeah, nice try," I said. "She had to make up mine or it'd be totally obvious she has a crush on you, which she does."

"Jeez," Ty blustered, "a girl other than Aunt Andi is nice to me, FOR ONCE, and it has to be a crush? Give me a break. I know a crush when I see one, and this is definitely not it."

"Oh," I responded, "so you're a crush expert now?"

"Yes, I am," Ty said. "For instance, have you noticed how Kinnard and Bellana have become so chummy lately?"

I lay down and pulled up my nice, new covers. My body sunk into the very comfortable couch, which felt extra nice because my shoulder was still killing me.

"Uh-huh, saw that," I said. "Oh, well. She's been here alone a long time."

"Yep, and I guess *you* missed *your* chance," Ty said, trying to be insightful. "Toooooo slooooooow, Marcooooooo. Ha ha!"

I didn't know why Ty was getting such a kick out of razzing me about Bellana.

"Still," he continued, "I know people, and you and Bellana would be perfect together. Kinnard is all right, but trust me."

If Ty said anything after that, I didn't hear it.

I wasn't asleep for very long when, through my closed eyelids, it looked like someone was flipping the lights on and off or lightning was flashing outside. I remembered how Mr. Leiding, my science teacher, told us we could figure out how many miles away a storm was by counting the seconds between the lightning flash and the thunder. Then again, being five floors underground, I probably wasn't going to see much lightning or hear much thunder.

Staggering pain suddenly rampaged through my skull like a monster truck on steroids. I opened my eyes to find I was surrounded by static . . . like how the TV looks when the satellite signal starts to go out. It was tremendously bright and was immediately accompanied by an ear-splitting *CRACK!* that sounded like lightning had struck right in front of me.

CRRRRAAAAAAACK! A mammoth, jagged white lightning arc shot across in front of me and exploded. I covered my ears and closed my eyes again, just hoping it would all go away. Through all the chaos, I somehow heard voices, but they were all mixed up and blended together so nothing they said made any sense. Some sounded far away, while others were so

120

close I thought I'd be able to see whoever was talking if I ever opened my eyes again.

All of the sudden, clear as a bell, I heard a man say, "Then the building of Vanidicus will take place, my liege, with you at my side."

The voice was distorted and unrecognizable, but I got the impression the person behind it was old or sick and having trouble breathing.

The static and noise kicked back in, and the free-for-all was back on. The dizziness finally got to my stomach, and I had to concentrate just to keep from blowing chunks. Another big *CRRRRAAAAAAACK!* rang out, and the insanity instantly stopped.

With my head still throbbing, I cautiously opened my eyes. A man with long black and gray hair and a beard that reached to his chest was lying on his back on the ground ten feet away. His clothes were black and brown and shiny, like satin, but much heavier and tougher-looking, like a uniform. I couldn't tell if he was even alive, so I tried to stand up to get a closer look, which took a few seconds as I regained control of my vision and balance. As I wobbily reached my feet, the static and screeching flashed for a split second, went away, and flickered again. Just when I thought I was going to lose my sanity, it stopped again. I looked up, and the man with the long hair and beard was standing over me.

"Ahhhhhhh!" I shrieked and jumped back, terrified. "Stop! Who are you? What is this place?"

I put my fists up as if I was ready to fight, not that it would've mattered. This guy was at least six feet, five inches tall and built like a professional wrestler. He just stood and watched me intensely with his dark, scary eyes. His right eye had an eerie green glow around the pupil.

"What are you?" I asked. "Some kind of robot?"

He turned his head slightly, revealing a scar running from the corner of his right eye with the green pupil straight back to his ear.

"Marconis," he mumbled.

It took me a second to process what he said.

"What?" I asked, exasperated and afraid he was going to come at me. "This place is called Marconis? Where's that?"

I couldn't see much other than the space around him. The air had a visible motion to it, like it was full of steam or smoke, but I didn't smell or feel anything. Every so often, a red line passed in between me and the wrestler, from right to left.

"What did you say?" I asked again.

"Tymaeus," he replied.

"What does that mean?" I said. "Is that your name?"

Hercules and I were having a real communication problem . . . just what I needed.

"My name?" he questioned. "I am called Forticus of the Order of Bellator."

WHAT? Had I just heard what I thought I heard? This was Bellana's father, in my dream?

"Commander of Sapertys?" I asked.

"That's right," he said, raising an eyebrow, obviously surprised I'd heard of him. "Guelphic Commander of Sapertys, to be exact. How do you know that?"

"Bellana told us about you," I answered.

"Bellana?" he shot back, his face suddenly lighting up with hope and relief. "She's alive!"

"Yeah, she's fine," I said. "She's been all alone in Spartanica for a long time, though."

His expression quickly got serious again, as if he was thinking very hard about what to say next.

"What are you doing here, on Sapertys?" he asked.

"Am I still on Sapertys?" I replied. "Is this the basement or something? Why did you bring me here?"

"I didn't," he said. "You brought yourself here."

The static and screeching blinked in and out a couple times again. I put my hands back over my ears until it stopped. Forticus was talking but I couldn't make out his words.

Then I heard him yell, "Marconis!" and everything cleared. "Focus on my voice. We don't have much time. Your body and mind are just beginning to adapt to the majinecity. Your Guelphic abilities will be weak and sporadic until you fully adjust. You won't be able to maintain this projection much longer." He paused briefly and said, "You are called Marconis of the Order of Bellator."

I froze as my mind tried to digest what Forticus just said.

I shook my head in disbelief and said, "No. My name is Marcus Mitchell."

"Listen to me," he insisted, "and understand. Focus your projection. You are called Marconis of the Order of Bellator." He paused again and said, "You are my eldest son."

The chaos flashed again, but I hardly noticed.

"Focus, Marconis!" he yelled.

I had to squint to see him because my head hurt so much.

"Your life is in tremendous danger here," he continued. "You must return . . . gateway . . . home. Do . . . understand?"

The chaos flashed ever more intensely. Forticus' voice faded into the noise.

I barely heard him say, "Find other blood . . . mother . . ." before he was completely gone.

I lurched up into a sitting position back on my couch in 0619 in a sweaty panic. The room was dark and quiet. My heart was racing, my head still pounding. Ty was on his couch, whimpering and talking in his sleep like usual. I had to tell him what just happened.

"Ty!" I whispered loudly. "Ty . . . wake up!"

"What? What?" he blurted out, all wild-eyed. "Is it time for school already?"

"No, we're in Spartanica," I said. "Remember?"

It took a few seconds, but he finally looked semi-conscious.

"Dude," I said, "I think I just met Bellana's dad."

"He's here?" Ty responded, looking at the door as if Forticus was going to walk through. "Where?"

"No," I said. "Chill out. I know this is going to sound totally sideways." I stopped and took a deep breath before saying, "I saw and talked to him in my mind. Like in a dream, but it wasn't a dream. He called it my *projection*. He was there, right in front of me, and you won't believe what else he said."

I took Ty through the whole surreal episode. He tried to tell me it was a dream, which I knew it wasn't . . . was it? Could it have been?

"I have to tell Bellana," I said.

"Tell Bellana what?" Ty scolded with an amused look on his face. "That you met her dad in a dream? That we're her brothers? How can that possibly be? You know our parents died when we were little. We've lived with Aunt Andi ever since. I mean, Marcus, come on! Duh! Remember?"

Ty was usually the one with the active imagination, so he was thoroughly enjoying being the rational brother for once.

"Dude, this was the most . . . ugh . . . ." I tried to say, but my head was still killing me, "the most real dream ever."

I was starting to question my own memory.

"If we had a sister," Ty said, "which we don't because we'd know if we did, wouldn't she be on Earth?"

"Uhhhh, my head," I groaned and leaned back down onto the couch, unable to keep it up. "Good night."

TWENTY-TWO

YOU'RE AS SILLY AS EVER
(TY)

I couldn't fall asleep after listening to Marcus' Forticus story, so I got up and went back to the dressing room on level three where Bellana had pulled her disappearing act. Once inside, I looked all over the room again for another exit but, like before, didn't find one.

I took an extra close look at the large wall mirror, thinking maybe it had a secret opening or that it was a two-way mirror, like the one we saw when my class visited the Newkastel Police Department. The cops let us go into actual jail cells and the command center where 911 calls were taken. They even took us to their shooting range and let us look into their munitions room where all the guns and ammo were kept. But the coolest part was the interrogation room where they questioned suspects about crimes. It had a big two-way mirror on the wall, just like the one in this room, except this one was a lot bigger. The mirror let people in the observation room next door watch what was happening without being seen.

So I wondered . . . could there be an observation room on the other side of this mirror that Bellana somehow snuck into when Marcus and I weren't looking? I leaned against it and peered in as hard as I could but didn't see anything but my reflection.

Defeated, I tried to step back, but couldn't. My nose and forehead were stuck, like my face had been instantly super glued to the mirror. I pushed back hard with my hands to break loose, and they got stuck, too!

But it didn't feel like they were just stuck. It was more like the mirror had wrapped around them, like the glass was slowly swallowing me. What if this was a trap . . . some evil, camouflaged people catcher that I'd fallen into? If there was a time to panic, this was it!

"Help!" I pathetically bellowed. "Uh, yes, uh, please . . . help! I'm stuck to the . . . help! To the mirror! Uh . . . actually, IN the mirror! Help!"

Then a scary thought hit me. What if this was like quicksand, and the more I struggled, the more it'd pull me in?

I stopped moving and whispered, "Heeeeeeellllllllllpppppp! Heeeeeelllllppppp!"

It was pointless. No one was ever going to hear me!

"Tymaeus," a woman's voice I didn't recognize said from behind me.

I jumped when I heard it and slid even further into the mirror. Now my nose was completely submerged, and I could only breathe through the corners of my mouth.

"Close your eyes," she said, "take a deep breath, and step back slowly. Everything will be okay."

She had a very calming and reassuring manner. I did as she said and jerked back hard.

"Ow!" I screeched. "It didn't work! It didn't work!"

"Calm down," she said patiently. "Pull back slowly, like you're sneaking out of an instruction you don't like and you don't want the teacher to see."

"Out of an instruction?" I asked. "You mean like gym class? I really hate gym class!"

She didn't reply. I pulled my head back very slowly.

"It's working!" I whispered jubilantly.

My head slowly peeled all the way out of the glass, followed by my hands and knees. Finally free, I put some space between me and my personal fly trap. The mirror just looked like, you know, a mirror. I spun around and saw Anina standing behind me.

"Hey!" I exclaimed happily, but was confused by her presence. "How did you know how to get me out of that?"

She smiled a very kind, understanding smile, walked up, put her hand on my cheek, and said, "Tymaeus, my boy, you're as silly as ever."

Huh?

"What did you call me?" I asked.

"By your proper name, of course, Tymaeus," she answered.

That was one of the names Marcus said Forticus used in his dream.

"Why are you talking like that?" I asked.

Anina's eyes rolled back into her head and she collapsed.

"Anina!" I yelled. "Are you okay? Anina!"

She opened her eyes and looked around.

"What am I doing here?" she asked.

"I don't know," I said. "You were just suddenly here talking to me. Don't you remember?"

She got a freaked-out look on her face.

"No," she responded, "the last thing I did was go to bed when everybody else did."

"You must have been sleepwalking," I said. "Can you get up?"

She nodded, and I helped her up slowly.

"Let's get you back to your room," I said.

With her arm around me for support, we walked through the dressing room door and started down the hall when I heard Bellana behind us.

"Hey!" Bellana said. "Is everything all right? What're you two doing around here?"

Believing I'd caught Bellana in the middle of her disappearing act, I completely forgot about Anina, who dizzily leaned up against a wall and slowly slumped back to the floor.

"Where did you just come from?" I insisted with my finger pointed at her.

"In the barbery," Bellana answered, pointing to the dressing room Anina just came out of. "That's where I fell asleep."

"No, no, no way," I said, still approaching.

"Zah!" Bellana gasped as she ran by me. "Ty! Anina . . . what's wrong?"

"I feel so slappy," Anina said.

"I'll take her back to main medica on six," Bellana said, putting her arm around Anina. They both continued down the hall.

"That's fine, but then I want to know where you were, Bellana," I hollered as they shuffled away. "I know you weren't in there."

I walked back into the barbery and looked warily at the big mirror. No way was I getting close to that thing again. I barely survived the first time.

I headed back to 0619 and woke a very groggy Marcus.

"Hey," I said as he tried to shake the cobwebs, "what names did Forticus say to you?"

"What?" Marcus said, shielding his eyes from the light that turned on when I came in. "Oh, he, um, he called me Marconis."

"No," I said, "the other thing he said that you thought was a name. What was it?"

He had to think for a moment.

"Uhhhhh, Typhus," he answered. "Tymus. Something like that."

"Tymaeus?" I offered.

"Yeah, that's it," he confirmed. "Tymaeus. Why?"

"Anina just called me that name," I explained. "She was in some kind of trance, but she called me Tymaeus and said I was her silly boy. Wait, come on."

I tugged on Marcus' shirt to follow me to the back of the room where a smaller version of the viewtop we'd used in the dining module sat. Just as before, the unit turned on and displayed the three-dimensional Spartanica symbol as soon as I sat down.

"Display the most recent image of Forticus of the Order of Bellator," I commanded.

A three-dimensional image of a man, a big man, standing at a podium in a funky-looking uniform materialized in front of us.

"Is that the guy you saw in your dream?" I asked.

Marcus, visibly shocked, nodded his head and said, "That's him. That's definitely the guy I talked to. That's Forticus."

"Dude," I said, chills running down my back, "I don't understand any of this, but I'm seriously starting to think you didn't have a dream."

TWENTY-THREE

IT'S STARTING TO MAKE SENSE NOW
(BELLANA)

"Fazah!" Arianas yelled as the door to room 0627 opened. "What happened?"

I helped Anina walk into the room and sit down on her bed.

"I don't know," Anina responded. "I woke up on level three. I have no idea how I got there."

Nekitys hurried over and clasped two fingers on her right wrist. Iryni got up and came over as well.

"Her heart rate is elevated," he said. "Here, lay back."

He fluffed her pillow and helped her ease back onto it. He activated the overhead vitalscan and reviewed the readout panel on the wall as Anina's body was enveloped by a yellow light.

"She's fine," he surmised. "Anina, have you ever walked in your sleep before?"

"No," she responded while yawning. "At least no one's ever told me I did."

"It looks like you could use some rest," I said. I looked at Nekitys and said, "As long as she's all right, how about we all do the same?"

Arianas, Iryni, and Nekitys agreed.

"Well then," I said with a smile, "no more wandering the halls, Anina."

"We'll keep an eye on her," Iryni said and waved goodbye, as did the others.

I left the room, but as I reached the stairway door, Kinnard came around a corner at the distant end of a hall that was nowhere near any of the rooms anyone was using. He looked surprised and slowed down when he saw me.

"What're you doing up?" he yelled as he approached. "I thought you'd be resting."

"I was," I replied. "I thought you were resting, too. What were you doing way down there?"

"Oh," he said as he made it to where I was standing, "I used the lavatory and took a wrong turn when I came out. I got a little lost."

"Your room's only three doors away from the lavatory," I point out. "You got lost?"

"I guess I, uh, wasn't quite awake," Kinnard responded with an embarrassed smile. "Hey, I feel stupid enough as it is. Don't rub it in."

"Sorry," I said, still oddly suspicious about the whole scene. "Do you need directions back to your room?"

"No!" he said, getting a little agitated. "I know where I am now, thank you. Good rest."

Kinnard walked off down the hall. I stayed and watched to make sure he got where he was supposed to go, but I had another problem. Ty said he knew I wasn't in the barbery before I found him and Anina in the hallway on level three. How could I have been so careless before? It wasn't like Ty and Marcus were dumb. I never should have brought them there in the first place, but I was so tired and didn't think I'd make it much farther once I sat down.

Truth be known . . . Kinnard was right. I could do some stuff. Special stuff. I was really strong. And fast. In fact, I could run faster than a quagga at full speed.

They roamed all over the outlands looking for water and plants to eat. They weren't quite as quick as hartebeest but still easily outran most arduszone predators. One day I decided to have some fun and started chasing a herd grazing outside the city. I isolated a couple and ran right behind them until *HA!* I blew right past. I totally felt like a hungry sabre hunting my prey! It was incredible! The funny part was they kept running behind me after I passed them. I was like, *hey, guys . . . I'm not chasing you anymore . . . why are you still running?*

I didn't mind everybody knowing about that stuff so much. But some of the other abilities, like stepping through reflectors into the darkways, I wasn't so sure they'd understand. I didn't even really understand how I could do those things. If some *other* kid could do all this stuff, I'd think that kid was a freak. I hoped these kids didn't think *I* was a freak.

But I had to admit . . . I was glad I could do that stuff. I figured out by accident how to move through a reflector, like the big one in the barbery, and sneak down to my little hideout when I needed a safe place to sleep. There was no other way in or out of my bedroom down on level twelve except through the reflectors.

"Priority one notification," SMILEy announced.

I couldn't believe it. Not again.

"Priority one notification, proceed," I answered.

"Two intruder life forms have entered the facility at location Zetta One," SMILEy announced.

I really needed to figure out a way to barricade that door!

"Are they human?" I asked.

"With ninety-seven percent probability, intruder life form species is not Homo sapiens," SMILEy responded.

FAZAH!

"Well, what are they, SMILEy?" I blurted.

"With ninety-five percent probability, the intruder life forms are Canis sapiens," SMILEy replied.

"What the gehanna is that, SMILEy?" I asked as my panic level went vertical.

"It's the 'rats!" Kinnard hollered as he came running back down the hall.

Nekitys poked his head around a corner at the far end of the corridor and started jogging toward me. Yra and Naetth tumbled through a door behind Nekitys and followed as they struggled to pull on their clothes.

"It's the 'rats!" Kinnard said again as he got to where I was standing. "Do you have your rifle?"

I shook my head and said, "No. Let's just hide in a room until they leave."

"We can't!" Kinnard said. "'Rats have an infallible sense of smell. They can track prey from milles away just by sniffing the air. They'll walk every bit of this place until they find us. Where's your rifle?"

"I left it up on level four," I replied.

"Any other weapons?" he asked. "Anything the rest of us can use?"

"No!" I exclaimed. "You're not qualified yet. They won't work for you."

"Great!" Kinnard said, exasperated at the prospect of having to fend off our attackers with nothing more than his bare hands. "Tell that to the 'rats!"

"Update," SMILEy announced. "Canis sapiens life forms have entered stairway C on level one."

Kinnard and I looked at each other and both said, "Let's go!"

We headed up the stairway. I was way ahead of everyone else by the time I reached the door on level four and hustled into the dining module as the illumination turned on. I opened the cafeteria closet where I'd left my rifle on a shelf, but it wasn't there.

"What?" I uttered out loud, hurriedly glancing all around in a panic.

"Update," SMILEy said. "Canis sapiens life forms have reached level two in stairway C."

"I know!" I yelled in desperation, tearing everything apart to find my rifle. "They're coming! Where is it?"

I heard the stairway door open and close. That meant they were right outside the door to the hallway. I'd have to hide until they left so I could find my rifle. I hustled into an open vestibule at the back of the room but left the door open a crack so I could peek out without being seen. Menacing shadows slid silently across the floor under the door to the hallway. The door opened.

"Bellana?" Kinnard whisper-yelled. "Bellana?"

I exhaled so hard I almost collapsed, stepped back into the room, and leaned over onto my knees to catch my breath.

"Ugh," I groaned. "I thought you were them. I can't find my rifle. It's not in there where I always keep it."

"Ask SMILE where it is," Kinnard said. "Hurry!"

"SMILEy can tell me where my rifle is?" I asked.

"Of course," he said. "It knows which rifle is assigned to you, and it can locate it by its serial number. Ask it!"

I was surprised that I didn't know SMILEy could do that. Then again, being here alone forever, I hadn't exactly had issues keeping track of stuff.

"Smiley, locate my—" I started to say.

"Wait!" Yra cried. "Wait! It was me! I took it! I wanted to try a real one, but it wouldn't work, and then—"

BANG! The door to the hallway erupted through its instantly shattered frame and flew across the room. Two of the ugliest living creatures I'd ever seen ran in.

They growled and snarled dauntingly, baring their canine-like teeth as drool dangled and flapped all around from the corners of their mouths. They were easily twice my height with ominously oversized, hairy, human-shaped bodies. Instead of hands, they had paws, each with four thick, yet surprisingly nimble digits, all with long, razor-sharp nails jutting out like ready-made daggers. Their barrel-chested physiques with grotesquely broad shoulders and cannon-sized arms were bigger and more muscular than anything I'd ever seen. Their strong, foreboding faces, with flat mouths and pushed-in noses that sat higher than their pitch-black recessed eyes vaguely reminded me of a bulldog. Unlike a bulldog, their heads were hairless with taut, dark gray skin over chiseled muscle and bone. I couldn't tell whether their dark-brown skin was shiny or if they were wet, or maybe sweating. While they looked like animals, each one wore a black, military-style uniform with the sleeves torn off, undersized pants with frayed bottoms that stopped mid-shin, and ratty black army-style boots. As barbaric as these things appeared at first glance, they were definitely more than just wild beasts.

"What do you want?" I yelled.

These things had broken into *my* home. Rifle or not, I was not just going to stand there and be afraid. If they wanted this place, they were going to have to take it from me.

"Weeeee waaaaaaant our property baaaaaaaaaaaack," the taller thing said, gesturing at Kinnard, Yra, and Naetth.

"We're not your property, 'rat face!" Yra yelled.

Both things scowled at him. Kinnard ran at the smaller one, jumped up, and kicked it with both feet. The thing took a couple steps back while Kinnard dropped to the floor and slid backwards. Before Kinnard could get up, the small thing put its foot over his throat and pressed forcefully down. I thought it was going to kill Kinnard, but the bigger thing yelped and the smaller one eased up a little.

"Yooooouuuuuu wiiiiiilllllllll come with us or weeeeee wiiiiiiillllllll crush him like the human filth he is," the bigger thing said.

Kinnard's face turned dark red as he futilely thrashed about trying to get the small thing's leg off his neck.

"Let him go!" I yelled.

Kinnard started turning blue as his arms fell lifelessly to the floor. He was dying!

In the blink of an eye, I sprinted at the smaller thing, drove my hands into its chest, and sent it crashing through one side of the cafeteria doorframe into the eating area, where it vanished from sight. I saw stars for a few seconds but heard Kinnard coughing. He was alive!

Big clomping footsteps came up quickly behind me. The big thing grabbed the back of my shirt and effortlessly heaved me through the air. I landed on my back and bounced a couple of times as I slid across the floor. That thing was seriously strong! I tried to stand up, but it clamped onto my neck with its left paw, lifted me off the ground, and slammed me up against the wall.

"IIIIIIIIIIIIIIIII was going to leeeeeeeetttttttttt you allllllllll liiiiiiiivvvvvve," it said.

He swung his right paw out to the side and extended long, sharp claws from each finger and thumb. Drool was spewing from all over its mouth and leapt out at me each time it spoke.

"But noooooooowwwwwww you wiiiiiiillllllll diiiiiiiiiieeeeeeee," he finished, gritting and showing his yellow and black fang-like teeth. I closed my eyes and braced for the end.

"Rrrrrrrrrrrrrr. NO!" I heard someone yell.

My death blow never came. I opened my eyes to see Marcus barely holding the big thing's right arm back, keeping it from slicing me to pieces. How could he do that?

Marcus looked at me as if to say *do something!* I clasped both of my hands together into one big fist and pounded down across the thing's left arm. Its elbow bent a little but it didn't loosen its grip. I hit it again and broke free, dropped to my feet, and gasped for every breath of air I could get. Marcus let go of its other arm and quickly backed out of reach. The thing, noticeably stunned, looked quickly back and forth in confusion between the two of us.

"Huuuuuuuuumans with the power of hardened Desrata battlers?" it postulated. "Impressive. You will harvest twice that of the normal puny human servant."

"Bellana!" Kinnard yelled from behind, holding my rifle up where I could see it.

The Atlantean boys had snuck out and found it while the big thing was tossing me around.

"Here!" he said and lobbed it to me.

I caught it and slid it on. It hugged my arm like an old friend and lit up, ready to go.

"Whaaaaaat is this?" the big thing asked. "A puny huuuuuuman toy?"

I debated whether to adjust my rifle to *kill* but left it on *knock out*. If this thing had information about the Desrata, I wanted it.

I motioned with my head for Marcus to get out of the way. Dropping a few thousand tessles of majinecity on this thing would launch it airborne, and Marcus was in the flight path. He looked at me as if he was confused, so I motioned again. He still didn't get it. The thing, noticing I was distracted, snarled and made a quick move toward me. Its reward was a perfect maj strike to the middle of its barrel-sized chest. It launched by Marcus on its way to being embedded in the wall behind them both. It was no longer moving or snarling . . . just drooling.

Marcus stood ready for it to get up, but when it didn't, he turned to me and said, "Were you trying to tell me something?"

"Trying?" I hollered, completely exasperated and still fully amped up for a fight. "What do you think, genius? Fazah!" I turned back to Yra and yelled, "Where the gehanna was my rifle?"

Yra looked up at Kinnard and explained, "Like I was saying before, I wanted to try a real one—"

"You wanted to try a real one," I interrupted, "so you stole mine? If you had watched the instruction you would've known it won't work for you!"

"Bellana," Kinnard interjected, "he risked his life with me and Naeth to sneak out and go get it. He brought it back here so you'd have it."

"And that's supposed to make it all better?" I yelled, my throat getting hoarse. "We could've died!"

Kinnard gestured at the big thing and said, "How long before they wake up? Do you have someplace we can secure them?"

"Fazah, where's the other one?" I thought, annoyed that I'd forgotten about it.

Marcus and I ran to the cafeteria doorway. The small thing was sprawled out, face down and unconscious on top of several tables that got shoved together when it landed. I walked over and fired a pulse into its chest, just to be sure.

We walked back into the dispensary room.

"These are the Desrata you've been talking about?" I asked Kinnard.

He nodded.

"These are the same things I had to scare off a couple of annos prior," I said. "And, yeah, I know where we can lock them up."

"Why didn't you change the rifle to kill?" Naetth asked. "I say we take 'em outside and blast 'em one last time."

"Maybe later," I said. "Right now, I want to know why they came to *this* building. They have the entire city to mess around, yet they came directly here, to us."

"Good point," Kinnard said, looking at Naetth and Yra. "That can't be a coincidence. Hey, I don't think we'll be much help with these things. Do you mind if we go check on the girls?"

He was right. The Desrata were so heavy I didn't think anyone other than I could move them . . . except . . . Marcus?

No," I answered Kinnard, "I don't mind. Go ahead."

Kinnard, Yra, and Naetth took off through the now doorless exit to the hallway.

"Nekitys," I said, "have you seen any extra-large full-body immobilizers in medica?"

"I have seen three size extra-large full body immobilizers," he responded.

"Ah, that's great," I said, feeling relieved for the first time all day.

We could put an immobilizer around each 'rat's neck to impede messages from their brains to the rest of their bodies. Immobilizers were normally used to expedite the healing process by temporarily keeping patients from moving, usually with back injuries.

"Can you please bring them here as soon as possible?" I asked Nekitys. "And bring the remote controller for each one, too."

Nekitys nodded and left the room.

"We'll get these things turned off and locked up," I said.

With everyone else dispatched, it was just me, Marcus, and Ty in the room. We stood around without talking for a bit while we waited for Nekitys to come back. I finally decided to break the awkward silence.

"So," I asked, "are all the kids on, what's it called, Earth, as strong as you?"

Ty looked at Marcus as if he wasn't sure how Marcus would answer.

Marcus looked at me and said, "Not exactly."

"Not exactly?" Ty yelped. "Not exactly? That was amazing! How did you do that, dude?"

"Well, I couldn't let that thing kill Bellana!" he yelled back.

"So you were being false outside the armory when we were opening the tunnel," I pointed out. "You probably could've moved all the exorbalis blocks by yourself. Why did you act like you couldn't?"

"He wasn't being false," Ty chimed in. "He's not really that strong."

Ty was officially on my nerves.

"I wasn't misleading you before," Marcus said. "I didn't used to be this strong. It just kind of happened in the past day or so."

"Yeah, I can vouch for that!" Ty felt compelled to add.

"We need to talk to you about something," Marcus said.

With the way he suddenly got so serious, I wasn't sure I wanted to hear what he was going to say.

"I had a . . . not a dream . . . a . . . I don't know . . . vision . . . last night," Marcus explained. "I talked to your dad . . . uh . . . father."

"Excuse me?" I said, needing to hear what Marcus said again just to make sure I hadn't misunderstood.

"Your father," Marcus continued, "Forticus, I spoke to him last night."

His words sliced through me like a meat cleaver. It was bad enough knowing my parents deserted me here, but I'd always more or less assumed they'd died on the last jorno. Now this kid, this stranger, was telling me he spoke with Father? Marcus was either seriously disturbed or my Father, whom I loved more than anything, was alive and had left me alone in this prison all these annos.

"Is that supposed to be funny, Marcus?" I asked, trying not to become visibly upset.

"No," he said, "I'm totally serious."

"What do you mean *you* talked to *my* Father last night?" I asked, struggling to fight back the stream of tears that wanted so desperately to pour out of my eyes.

"I went to sleep in our room and somehow ended up sitting in front of Forticus and talking with him," Marcus elaborated. "But here's where it gets crazy."

"Oh, really?" I said. "Talking to my dead father isn't crazy enough?"

"Yeah, I know," Marcus continued. "He said I am called Marconis of the Order of Bellator. He also said . . . I'm his oldest son."

Chills raced up and down my body as I digested those last two sentences. Questions started firing through my brain like shooting stars across the night sky. How could any of this be true? Wouldn't I know if I had a brother? But then again, oddly enough, Marconis was how my grandfather, my father's father, was called.

"What else did he say?" I asked, hoping the answer was *nothing*.

"Well," Ty chimed in excitedly, "he called me Tymaeus. Well, not really, but he said that name to Marcus, and then Anina called me that later, in the barbery. Before you came, she was in some kind of trance."

I put my hand up so Ty would stop talking. I needed to hear the story from Marcus. But then something Ty said resonated with me.

"Wait," I said. "Did you say Tymaeus?"

Ty nodded his head. Tymaeus was how my other grandfather was called . . . Tymaeus of the Order of Acutulus. How could these guys have those exact names? I didn't know what to think, much less say.

"Anything else?" I finally managed.

"Forticus said it was really important for me and Ty to go home because we're in great danger here," Marcus explained. "Oh, and he got a big smile on his face when I told him you were safe."

Father smiled when he heard I was safe. I could see that smile in my mind.

"You really talked to my Father?" I asked, somehow beginning to believe a little of the absurdity coming from Marcus.

"Ty and I looked up his image on a viewtop," Marcus said. "It was definitely him. All the way down to the scar next to his right eye. And if we believe what he told me, I actually talked to *our* father, and you're our sister."

Silence hung in the air like thick haze on a hot summer day while the three of us absorbed that last statement.

"He also said that my projection, whatever that is," Marcus continued, "was weak because I was still adjusting to the majinecity. Right before I woke up, he said *mother* and *find other blood*. Then he was gone and I woke up in my room."

"Otherblood," Nekitys said, unexpectedly standing in the doorway with the collars I asked for. "Otherblood. Otherblood. Quaesitor of the Order of Otherblood. Spartanican Magister of Science."

"Oh, good, your back," I said and ran over to get the collars.

I snapped one around the bigger thing's neck. It barely fit, even when expanded to maximum diameter. It was much easier to get an immobilizer around the smaller thing in the other room.

"Are you positive those things aren't going to wake up?" Ty asked as I walked back into the dispensary.

"Very sure," I said. "I tuned down the immobilizers so they can't do much more than breathe. And if they do wake up, bing bing," I said, acting like I was shooting the big one with my rifle.

142

"They'll die if you leave them in that state for more than a jorno," Nekitys said.

"I know," Bellana responded. "We'll put them where they can't hurt anybody before it's a problem."

Marcus looked at me and said, "You have to hear this." He turned to Nekitys and said, "Tell her what you just told us."

"Quaesitor of the Order of Otherblood, Professor of Natural Phenomena and Spartanican Magister of Science," Nekitys recited. "Appointed to the Guelphic Command Staff in 72266 by Forticus of the Order of Bellator."

I thought for a second and said, "Professor Otherblood. I remember the name. So what?"

"Forticus mentioned him to me," Marcus said. "He said *find other blood* and then *mother*. I don't know what it means, but I'll bet he was talking about this scientist."

I turned to Nekitys and said, "How do you know so much about this guy?"

Nekitys' gaze dropped to the floor and then rose back up to me. "I don't know," he said, "I just do."

"Do you know where he lived?" I prompted. "Or how about where he worked? If he was a sciencer, he must've had a place where he did experimentals."

"I don't know anything else," Nekitys replied.

"Thanks, Nekitys," I said, resigned to the fact that we now knew as much as we were going to know about this genius that worked for Father. "Can you check on Anina? I'd like to make sure she's okay after all the excitement."

Nekitys nodded and left the room.

I couldn't really comprehend what was going on, but I figured these guys should know what I knew. After all, Marcus had just saved my life. That bought him some small measure of credibility.

"Well, Marconis is how Father's father was called," I said.

After a few seconds, Ty asked, "How about Tymaeus? Have you heard that name before?"

I gazed over at him and said, "Yes. Mother's father was called Tymaeus."

"Yes!" Ty said, pumping his fists and strutting around the room, noticeably pleased. "I'm in the family! Tymaeus of the Order of Bellator. Now that's a cool name! *Hi, I'm Tymaeus of the Order of Bellator.* It just rolls off the tongue, doesn't it? Watch . . . *Tie May Us . . . .*"

Distracted by his own theatrics, Ty had moved within a couple of steps of the big Desrata, whose legs and arms unexpectedly flinched.

"Aaaaaahhhhhhhh!!!!" he yelled, fell sideways over a chair, and crawled faster than I'd ever seen a human crawl to get back by me and Marcus. "I thought you said they couldn't move?"

"Guess I was wrong," I said.

I looked up, raised my rifle over Ty's shoulder toward the Desrata, and yelled, "Watch out!"

"Aaaaahhhhhhhh!" he screamed again and scooted behind me, shielding his head with his arms.

The 'rat hadn't actually moved again, but I just couldn't resist. Marcus laughed and gave me an enthusiastic thumbs-up. Ty finally looked up and realized I'd been funning him.

"Real hilarious," he complained. "Can you please just get those things out of here?"

"In a minute," I said. "Recognize."

SMILEy responded.

"Identify humans in this room," I commanded.

"Answer," SMILEy replied, "humans presently in the level four dining module include Bellana of the Order of Bellator, Ty, Marcus, and two unidentified individuals."

"That must be the Desrata," Marcus said.

"No, they're not human," Ty countered.

"And SMILEy would call them *intruders*," I clarified, "because they don't have shadowcomm IDs. I've never heard him call someone *unidentified*. SMILEy, define the term *unidentified individual*."

"Answer, an unidentified individual has an anonyma shadowcomm registration."

"Anonyma registration?" I wondered out loud. "I didn't know that was even possible. SMILEy, how can a shadowcomm registration be created without a name?"

"Answer," SMILEy responded, "an anonyma registration is only allowed with voice-recognized level zero approval."

"Level zero?" I said, exasperated by the fact that I didn't know level zero even existed.

Even after all this time here, I was beginning to think I knew nothing about my home.

"Who has level zero access?" I asked.

"Answer, level zero access can be assigned to one person only," SMILEy said. "That person must first be recognized as Guelphic Commander of Sapertys."

"Father?" I blurted. "Father erased your names from your shadowcomm registrations? So you were born here, given shadowcomms like everybody else, and then, for some reason, Father hid you. Let me have the shadowcomms I gave you."

Ty and Marcus reached into their pockets and handed them over. I smashed them between my thumb and forefinger.

"SMILEy," I said. "How many humans are in this room?"

"Answer, there are three humans in the level four dining module."

"Ugh, that's it!" I announced. "You can open secured doors and walk through security fields because you have the same access level I do! Not as Ty and Marcus, but as Tymaeus and Marconis. Oh

145

my, so it's all true then. You two are from here. You're Spartanican."

I had to think very carefully about my next sentence because it made absolutely no sense. I had absolutely no memories of either one of these guys. No memories of Mother or Father talking about them. No fond recollections of ever playing with them, arguing about a toy, or even watching a leadoje match, which Father absolutely loved. How could the knowledge that I had two brothers be completely foreign to me? I didn't know the answer but, for right now, I had no reason to doubt the obvious conclusion.

"Fazah," I finally admitted, hardly believing the words were rolling off my tongue, "you're my brothers."

TWENTY-FOUR

GREEN GOO FROM THE SKY
(TY)

Well, this was all just great! I was supposedly a direct descendant of the so-called famous Guelphic Varkis, the high and mighty Spartanican super club, but do you think I had a single super skill? No! Not one! I watched Marcus and Bellana carry the Desrata battlers, one at a time, up four flights of stairs. Even the small one had to easily weigh over three hundred pounds, but, together, Marcus and Bellana hardly even struggled with it.

They repeatedly carried one up one flight and went back for the other so we wouldn't leave either alone for too long, which I really liked. The last thing we needed was for one of those things to somehow wake up when we weren't around. I tried moving one, you know, because I figured I'd have the super strength, too, but I could hardly lift a leg. Not even a dang leg! I was annoyed beyond words, which is saying a lot for me. While Marcus got to be Superboy, I was still Supernobody, left to hold open doors and push stuff out of the way, like some mindless drone.

We finally got both Desrata to level one. Bellana didn't want to keep them in the coliseum building with us, which I had absolutely no problem with. I could tell she was related to me because she was actually pretty smart. She said there was a bunch of isolation rooms in another building that were used to hold people awaiting review by the Guelphic Judico. By the way she explained it, they sounded like jail cells people stayed in until they went to trial.

"No one's ever escaped from an isolation room," Bellana said. "It'll take a while to drag these things there, and we'll probably have to dig our way in, but they'll never escape."

I didn't have to carry them, so it sounded fine to me.

Marcus and Bellana lugged the big Desrata outside through entrance Zetta One and set him down to go get the smaller one.

"These things are getting heavy," Marcus complained.

"Aw, come on," Bellana jibed, "you're not quitting on me, are you?"

"No, just sayin'," Marcus said and smiled.

As they carried the second one through the outside door, we heard three muffled beeps. They stopped and beeped three times again a few seconds later. They sounded like they were coming from the first Desrata we'd brought out.

The pitch got higher, and the volume got louder each time three more beeps sounded.

"What's going on?" Marcus asked suspiciously.

The big Desrata's entire body started to glow dark red.

"Run!" Bellana yelled.

I heard them drop the second Desrata as I took off in the diametrically opposite direction of the glowing one. Marcus and Bellana blew by me as if I was standing still.

KABOOM!

A huge explosion blew me forward through the air and onto my stomach. A bunch of rocks and dirt fell from the sky, followed by a torrent of heavier wet stuff that slapped down like raw steak on a grill. I kept my eyes closed until the aerial barrage stopped and wiped my forehead to clear off the sweat rolling down before it got into my eyes.

There was just one problem. The stuff rolling down my forehead wasn't sweat. It was green and thick, like paint or Slushee syrup. I glanced back over my right shoulder. One of the Desrata's boots was leaning up against my rib cage . . . with the foot and lower leg still in it and green stuff spouting out of the top of a severed knee!

"Yuuuuuuuuuck!" I yelled and jumped up, kicking the 'rat leg away from me. "Pieces of that thing are all over me."

I shook my hands and Desrata gunk flew everywhere.

"This is soooo totally disgusting!" I yelled.

"Ty!" Marcus hollered, pointing at something behind me. "The other one! The other one is going to—"

KABOOM!

I ducked back down and covered my head. A whole new microburst of gross stuff came raining down. It was like living in an M-rated video game, and I couldn't turn it off.

Marcus ran over and said, "Dude, dude, are you okay?"

He put his hand on my back and immediately yanked it back off.

"Uhhh, is this—" he started.

"Desrata blood and guts?" I said, finishing Marcus' sentence. "Yes, and it's all over me."

Marcus shook his hand, trying to get the goo off. I stood up and did the same with both hands and feet.

"How did they blow up?" I asked. "I thought they could barely even breathe with those things around their necks."

"I don't think they blew themselves up," Marcus said. "It's more like they had time bombs on them. It's a good thing we got them out of the building when we did."

A light went on in my head.

"Or they were carrying remotely detonated explosives," I postulated. "They didn't blow up until we took them outside. I bet the building blocked the trigger signals. Once we brought them outside, the signals connected and *boom*." I looked around and said, "Where's Bellana?"

Marcus glanced back and exclaimed, "She was right behind me."

He ran over to where they had hid while I was getting gooed.

"Bellana!" he called out. "Bellana!"

The ground began to rumble, and a loud noise filled the air.

"Oh, no," Marcus said, "hamster ball!"

"Go!" I yelled, motioning for Marcus to take off. "Go!"

Marcus sprinted away and was out of sight almost instantly. I started running my usual slow way and got nowhere particularly fast. Would I ever be able to do the cool stuff Marcus was doing?

The quickly escalating tremors made it hard to move in a straight line. After a short while, I came around a corner and could see out of the city as the top of a hamster ball disappeared over the other side of a sand dune. Marcus was already out of the city and quickly disappeared over the horizon as well. I walked to the edge of the desert. I wasn't going to catch anything out there so I stopped.

"Ty!" someone yelled from behind.

I turned to see the Atlantean kids running at me. I looked back toward the desert, hoping to see Marcus coming back.

"Oh, Ty!" I heard.

"They took Bellana and Marcus and, oomph—"

Iryni ran up from behind and hugged me before I could finish my sentence.

"We thought you were dead," she said.

She obviously hadn't realized I was covered in Desrata remains. I felt her sticking to me as she slowly peeled away and stepped back.

"Uhhh," she exclaimed, looking down at her thoroughly slimed clothes and hands, "what is all over you? What is that smell?"

She tried, in vain, to wipe off her left cheek, which she had pressed up against my back when she hugged me. Her hands were so mucked up that it didn't help at all. Her front half was hopelessly slathered in Desrata gunk. I felt so bad for her.

"I'm sorry!" I pleaded. "I'm sorry! I didn't know you were going to do that!"

"Ty, what happened?" Kinnard asked. "Where are Marcus and Bellana?"

"Well, first the Desrata exploded, and then Bellana disappeared, and then the hamster ball, and then Marcus ran after them."

I knew I was too hyper to be making much sense but hoped Kinnard would piece my ranting together.

"So are you telling me this stuff is . . . Desrata guts?" Iryni asked, looking seriously freaked out.

I nodded slowly. She turned and walked stiffly behind a nearby exorbalis pile.

"I'm so sorry, Iryni," I said again. "Honest, I would have—"

My words were drowned out by the sound of her blowing chunks, and I mean really loudly, like a train horn. How could that little girl make so much noise?

"Kinnard, I—" I started to explain further, only to be muffled out by Iryni. "Anyway, the Desrata kidnapped Bellana, and in all the—"

Ugh, I got cut off again. Poor girl.

After a momentary pause, I said, "The Desrata took Bellana that way in one of those big, clear balls."

I pointed over the sand dune. "Marcus ran after them," I continued.

Iryni stepped out from behind her makeshift fortress of puke-a-tude and headed back into the city.

"I'll go with her," Arianas said.

"No, wait," Kinnard insisted. "We go together. There's no telling how many more 'rats are here."

I heard motion behind me and turned to see Marcus walking into the city, breathing heavily.

"I couldn't . . . I couldn't catch them," he said, kneeling down to catch his breath. "They move too fast."

"You chased them on foot?" Kinnard asked, obviously thinking Marcus was an idiot for even trying.

"They took Bellana," Marcus replied. "We have to go get her."

Kinnard shook his head in disagreement.

"What?" Marcus said emphatically. "Maybe you're willing to let her die, but I'm not!"

"The fields are three jornos away on foot," Kinnard responded. "And what will we do when we get there? Throw exorbalis blocks at them? You saw the size of those things. What chance do *we* have against them?"

"You might be used to losing people, but I'm not!" Marcus yelled. "We're not letting them take her!"

"Okay!" Kinnard yelled back. He paused momentarily before saying, "First, we finish the maj training so we at least have weapons. Yeah?"

Marcus backed off a little.

"While we're training, we put together an attack plan," Kinnard continued. "The seven of us know the fields as well as anyone. We know where the guards go and when. We also know their weapons. Then, and only then, we go get Bellana." Kinnard turned toward the Atlantean kids and finished by saying, "And Kalahn and Perditus."

On the way back to the coliseum, Marcus suddenly noticed Anina was with us. With all the commotion, I'd completely missed her.

"Hey, how are you doing?" Marcus said. "I can't believe I didn't see you there! Sorry."

Anina smiled shyly and replied, "Oh, that's okay. I'm fine. Don't worry about me." She looked past Marcus at me. "Hi, Ty. Leg still broken?"

And to think I was genuinely concerned about this girl.

"Uh, no, it's better," I replied with a sarcastic grin. "But no thank you for asking."

"When was your leg broken?" Iryni asked with concern.

Marcus and Anina obviously loved the whole discussion.

"Never," I said flippantly. "It wasn't broken. But it felt like it was! Aw, just forget it."

We reached the coliseum and found Desrata parts all over the ground and building.

"I say we move permanently into the armory," Marcus said. "The weapons and training are there, and the Desrata will probably come looking for us here."

"Works for me," Iryni said, "as long as it has reinigens."

"How will we get in?" Arianas asked. "Bellana is the only one who can open and close the tunnel in less than four oras."

"That won't be a problem," Marcus said, starting to walk away.

"Why not?" Kinnard asked. "Do you know another way in?"

"No," Marcus said as he turned back around to face all of us, "I don't. Let's just say I'm feeling a lot stronger the last couple of days. Can we please go now?"

"No, we can't," Kinnard said, getting right up in Marcus' face. "We don't know you, and it's awfully strange Bellana disappeared when she was with *you*. Who exactly are you?"

Marcus shook his head and turned to walk away.

"Hey," Kinnard said, grabbing Marcus' shoulder.

Marcus spun and shoved Kinnard, who flew back at least ten feet and rolled across the ground another ten. Naetth and Yra started yelling and stomped toward Marcus as if they were ready to attack.

"Stop it," Kinnard yelled. "Naetth! Yra! Stop it!" He looked at Marcus and asked, "Why didn't you say something?"

"Why didn't he say something about what?" Yra yelled, still trying to look tough.

"It just sort of happened in the last day or two," Marcus said.

"What just sort of happened?" Yra and Naetth pleaded.

Marcus nodded at Kinnard as if to say it was okay for Kinnard to explain.

"Marcus is a direct Guelph descendant, too, like Bellana," Kinnard elaborated without taking his eyes off Marcus.

Marcus shifted his gaze to Yra and Naetth without moving his head.

"Can we go now?" he asked. "This Desrata gunk stinks."

"Tell me about it," Iryni said, looking at me with a *thanks a lot* look on her face.

154

"Are you and Bellana related?" Anina asked hopefully.

"Yeah," Marcus said, gesturing at me. "She's our sister, actually."

Kinnard kept staring at Marcus, as if he couldn't believe what he'd just heard.

"Can we go now?" Marcus repeated, becoming impatient with the whole discussion.

"Well, yeah, let's go," Yra said. "If you can open the tunnel, why not?"

Kinnard slowly stood up and brushed himself off with a sigh, his clothes now spotted with Desrata remains.

"Yeah, let's go," Kinnard said in an oddly resigned tone, "but I call the first reinigen."

We walked to the armory and skittered down the tunnel after Marcus opened it. It was funny, though. Yra and Naetth didn't say a word to me the whole way. Usually they'd mess around and bump into me, you know, the usual stuff. But this time they totally stayed away. I think they were a little afraid of me. Guess they didn't want to be messin' with a Bellator!

TWENTY-FIVE

ACCOMPLISHMENT 13
(MARCUS)

So I had a sister for like an hour and then lost her to a bunch of animals. No way. *Nothing* was going to stop me from getting Bellana back.

Everybody got into the armory and I closed up the entrance. The exorbalis, which used to feel like lead bricks, was now like tossing around Styrofoam. Seriously, I felt like Superman, except I couldn't fly and wasn't sure bullets would bounce off my chest.

While everyone else went off to find reinigens, Nekitys and I headed to the sim room. Bellana had said rifle certification would take a couple of weeks, but that was if we only trained an hour per day. We'd done a lot more than that the day before, and I was already getting pretty comfortable using the appendage. If we were going to get Bellana back alive, we had to get certified with the rifle quickly.

My next training sim called for one-on-one combat with another trainee at the same level or higher. Up until that point, we'd been firing at moving and stationary virtual targets. Thinking about it, if Bellana had been here alone so long, I wondered how she had done this part of the training.

"Have you completed accomp twelve yet?" I asked Nekitys as we walked into the sim room.

"Yes, I completed accomplishment twelve yesterday," he responded.

"So, do you want to try thirteen?" I asked. "It'll take both of us to run that one."

"Yes," he replied. "That is a good idea. Thank you."

He hadn't exactly done anything wrong, but I still thought if there was a serial killer among these guys, it was him.

My shoulder was still sore, so I sat down and started moving it around to loosen up. When I looked up, the room was dark.

"Nekitys?" I yelled but heard nothing back.

After a short burst of light and a momentary screech, I suddenly wasn't in the sim room anymore. Forticus was sitting on the floor in front of me.

"Hello, Marconis," he glanced up and said, as if he'd been expecting me.

It took me a couple seconds to recognize I had to be in another projection. The random nature of these things was unnerving.

Forticus got to his feet. He was a truly imposing figure. Even just standing up, the guy exuded power and strength. I could swear he was bigger and more daunting than the first time I'd seen him.

"They took Bellana!" I blurted, sounding like a pathetic little kid who knew he was in big trouble. "There was nothing I could do!"

Forticus' face turned sullen, making his presence all the more intimidating.

"*Who* took Bellana?" he asked in a surly tone.

"The Desrata," I answered, my eyes filling with tears.

I realized I wasn't actually afraid of Forticus himself, but I was terrified of disappointing him.

"The Desrata are arduszone animals," he said. "They never would have taken Bellana."

"I was there," I insisted. "I saw it happen. They wear uniforms now and drive big transparent rolling balls with draiders on them."

Forticus looked down and shook his head.

"No," he argued. "The Desrata do little more than hunt and live on their settlement. If they are now as you describe, something has drastically changed."

"Did you know Atlantis was destroyed, too?" I asked.

"Yes," Forticus acknowledged. "We heard their distress calls but we were under siege as well."

"By whom?" I demanded. "Who did this?"

"You and Tymaeus and Bellana must leave this world immediately," Forticus said. "The evil that lives here grows stronger every protoka. Your lives are in danger, even more so than when we sent you away the first time."

"*You* sent us?" I asked, struggling to believe what I'd just heard.

My own father had abandoned me to another world.

"Why did you send us away?" I continued. "Why don't we remember any of this?"

"Listen to me!" Father replied. "If you stay in this projection too long, they'll sense your presence. The evil in this world grew stronger than our ability to stop it. I was an arrogant fool and was betrayed by someone close to me. We sent you and Tymaeus through the gateway to protect you. It could only sustain two of you at one time, so we kept Bellana here, but only until the next majstice, but we never got there."

"But who—"

"No, listen to me, Marconis," Father interrupted. "You must find Otherblood. He was outside the city on the last jorno. He knows how the gateway works and will get you back to Earth."

"We have to get Bellana back first!" I yelled. "We can't leave without Bellana!"

"My son," Father paused again and sighed, "do all you can to get your sister back, but promise me whomever of the three of you can make it will do everything possible to leave this world by the next majstice and never come back, regardless of anything else. Not leaving means certain death. I can't risk losing all of you. And stay out of the darkways at all costs. Evil uses them to hide and grow. They're deadly." He hesitated, looking and sounding desperate and out of breath before saying, "Go now and never project yourself here again. You must remain undetected so you can get back through the gateway. Goodbye, my son."

He waved his arms in front of his face and everything went dark again.

I was back in the sim room. Nekitys was standing right where he was before. It was like time stopped while I was projecting. Could this get any more sideways?

I sat and got my bearings for a minute.

"Are you ready?" Nekitys asked, startling me out of my fog.

"Oh, yeah," I mumbled. "Hey, do you know when the next majstice is?"

"Yes," Nekitys replied. "The next majstice is in approximately seven jornos."

Seven jornos? We had seven days to get Bellana back, find Otherblood, and figure out how to get home.

"When's the next one after that?" I asked.

"The second nearest majstice will take place a little over two annos after the next majstice."

"Two annos?" I asked. "Why so long? Didn't we just have one?"

"Yes," Nekitys explained. "A majstice occurred three jornos prior. Majstice frequency is predictable but irregular because of the asynchronous orbits of Primus and Beta. Both moons are presently almost within proximity to sufficiently magnify the planet's majineic field for majstice to be achieved."

"So, seven jornos and then two years, I mean annos," I summarized.

Forticus had said only two of us could go through the gateway at a time. I'd have to stay behind.

"Approximately," Nekitys confirmed.

"Then, let's get trained," I said. "Simulator, recognize."

"Recognized," the simulator voice announced, "proceed."

Nekitys looked at me with a confused expression. The simulator had acknowledged my request without confirming my name like it did for everyone else, probably because of my anonymous shadowcomm number.

"I guess it forgot my name," I said with an uncertain smile. "Activate warrior sim pads one through nine, majrifles, current model, two warrior sim, random obstacles, no virtual targets."

"Identify second warrior," the sim voice responded.

"Simulator, recognize second warrior," Nekitys announced.

"Second warrior recognized," the simulator confirmed. "Nekitys of the Order of Aliugenus."

Hearing his full name made me wonder where he was from. The Atlantean kids said they didn't know him before the fields.

A big green sim box with digital boulders and other obstructions lit up half the mats. My rifle materialized as expected. Nekitys was ready, too.

"Simulation begin," I announced.

Before I could get behind anything, Nekitys hit me with a blast and disappeared. The instruction video said virtual sim rifles only used knock-down intensity when more than one person was in the same sim. Wow! Knock-down definitely lived up to its name!

Nekitys' blast sent me flying back against the green perimeter wall, where I dropped like a rock to the mat. I quickly rolled to my left and got behind a pile of simulated rocks. Another blast whizzed by as I pulled my legs in. I was surprised by how fast Nekitys was! With the way he walked around in a daze all the time, who would've thought the guy had any speed?

Pop, pop, pop. Three more blasts hit behind me to my right, so I rolled left, but just as I did, I saw Nekitys out of the corner of my eye, poking around the corner of a fake building. That was the last thing I remembered before he pegged me again, this time in the stomach. By the time I looked up, Nekitys was standing over me, pointing his rifle at my head.

"Another?" he asked, completely devoid of emotion.

"Yes," I answered, aggravated I was such a helpless foe. "Just give me a minute."

I closed my eyes and lay on the mat, catching my breath. When I went to get back up, Nekitys was still standing over me, staring.

"Aaahhh!" I yelped and skidded back. "What are you doing?"

"I am waiting for you to be ready," he said.

"Well, go wait over there," I snapped and gestured toward the far end of the sim box. I stood up and said, "This time you tell the sim to start."

"Very well," he agreed.

He raised his voice and said, "Simulation begin."

I immediately ripped a round at him just as he'd done to me, but he ducked into a small building before it hit him. I ran diagonally across sim pads one and five to reach nine and crouched down next to an open door to the building he was in. It was wild. The building was virtual, but I could actually lean up against it. How could I lean against something that wasn't even there?

Nekitys let several blasts go out a window directly over my head and tried to run out a back door, but I blasted him twice before he got there, sending him face first into the rear wall. He crumpled to the floor and started convulsing.

"Nekitys!" I yelled and ran over to him. "Hey! Hey, Nekitys!"

I gently tapped his cheek, trying to get him to come around, but he made weird gurgling noises like he was choking. His eyes rolled around and his body twitched uncontrollably. Then he stopped moving altogether and went limp. Had I actually killed him?

Just when I thought he was truly gone, his eyes popped open. He sat up and pushed himself against the wall next to the rear door and shook his head as if he was trying to see straight.

"Dude, are you okay?" I asked, trembling a little. "I didn't mean to pop you twice. Dude?"

He started to settle down.

"Can I get you anything?" I asked.

"Otherblood!" he announced, suddenly grabbing and pulling my arm. "Otherblood."

His eyes blinked rapidly and his voice sounded almost mechanical.

"I know where to find Professor Otherblood," he said. "He's calling me."

His eyes fluttered a few more times before they closed and his chin dropped to his chest.

"Recognize," I yelled.

"You are already recognized," the deep, tough-sounding sim voice said.

I felt like it wanted me to apologize for not knowing I was recognized.

"Where's the medica room on this level?" I yelled.

"The medica facility on level twelve is room 1219," it responded. "Exit simulation room 1223. Room 1219 will be to the left, two doors away."

I gently lifted Nekitys over my left shoulder. The kid was solid. He was nowhere near as heavy as a Desrata, but I had to put some real effort into carrying him.

The others walked in as we approached the door to the sim room.

"What happened?" Kinnard asked.

"We were training on accomp thirteen and he hit his head," I said. "I'm taking him to medica."

"Maybe he'll wake up with a personality," Naetth remarked sarcastically.

Yra smirked.

"Ty," I said, "come with me. You guys can keep training. Let's see if everyone can complete two or three accomps today. And watch the rifle. It's easy to pop more than one pulse out when you don't mean to."

Ty and I left the others in the sim room and found 1219. I put Nekitys on a bed, and Ty and I sat down.

"Now what?" Ty asked. "Do you have super-secret Guelphic doctor powers, too?"

"Funny," I said. "No. I don't know what to do. But listen, I saw Forticus again."

Ty didn't say anything. It caught me off-guard, and I hesitated momentarily. Ty always had something to say.

"What's wrong with you?" I asked. "Did you hear me?"

"Yes!" Ty replied. "What? Do you need an invitation? Tell me what happened!"

I took Ty through the Forticus and Nekitys excitement.

"So we're going home?" was all Ty could say. "For real?"

"Yeah, sure," I elaborated. "All we have to do is get Bellana out of the Desrata camp, find this Professor Otherblood, and figure out where the gateway is. After that, we just need to get all three of us through the gateway on the majstice. Seven days. We have seven days to do all that."

Ty started talking slowly, as he always did when he was figuring stuff out.

"So the gateway is powered by a majinecity surge," he contemplated. "That's brilliant but a total pain. It only works when the moons are in the right place."

"Dude," I replied, "what if we can't get Bellana out of the 'rat settlement in time? What do we do?"

The question hung in the air like a two-day old helium balloon.

"We don't go home until Bellana is safe, right?" Ty said. "I mean, we *all* go or we *all* stay."

It staggered me to hear Ty be so, I don't know, *brave*, but I nodded in agreement.

So there it was, we had seven days to do the impossible or get stuck here facing an evil we didn't even understand.

"I checked SMILEy," Ty said, "and there's information about Professor Otherblood but nothing about where he might be now. SMILEy said he's not in any of the city buildings, at least the ones SMILEy still operates."

"Professor Otherblood is approximately two jorno's walk from here," Nekitys said, without moving or opening his eyes.

Ty and I looked at him, expecting him to wake up, but he didn't.

"Nekitys?" I asked, but got no reply. I looked at Ty and said, "You heard him talk, right?"

Ty nodded, and we both stepped next to his bed.

"Nekitys?" I tried again, nudging his shoulder.

His eyes sprung open as if he'd just been scared out of his mind. Ty and I jumped back.

"Jeez!" I blurted. "Are you okay?"

"Oh, yes," he responded enthusiastically and sat up. "I feel grand! How are you?"

Ty and I stepped back, stunned by Nekitys' sudden jubilance.

"We're fine," I answered. "Why are you smiling?"

"Why not smile?" Nekitys replied. "Isn't it a great day to be alive? I haven't felt this good in annos!" He jumped off the bed and said, "Now we have to get to Professor O, right? I know exactly where the good man is. Let's go!"

"Whoa," I said. "Wait, you mean right now? We can't. We need to finish rifle training and get Bellana back. Don't you remember?"

"You know, my amicu," Nekitys said, "you were handling that majjy like a pro today. Zah! You about blew me to Lemuria! How about we make it possible to use majjys before we're fully certified? Wouldn't that just be a huge help?"

"You can do that?" Ty asked. "How?"

"Oh, ho ho," Nekitys exclaimed, "watch this, my amicu."

He bounced over to a flat white table with rounded sides. He put his hands in the middle of the table and slid them in opposite directions across the top. Out of nowhere, the surface lit and displayed a computer-like screen with graphics, Spartanican words, and flashing symbols.

"Ah, let's get this up where we can work with it," Nekitys said.

He put his fingers and thumbs down on the table and slid the control panel up into the air where it hung almost transparently. Ty and I were standing behind it but could see Nekitys through it on the other side. He moved stuff around on the screen as if he'd been doing it for years.

"What are you doing?" Ty asked, completely awestruck.

"Simple, really," Nekitys replied. "We're going to allow all of us to get certified just by completing level one."

"No way!" Ty said. "You can do that?"

"Of course, amicu," Nekitys replied. "Calculos do what we tell them to do. We need to help Bellana right now, yes?"

Ty and I nodded in agreement.

"We can't stand around for jornos getting trained," Nekitys continued. "Besides, all the accomplishments above number twelve focus more on battlefield strategy than actually using the rifle. Uh-oh."

"What?" I asked. "What is it?"

"It's requiring two level-one approvals," Nekitys said.

He looked at us through the hovering control panel screen.

"Do you suppose a couple Bellator boys might have level one high exalted supreme access?" Nekitys asked.

Who was this guy? He had been so blah since we met him but had morphed into some super-smart surfer dude. Banging his head in the sim had somehow rebooted his entire personality.

"We can try!" Ty answered, excited at the thought of doing whatever Nekitys was doing.

"Hang with me, amicu," Nekitys said. "When you hear the voice, say how you're called."

Nekitys did a few more things on the panel.

"When I hear the voice say how I'm called, do what?" Ty asked.

"Say how you're called," Nekitys replied.

Ty still looked confused.

"Yeah," Ty said, "it's going to say how I'm called, then what do I do?"

"It's not going to say how you're called, you are," Nekitys said.

"I am what?" Ty asked.

"Going to say how you're called when you hear the voice prompt," Nekitys answered.

"Ohhhhhh . . . I got ya," Ty responded. He looked at me and said, "Wait for the voice and then—"

"Yeah," I interrupted, annoyed with the whole discussion, "I get it, Ty. I got it the first time."

After a few seconds, a rather pleasant lady's voice from the panel said, "First approval."

Nekitys gestured for us to say something.

Ty and I both looked at each other, each expecting the other to speak, but neither of us did.

"First approval failure," the voice responded.

"Oh, great," Ty complained. "Now what?"

"How are you called?" Nekitys asked Ty.

"Uh," Ty replied, "Tymaeus of the Order of Bellator."

"I didn't know your name started with *Uh*," Nekitys said.

"Uh, it doesn't," Ty replied.

Nekitys glared at Ty through the control panel.

"Then why did you say *uh*?" Nekitys protested. "Don't you know your own name, amicu?"

Ty rolled his eyes, realizing the point Nekitys was trying to make.

"Just have it ask me again," Ty snorted impatiently, "I'll go first."

Nekitys moved his hands around the console some more and again we heard, "First approval."

"Tymaeus of the Order of Bellator," Ty very pointedly responded.

"First approval success," the voice said. "Second approval."

"Marconis of the Order of Bellator," I said.

"Second approval success," the voice confirmed. "Majrifle certification level modified to accomplishment one."

"Success!" Nekitys happily announced. "Shall we go tell the others?"

"Wait," I said, "Bellana said our shadowcomm IDs were anonymous. How is it recognizing our names?"

"Hmmm," Nekitys replied, still working feverishly on the control panel, "good question. When you speak, the SMILE scans your shadowcomm ID. Then it uses your verbal response and your shadowcomm ID to verify your access level. If you have an anonyma registration, it must just use your shadowcomm ID. "

"Then we could have said anything and it would've worked," Ty concluded.

"Yeah, I guess," Nekitys said. "I've never heard of an anonyma shadowcomm registration before but that sounds logical."

Nekitys quickly did a few more things on the control panel and it disappeared.

"That is so ultimately cool!" Ty said. "You have to show me how that works."

"Did you say you knew where to find Professor Otherblood ?" I asked.

"He has a studium in the outlands," Nekitys answered, "where he works on his most important experimentals. It's very secret, very secure, and very hard to find. Something tells me he's there."

"Do you actually know he's there?" I said.

"Not exactly," Nekitys admitted. "I can't explain it. I just know he'll be there."

This was great. Nekitys wanted us to trudge around the desert because he had a hunch Professor Otherblood was out there somewhere.

"It's not like we have any better ideas, if he's even alive," Ty said.

"He's alive," Nekitys said. "I know he's alive."

I went to say something, but Nekitys cut me off.

"And before you ask," he said, "I don't know how I know. I just know. "

How was that for a kind of maybe definite answer?

"Aren't you even a little interested in why we want to find him so much?" Ty asked Nekitys.

I had wondered the same thing about Nekitys, but he was so eager to help I didn't think it mattered.

"I heard you say you talked to Forticus, yes?" Nekitys asked.

I hesitated but slowly nodded my head.

"I don't understand how that can be because he's supposed to be dead," Nekitys continued. "However, Professor Otherblood is my best friend in the entire world. He worked for your father and considered him to be a very honorable man. If you say your father told you, his son, to find Professor Otherblood, then I must help you do so."

I was really starting to like this new-and-improved Nekitys.

"That's really cool," I said. "Thanks, Nekitys. Can we keep this between the three of us? I don't know that the others will be as understanding as you are."

"Of course, amicu," Nekitys said. "Just promise to take me with you to find the good professor."

Ty and I looked at each other with smiles and both said, "Absolutely."

"You said he was two jornos from here?" I asked.

"Yes," Nekitys answered, "if we have to walk. But there might be a usable arduszone freighter somewhere in the city. I know where they're usually stored. We can check." Nekitys paused and said, "But if you're Bellators, you can use the darkways, right? I don't know how those work, but Guelphies are supposed to be experts."

In my last projection, Father specifically said to stay out of the darkways, but I didn't want to have that conversation right now. I didn't know anything about the darkways and we didn't have time to learn. We needed to focus on what we knew. Ty's blank expression told me he was clueless as well.

"Yeah," I said, "I guess we haven't gotten to that chapter in the Varkis handbook yet."

"No surprise," Nekitys added. "That knowledge transfer doesn't normally start until you have thirteen annos, to ensure your bodies have matured enough to properly synthesize and magnify polar majinecity."

"So that's where the super powers come from?" Ty asked. "The speed and the strength? Our bodies somehow use majinecity?"

"Of course," Nekitys said. "Your bodies are genetically enabled majineic amplifiers. How else could you be so strong?"

I had to put my hands up and rein these guys in before I got too lost.

"Sorry to break up science class, but we gotta move," I said. "Nekitys, can you check around for a freighter while Ty and I get everyone real rifles? Actually, find as many freighters as you can."

"On it, amicu," Nekitys responded and restarted the control panel.

"Bellana said there were draiders and lofters in this building," I said. "Can you find them, too?"

"Yes," Nekitys answered, already deep into whatever he was doing on the panel.

"But the instruction said we couldn't use those until we were certified on rifles and cutters first," Ty protested.

Nekitys and I looked at each other, nodded, and smiled.

"Great minds think alike, amicu," Nekitys said.

Ty glanced back and forth between me and Nekitys, not quite understanding what had just taken place.

"Wait," Ty said, with a smile creeping across his face. "What? Oh, no way. You're going to change the certification levels on those, too? This is so cool."

"I'll get started," Nekitys said.

I looked at Ty and said, "Let's go give everyone their very own real live majjy."

TWENTY-SIX

YES, MY NOBILIS

(BELLANA)

"Do you have the Bellator girl?" a woman's voice asked.

It sounded as if she was talking at the other end of a communicator.

Wherever I was, I was barely conscious, unable to open my eyes or move, yet it definitely felt as if I was moving. The last thing I remembered was being in the city. The 'rats. They had exploded, hadn't they? In my barely conscious state, it all felt like a distant dream.

"Yes, my nobilis," another voice answered. "She is in the restraint and hasn't moved."

"She is undamaged, as commanded?" the woman asked.

"Yes, my nobilis, as you commanded."

"Were the animals of any assistance?" the woman asked.

"Yes, my nobilis," the voice near me said. "Once she was de-animated, they quickly retrieved her body without alarming the others and brought her to the sphaera."

"Very good," the woman said. "They may prove of some usefulness after all."

"Yes, my nobilis."

"Bring her to me, Centurio, as we discussed," the woman said.

"Yes, my nobilis," Centurio responded.

The voices were human and they knew who I was. I had to figure out *where* I was and what was happening, but I couldn't even open my eyes. What was wrong with me? I had to wake up, but I couldn't. I was completely and utterly defenseless as consciousness faded once again.

TWENTY-SEVEN

WE DIDN'T KNOW
(TY)

"Woooo hooooo!" Yra yelled when we told him majrifle training was over.

He and Naetth tapped each other on the cheeks with both hands in what must have been some kind of Atlantean high five.

"The cutters, too?" Naetth asked.

"Yes," I said, "but Nekitys needs to show us how to use them first."

"Rockadockadeemer!" Yra exclaimed joyfully. "Let's go get a weapon! Can we go outside and try them?"

"Nekitys figured this out?" Kinnard asked, shaking his head skeptically.

"Yeah," Marcus said, shrugging his shoulders, "he's a different guy since I blasted him in the sim."

Everyone except Kinnard laughed.

"Is everybody okay with this?" Kinnard asked. "I mean, is everyone confident you can handle a real majrifle without hurting yourself or one of us?"

Everybody eagerly nodded.

"Okay, I guess," Kinnard conceded, "let's go."

We all headed for the stairs when Nekitys came up from behind.

"We just need your approvals for the other weapons," Nekitys said to me and Marcus, "but we can do that upstairs."

"Exactly when did you become a calculo expert?" Kinnard asked suspiciously.

"I'm being helpful," Nekitys responded with attitude. "Is that a problem? Would it make you happier if I just did nothing, like you?"

Nekitys' newfound confidence was taking us all by surprise.

"Oh, give me a break, mortus boy," Kinnard said, his voice getting louder. "You walk around in a daze for two years, staring at everybody, barely saying a word, and now you want us to believe you're mister helpful? Funny how you're so helpful right when we're talking about going back to the fields."

"What does that mean?" Marcus asked.

"I'll wager he's leading us right into a 'rat trap," Kinnard answered. "If he knows how to use the calculo, then he probably knows how to communicate with them too."

"Why would I do that?" Nekitys protested. "So I can go back to the fields? Those 'rats tortured me! Over and over! Why would I ever want to go back?"

"What do you mean they tortured you?" Kinnard said skeptically. "How?"

"They'd come and take me away," Nekitys explained, "late at night, and drag me somewhere with a bag over my head so I couldn't see. They hooked me up to a machine and majineically shocked me . . . sometimes for oras, sometimes for jornos. One time they shocked me so hard their machine broke, so they brought me back the next day and fried me with a bigger, more powerful one. They couldn't understand why I wouldn't die, so they kept trying harder." He looked at Naetth and Yra and said, "Mortus boy? You think that's funny? Let's see how you feel after a few million tessles of majinecity is pumped through your body and soul." He turned to Kinnard, "So help me understand why I would want to go back to that."

Silence suddenly and awkwardly consumed the space around us. The Atlantean kids, utterly shocked, stood motionless with their eyes agape, obviously caught completely off-guard by the horrific picture Nekitys had painted.

Kinnard shook his head and muttered, "We didn't know."

"Why didn't you ever say anything?" Anina, clearly shaken, barely managed to articulate. "Why didn't you tell us before?"

"Because I didn't remember any of it until a little bit ago," Nekitys replied. "Ever since I banged my head in the sim, these unbelievably vivid memories have been sporadically playing over and over as if they just happened. Each one is like living through the worst nightmare ever."

Nekitys covered his face with his hands.

"I don't want to remember," he said as if he was desperately commanding himself to forget. "I just want it all to stop."

Kinnard briefly glanced at the ceiling before looking at Nekitys and said, "I'm really sorry."

Nekitys lowered his hands from his face and said, "Don't sweat it. You didn't know."

"I'm so sorry, Nekitys," Iryni said, fighting back tears. Anina and Arianas, similarly distressed, nodded in agreement.

"Okay," Nekitys said, sounding as if he was ready to move on, "let's go get our rifles. We have friends in the fields that need our help."

We took the stairs up to the level-five armory. The Atlantean kids were seriously wigged out about Nekitys. This guy they'd made fun of and kept at arm's length for years was turning out to be okay. Of course, I couldn't talk. I thought he was an oddball, too. I treated him the way other kids sometimes treated me. Totally not cool.

Marcus opened the door to armory 5a. It was an expansive room with a gray floor and walls and a white ceiling. An overwhelming number of maj-appendages were lined up neatly, side-by-side, like little soldiers on six-foot-tall, gray shelves that filled the room as far as the eye could see.

"Whoa," I gasped, "so many weapons. Why are they all gray? Bellana's was light brown."

"They auto-camouflage," Nekitys said. "I mean, they automatically adjust to the colors of their surroundings to be less conspicuous."

"Seriously?" I said, once again amazed. "Is there no end to the cool stuff here?"

"Too bad there's only a few of us," Kinnard said. "We could take over the entire planet with just the firepower in this room if we had the soldiers."

Marcus and I had approved Nekitys' access to the armories earlier. He stepped in and activated a control panel just inside the entry. Yra tried to follow him, but the security field knocked him back on his butt again.

"Ugh, I *hate* those things!" he protested and got back up.

Marcus cautiously poked his way into the room, not quite confident he'd make it through without ending up like Yra. I blew by Marcus without a problem and started handing majrifles to everyone through the door as Nekitys used the control panel to formally assign each one so they'd actually work. Each time I handed a rifle through the door, it turned a darker gray to match the colors in the hallway.

"Amazing," Naeth said, waving his rifle around and playfully moving through mock attack poses. "These feel exactly the same as in the sims."

"Everybody please leave your safety switch on," Kinnard directed. "Let's not accidentally blast each other."

"So when can we go outside and shoot stuff?" Yra asked. "I really want to try this thing. Please!"

"It'll have to be later," Marcus said, looking at Kinnard. "It kills me to think the 'rats are treating Bellana like they treated Nekitys. We need to put together a plan as soon as possible and go get her."

"Don't forget the cutters, draiders, and lofters," Nekitys said. "You two just need to approve the cert changes and we'll have those, too."

Kinnard smiled and looked at Nekitys.

"Did you say draiders and lofters?" Kinnard asked.

The other Atlantean kids' eyes lit up with anticipation as well.

"If we can draid and loft the 'rats," Kinnard continued, "we have a real wager at this thing. Just one question . . . does anybody know how to use them?"

"Yes," Nekitys said. "I can show you how they work."

"How exactly," Kinnard started to say before catching himself, "wait, let me guess . . . you don't know, you just know."

Nekitys just smiled and kept working on the control panel.

"Now you're getting the hang of it," Marcus snickered.

"I also found the idlelot where arduszone freighters were kept," Nekitys said. "It's not far from here, but they were housed above ground so don't get your hopes up."

"Let's go check out the lofters and draiders first," Marcus said. "Then we can try to find a freighter." He turned to Yra and Naetth and said, "You can try out your rifles along the way."

They both pumped their fists exuberantly at that bit of good news.

TWENTY-EIGHT

LOFTERS AND DRAIDERS
(MARCUS)

We followed Nekitys up to the heavy armory room on level three. It was as big as the sim room, maybe bigger. Ty, Nekitys, and I entered and walked over to a control panel where Ty and I approved the cert level changes for the lofters and draiders. We also granted access for everybody else to the room, which had gray floors and walls just like the appendage room, but no shelving. Yra, skeptical about being able to pass through the security field, let the others go first before he tempted fate again.

We all followed Nekitys over to a twelve-foot tall, five-foot wide, otherwise featureless obelisk with an octagonal base that became square two-thirds of the way up. There had to be another couple hundred of them lined up behind Nekitys. They must have had auto-camouflage like the appendages because they were all the exact same color gray as the floor and walls.

"This is the Sparta GT10 low profile, gyro-stabilized, auto-charging, super-distance demolition lofter," Nekitys said, casually leaning up against it.

He turned and slid open a panel at chest level on one side and started tapping on a small monitor that lit up. The lofter began to hum and hovered motionlessly three or four inches above the floor. Everyone took a couple of steps back to give it room.

"The GT10 is majineically suspended at a constant five unicas off the ground," Nekitys explained. "Once targeted on a geographic location, the square turret on top uses gyroscopic dampening to remain fixated on that location, regardless of where the unit is moved."

Nekitys tapped more on the monitor. The turret rotated effortlessly to a forty-five degree angle pointing away from him. Even though the entire unit looked very solid, the top two feet or so somehow rounded off into a three-dimensional parabola protruding from the top of the turret.

"How did it do that?" Ty asked, astonished by what we'd seen.

"I don't know," Nekitys said. "It's a classified military secret. I don't have the authority to access the information. Believe me, I tried."

Kinnard walked right under the turret, his gaze locked onto it as if he was trying to memorize its features.

"That's the business end of the lofter," Nekitys said, pointing at the rounded end Kinnard was mesmerized by. "You don't want to be on that side when it's firing."

Nekitys tapped a couple more times and grabbed a pair of handles that extended below the monitor. He swung the lofter around as if it didn't weigh anything. He pushed it toward Yra, who tripped backwards trying to avoid it.

"Fazah!" Yra exclaimed. "Watch it, Nekitys!"

"Oops," Nekitys replied with a grin, still guiding the lofter across the floor. "Sorry about that."

"This beauty will send up to a ten giga-tessle burst of directed majinecity anywhere from one to ten milles in any direction," Nekitys explained. "It's not the most precise weapon, but it'll level half a settlement before anyone even knows you were there."

He stopped sliding it and tapped the monitor again.

"Once you lock it down," Nekitys continued, "it won't move anymore. Go ahead, try to move it."

Kinnard, still absorbed with the lofter, walked over and gave it everything he had while we all watched but couldn't get it to budge.

"And watch this," Nekitys said as he turned on another unit.

Neither lofter emitted any sound. They were as silent as they were deadly.

"If you need more than one GT10 for some reason," Nekitys said as he slid the second one next to the first until they made a clicking sound, "they interlock to become one weapon so you can double your blast intensity. You can actually interlock up to ten units and control the group of them from any connected monitor."

"Ten?" Kinnard said. "That'd be a tera-tessle of majineic destruction. I bet that's more than enough to take out a cupola."

"No," Nekitys replied. "Typical cupola energy levels are in the upper peta range. You'd need tens of thousands of tera-tessles to even scratch a cupola."

I knew what Kinnard was thinking. He was trying to figure whether lofters like these could have been used to wipe out Atlantis and Spartanica.

"The only thing is," Kinnard said, "we can't just roll up outside the 'rat settlement and start lofting giga-tessle blasts. We don't know where Bellana, Perditus, and Kalahn are. We could accidentally kill them."

"Yeah," Naetth said, "but once we get them out, we definitely go back with a few ten-packs and let 'em rip."

Nekitys powered off both lofters. They dropped gingerly back down to the floor. He gestured for us to follow him to a different part of the room.

"This, over here," he said, "is the Sparta MT100 target-locking, short-range, gyro-stabilized, auto-charging, precision destruction draider."

It was smaller than the lofter but still six feet tall and three feet wide. It looked like nothing more than a three-dimensional rectangle standing on one of the short ends.

"With these, you just lift off the cover," Nekitys said, sliding off the top three feet of the draider to expose equipment underneath, "and push to unhinge the intensifiers out this way."

Nekitys nudged a three-foot high bundle of packed components sticking up from the center of the unit. It rotated away from him and unfurled into four separate four-inch wide cylinders with concave tips that looked like mini-versions of the rounded end on the lofter.

"Each of the four intensifiers discharges independently," Nekitys explained. "That way, one is always firing while the other three quickly recharge. All four are always aimed at the same target, so there's no need to adjust your aim between pulses. You'll just end up spraying blasts all over the place."

Nekitys slid open an access panel and flipped a switch. A small monitor, just like on the lofters, lit up as a two-handed control stick rotated out.

"A draider can be used in one of two modes," he explained, "free-fire and target-lock. Target-lock requires the warrior to visually acquire the target on the monitor."

He looked at the display and manipulated the control stick to guide the intensifiers until they tilted down and found Ty, whose wigged-out face displayed on the monitor.

"Hey, dude, don't point those things at me!" Ty complained, backing up.

Nekitys touched the monitor and Ty's face was instantly framed in a red box on the screen. The word *LOCKED* appeared in bold red letters in the upper left as well.

"Once locked," Nekitys continued, "the draider targeting system will follow its target until it's destroyed or out of range. Ty, move around a little."

"All right," Ty said hesitantly, "but I don't agree with this approach at all."

"We promise not to blast unless you keep whining," I said.

Ty sneered at me, walked to his left, and then zigzagged down an aisle, trying to get out of the draider's lock. The intensifiers smoothly followed his every move. Even pretty far away, his image stayed full size on the monitor.

"Note how the targeter zooms in on distant targets to make it easy to lock onto things further away," Nekitys said.

"So turn it off now," Ty hollered, waving his arms from the far side of the room. "I'm coming back."

Nekitys did so, and the monitor let go of Ty's image. The intensifiers turned back to facing straight ahead.

"Free fire is just what it sounds like," Nekitys said. "Use the control stick to point and shoot. You still want to use the monitor to see where you're aiming, but it won't automatically follow anything. And draiders don't interlock, either."

"How are we going to get these things outside?" I asked, hoping we wouldn't have to float them up the stairs. I sincerely hoped these people, as advanced as they were, had elevators, but I hadn't seen one.

"Yeah," Yra chimed in, "so we can practice blowing up some stuff."

"There's a hoister in the back corner of this room," Nekitys said. "The building specs show that it elevates to the surface but I haven't checked yet."

"Let's go have a look," Kinnard said.

Nekitys shut down the draider and led us down the main walkway in the center of the room. Everyone looked around in wonder, astonished by the sheer number of heavy weapons in the room, all lined up perfectly, side-by-side, waiting to be used.

Nekitys stopped as we approached the back left corner of the room. A big red rectangle with a large black "X" in the middle was painted on the floor. The same was painted on the ceiling above it.

"This is it," he said.

We all stared at the open space, confused by the lack of anything in it.

"I give up," Kinnard said. "How does it work?"

"Easy," Nekitys explained, walking into the red box as he did. "Just step on the hoister pad."

The red boxes on the floor and ceiling started to glow brightly.

"Recognize and verify hoister ready to engage," Nekitys said.

A security field instantly surrounded the red box from floor to the ceiling, encasing Nekitys within.

"Can all of us use that thing?" Kinnard asked me.

"Yeah," I responded. "We changed everybody's access to be able to do it."

"Hoister ready to engage," a man's voice, presumably SMILEy's, responded from overhead.

"Now it's ready to slide this entire space directly up to ground level," Nekitys said. "The security field will stay on until it's verbally disengaged. That way, we stay protected inside until we're ready to step out. Quite ingenious, actually."

Nekitys looked thoroughly impressed as he scanned the inside of the field.

"Well, let's try it," I said to Nekitys. "How about we take a couple draiders up and go find those freighters you were talking about."

"Disengage hoist," Nekitys said, and the security field dropped. "It'll be an ora walk from here, but that'll give everybody a chance to handle a draider." He looked around and asked, "Who wants to go first?"

Everyone put a hand in the air.

"Me!" Arianas yelled loudest.

"Arianas, Iryni, and Anina, come with me, please," Nekitys said.

"Awwww," Naetth and Yra whined, looking disappointed.

"Just relax," Kinnard said. "You two can go next. Practice using your rifles until it's your turn."

Naetth and Yra, suddenly remembering the new toys wrapped around their right forearms, got excited all over again.

TWENTY-NINE

HOISTER

(TY)

The Atlantean kids followed Nekitys back to get draiders, leaving me and Marcus alone by the hoister. All day we'd talked about rescuing Bellana, which obviously was really important. But, if Marcus and I were going to get home, there was something else we had to figure out.

"So when do we tell Kinnard and those guys about Professor Otherblood?" I asked. "I mean, somebody has to go find him if we're going to get home like Forticus said."

"I know," Marcus said, "but it's one thing to tell these guys we're Bellana's brothers. It's another to explain we need to find some scientist so he can help us get back to a parallel reality. I just don't think we have the time to explain it all, answer questions, and get those guys past being suspicious. They're so guarded about everything. I was thinking about telling them we needed to leave someone behind to protect the city in case it's attacked while we're gone. Kinnard would probably jump at the chance to leave Nekitys here. Then Nekitys could go find Otherblood after we leave."

That was actually a smart idea. Marcus had obviously been thinking about this a while.

"Do you think anybody should go with Nekitys?" I asked.

"Not me," Marcus answered. "I'm not doing anything else until we have Bellana back."

"I think I should go with him," I said.

Marcus wanted to say something, but I cut him off.

"Now just wait, Marcus," I whisper-yelled so the others couldn't hear. "First of all, at least two people should go in case one doesn't make it back. If it wasn't for Bellana, wouldn't we all go? Second, this gateway was built for you, me, and Bellana. What if there's some special knowledge only we have, or the professor needs our DNA to prove our identity or something? If one of us doesn't go, it could be a totally wasted trip. And third . . . ."

I knew Marcus was going to think I was just too scared to fight the Desrata. He would think I was trying to get out of it. I just knew he was going to start making fun of me.

"Okay," he replied.

"Okay?" I asked, stunned by his apparent insult-free agreement with my suggestion.

"Yeah, okay," he reaffirmed. "It makes sense to have each of us on one of the missions."

"Well, uh, yeah, that's, uh, that's exactly, you know, uh, my point," I said.

Marcus was freaking me out. He always had a smack down ready for me. Could he have been growing into a strategic, mature Spartanican leader?

"But we both know," he continued with a smirk, "you're just too chicken to square off against the 'rats."

So much for that.

Three draiders came floating around the corner behind us with each of the Atlantean girls guiding one. Nekitys walked between them, giving instructions as they approached.

"They'll move as fast as you want to push them," Nekitys said. "Go ahead and run."

Each girl took off. The draiders moved right along with them, not slowing them down a bit.

"Now stop!" Nekitys yelled.

Each draider immediately halted just as Nekitys indicated they would.

"These things aren't heavy at all, Ty," Iryni said. "It's like pushing a feather. Come and try this."

I walked over and gave it a whirl. She was right. There was absolutely no friction between these things and the floor, yet once I stopped, they stayed exactly in place. They didn't float away or vibrate or anything.

Iryni gently took my hand and guided it to her draider's monitor. It startled me, and I glanced at her sideways, unsure of exactly what was going on.

"And if you push here," she said, moving my forefinger onto a command button on the screen, "it stays locked in place. See? Bet you can't move it now."

She was right again. I couldn't get the draider to budge even though it was still hovering.

"Oh, uh, yeah, hmmm," I sputtered with her still holding my hand and smiling, "yep, it's stuck in place all right. We should probably get going, huh?"

"Draiders and lofters will not fire unless anchored," Nekitys explained, "like Ty and Iryni just did with theirs. They'll move like skimmers across a frozen inlet and they'll rip your enemies to pieces, just not at the same time. Let's slip them onto the hoister pad and head up."

The other girls slid their draiders onto the pad. Iryni took hers back from me but kept holding my hand.

"Ah, you should really use both hands to control this thing," I insisted, gracefully taking my hand back.

"Okay," Iryni said. "Whatever you say."

I was beginning to think this girl liked me, like more than just a friend.

"Recognize and verify hoister ready to engage," Nekitys said.

"Not ready to engage," the voice responded. "Verify perimeter clearance."

Nekitys looked around the edges of the pad and said, "Anina, you need to pull yours in a little. It's sticking over the edge."

"Oh," she said, taking a step back, directly into Marcus.

She turned her head, smiled, and said, "Sorry about that."

"Anytime," Marcus said, grinning awkwardly. "Uh, no, I didn't mean bump into me anytime. Just, uh, that's okay."

Marcus really needed to learn how to talk to girls. He looked and sounded like a total doofus.

"Verify hoister ready to engage," Nekitys repeated.

"Hoister ready to engage," the voice responded.

"Ascend hoister," Nekitys ordered.

We lifted off without a sound. Although we were moving up, the floor beneath us wasn't.

"Whoa," I yelled, hastily grabbing onto Iryni's draider. "Why aren't we falling?"

"The hoister is essentially a mobile security field," Nekitys said.

"So we're moving inside a big transparent majineic box?" Kinnard translated.

"Exactly," Nekitys responded.

"It feels like we're floating," Anina said, looking down with her eyes wide open.

The space over our heads went black as the hoister slid into the ceiling. Several of us crouched down.

"No need," Nekitys said. "It'll be dark as we move through the building up to the surface."

We passed through the ceiling as if it wasn't even there. The only light came from the room under us until even that disappeared, immersing us in total darkness. Iryni grabbed onto my shirt with both hands. After another five seconds or so, sunlight poured in from overhead. As we elevated fully above ground, I had to squint because the sun was directly in front of us. Iryni buried her face against my shoulder.

I held my left hand up in a useless attempt to shield my vision but saw something big move out of the corner of my left eye.

"Aaaaahhhh, Ty!" Iryni yelled, pulling my shirt so tightly it ripped as I struggled to get a glimpse at what was freaking her out.

Suddenly, I heard what was terrifying Iryni before I could even attempt to focus on it. It was a sound I'd only heard once before, and once would have been enough for a lifetime.

"Huuuuuummmmmmmaaaaaaans . . . ."

THIRTY

YES, I KNEW YOUR FATHER
(BELLANA)

"Do you like your new outfit, dear?" a woman's voice asked, jolting me awake.

I tried to stand up but the best I could manage was flopping clumsily onto my stomach.

"We made it especially for you," she said, "and, I must say, it does look oh-so-nice."

"Grrrrrrrr, why can't I move?" I yelled, my speech so garbled I hardly understood it myself.

"Oh, that," she said.

She sounded like the woman I'd heard before, except now we were together in the same room.

"Here," she said, "let me help you."

I suddenly felt empowered, strong enough to get to my feet. As my head cleared, I realized I was standing in a small circle of illumination encased by utter darkness. I couldn't see the woman speaking to me, but her voice echoed in a way that made me think we were in a large room. I was wearing a full-length black body suit that hugged me like a second skin.

"Where am I?" I demanded in a stern voice. "Why did you kidnap me?"

Any semblance of strength immediately evacuated my body, and I dropped like a rock to the floor.

"No, no, my dear," the woman chided. "Don't get testy with me. You see, when little lady Bellator is respectful and does as she's told, she gets rewarded."

My strength suddenly surged back, and I warily stood up again.

"But when little lady Bellator is disrespectful," she continued, "she will feel my displeasure."

"Uggghhh," I grunted, falling flat on my face again, completely unable to move as blood gushed out of my nose and onto the floor.

"Now apologize, little lady Bellator," the woman demanded, sounding irritated and angry.

I couldn't even speak.

"Answer me, you traitorous little witch!" she yelled.

"My Nobilis," a male voice interjected.

"What?" the woman yelled.

"I beg your kind forgiveness," he said, "but the restraint is at full effectiveness. She can do little more than struggle to breathe at this setting."

There was a pause.

"So it is," the woman said. "Yes. Quite the toy you've created, Pediseca. You have done well. I must learn to better control it."

There was another pause. Some small parcel of energy crept back into my body. I labored onto my back, sucking air through my nose to stop the blood flow.

"Sit up!" she commanded.

I sluggishly did as she said, using my left forearm to wipe off my upper lip.

"Hmmmm," she continued, "from this angle, you look like your father . . . sorry to break it to you."

"You knew my father?" I asked without thinking.

WHAM!

The back of my head slammed into the floor as I once again lost any and all ability to maintain a semblance of bodily coordination. I fought to stay conscious as my world spun out of control.

"I do not remember granting permission to address me!" the woman yelled angrily. She cleared her throat and said, "Yes, I knew your father; wretch of a man if there ever was one, and a traitor to all Sapertyns. He destroyed our beautiful cities, including that pile of twisted waste you still call home."

I desperately wanted to ask what she meant but I was still paralyzed. How could Father have destroyed the city? He loved Spartanica!

"And now," she blustered, "with you out of the way, we will reclaim Spartanica and rebuild it in our own image, as it was intended to be. And you, my dear Bellator girl, will join us. You will join us or you will never again leave this room in one piece."

"Please pardon the interruption, my Nobilis," Pediseca said.

"You may speak," she replied.

"An urgent communication awaits your attention," he explained, "and we are nearing the time for you to contact the Great One."

"Ugh, please, again?" the woman grumbled. "Very well. Take me. Oh, and my dear Bellator girl, wait for me here, won't you?"

Like I really had a choice.

THIRTY-ONE

I'M GONNA HURL!
(MARCUS)

"Don't shoot! Don't shoot!" Nekitys yelled, reaching over to push Yra's and Kinnard's rifles down. "It can't get to us in here. Your blasts will ricochet off the security field and kill us all!"

The 'rat stood motionless, inches away on the other side of the field, staring down at all of us.

"Huuummmaaaaaans," it said, "I come alone. Nooooo weapon. I escape settlement to help you."

Needless to say, that wasn't what we expected to hear.

"Everybody get ready," Kinnard said. "Nekitys, prepare to drop the field. We're going to put as many holes as we can through this thing."

The Atlantean kids all put our uninvited visitor squarely in the cross-hairs.

"Waaaaaaiiiiiiiiiiit," it said, stepping back with its paw in front of it. "Desrata Kingdom has your female. They kiiiiilllllllll if she not escape soon. I help you get her back. If I die, you fail, she die."

"No!" Naetth yelled. "You're a stinkin' 'rat! You're a liar! You're a killer! You would never help us!"

The 'rat backed up several more steps and eased itself down to the ground. Even sitting, it was almost at eye level with me.

"Desrata Kingdom has lost way, become evil," it said. "Not always so. Our leaders listen to evil humans now. Evil humans promise eternal Elisii if we help take your city. They make us work. They make us slaves. They make us take slaves. These not Desrata ways. These not *my* ways."

"Fazah!" Kinnard blurted sarcastically. "A 'rat with a conscience? Now I've seen everything."

"He says he knows where Bellana is," I said.

"He's lying!" Kinnard insisted. "I say we take our first live target practice right here. Nekitys, drop the field!"

"No!" I yelled. "Look around! Do you see any more 'rats? There's nothing out there except this thing." I yelled out to the 'rat, "How do we know this isn't a trap?"

"You many," it replied. "I one. You weapons. I none."

It leaned back and lay on the ground.

"No food for five sundowns," it explained, looking oddly frail. "I hunger. I tire."

"So, we're just going to drop the field and give this thing a big hug?" Kinnard said, looking at me incredulously. "Can you even be for real? You don't know what you're dealing with. You don't know these things like we do. They are pure evil!"

"I'm not saying be its best friend," I shot back defensively. "Let's lock it up and hear what it has to say. That's all. We can kill it anytime." I thought for a second, looked at Ty, and asked, "How can we make sure he won't explode like the other two?"

"IIIIIIIIIIIIIIIIIIIIII no wear human clothes," the 'rat replied. "I throw away. Desrata not explode. Human clothes explode."

"The uniforms?" Ty said. "Of course! I can't believe I didn't think of that! The explosives are in the uniforms!"

"So you escaped from the settlement," Nekitys said, "and came here just to help us get our friend back. Is that what we're supposed to believe?"

"No," it responded, "I help with female but you help me."

"Help you?" Kinnard said as if he couldn't believe the 'rat had the nerve to even ask. "How exactly are we going to help you?"

"After free female," the 'rat explained, "we use big weapons here to destroy humans that make Desrata slaves. I know where female is, different part of settlement. Others, like me, want humans go, want Desrata live for Desrata again. No more human clothes. No more human rules. Only Desrata."

Kinnard had a distant look like he was thinking really hard about something.

"If this thing is telling the truth," he said, turning to the other Atlantean kids, "it means it was humans that locked us up and starved us in the fields all that time." He turned to Nekitys and said, "It means you were tortured by humans. The 'rats were just dumb animals doing what they were told."

"See!" Naetth yelled. "I told you! I told you I saw humans there! I knew it! Fazah, nobody ever listens to me."

"Yeah, me either," Yra added.

"Oh, shut up," Anina chastened.

"Huuuuuummmmmmmmmaaaaaaaannnnnnnnns tell Desrata leaders to kill our little ones if we disobey," the 'rat added.

The Atlantean kids all glared at Kinnard, clearly stunned to learn that their actual tormenters hadn't been the animals they'd come to so ardently detest. Their true enemy had, in fact, been human.

"Humans order Desrata conquer this place now that female taken," the 'rat said, sounding weaker. "Humans promise Desrata eternal Elisii when they rule this place. They come soon."

"Why?" I demanded. "What is so important about a destroyed city, and why take our friend first?"

"I not know," it replied. "Human ways strange."

"You must understand," Nekitys explained to the 'rat, "we don't trust you."

"I no trust you either," it replied.

"I can get an immobilizer from inside the armory," Nekitys offered. "We can use the remote to make sure he behaves."

Precious time was slipping away like grains of sand through our fingers. We desperately needed a plan and had to get moving.

"Here's what we do," I said. "Leave the draiders here in the center of the hoister. Everybody spread out along the edges. Kinnard, you and me over here watching the 'rat. Ty, Iryni, and Arianas on that side. Naeth and Yra, you two over there. Nekitys and Anina, take the other end. Everybody look all around in front of you and to the sides. When Nekitys drops the security field, shoot anything that moves. If everything stays calm, we'll all take a step forward, off the hoister, except for Nekitys, who will stay on to go get the immobilizer. Any questions?"

No one said a word.

"Arianas," I continued, "when Nekitys heads down, you slide over into his spot, okay?"

She nodded in agreement.

"Make sure your safety's off," I said. Everyone briefly glanced down at their appendage.

Everything was suddenly very real. We were heavily armed with high-powered, deadly weapons and could very possibly have to kill or be killed. Up until now, it had all felt like part of some elaborate board game. Not anymore. This was intense.

"Ty . . . ready?" I asked.

He glanced at me over his shoulder and nodded. If anyone was afraid, they weren't showing it.

"Nekitys," I said, "drop the field."

The almost-transparent virtual window protecting us vanished. Everything was eerily quiet until a gust of wind blew across, causing a loose piece of exorbalis at the top of a pile across from Ty, Iryni, and Arianas to tip over and trundle down noisily. Without hesitation, all three of them adjusted their aim and ripped off several pulses, blasting the top four feet off the offending pile.

Kinnard and I, momentarily distracted by the fireworks, immediately refocused on the 'rat, which hadn't moved.

"Everybody okay?" I asked.

Nobody said anything.

"Hey!" I yelled. "Is everybody okay?"

"Yeah," Ty finally said, still searching intently for impending threats. "We're fine."

"Okay," I continued, "everybody except Nekitys step off the hoister."

Everyone did so.

"Verify hoister ready to engage and descend," Nekitys ordered.

"Hoister ready to engage," the computer voice responded.

Nekitys and the heavy weapons dropped back into the armory, leaving no trace whatsoever the hoister had ever been there.

"Good thing you guys killed that rock," Yra said, trying to lighten the mood but noticeably shaken by the whole exchange.

The wind gusted a few more times but nobody noticed. Eyes were peeled, nerves were frayed, and trigger fingers were itchy. For the first time, I realized that, although we were just a bunch of lost kids with a lot to learn, we were going to stand up to anything that came our way.

Nekitys re-emerged on the hoister after ten minutes or so with the immobilizer and a couple buckets of the most offensively putrid stuff I'd ever smelled. It was so pungent, Kinnard and I backed up to get away from it.

"Foooooooood," the 'rat said, sounding relieved and sitting up.

"Yes," Nekitys confirmed, gesturing to the immobilizer, "quagga and hartebeest sweetbreads. You can have all you want right after I put this around your neck. It gives us the ability to restrain you. May I put in on?"

"Yes," the 'rat replied without taking his eyes off the buckets.

Nekitys walked over and looped the immobilizer around its neck until the two ends clicked together. Then he handed me a small box with knobs.

"Very simple," he said. "With the adjuster at the top, he can do anything as he normally would. As the adjuster slides down, messages from his brain are slowed. He won't be able to move as quickly, or at all, depending on how low it's set. There's no pain involved, just decreased ability to move and otherwise react."

Nekitys brought the disgusting concoction over to the 'rat, which immediately stuffed two gushing paw-fuls into its mouth, with extras sticking out and splashing all over. The slurping and smunching were enough to make me swear off food forever.

"Ugh, I'm gonna hurl," I said, walking away.

"Actually," Kinnard replied, "I'm feeling pretty hungry, too."

Everyone else somehow agreed.

"Let's get something to eat and find somewhere to sleep," Kinnard suggested. "We can track down a freighter after we wake up." He looked at Nekitys and asked, "Any suggestions where to keep this thing so it can't cause any trouble?"

"There are many secure rooms," Nekitys responded. "I will take him."

"No," I objected, gesturing to Nekitys and Kinnard. "The three of us will take it together. The last thing we need is for this thing to bust loose inside the armory. Everyone else can head inside. We'll let this thing . . . ." I stopped and turned to the 'rat. "How are you called?"

It stopped chewing and looked up at me with intestines dangling from its lips down to the ground.

"Proditor," it said as chunks of drool-laden entrails spewed out of its mouth.

A good-sized chunk launched and landed squarely on Ty's forehead, above his right eye. He stood frozen like a statue, absolutely mortified.

"Uhhhh, uhhhhh, get it off!" he cried out. "Get it off! Uhhhhhh!"

He shook his head wildly, like a wet dog trying to get dry. The panic in his voice grew with every frenzied syllable.

"Uhhhhhhhh!" he screamed.

"Wait, Ty!" Iryni said, trying to hold onto his right sleeve. "Wait! Stand still! I can't get it off with you moving like that."

Ty barely stopped flailing long enough for Iryni to flick the offending niblet off using a flat piece of exorbalis she'd quickly picked up.

"There," she said, "it's gone. Now just take a deep breath. You're okay."

"Uh, thank you, Iryni," Ty said, still borderline hysterical, "but I won't be okay until I can disinfect my entire body. I can still feel the wet part up there! What if it's made out of acid like Alien blood?"

"Big tough Bellator boy," Naetth said mockingly, looking at Yra, who nodded and grinned. "Can we go back inside now?"

"Yeah," I said, "Kinnard and I will stay here until Predator finishes eating."

"Proditor!" the 'rat grunted, slurpily correcting my mispronunciation of its name. Ty immediately ducked and covered his head to evade any additional partially chewed projectiles.

"Okay," I said, not realizing it was possible to actually offend a 'rat, "until *Proditor* finishes eating."

THIRTY-TWO

THE ANONYMA PROJECTOR
(TY)

The human mouth has thousands of species of bacteria, viruses, yeast, fungi, microorganisms, and other simply disgusting stuff living in it. I understood some of them were the so-called *good* kinds that helped break down food for digestion and all that, but I was sure a few thousand of those grotesque little buggers were also the not-so-good kinds that were just looking for a way to make a person sick and die . . . especially me!

That was the human mouth. I couldn't even imagine how many *millions* of species lived in a Desrata mouth! And, as if that wasn't bad enough, our 'rat, Proditor, was eating uncooked wild animal guts. Nekitys called its disgusting dinner "sweetbreads," but I wasn't fooled by the pretty name. That 'rat was scarfing down beast intestines! I couldn't even imagine how many billions of lethal organisms must have been swishing around in its mouth. I got dizzy just thinking about it. That or I was dizzy because the 'rat slime on my forehead infected me with an incurable foreign pathogen! Ugh, what I wouldn't have given for a good old-fashioned physical at the doctor's office. Oh, well, dizzy or not, I wasn't going to let some 'rat-saliva infection beat me. I'd been ill before and battled through. The team needed leadership, and I wasn't going to let them down. I wouldn't say anything about feeling sick unless I simply couldn't go on. My immune system might just fight this thing off. Yes, it was dangerous and maybe even reckless, but, hey, that was just me, baby.

I actually started feeling a little better after I cleaned up and ate. I was tired, but this place had totally messed up my sleep cycle. The sun only went down for a few hours every jorno, so I was never quite sure when we were supposed to slumber. Being tired just kind of happened and I had to hope everybody else was ready to take a break, too.

Nekitys led all of us down to the barracks on level eight. He said there was enough sleeping space for over five thousand warriors on that level, and I believed him. There were eight big rooms, each with a bunch of smaller rooms inside, and they were all chock full of beds. The Atlantean girls took a room. The boys, including Nekitys, took another, and Marcus and I took a third.

"When we wake up," Marcus said, staring up at the ceiling from under his blanket, "we'll only have six days to get Bellana and get home. We have to leave Spartanica tomorrow, all of us. You and Nekitys gotta go find Otherblood."

I wanted to agree, but Marcus's voice was fading fast. My new bed wasn't as comfortable as the couch in the coliseum, but it did the trick in a matter of seconds.

I had a couple of my regular dreams to start my REM cycle, but nothing out of the ordinary. There was the one where I was an eighth-degree black belt martial arts expert defending Earth against an invading force of flying super-ninja aliens from planet Gliese 758 B. Those aliens were almost unstoppable until I . . . well, anyway, it was just a dream.

But just when I was about to defeat the evil Gliesean emperor with a flying pile driver, a tsunami of overpowering dizziness washed over me so ferociously I thought I was going to lose my dinner right in the dream. The super-ninja aliens disappeared into a thick veil of intensely loud static, like when the television was on but there was no signal, peppered with randomly flashing bolts of lightning all around.

This was *not* one of my usual dreams. Terrified, I covered my ears and closed my eyes, hoping to wake back up in the armory. The clamor died down after a few seconds and I warily took my hands off my ears and opened my eyes.

"Then the girl has been acquired?" a man's voice said.

"Yes, my Nobilis," a woman responded. "She is here with us and fully restrained."

I suddenly saw the woman that was speaking. She was on a viewtop right in front of me. Her face was heavy and round and looked like she'd been yelling because her skin was red with veins bulging out of her temples. She had ratty brown hair that looked like she'd never tried to do anything nice with it. She actually kind of looked like a 'rat. A human and 'rat hybrid, maybe? A *Humrata*? Okay, not really, but I was definitely going to have a hard time forgetting that face.

"Excellent!" the man proclaimed. "Yes, excellent! So we will take the city then, immediately."

I couldn't actually see the man that was talking, but it felt like I was sitting right next to him.

"My Nobilis," the woman replied, "we are fully prepared to march on the ruins but we have only recently become aware of a, shall we say, complication."

There was a pause.

"What is it?" the man insisted cynically, as if he'd been disappointed before. "Exactly!"

The woman fidgeted apprehensively. I couldn't blame her. This guy sounded downright evil.

"We just learned there are others in the city with the girl's abilities," she said.

"What?" the man replied emphatically. "How can that be? Why have we only learned of this now? You assured me only the girl had the knowledge and Guelphic virtues to be a threat. Once she was removed, we would take the city and enslave the others."

"Yes, my Nobilis," the woman countered, "but we have only just now become aware of more. The girl has siblings, two boys, and they are with the escapees in the city. We have also learned the boy escapee, Nekitys, is very knowledgeable regarding the weapons there. He is teaching the others to use them."

I couldn't believe what I'd just heard. It sounded like she was talking about me, Marcus, and Bellana. She actually said Nekitys' name!

"How can that be?" the man demanded. "You said he was valueless, a mindless drone."

"I do not understand, my Nobilis, how this can be," the woman responded. "I personally supervised as the animals majnecuted that boy a dozen times or more. Not only was he valueless, he should be dead. He was a walking corpse, unable to understand or contribute. He couldn't even die properly."

"And yet these *children* found a way to make him useful!" the man yelled. "He is teaching them to defend and keep us from the center of our future empire. We can have no further delays, Crivera! This is a great failure, a great incompetence!" The man lowered his voice and said, "But then I've come to expect that from your miserable Order of Malus, haven't I?"

"My Nobilis," Crivera responded, "we have a plan that will work."

"Oh, we do, do we?" the man said sarcastically, still highly skeptical. "So will this plan fix your last plan that didn't work? Please, I can't wait. Enlighten me."

"My Nobilis," the woman said, "we expect them to attack the settlement to try to recover the girl. We will wait for and repel their attack. The city will be deserted and we will simply walk in and take it in their absence."

There was silence for at least ten seconds.

"My Nobilis?" Crivera prompted.

"Quiet!" the man yelled. "I am considering your so-called plan. As soon as the children step outside the city, they give away their biggest advantage . . . seemingly limitless weaponry. They will only be able to take a small number of heavy weapons with them. You must let them venture far into the arduszone so they can't easily retreat. Once they've stranded themselves, you can surround them and bring an end to this annoyance. They will be dangerous at first because their weapons are powerful. Use the animals to attack them in large numbers and overwhelm them. Then capture them and turn them over to the animals. It will be a cheap reward for the animals that die in the attack and will keep them believing we are allies."

"My Nobilis," Crivera started, "we will try to take them alive, but—"

"No buts!" the man interrupted. "No, no, no. No buts about it. We need to give the animals a common enemy with us. These children will be that common enemy. When we help them capture that enemy, they will forever see us as allies, and we will maintain our control over them until we no longer need them."

"Of course, my Nobilis," Crivera said. "We will take every precaution—"

"No, Crivera!" the man demanded. "You will succeed, for you have no other option! I will accept no further failure from the Order of Malus."

"By your will, my Nobilis," she replied.

"Yes, indeed, by my will," he said. "Leave. Pediseca, you stay."

Crivera's face disappeared and another came on. It was a definite improvement. Anything would have been.

"My Nobilis," he said, closing his eyes and bowing his head.

"Do you trust the information coming from the city?" the man asked.

"My Nobilis," Pediseca replied, "I do trust what has been said."

"But the animals have never reported anyone other than the girl," the man said. "Could this all be a ruse to catch us off guard? A trick, perhaps, to keep us from taking the city?"

"My Nobilis," Pediseca said, "with deepest respect, I do not believe so. When we captured the girl, I saw two boys with her. They were not with the group we let escape from the field. One of them chased us into the arduszone with the speed of a champion quagga."

"And we are to believe these children are related to the girl?" the man asked.

"My Nobilis," Pediseca responded, "that is the information we received from the city. I have no further insight or reason to doubt."

"I assumed they and their mother were killed by the overload," the man, barely audible, muttered to himself.

"My Nobilis?" Pediseca inquired, looking confused.

"Nothing," the man said, "you may go."

"My Nobilis," Pediseca responded, bowing his head again.

The viewtop went dark.

"No matter," the man said, "we shall overcome this distraction as well."

Fierce static and lightning erupted again and rousted me awake. Even though I was ecstatic to be back in my and Marcus' room, I'd been sweating like an MMA fighter and my clothes and sheets were soaking wet. It was so disgusting I had to stand up just to try to dry off.

I paced back and forth impatiently for a minute, waiting for Marcus to wake up, but finally couldn't stand it. I had to tell him what I'd just seen.

"Marcus, are you awake?" I said, nudging his shoulder. "Marcus!"

His body lurched and he sat up.

"What?" he blurted, rubbing his eyes. "Jeez, Ty, what's your problem?"

"Nothing." I said. "Are you awake?"

He stopped and glared at me with one open eye, collapsed back onto his bed, and buried his face under his pillow.

"Marcus, seriously," I persisted. "We have a big problem!"

He didn't move.

"I think the 'rat is somehow communicating back to their settlement," I explained.

Marcus immediately popped up, his pillow tumbling to the floor.

"What?" he asked. "How?"

His hair was sticking up all over the place, making it difficult to explain without laughing.

"I had this dream," I said.

"Oh, please, not the alien ninjas again," he said, immediately laying back down and pulling his blanket over his head.

"No, listen," I insisted. "Remember how we thought the first time you talked with Forticus was a dream?"

Marcus didn't move.

"It was just like that," I finished.

"Seriously?" he asked, sitting up, suddenly interested to hear what I had to say. "Did *you* talk to Forticus?"

"No," I said. "It was more like I was eavesdropping on a conversation. Some guy, who was like a boss, was talking to a truly hideous woman named Crivera."

I filled Marcus in on the rest, including the static and electrical stuff.

"That doesn't sound like a dream," he said after hearing the whole account. "They were talking about Bellana, you, and me. And the guy actually said Nekitys' name. You must have projected into the room where they were talking."

Yes! A super skill! Finally!

"How do they know about us?" Marcus asked rhetorically. "How do they know what we're doing?"

"It has to be Proditor," I said. "I'll bet he's a 'rat spy secretly communicating back to them."

"Yeah, maybe," Marcus said, "but Proditor doesn't know the three of us are related and it doesn't know Nekitys showed us how to use the weapons. No, it can't be the 'rat, not unless it reads minds."

"Well, what then?" I asked.

There was a knock on our door.

"Are you guys awake?" Kinnard asked through the door.

"We have to tell him," Marcus said. "This puts everybody in danger."

I reluctantly nodded in agreement.

"Come on in," Marcus said.

"We're heading up to eat if you want to come with," Kinnard said.

"Yeah, in a minute," Marcus said. "Close the door and sit down for a second." Marcus looked at me and said, "Tell him."

I took Kinnard through what I had seen. He listened intently but none of it seemed to faze him.

"Do you guys really not understand what's going on?" he asked.

We shook our heads, obviously clueless.

"Mental projection is a Guelphic Varkis ability," he said. "You may have just started being able to do it. Father said the special abilities don't surface until right around our age now."

It was a good thing Kinnard's dad had told him about Guelphic Varkis stuff. Otherwise, we would've thought we were losing our minds.

"How does it work?" Marcus asked.

"Father said each direct descendant had the ability to mentally channel to one family member," Kinnard explained. "The person that does the channeling is called the 'projector.' The projector has a direct link to the consciousness of the subject. It's a one-way path. The subject can't project back to the projector."

"What?" Ty exclaimed. "I'm related to that guy? He's totally evil! Who the heck is he?"

"Did you hear a name?" Kinnard asked.

"No," Ty replied. "They just called him 'my Nobilis,' whatever that means. Well, at least he can't project back through me."

"Yeah," Kinnard continued, "but there's bad news, too. Since you projected into somebody, another relative can project through you. You are somebody else's subject, and you won't know who it is unless he or she tells you."

"So Ty's projector could be watching and listening to this conversation right now?" Marcus asked.

"Yes," Kinnard responded.

"So that's how the humans working with the Desrata know all about us," I said, putting the puzzle pieces together. "They're watching everything we do through my eyes."

"Probably," Kinnard said, "unless we can think of another way they're getting their information."

"This is nuts," Marcus said, looking at me.

"You said Crivera and Pediseca were looking right at you when they were talking, right?" Kinnard asked. "But the guy they were talking to had no idea you were there?"

"Right," I said.

"Fazah," Kinnard gasped, "you had an anonyma projection, Ty. You were projecting through the eyes of the guy Crivera and Pediseca were talking to. I'm sure of it." He turned to Marcus and asked, "Have you had a projection?"

Marcus shook his head and said, "No."

"Then you're probably fine," Kinnard said. "There weren't that many direct descendants around even before the last jorno. Your projector and subject are most likely dead. It's hard to believe Ty's is still alive. The truly weird thing is, less than one percent of projection links are anonyma. Almost all of them are 'named.' That's where the projector sees and interacts with the subject as if they were physically together."

"Hmmph," Marcus said, "guess I'll just have to wait and see what happens."

He obviously didn't want Kinnard knowing about his discussions with Forticus.

"One thing's for sure," Kinnard said, looking at me, "you can't be a part of anything we're doing until we figure out who your projector is."

"But what if my projector's already dead?" I asked.

"What if he or she isn't?" Kinnard fired back. "Can we really take that chance? The people in your projection knew stuff about us that only we know. How else could they know so much?"

"I agree!" Marcus said. "Ty, you need to leave the room so Kinnard and I can talk. And don't go with the others. Just sit in the other room until I come get you."

So there it was. Without even knowing it, I'd become a spy for the humans using the Desrata to take over the ruins of Spartanica so they could jumpstart their own empire. I'd become an outcast among my own people. After patiently waiting while Bellana and Marcus showed off for everybody, I finally got a special power, and all it did was make me a traitor.

THIRTY-THREE

WHAT WERE THOSE THINGS?
(MARCUS)

"There's no way he can help get Bellana back," Kinnard said, referring to Ty.

"Yeah, I know," I responded. "We'll have to leave him when we go. But I don't want him here alone, just in case the 'rats come back into the city while we're gone."

"That's a good point," Kinnard said, looking like I'd surprised him by thinking of it so quickly. "Who do you think should stay with him? I can tell you right now, you won't be able to leave one of my crew behind. They want to do everything possible to get Kalahn and Perditus out."

"How about Nekitys?" I offered, just as I'd planned all along. "We could set up lofters and draiders at the edge of the city and have Ty and Nekitys provide cover if we're being chased on the way back."

"Yeah," Kinnard agreed, deep in thought, "and it'd be *smart* to leave a small crew behind to come rescue us in case we don't make it back. Don't think for a minute this is going to be easy. We could all end up dead or worse."

I was sure worse meant alive, working in the fields.

"I'm fine if Nekitys stays," Kinnard continued, "as long as we have a solid attack plan and everybody's confident about using the weapons."

I couldn't believe how well that discussion had gone. In one fell swoop, Ty and Nekitys were set up to find Professor Otherblood while the rest of us went after Bellana. Most importantly, I wouldn't have to explain a single thing about the gateway or Forticus. Everything was going perfectly, considering.

We finished breakfast and headed out to find a freighter. Everyone came along except Ty, of course, who, as expected, was feeling all sorry for himself. We left Proditor locked up with his collar on as well. We wouldn't need him until it was time to plan the attack after we got back.

After an hour and a half or so, Nekitys finally said we'd reached our destination. It wasn't a good thing.

"This is it, Nekitys?" an exasperated Kinnard bellowed. "We risked our lives to come here for this? There's nothing here."

"This is where the freighters should be, if there are any," Nekitys responded. "Let's look around."

We walked in a circle for ten more minutes and found nothing remotely resembling a vehicle.

"Even if all the freighters were destroyed," Yra said, "you'd think we'd at least see the remains of one in pieces somewhere."

"Could they have been moved?" I asked. "Maybe taken inside for protection? Maybe there was some kind of warning and one or two got stashed away."

"Fazah," Kinnard said, "now we're grasping at air."

"Any better ideas?" I shot back at him.

"The only place nearby large enough to hold a freighter is the water control building," Nekitys said. "It has two large underground artificial reservoirs that were used for storing water before the SMILE was activated. Since then, they've just been big, empty, underground caverns."

Nekitys looked around for a bit, like he was trying to get his bearings.

"Over here," he finally said.

We walked around a corner and saw yet another ten-foot-high pile of exorbalis destruction.

"This is it," Nekitys said.

He walked a little further down, glanced all around, and pointed at the rubble.

"This is where the entrance to the water control building would have been," Nekitys explained. "The outer wall would have run along over there. The top of the tanks should be on level three. One tank is on the right side of the entrance, and the other tank on the left."

"Well, it's a longshot," Kinnard said, "but at least it's a shot. It's not like we have a plan B."

"Exactly!" I exclaimed, relieved to hear Kinnard finally coming around. "How about the rest of you go do some target practice while I dig my way in?"

"Yes!" all the Atlantean kids except Kinnard yelled.

"Finally!" Yra added.

"Can you or Nekitys stay here while I'm tunneling," I asked Kinnard, "just in case we have uninvited guests?"

"Yeah," Kinnard said, "I'll stay. These guys may have questions about the weapons only Nekitys can answer."

"There should be some open space not far from here to let a few blasts go without hurting anyone," Nekitys said, motioning for the Atlantean kids to follow him. "Come on."

Anina smiled and waved goodbye, and the gang of them was off.

"I'm leaving my rifle right here," I said, setting it down on an exorbalis block. "Don't let me forget it."

Kinnard nodded, and I started burrowing through debris in hopes of finding the top of one of the storage tanks. After twenty minutes or so, I'd opened up a narrow shaft, similar to the passage Bellana dug at the armory, and found a flat surface that must have been the floor of level one.

It was relatively dark, dead silent, and definitely creepy in the shaft as I lay on my back and took a moment to catch my breath. Up until then, I'd never even considered being claustrophobic, but I could swear the walls were slowly squeezing in around me. I shut my eyes, desperate to maintain my last shred of sanity, when a pitter-pattering noise suddenly resonated from overhead. I slowed my breathing to listen more closely and faintly heard an animal sniffing the air directly above me.

"Aoooor, aoooor," something outside yelped. It happened again except this time there were more howls than I could count.

The tunnel walls ominously shifted, and bits of exorbalis drizzled down as the fervor above escalated. I braced my arms and legs up against the sides in a desperate attempt to keep from being buried alive, hoping that whatever was running around outside would move on before I became entombed in Spartanica's ruins.

Slowly but surely, the commotion died down to the point where I was confident my interlopers had taken off. I guardedly lowered my feet and then my hands. Much to my relief, the tunnel held without much drama.

I needed to get my rifle in case one of those things figured out where the entrance was. My passageway wasn't exactly built for two-way traffic, so turning around was going to be a real job. I had visions of getting wedged in some awkward position and dying in there. That would have been just great. The eldest son of the great Forticus survives a trip through the gateway and helps fight off hardened Desrata battlers only to die in a coffin of his own construction, scrunched up like a baby bird trying to break out of its shell. I wondered if all that would actually fit on my tombstone.

I slowly and delicately contorted myself around like an earthworm, twisting into angles I didn't know my spine could even go, but finally ended up facing the exit. I shimmied toward the opening until I abruptly came face to face with what I'd only heard before: the head of a wild, snarling, angry beast with shoulders so broad they wedged against the outside of the tunnel entrance. It obviously had nothing but dinner on its mind. At first glance, it reminded me of a giant, hairless light-brown hyena except it didn't have ears sticking up off its head, which made it look even more savage.

I froze, hoping it could only see motion, like a squirrel or a deer. If so, it'd get bored and leave as long as I stayed perfectly still.

"Rrrrrrrrrrrrr," it ferociously grumbled deep in its throat like it was ready to pounce, but I didn't so much as flinch. It wasn't like I could go anywhere.

"Aooooor," it yelped, the vibrations from its voice rattling the now frail tunnel walls as it violently and repeatedly snapped its powerful jaws at me. Then, without warning, it backed out of the tunnel and left. Maybe it had realized it was too big to squeeze in and gave up. I didn't know and I didn't care. It was gone, and that was all that mattered.

After another very long minute of motionless silence, desperately hoping to avoid another confrontation, I cautiously started inching forward again when *BOOM!* - the face of a much bigger version of the same animal exploded into the opening, yelping, drooling, and whipping its head viciously side-to-side in a furiously malevolent attempt to widen the opening so it could get to me. Only its grotesquely oversized body jammed up against the tunnel entrance kept it from locking its merciless jaws squarely around the entirety of my skull.

I frantically scurried back away from the beast in a total panic until the tunnel promptly gave way, burying me under at least four feet of exorbalis and pinning my arms under my body. The animal squealed momentarily but shook off the debris that had fallen on its head and started rooting through the rubble to find me.

After frantically wriggling my body back and forth several times, I managed to free my right arm and glance up just in time to see the beast effortlessly smash away the exorbalis blocks above me. As its voracious jowls lunged down to deliver the death blow, I reached up and grabbed it by the throat, halting the attack with its fangs so close its tongue lashed up against my forehead.

"Stop!" I grunted as it fought aggressively to lower the boom. "Stop!"

The monster's skin was smooth and slippery, and my grip started to give way. It was simply too strong and fighting too hard.

"STOP!" I yelled, desperate to stay alive.

As I put every last remnant of strength into staying alive, a powerful warming sensation flared across my chest from the inside, compelling me to draw two lungsful of air while still holding off the beast. A surge of strength pulsed through my body and intensified up my right arm. The hand keeping me alive became intensely hot and started to glow a brilliant blue.

"Go . . . a . . . way!" I yelled, forcing my arm to full extension.

The animal cried out loudly in agony as it literally blasted out of my hand, flying backward through the air until it was out of sight. It yelped again as I heard it collide violently with a pile of exorbalis in the distance.

More animals started howling, but it sounded like they were moving away from me. Out of nowhere, the welcome sound of majrifle pulses filled the air. Several more beasts flew clumsily overhead. One landed and slid nearby, pushing exorbalis blocks back on top of me as I turned and covered my face with my free hand. The animal clumsily scrambled away over the top of me.

"Marcus!" I heard the Atlantean kids yell. "Marcus!"

"Over here," I answered hoarsely, my throat completely devoid of moisture. "Over here!"

"Fazah! Amicu!" Nekitys blurted, having spotted me through the rubble.

He knelt down over the top of me and started sliding exorbalis off. The Atlantean kids ran over and helped.

"Marcus!" Anina yelled, reaching down to find me. "Are you okay?"

"Yeah," I said, clearing my throat, "I'm fine."

"All right, just lay still," Naetth yelled. "We'll get you out."

As they slowly peeled away my impromptu sarcophagus, I managed to push through and sit up.

"Am I glad you guys came back when you did," I said.

In all the chaos, I'd forgotten they hadn't left me there alone.

"Where's Kinnard?" I asked.

"We haven't seen him," Nekitys responded. "He stayed here with you, remember?"

"Oh, no," I fretted. "Those things must've attacked him."

Enough debris had been removed for me to do the rest.

"Thanks, guys," I said, "I can take it from here."

I pushed up through a half dozen or so fairly large exorbalis blocks and stood up.

"Kinnard!" I yelled, stepping down off the top of my former tunnel.

Everyone followed me down.

"Kinnard!" I tried again.

The big hyena-thing that almost devoured me had left a huge impression in an exorbalis pile fifty or so feet away, but, thankfully, the beast and its pack were nowhere in sight.

"Thanks for getting that thing off me," I said, assuming someone had hit it with a rifle pulse. "I wasn't going to be able to hold if off much longer."

"You mean the big thing that was on its back over there?" Arianas asked, pointing at the dented pile. "It was already flailing around by the time we saw it."

"Yeah," Yra said, "I blasted a couple of the smaller ones that came at us but not the big one."

"I got one, too," Naetth added, obviously very proud of his marksmanship. "Did you see how they flew through the air? It was totally prodigious!"

I didn't understand how I'd fought off the beast but didn't have time to dwell on it. Kinnard was missing and we had no idea where to start looking for him. As we hollered for him again, he came running around a corner to our right.

"Hey, what happened?" he said, catching his breath. "I thought I heard rifle fire."

"What happened?" I yelled, getting right up in his face. "I almost got eaten alive! That's what happened! Where were you? You were supposed to keep watch!"

"I heard a loud noise over there," he explained, pointing in the direction from which he'd come. "I thought it could be 'rats, so I checked it out but didn't find anything."

"You went and looked by yourself?" I screamed. "And left me alone in there? Brilliant, Kinnard! Really brilliant!"

"I tried to yell to you in the tunnel but you were too far in," Kinnard responded. "What was I supposed to do? Wait for a bunch of 'rats to come walking up?"

"What were those things?" Arianas asked, referring to the hairless hyenas that had attacked me. "We walked the arduszone for two annos and never saw anything like that."

"They look like ancient drawings I've seen of chycrotas," Nekitys said, "but they can't be. Chycrotas have been extinct for over eight centurias, since the Carlidian era."

"Whatever they were," I said, "they're gone and everybody's okay. Let's focus. We still need to find a freighter. I'll start digging again if *everybody* will stay and cover me."

Kinnard sighed and rolled his eyes, knowing my comment was directed squarely at him.

It took a while, but I cobbled together a new tunnel. I made sure to make it a little wider than the first one and aimed for the main entrance instead of directly at a tank. I figured the tanks had to be pretty big and deep. If I pounded my way through the top of one, it could be a long drop down to the bottom.

I finally reach the first-level floor and punched a hole down through the second-level ceiling big enough to poke my head through. There was nothing but open darkness below.

"Recognize," I said.

Nothing. No response at all. This was going to be really hard if we couldn't get the lights on.

I lifted back up, tore the hole wider, and leaned my upper body down through, grabbing onto the topside of the level-two ceiling to keep from dropping to the floor.

"Recognize!" I said, much louder.

"Recognized," SMILEy responded, its voice echoing through the empty hallway.

"Yes!" I exclaimed. "Turn on all illumination in this building."

The hallway lights lit up just as I started losing my grip. I clutched the ceiling harder, desperate to keep from falling.

"Oh, come on!" I muttered to myself. "Hold on, Marcus, hold on!"

I squeezed so hard that the ceiling finally crumbled in my hands. Any leverage I had to keep myself elevated was instantaneously gone.

"Ooomph," I involuntarily grunted as I crashed to the floor.

I took a few seconds to let the stars circling my skull fade away.

"What's the status of the water tanks in this building?" I asked without getting up.

"Answer, reservoir one has been compromised," SMILEy responded. "Reservoir two has been compromised."

Compromised? I figured that was SMILEy's was of saying the tanks, and anything in them, were trashed.

"Is there somewhere I can see into each reservoir?" I asked.

"Answer, yes," SMILEy said. "The contents of each reservoir can be viewed via the level-three observation windows."

SMILEy gave me directions down to the windows. When I got there, all I saw were walls.

"I don't see any observation windows," I said.

"Answer," SMILEy replied, "the observation windows are closed."

SMILEy was reminding me of Ty again.

"Ugh," I exclaimed. "Open reservoir observation windows."

The walls on both sides of the hallway split horizontally with the top half sliding up, the bottom half down. Thick glass behind the walls didn't expose the wide-open caverns I'd hoped for. Instead, the spaces on the other sides were completely filled with collapsed building debris.

"So much for that," I said, sounding and feeling defeated. "All this way and no transportation."

"Answer," SMILEy announced, "liquid transports are available in the rear hangar."

"What?" I blurted. "Liquid transports?"

I didn't know what a liquid transport was, but it sounded remotely promising.

"How do I find them?" I asked.

SMILEy directed me to the far end of the hallway and down to level four. Along the way, he explained that liquid transports were originally built to carry large quantities of water on longer trips outside the city but that they hadn't been used in over twenty annos.

The rear hangar entrance opened to a giant, mostly empty room with a high ceiling. Parked along the far wall were three large vehicles that looked like they could qualify as transports.

"Yes!" I exalted. "SMILEy, I love you!"

My exuberance, however, quickly faded as they came into view. The first one was missing most of its back end. The second was propped up on blocks.

"Please," I begged, "oh please let the last one be okay."

To my surprise and relief, the third transport looked intact.

"SMILEy," I said, "how do I get this thing outside?"

"Answer," SMILEy responded, "execute the auto-staging sequence."

"Auto-staging sequence?" I asked. "Are you saying this thing can move itself outside automatically?"

"Answer," SMILEy replied, "yes."

I saw why Bellana liked SMILEy so much. He was a seriously helpful dude!

"Initiate liquid transport auto-staging sequence," I announced.

"Please identify transport number," SMILEy responded.

There was a symbol in the center above the windshields.

Now I really wished Ty was around. I had no idea how the Spartanican numbers worked. Based on the level numbers I'd seen on the stairway doors in the coliseum and armory, I knew the symbol wasn't three. I hoped it was either eight or thirteen.

"Initiate liquid transport eight auto-staging sequence," I guessed.

"Engaging," SMILEy replied.

"Yes!" I blurted as the transport whirred and came to life.

Lights flashed on each side and in front as the transport lifted up, hovered a few inches off the floor, and carefully slid forward. It was easily fifteen feet tall and maybe twice as long. As it glided past me out of its parking spot, it looked like an oversized Lego block with a cab in front and a bunch of knobs and dials on the side.

I followed closely as the transport, without turning, slid sideways fifty feet onto an oversized hoister which automatically elevated us through the building but almost slowed to a stop as we broke above ground. It hadn't occurred to me that we'd have to slog through ten or more feet of debris on the surface. Dozens of chunks of exorbalis rolled off on three sides as we gradually emerged. The fourth side, behind the transport, was open and relatively rubble-free.

Once the view cleared, I saw Nekitys and the Atlantean kids surrounding the hoister, each with at least one weapon trained right at me.

I didn't move, hoping to keep from startling anyone into an inadvertent rifle blast. I wasn't sure if the hoister security field would stop a maj-pulse, and I didn't want to find out.

I heard Kinnard yell something and everyone lowered their weapons. I exhaled in relief and dropped the field.

"So," I said, looking at the transport, "whaddaya think?"

"I am not familiar with this vehicle," Nekitys replied, inspecting it as he walked around.

"It's a water transport," I said. "I was hoping you'd know how to drive it."

Nekitys climbed into the cab and surveyed the array of buttons, levers, and dials.

"Well, yes," he said. "Theoretically."

"Great," Iryni said, sounding tired, "then can we please go back to the armory now?"

"Sure," Nekitys said, looking hesitant. "Climb in. Let's give it a whirl."

The cab was small and only had two seats with a narrow space behind them. Arianas climbed in first and stepped to the back, followed by Iryni, Naetth, and Yra.

"Are you getting in, Marcus?" Anina asked.

"You can go ahead, thanks," I replied. "Kinnard and I need to watch how Nekitys handles this thing."

"Okay," Anina responded, tugging at my hand playfully. "But you come in next then. I'll save you the place next to me."

I smiled back and stepped up after her, followed by Kinnard, who took the other seat. Those of us standing had to turn sideways so everyone could fit.

"Well, isn't this cozy," Naetth said sarcastically.

"All right," Nekitys said. "Ready, everybody? It might take a couple tries to work out the glitches, so be patient, please. I'm not sure where the speed control is, but I think this is the drive engage button."

Nekitys pushed it and nothing happened.

"Hmmmm," he murmured.

He tried to slide a large lever in the middle of the console but it wouldn't move. He leaned on it and it abruptly gave way all the way to the down position.

The transport took off like a rocket . . . backwards . . . and bounced off several deep piles of debris as we all were thrown forward onto Nekitys and Kinnard.

"Let me up!" Nekitys yelled with his head pinned against the control panel. "Let me up! We have to stop!"

We banged into several more rubble piles, like a bowling ball flying down a lane with small boulders for bumpers on each side. I finally got a little balance back, reached across, and jerked the lever back up, which sent everyone crashing toward the back of the cab but stopped the transport.

"Ugh," Yra complained. "How about a little warning next time, Nekitys!"

"I'm sorry," Nekitys replied. "The lever just let loose all of the sudden. Is everybody okay?"

We all grumbled but no one said anything about being injured.

"Good," Nekitys said. "I can't deduce how to make it go forward."

"It went forward when it skimmed over to the hoister," I said.

Nekitys scrutinized the control panel for a few seconds while we all waited.

"Ugh, can we just go backwards to the armory?" Kinnard asked while rubbing his forehead, which had banged into something when we took off. "Can we do that?"

"Yes, of course," Nekitys paused. "Just one problem. That means we need to turn around. Hmmmmm. I wonder what this lever does."

"No!" everyone yelled.

"Okay! Okay!" Nekitys said. "Don't worry! We'll take it very slowly."

THIRTY-FOUR

HELLLLLLLLPPPPPPPP!

(TY)

It was probably better that I didn't go along to find a freighter. Since the others had left, I'd been synthesizing food and drinks for our trips and moved a bunch of lofters and draiders outside. Not only were lofters and draiders seriously awesome weapons, but they could be controlled using remotes. One remote could control all of them or different remotes could be used in combinations. I wished I would've had something like them in school. There were a few boneheads (not to mention any names . . . like Toby Cruz) I would have loved to zap remotely and laugh while they tried to figure out how it happened.

As I went to drop the hoister back into the armory, I heard a whirring noise in the distance that sounded like it was getting closer. Had the 'rats been watching, just waiting for me to move the weapons outside? Now what was I going to do? Sure, I was a fearless, hardened soldier myself but I couldn't take on an entire 'rat battalion by myself. Who could?

My first, and natural, instinct was to stay on the hoister, bring up the security field, and retreat into the armory, but then the 'rats could take all the weapons. Then they could force Bellana to teach them how they worked, and the entire 'rat nation would use our own weapons against us in a massive, overwhelming, decisive strike. We'd all be captured and made into slaves in the fields. This was terrible! I should have just stayed inside and done nothing!

Not wanting to be ultimately responsible for the fall of Spartanica, I darted off the hoister, ran toward where the sound was coming from, and hid behind a pile of rocks. From there, it sounded like the noise would pass right by me. The ground wasn't rumbling, so I didn't think it was a hamster ball. I poked my head around the corner to get a quick peek and saw a big gray brick-looking thing only ten feet away and bearing down on me quickly! All I could do was pull back and duck.

BANG!

Exorbalis blocks came crashing down, bashing me violently face-first to the ground, entombing me in a makeshift sarcophagus. I was more worried the big brick thing was going to drive over the top of me but luckily it didn't. I was, however, imprisoned beneath a behemoth pile of rubble, unlikely to ever see sunlight again.

"Helllllllpppp!" I attempted to yell with my mouth smashed against the ground.

There were voices in the distance. They sounded human!

"Hellllpppppp!" I tried again in muffled futility.

"Thank Primus that's over," I barely heard someone say.

"Helllllllpppppp!"

"I'll go review the instruction and figure this thing out," someone else said.

"Yeah, I'd rather not go fight the 'rats backwards," Marcus said.

It was Marcus!

"Helllllllpppppp!"

"What's wrong with you?" I heard Kinnard ask.

"Something's not right," Marcus replied.

"Helllllppppp!"

"What do you mean?" Kinnard said.

"I don't know," Marcus said. "Just a strange feeling . . . something over there."

I could only hope they were coming toward me.

"Helllllppppp!"

"Did you hear that?" Marcus asked.

"Yes," Kinnard said. "That time I did. It came from over there."

"Helllllppppp!"

I heard the exorbalis blocks above me being moved away. A giant wave of relief poured over me as I realized they were digging me out.

"Ty!" Marcus yelled.

The blocks started flying off much more quickly until I finally had enough space to slowly roll over onto my back.

"Don't move!" Marcus said. "Just stay down! Jeez, what happened?"

"What happened?" I said, sitting up and brushing myself off. "What happened? You guys ran me over in your big gray brick, that's what happened. Don't you know you're supposed to drive on the road and not through the rocks?"

"We're sorry!" Kinnard said. "Look, it's a long story. Can you get up or should we have Nekitys take a look first?"

"I should probably be on bed rest for a week, but we have things to do," I insisted. "Help me up."

Marcus and Kinnard each took a hand and pulled.

"I've been working my butt off since you left," I said, gesturing to the lofters and draiders lined up nice and straight. "I even got food and water all ready to go, and all you can do is come back and run me over with . . . whatever that thing is."

"I'll explain it later," Marcus said. "Can you walk?"

"I'm fine," I said, justifiably aggravated by the whole thing. "Just look out already."

"Let's head inside," Marcus said.

We walked around the corner and saw everyone else waiting on the hoister. Naetth went to say something.

"No, no, don't—" Marcus pleaded, trying to shush Naetth by putting his forefinger to his lip.

"What the gehanna happened to you?" Naetth ultimately asked, unquestionably referring to my disheveled appearance.

"What happened to me?" I said, getting more animated each time I said it. "You want to know what happened to me?"

Kinnard exhaled sarcastically and rolled his eyes.

"Fine!" I blurted. "Nothing. Okay? Nothing happened to me. Let's just go."

THIRTY-FIVE

ATTACK PLAN
(MARCUS)

We all ate and headed down to where Proditor was locked up so we could work together on a plan of attack. Everybody, that is, except Ty, of course, who had to go off by himself. He actually did a lot of stuff while we were gone. As much of a pain as he could be sometimes, I missed having him around. He was good at noticing stuff that others, including me, usually missed. And, quite honestly, I always knew Ty had my back. He could be a knucklehead, but he was my knucklehead.

We let Proditor out and went to another, larger room Nekitys suggested that had a big round table surrounded by a dozen chairs.

"Everybody can sit down," Nekitys said. "This is the Guelphic Strategic Planning Center. Spartanica's military elite used this room to coordinate missions. I read all about it in the SMILE."

"Okay, Nekitys," Kinnard said impatiently. "Nice room, but we need something to draw on if we're going to lay things out."

"How about this," Nekitys said. "Display topographical map of Spartanica and the Desrata settlement including visual demarcations for each."

The entire tabletop lit up and displayed a two-dimensional geographic map with a large dark blue area bordered by water on one end and a much smaller, red area to the southeast. Spartanican letters identified each highlighted area, not that I could read them.

"Zoom in on the Desrata settlement while leaving the nearest portion of Spartanica in the view," Nekitys commanded.

The tabletop display adjusted as Nekitys directed. The Desrata settlement got much bigger in the lower-right corner of the display. Only a small portion of Spartanica could be seen in the upper-left corner. A vast expanse of orange desert separated the two.

"Now display the location of this facility," Nekitys said.

A small green dot started blinking at the edge of the table in the Spartanica section.

"There are light pens in the pockets on the right sides of each chair," Nekitys explained. "You can use them to mark up the map. Just call out the color you want to use and draw. Double tapping on anything you've drawn erases it."

"This is perfect!" I said. "Thanks, Nekitys."

"Sure," he responded, walking toward the door. "And you can slide the map around with your hands."

Nekitys watched as several of us tried out our new toy.

"I'll go figure out the transport while you guys strategize," Nekitys said.

The door opened and Nekitys hustled out.

"Can you show us where Bellana, Perditus, and Kalahn are being held?" I asked Proditor, whose light pen looked like a sewing needle in his monstrously large paw.

"Female not in fields," Proditor responded, waving dismissively at the red area on the map. "In building in human area, there."

Proditor pointed to one side of the Desrata settlement and explained that Bellana was being held in a large rectangular building surrounded by ten smaller buildings. He had trouble accurately manipulating the light pen so Arianas reached over and drew a couple Spartanican symbols where he said we'd find Bellana.

"No fences, but many soldiers," Proditor said about the human area, "mostly Desrata but some human."

We talked back and forth for another hour and came up with a blueprint that called for us to first stage one "diversion" lofter near the far end of the detention fields. Then we'd head over and stage two more "escape" lofters outside the human area before swinging around behind the buildings Proditor spoke of. Before heading in to get Bellana, we'd remotely trigger the "diversion" lofter to blast the far end of the detention fields to lure as many soldiers as possible out of the human area. Then, on the way back to Spartanica, we'd activate the "escape" lofters to lay down cover fire and flatten the human buildings.

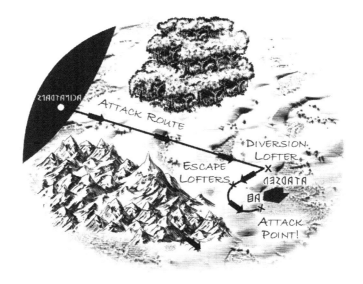

"Can you get your human uniform back?" Kinnard asked Proditor. "With it on, you can probably walk right into that big building and find the three of them a lot easier than any one of us can. You could even go in before we start lofting."

"No," Proditor replied. "I destroy human clothes. But Desrata will think I no have time to put on human clothes with fields under attack."

"But you can't just go strolling back into the human area," I said. "Won't they notice you've been gone for a while?"

"No," Proditor replied. "Desrata leave settlement to kill food, capture slaves, do what humans say. Then come back and no say what happen. But I must take prisoner to big building. I tell I stopped prisoner from escape and put in cell for beating."

"Makes sense," Kinnard agreed. "I'll go as Proditor's prisoner."

"No," Proditor immediately protested, motioning at the Atlantean kids. "You all escapees. Desrata know you."

Proditor gestured toward me.

"Him," he said. "Desrata and humans no know that one. They think he just new field slave."

Everyone looked at me for a long, silent second.

"You okay with that?" Kinnard asked.

"Yeah," I said in a resigned voice, "I'll go. Kinnard, you can set up the draiders outside the camp. You'll also be the getaway driver in the transport."

"Well, what are *we* going to do?" Anina asked, referring to herself, Arianas, Iryni, Naetth, and Yra.

"You'll help Kinnard set up and be ready to attack when we come back out," I said. "You are going to shoot every 'rat that comes out of there, except Proditor, of course."

"And humans not with us," Proditor added.

"Set rifles to kill, right?" Yra asked.

Kinnard and I looked at each other, instantly struck with the brazen reality that we were going to do whatever it took to get all of us back to Spartanica alive.

"I guess we're not there to just knock them out, huh?" Kinnard asked.

"You must kill or you will beeeeeeeeee kiiiiiillllllllleeeeedddd," Proditor said.

"Answer your question?" I asked Yra, who nodded but looked a little uneasy for the first time.

"What weapons will the Desrata have?" I asked.

"Whips, spears, swords," Kinnard responded. "They're also amazingly accurate throwing fist-sized rocks, which they stockpile near the fields."

"Yeeeeeessssssss," Proditor agreed. "Those Desrata weapons."

"Where are the sphaeras kept?" I asked Proditor, referring to the hamster balls. "Maybe we can blast those, too."

"I not know," Proditor responded. "Humans no allow Desrata by clear balls. I only see rolling in arduszone."

The door opened and Nekitys walked in.

"Hey, everybody," he said, "I got the transport figured out. That is one old machine. It was built way before any of us was even born."

"Who cares?" Kinnard said abruptly. "Did you figure out how to make it go forward?"

"Yes," Nekitys replied. "The primary control panel rolls up inside the dashboard. There's a button underneath that releases it, which explains why we couldn't find it."

"Let's go," I said to Kinnard. "Can the rest of you please bring up the food and water Ty put together?"

Everyone agreed.

"See everybody outside," I said as we all stood up.

Once we accessed the transport's control panel, steering it was a breeze. While it started out kind of slowly, it flew once it got a head of steam going. The tricky part was figuring out how to tether all the draiders and lofters to the back. We anchored six draiders to handles on both sides of the transport using a bunch of gray ribbon-like rope Nekitys found. The three lofters were easier because of the interlock. We clicked them together and used the ribbon to tie them to the draiders and the handles.

While Nekitys, Kinnard, and I figured all that out, the Atlantean kids brought up the food and water, which fit nicely into one side of an empty rear water tank. There was a lot more space back there than in the cab.

The transport wasn't quite as nimble with everything loaded and attached but still beat walking by a long shot. We figured it'd take two days to get there but only one coming back. Getting there would take longer because we'd be dragging the weapons and had to swing way out to the far side of the detention fields to set up the diversion lofter.

"If you leave in the next thirty protokas or so," Nekitys said, "you should make it to the diversion lofter site and set it up before umbra descends. Then get some sleep, head for the escape lofters staging location, and set out for the rear of the human area."

It all sounded so simple when he said it like that. Sure, the first part, the travel and set up, would be easy enough, but after that we were talking about real live warfare against the Desrata and whatever humans were with them.

"How about medical supplies?" I asked. "Do we have any? We should be able to help anybody that gets hurt until we can get back here."

Nekitys popped open the top of a rear water tank and pulled up a big square bucket.

"Right here, amicu," he said. "Coverings, medica supplies, and other stuff like that. I showed Yra and Arianas how to use all of it while everything else was getting loaded. And here are the remote talkers you wanted."

I had asked Nekitys to find walkie-talkies or some other kind of long-distance communicators so the two groups could stay in touch.

"I don't know over what distance they'll work," Nekitys said. "They use far-field majineic induction technology, which I think only transmits a couple of milles. I couldn't find anything for longer distances."

Two pairs of small, barely visible, skin-colored pieces of tape were laid out across his left forefinger.

"These stick on the inner part of your outer ear," he said, "near the auditory canal. They're paired so each one can only communicate with one other one."

"How about I pair up with Ty," I said to Kinnard, "you with Nekitys."

"But if we give one to Ty," Kinnard said, "won't his projector be able to hear whatever you say to him and vice versa?"

This projection thing was a real pain.

"Dang," I complained, annoyed I hadn't thought of that before saying anything. "I'll have to leave mine off until after we attack the human area, just in case."

Nekitys handed a talker to Kinnard.

"Put it on like this," Nekitys said, pushing his onto the bottom side of a ridge in his ear.

Kinnard did the same. They were practically invisible once they were in.

"Touch it when you want to open the channel and talk," Nekitys explained.

Nekitys touched his and spoke. Kinnard nodded to signify he'd heard Nekitys.

"There's no volume control," Nekitys said, "but I think it automatically adjusts based on the noise around you."

"Let me have mine," I said and attached it to my right ear.

"I thought you were going to wait," Kinnard said.

"Nekitys," I replied, "put the one that matches mine in your other ear."

"Seriously?" Kinnard said.

"I'll lose it if I don't put it in now," I said. "We can't let Ty have one, but I have to be able to communicate with these guys once we leave."

"No problem," Nekitys insisted. "Just don't both be jabbering at me at the same time."

"I think that's everything," I said. "Let's roll."

"Everybody grab your rifle and load up," Kinnard announced to the others.

I motioned for Nekitys to walk with me away from the group.

"You and Ty take off as soon as we're out of sight," I said, "and don't say anything to him about the attack plan."

"I know, amicu," Nekitys said. "No worries."

"Thank you, Nekitys," I said, truly grateful. "You've been a huge help."

"Be safe, amicu," he replied. "See you back here in a few jornos."

THIRTY-SIX

MOST DISTINGUISHED SCIENCER
(TY)

Nekitys finally walked into the armory room where I'd been waiting and nodded. That, I assumed, was to tell me the others had left. He tossed a pair of pants and a shirt at me.

"Here," he said, "I thought new clothes might be nice. I found these in a room upstairs."

Even with the reinigens, the pajamas I'd been wearing since being beamed here were getting a little ripe, so fresh attire was more than welcome. The long-sleeve shirt was dark gray with the Spartanica insignia on the left side of the chest. The pants were dark gray, too. Together, they looked like some sort of uniform. Nekitys changed into a similar-looking setup. We picked up the packs I'd filled with food and water, slid on our rifles, and took the hoister up to the surface.

"Where's the transport?" I asked, expecting to see the gray brick that almost killed me waiting for us.

Nekitys just looked at me without saying a word.

"Oh, you have to be kidding!" I said. "I thought that was for us. Didn't we say we were getting a freighter to go find Professor Otherblood?"

I thought about it for a second and figured the others taking the transport made sense, given what they had to do.

"Are we on the same page, amicu?" Nekitys asked.

I nodded to let him know I understood.

"Then let's get walking," he finished.

Our path was going to take us through parts of the city I hadn't seen before we'd reach desert, not that it mattered. One pile of rubble was the same as the next, and the next, and the next.

"You know what really gets me about all of this?" I said after twenty minutes or so. "What I really can't understand? Where did all the people go? Even after eight annos, I'd expect to see skeletons or even just random bones, but we haven't seen a single remnant of human life."

Nekitys stopped and quizzically glanced around.

"I have wondered the same more than once," he said.

He kneeled down, picked up several handfuls of dirt, and put them in a small pocket in his pack.

"We can analyze this soil for DNA traces when we get there," he said. "Professor Otherblood should be able to isolate any human biological characteristics."

"How will that help anything?" I asked.

"A significant sample of human DNA fragments in the soil would confirm a lot of people died here," he said. "Whatever destroyed the city may also have disintegrated its citizens at the cellular level. We could be looking at Spartanican remains right now and not realize it."

"Because they've been reduced to their sub-atomic components," I added, slowly catching up to Nekitys' thought process.

"Yes," he said. "It's a reach but worth a try."

It was more than a reach. It was brilliant. It wasn't often that I was genuinely impressed by a human. Nekitys had just done it. With absolutely nothing else to go on, he put together a very well-reasoned possible answer to the ultimate Spartanica question . . . where did all the people go?

We continued without talking until we reached the edge of the city. The desert in front of us looked like it went on forever. There was nothing ahead but flat, wide-open space. No mountains. Not even a sand dune. Just endless, barren nothingness.

"Two jornos' walk in this, huh?" I asked.

"Not a problem, amicu," Nekitys said. "I remembered a shortcut that'll knock off half a jorno."

"Does this place we're going have a name?" I asked.

"Petras," he replied. "At least it used to be called Petras when it was inhabited by an outlander tribe called the Petrans in centurios past. They stopped traveling the arduszone and carved out a large settlement. It's been deserted forever. Professor O found it while traveling in his younger days and built a studium there. It's his favorite place to do experimentals. I think your father helped him with it. I know your mother worked closely with him. She may have spent time there."

"My mother worked with Professor Otherblood?" I asked.

"Yeah, didn't you know?" Nekitys asked. "Decorias of the Order of Bellator was one of the most distinguished sciencers on the planet. She, Professor O, and their team worked on everything from more powerful calculos to advanced medica. They even dabbled in crazy stuff like inter-dimensional travel, all purely theoretical, of course."

All purely theoretical? Not exactly!

The more Nekitys talked, the more I became convinced of what Forticus told Marcus: Professor Otherblood, assuming he was still alive and we could find him, was the one guy on Sapertys that could get us home. If we couldn't find him, I didn't know what we'd do. And the fact that my mother was so smart   .

. . correction . . . one of the most distinguished sciencers on the planet, only made sense. After all, it totally explained where *my* superior intellect came from.

THIRTY-SEVEN

A FRIEND IN GEHANNA?

(BELLANA)

"Please stand up, dear," a woman's voice requested in a gentle tone from the darkness.

It was a different voice than before, friendlier, more caring, and not evil. It startled me and I would've jumped if I could actually move. I'd been there alone, immobile, in my little circle of light surrounded by gloom for an eternity. Warmth suddenly returned to my muscles and I slowly stood up. Footsteps came toward me and a woman emerged into my illumination. Her face was heavy and round but she had a kind expression and caring eyes. Her skin was red, like she'd been yelling, and her hair was an unkempt mess.

"Hello, dear," she said with a smile. "My name is Crivera. I'm sorry you've been treated so poorly. There are those here who harbor resentment against the former rulers of the central cities, even after all these annos. I know it must be hard for you to understand, as young as you were then."

I didn't say a word. She noticed me looking at something in her left hand.

"Oh, this?" she asked. "Yes, this is the device they gave me to restrain you. Quite barbaric, actually. You see, we know who you are . . . and what you are . . . and what you're capable of. As rare as human life is these days, you are in a category all your own. A direct descendant of the Guelphic Varkis. You're the only one left, you see, and the truth is we want you to be an important part of the future we're planning. We want to rebuild Spartanica and Atlantis to their former splendor, and we want you to be a willing participant in that process, but it has to be your decision. We're not in the business of forcing people to do anything against their will."

She stopped and looked at me.

"You're awfully quiet," she said. "Any thoughts, dear?"

"Where's the other woman?" I asked. "The one that tortured me."

"She's nearby," Crivera said, "but I convinced our leader you should be given the opportunity to understand what we're doing. There's no room for personal vendettas here. Can you and I have an adult conversation?"

She held up the device in her hand.

I nodded and said, "Yes, if you promise not to zap me again because you don't like what I say."

"Oh, no, no dear, never," she said. "We're not concerned about what you say, but rather what you can do. Do you understand?"

I nodded. They didn't want me using my strength or speed to fight them or escape.

"I had our expert set this to allow you normal human movement," she said with her reassuring smile, "which is only fair, wouldn't you agree? I will not use the device to hurt you, so long as we can all be civilized."

SPARTANICA

She walked out of the light and returned a few seconds later holding both hands up to show me she no longer had the device.

"There now, is that better?" she asked.

I nodded. While I was glad that thing was gone, I was sure it wasn't too far away.

While Crivera made it sound like she was doing me a huge favor, I really had no choice but to go along with her. But, regardless of what she said, I needed to get back to the city as soon as possible. Until she came in, I thought these people would just let me suffer and die on the floor, helpless and isolated. At least now, if I played my cards right, it sounded like I could get out of that room and start looking for ways to get away.

"What do you want me to do?" I asked.

"Just come with me, dear," Crivera said, "with an open mind, and understand how you can fit into the plans we have. That's all we ask. You'll see this is all just a big misunderstanding."

She reached out and gestured for me to go with her. While I knew I couldn't trust her, she was my only ticket out.

I took Crivera's hand and we stepped into the darkness.

THIRTY-EIGHT

DON'T DIE, MAN!
(MARCUS)

"Are we there yet?" Yra whined from behind me.

I had to laugh. That's what every kid said on a long, boring trip. Nobody else in the transport got it. It must have been an Earth-only inside joke.

Funny or not, it had been a long, hot, bumpy trip, and we were still on the move. It was already dark, and we'd expected to be done staging the diversion lofter long before sunset. We had to go slower than planned because the lofters and draiders bounced around too much if we went too fast. We wouldn't be going slowly on the way back, though. Once we were on the run, it'd be *pedal-to-the-metal*, or *lever-to-the-top*, since we were talking about the transport.

"There," Kinnard pointed, "over there. That's the spot."

Each lofter had a built-in targeting system that displayed a geographically accurate screen that enabled us to lock-in where we wanted the pulses to land. Then it plotted a circle around that target to indicate where the lofter could be positioned to be within range of the target. Once the lofter was locked down inside that circle, it was ready to go. I was pretty sure there was no GPS on Sapertys, so I didn't understand how the targeting worked, but we'd been driving to that location based on where the diversion lofter needed to be to hit the detention fields.

"Ugh, finally," Anina said.

Everybody stretched a little in anticipation of getting out of the transport.

"Yeah," Kinnard said as we stopped, "let's set up the lofter and get some sleep."

"I'll go let Proditor out," I said.

Proditor sat in the rear water tank, where it could keep an eye on the heavy weapons through a small window that peered out the back. To be perfectly honest, there wasn't nearly enough room for it in the cab with the rest of us. To be even more perfectly honest, Proditor stunk, and bad enough to make us all turn green and gag. I was glad when it took the rear lookout job so we didn't have to explain why we really needed it to be far away and, more importantly, downwind.

By the time I got back there, Proditor was already climbing out and sniffing the air.

"Something wrong," it said.

"What do you mean?" I asked, nervously scanning the horizon. "Are there Desrata or humans nearby?"

It sniffed again a couple of times.

"Not Desrata," it said. "Not huuummmmmmmannnnnn. Something. Noooooootttttt coming. It here."

I frantically searched all around, half-expecting something to jump out at us. But we were in a flat, barren desert and could see to the skyline in every direction. It wasn't like there was anywhere to hide.

"There's nothing here but us," I said.

"What's going on?" Kinnard walked up and asked.

"Proditor says he smells something strange nearby," I replied.

"Not nearby," Proditor emphasized. "Here."

"Desrata are known for their sense of smell," Kinnard said. "They can zero in on the exact location of another living being long before they can see it." He looked at Proditor and asked, "Do we need to leave?"

Proditor closed his eyes and drew another exaggeratedly long, deep breath.

"Noooooooooooo," he said. "Smell is so close we must see, but nothing here. I no understand."

"It's another six oras to the next lofter site," I said. "I really don't want to get back in the transport right now."

The look on Kinnard's face told me he agreed.

"Let's bed down here," I said. "I'll take the first watch for four oras."

Kinnard nodded in agreement. "Works for me," he said. "Wake me up when it's my turn." He walked over to the others and, in a louder voice, said, "Go ahead and find a place to lay down. Stay close in case we need to get moving in a hurry."

Naetth and Yra headed to the other side of the transport while the girls set down not far from where Proditor and I were standing. The green and blue swirly moon, which Nekitys told me was called Beta, hung menacingly overhead.

Naetth and Yra came back around where the girls were.

"Move over," Yra said. "It's too bright over there."

"Would it kill you to ask nicely?" Arianas asked.

"Okay, move over right now . . . please," Yra replied.

Arianas just sighed and shook her head. The girls scooted over to make room. Yra and Naetth lay down in the meager shade created by the transport.

"I'll be in the cab," I said to Kinnard.

He nodded and lay down next to Naetth. Proditor suspiciously sniffed the air one more time, jumped back into the rear water tank, and closed the lid. It didn't even take five minutes for everyone to pass out. Quite honestly, I wished I could join them.

Nekitys said Beta was the smaller of the two moons but it had been closest to Sapertys since Ty and I got here. The other moon, Primus, was much closer than it was just a couple of days ago but still a good ways away. Beta was completely covered by massive cyclones. I counted at least twenty-three pitch-black hurricane eyes with swirling blue or green clouds around each one, and that was just on the side facing us. The clouds at the outer rim of each hurricane blended into turquoise as they mixed with clouds from other storms. Beta's super-close proximity to Sapertys created a colored glow all around us that kept everything lit up well enough to see pretty far away. If I focused intently on a single storm long enough, I could actually see the clouds rotate around the eye. One time, two big eyes got so close to each other I thought they were going to combine into one massive storm, but they slowly bounced off each other and headed in different directions. It was like watching a big, silent, exceptionally relaxing, slow-motion pinball game.

My body suddenly shuddered and my head snapped up. I realized I'd dozed off. Beta was much further to my right than before. At least it was still dark, so I couldn't have passed out for very long. I poked my head out the cab door to check on everyone, but no one was there!

"Hey!" I jumped out and yelled. "Hey!"

My voice echoed into the distance but there was no response.

"Hey!" I tried again. "Guys! Where are you? Guys!"

I took a slow jog around the transport twice, searching intently all around, but there wasn't a single clue where they could have gone. I headed over to where everyone had laid down. There were impressions in the sand where each kid had been but nothing else. The shadow on that side of the transport made it challenging to see, but it looked like the sand where Iryni used to be was vibrating. I crouched down to get a better look and heard a rustling noise but still couldn't tell whether the sand was moving or if my eyes were playing tricks.

I inched my face down closer and squinted to narrow my focus, hoping reality would come into view, when something quickly jutted up out of the sand, wrapped around my neck, and forcefully pulled my head straight down into the ground. I clutched whatever was pulling (and strangling) me with my right hand and tried to rear back with my left. It took every Guelphic bit of hyper-strength I had, but I started powering away from the sand. The things in my right hand were long, thin, slippery, and squishy, like octopus tentacles, flexing and yanking, trying to force me underground.

As I pulled up a little more, a pair of human hands violently jutted out of the sand and flailed hysterically in the night air. I jerked back onto my knees, still squeezing the tentacles, used my left hand to grab both wrists grasping aimlessly for life, and pulled up as hard as I could. The tentacles gave way and Iryni's face eerily emerged like a ghostly apparition from under the ground. Her eyes opened and she involuntarily spewed a mouthful of grit right up into my eyes. I flinched sideways and lost my balance, falling on my right shoulder and losing my grip on her and the death ropes around my neck. As I clumsily hit the ground, my body was instantly encased by dozens more tentacles that erupted from beneath me and vibrated violently as they strained mightily to entomb my body in the sand. My arms were pinned at my sides, like a mummy's, and I realized that, even with every bit of Guelphic fortitude firing at full power, I was completely unable to move. Iryni's screams faded into the distance as my head shimmied under into dark silence.

How long could the human brain go without oxygen before it started dying? Ty would've known. I was still battling with everything I had, but it was useless, and I couldn't breathe in unless I wanted a couple of lungs full of sand. I couldn't believe it. I was going to die. Right there. This was going to be it for me.

Just as I prepared to accept the inevitable, two thick, tremendously powerful arms looped around the underside of my body and pulled me back toward the surface with the force of a diesel locomotive. Several tentacles around my waist and neck immediately snapped. A tremendously loud shriek rang out as the other tentacles loosened momentarily. My body flew up out of the ground, through the air, and landed on the surface as I wheezed in a mixed mouthful of air and sand. I was dizzy and disoriented, just trying to clear my eyes enough to see straight. Finally, after several big huffs of air, my vision cleared just enough to see Proditor, knee deep in sand, holding Iryni over his shoulder, battling tentacles wrapped around his thighs, arms, and chest. He twisted at the waist and heaved Iryni through the air in my direction.

I put my hands on her shoulders as she sat up and asked, "Are you okay?"

She coughed a few times and nodded.

"The others!" she urged. "Go, Marcus. Just Go!"

She rolled away, still hacking up sand.

Proditor snapped several tentacles holding him down and stepped back up to the surface.

"Squeeze until they break, human!" he hollered. "Until they break!"

He dove headfirst back down into the sand and disappeared. It was totally silent except for my and

Iryni's breathing until Proditor's head and torso shot back up with Arianas in his arms. Tentacles were snarled all around both of them.

"Human!" Proditor yelled. "Squeeeeeeeeeeeeeze!"

"Stay here," I said to Iryni.

I ran over and grabbed two handfuls of tentacles gripping Arianas and squeezed as hard as I could. I felt the thing's blood drain from the inside of my fist until there was almost nothing left, but they wouldn't break, so I yanked as hard as I could. They finally snapped and another loud shriek pierced the night.

Proditor tossed Arianas to the side and dove back into the sand. I helped her slide over by Iryni as Proditor emerged again, this time with Anina. Like before, I strangled the tentacles wrapped around them before he tossed her and dug his way back down. This cycle repeated several more times until everyone was back above ground. Kinnard was last, after which Proditor sat down with his legs buried up to the knees while countless more tentacles sprang up, wrapped around, and tried to plunge him into a subterranean morgue. I kept grabbing, squeezing, and ripping, but they were still coming too fast.

"Proditor," I yelled, "you have to move away now. Roll away! Hurry!"

"It is okay, human," he said. "Squeeze more. Break more."

We kept strangling and wrenching but it was a losing proposition. Proditor was gradually being engulfed in a death grip faster than we could fight back.

"It is okay, human," he said again, quickly fading into the sand.

"Proditor!" I screamed. "No!"

The Atlantean kids were hysterical behind me, actually screaming for Proditor to save himself. Kinnard ran over to help.

"No!" I yelled. "Go back! These things are too strong!"

Proditor sunk too far under the sand for me to help anymore. With my body flat on the ground and my arms reaching into the sand down to find him, a fresh bundle of tentacles rose up and glommed on to my upper body and head. I turned my face to the right just in time to keep my nose and mouth out of the sand so I could breathe.

That was the good news. The bad news? For every handful of tentacles I snapped off, another five sprang up out of the sand. Whatever this thing was, it had no intention whatsoever of giving up.

Abruptly, all the tentacles clutching me let go. I instinctively jerked up out of the sand and skittered away from the transport.

"You must have killed it!" Anina yelled. "Fazah! Marcus, you killed it!"

"No," I said, pulling my legs to the surface. "It just let go."

Although I was seriously winded, I still felt as strong as ever. It was as if my muscles refused to get tired, even after the insane ordeal I'd just somehow survived. I stumbled over to the others.

"I don't know what happened," I said. "It just let me go."

Anina crawled over and hugged me from behind. She was shaking, obviously rattled. I looked back over my shoulder at her.

"Are you okay?" I asked.

She just nodded with the side of her face buried in my back and hugged me even more tightly.

"Whoa," I gasped, trying to gently loosen her arms a little. "I'm glad you're all right, too, but I've had my fill of squeezing for a while."

"Rrrrrrrrrrrrrrrrrrrrrrrrrrrrrrrrrrrrr!" we heard in the distance and looked over to see Proditor's silhouette erupt from the sand with his arms vigilantly ensnaring something big that was viciously thrashing back and forth, slamming him on the ground from side to side.

"Rrrrrrrrrrrrrrrrrrrrrrrrrrraaaahhhhhhhhh!" he yelled again even louder.

A tremendous *CRACK*, like when loud thunder erupts right over your bedroom in the middle of the night, rang out. The creature fighting Proditor reared straight up in the air, let out an ear-piercing squeal, and fell dramatically sideways to the ground. Proditor bounced off due to the impact and landed with a thud heavy enough for us to actually feel the vibration.

I quickly ran over to him. He was lying on his back with green goo oozing from his mouth and nose. I watched as a huge bump literally swelled up to the size of half a baseball on the left side of his forehead as he lay motionless.

"Proditor!" I yelled, tapping his face, desperately watching and hoping for even the minutest sign of life. "Proditor!"

He didn't respond whatsoever.

"Proditor!" I urged again. "Come on, man! Don't die! Don't die! Proditor!"

THIRTY-NINE

THIS WON'T BE YOUR FATHER'S SPARTANICA

(BELLANA)

"This, my dear," Crivera said, "is our vision for a new Spartanica."

Before me was a three-dimensional rotating holographic model of a fully restored city, complete with upright buildings, travelways, and a reconstructed cupola.

"That's what it looked like before the last jorno," I said. "You really plan to rebuild it? I mean, who would live there? There aren't any people around anymore."

"There are more than you think," she said. "Pockets of survivors, here and there, more so in Atlantis and Lemuria than Spartanica."

"Lemuria?" I asked. "Lemuria was destroyed, too?"

"Yes, dear," Crivera explained. "The last jorno, as you call it, was an unforseen planet-wide event that overwhelmed all three cities. Our sciencers determined an abnormal sun flare during peak majstice caused a once-in-a-world majinecity event that devastated our civilization."

So there it was. My family. My friends. My world. My life. Gone in an instant because our sun burped at the wrong time.

"But where did all the people go?" I asked. "I can understand if everybody died, but there are no signs anyone was ever here. No bodies. No bones. Nothing."

Crivera's expression turned very sullen as her voice became quiet and sad. She put her hand on my shoulder.

"They were pulverized, my dear, instantly," she said. "The astronomical surge in majinecity reduced anyone who wasn't protected into their base elemental components and spread the building blocks of their existence into the atmosphere."

My knees went weak and I sat down. Crivera sat next to me.

"It was a tremendous, unforeseeable disaster that no one could have prepared for or prevented," she explained. "But now we have the opportunity to rebuild. We have the opportunity to prove some natural catastrophe can't just wipe us all out."

"Why didn't you just come to the city and ask me to help?" I asked. "Why all this stuff with the Desrata?"

"Because, my dear," she said, "there are so few of us remaining, we have teamed with our gracious allies, the Desrata, to start the process of rebuilding. We can't risk human lives. We're too rare and valuable now. We sent Desrata to the city some annos past and they were fired upon, by you, unfortunately. Several were killed. We watched the city closely and saw that you had powers that could only come from the Guelphic Varkis. Very few living humans were so endowed, even before the apocalypse. We knew you were likely the daughter of Forticus."

"Yeah, so?" I asked, getting defensive. "Forticus was my father. Why does that matter?"

"Your father was, shall we say, a very strong-willed man," Crivera answered, turning away. "He ruled Spartanica with a fist of durusaxam. While he enforced order and discipline, he was rarely open to opinions or ideas that differed from his own. We had to assume you'd be driven by your father's need for absolute control. When you killed the Desrata we sent to explore the city, we believed our fears were justified. The Desrata were enraged and immediately wanted to retaliate, but we were able to convince them a more diplomatic approach would be most beneficial for all."

Diplomatic? Desrata? I was somehow supposed to know they were just *exploring*? It didn't look like they were *exploring* when they were throwing spears and running at me by the dozen. It looked a whole lot more like they were there to kill me right then! They weren't exactly the most warm and inviting things I'd ever been around.

"You had weapons," Crivera said, "Guelphic powers, and, we feared, your father's unbending disposition, so you can understand that we were hesitant to approach, lest more Desrata be killed and the entire situation spin out of control. It was by pure chance we were able to bring you here unharmed so you could learn of our true motivations."

"To rebuild the city," I said.

"Not just the city," she explained, holding her hands up to emphasize the enormity of the plan, "the planet, my dear, and re-establish the human race! Spartanica will only be the start. It will again be the ruling or, rather, capital city."

This was a lot to get my head around. A natural disaster had wiped out the central cities. My father was, in simplest terms, a tyrant. I had misunderstood the Desrata. They were actually just a bunch of hairy good ol' boys that just wanted to help rebuild Spartanica.

"Why me?" I asked. "Why do you want me?"

"Because, my dear," Crivera answered, "you represent an irreplaceable part of Sapertyn heritage and culture. You are the only remaining direct descendant of the Guelphic Varkis, or," her tone suddenly became suspicious, "so we thought."

"What do you mean?" I asked, playing dumb.

If they'd been watching the city like she said, they could've seen Marcus doing Guelphic stuff they thought only I could do.

"When we took you from the city," Crivera said, "a boy about your age ran after our sphaera with speed unlike that of a normal human."

Marcus must have seen them take me and chased after them. He tried to save to me. He could've been killed, but he did it anyways. It was the first time someone had tried to protect me since Mother and Father were around.

"There were other kids with me in the city," I said, "but I haven't seen any of them do anything special. If someone ran after me like you're saying, it's news to me."

Crivera looked right at me and smiled.

"Of course, dear," she said. "The others. Did they escape from the Desrata detention fields?"

"I don't know," I said. "They just showed up one day and asked for food and shelter," I said.

"Hmm," she responded. "That's all right, dear. You don't have to pretend. Can I let you in on a little secret?"

I nodded.

"We arranged their escape," she continued, "as a good-will gesture to humans everywhere. It pained us to see them trapped in the fields, treated like animals. The outlanders are accustomed to such hardships, but not city dwellers. The Desrata are fiercely possessive of their slaves, so we went to great lengths to create a seemingly random opportunity for escape, and your friends were smart enough to take advantage. Oh, and please, don't bring this up around the Desrata. They won't, shall we say, appreciate the spirit of our generosity. You know, I find it noble, the way you protect your friends."

"So what now?" I asked.

"Now, my dear," she said, "we want you to come back to the city with us, together, as a team, as the future leaders of Sapertys, and help us explain all this to your friends so we can all work together, as humans with a common cause, a common vision, and a common understanding. I know this is a lot to absorb. I'm sure you need some time to digest it all. I want you to do so and we'll talk later."

"Do I have to go back to the dark room?" I asked.

"I'm afraid so, dear," she said. "Until we know you are with us, some draconian measures must remain. I tried to improve your accommodations but was overruled. Once we know you understand and support the dream, I will have leeway to improve your lodging."

So, basically, I had to agree to help or they'd let me rot under that light forever.

Crivera was desperately trying to make me believe that joining their "vision for the future" was some great privilege. It was so great, in fact, that they had to kidnap and hold me hostage to *volunteer* to help. Whatever she was selling, I wasn't buying it. Not now. Not ever.

FORTY

WELCOME TO THE JUNGLE
(TY)

"So here's the shortcut," Nekitys said, pointing into dense rainforest with some of the tallest trees I'd ever seen. I think Marcus and I slept on the outskirts of this place back when we first arrived, after we got thrown out of the complex, right before we met the Atlantean kids. That felt like forever ago.

"If we go through here," Nekitys said, "we'll easily save at least half a jorno. Otherwise we have to go all the way around."

A well-worn track laid out our route into the heart of the jungle ahead.

"Do we just stay on this path?" I asked.

"I think so," Nekitys said. "Do you see the mountains in the distance?"

He pointed straight ahead at a range of peaks barely visible well beyond the trees.

"We need to walk toward the tallest peak," he continued, "the one in the middle. Once we're through all this greenery, we're only another half-jorno's walk to Petras."

We'd actually been pretty lucky so far. We hadn't had a single delay. Cutting eight hours of walking time off our trip made perfect sense.

"Lead the way," I said, and motioned for Nekitys to go ahead. "Have you ever been through here before?"

"No," he replied, "but if you draw a straight line from Spartanica to Petras on a map, it goes directly through the middle of this place. I don't know why I was thinking we'd go around."

It only took half an hour of walking to realize why we should have gone around. At first, everything was peaceful, even serene. The plants were notably oversized compared to at home. There were ferns with leaves half as long as I was tall and even wider. The trees had trunks bigger around than the houses in my neighborhood, and I couldn't even see the tops from underneath.

For the first time since I'd been on Sapertys, it started raining. At the beginning, it was no problem, just like on Earth. But it came down harder and harder until the raindrops were the size of buckets, literally! One crash-landed on the back of my neck and knocked me face down onto the sopping wet ground. I hustled through the mud on all fours to the nearest tree and stood as close to the trunk as I could.

"Nekitys, what is this?" I yelled, pointing up. "What's going on?"

"I think the rain is collecting on the leaves," he hollered back, "and releasing in large quantities when the weight becomes too much to sus—"

A five-gallon liquid warhead from above exploded on his scalp, belly flopping him into the mire.

"Ow," he yelled, rubbing the back of his head, "that actually hurts!"

He crawled under the tree with me. Liquid grenades were detonating all over the place, but my plan to stay close to the tree kept us relatively unscathed.

"I think we'll be okay here until it stops," I leaned over and yelled. "The bigger leaves don't usually grow so close to the—"

KERSPLOOSH!

Nekitys got drenched again, almost falling to the ground due to the force of the impact. He shook his head several times, wiped his eyes, and glanced over at me.

"You were saying?" he finally hollered.

I shook my head dismissively, glad it wasn't me.

"Forget it!" I yelled.

The shelling continued for another twenty minutes or so. Once it let up, we stepped out from under the tree and back onto our path, which had turned into a soupy river of muck. We sloshed through it for a while until it disappeared into a wall of thick foliage.

"Do you think this'll pick up again," I asked, "or is this where it ends?"

"No way to tell," Nekitys responded, analyzing the six-foot-high intertwined knot of branches and leaves impeding our way, "but we're still lined up with the middle peak."

Since the rain let up, I'd noticed how quiet the jungle was. I'd been camping back home. I hated it, but I had to go for a sixth-grade class field trip. The entire time we were there, birds and other animals squawked and barked and chirped. The whole thing gave me a giant headache, but that wasn't why I despised being there.

The first night was unbearably hot and humid, and I'd forgotten my pajamas at home, so I snuck my shirt, socks, and pants off inside my sleeping bag after it got dark. Laying on the rocky, hard-as-granite, slanted ground in a tent was torture enough, but I got stuck with a bunch of dorks that decided to have an endless burping contest. Burp, giggle, burp, giggle, burp, giggle. It went on for over two hours before I finally gave up and went and sat with the teachers around the campfire, refusing to return to the whole putrid disgrace. I walked up next to my science teacher, Mr. Leiding, and told everybody what was going on. It was all they could do to keep from bursting out in laughter. I couldn't understand why they thought it was so funny. Personally, I didn't think the burping thing was at all amusing. Turns out, they weren't snickering at my story. After a minute or so, a mosquito bit me on the leg and I realized that, in my haste to escape, I'd forgotten to put my clothes back on when I left the tent. I was standing in front of all my teachers and Principal Brogdon wearing nothing but my underwear and a horrified expression.

So, yeah, anyway, I'd always hated camping.

But still, I hadn't seen or heard a single animal, or even an insect, since we'd strolled into this place. We saw a couple herds of four-legged antelope-looking things called quagga in the desert, but nothing since. Not that I was complaining. We had enough to worry about without a python slithering down off a branch or a bunch of mandrill monkeys chucking coconuts at us.

I pulled out my water bottle, closed my eyes, and tipped back a nice, long, cool swig. As drenched as I was on the outside, I was getting a bit parched inside after rigidly hugging that tree during the storm. When I brought the bottle back down, Nekitys was gone.

"Nekitys?" I said, looking all around. "Nekitys?"

He had been standing right next to me just ten seconds prior.

"Nekitys?!" I yelled.

Maybe I was wrong about there being no animals! Maybe Nekitys got dragged off by some big, hungry, noiseless carnivore. Or maybe an oversized bird swooped down silently and nabbed him before either of us knew what happened. I looked up to check just in time to have one last cup of rain pelt my face but didn't see anything flying away. He obviously wasn't behind me, so I decided to venture ahead into the great unknown before getting totally hysterical. There'd always be time for that later.

The leaves and brush blocking the trail made it impossible to see more than a step ahead. My feet sank four inches into watery slop with every blind stride. I finally came up against a wall of dense knotted vines that stubbornly blocked my way forward. Upon closer inspection, it looked like a single oversized branch running diagonally across was anchoring everything else. If I could just get past it, maybe I'd be able to see the path again and find Nekitys.

Oddly enough, a runny neon blue liquid was slowly dripping off the branch right where I wanted to put my hand. Not wanting to touch it but not seeing another clear place to grab, I leaned my shoulder into the obstruction and heaved with every ounce of strength I had.

Without warning, the branch gave way and I fell forward as the ground beneath me literally disappeared. It simply wasn't there anymore. I instantly found myself sliding helplessly down a steep incline, which normally wouldn't have been an issue but, with all the precipitation, our nice little trail had turned into a gravity-fed death trench. I reached out to grab onto anything that'd slow me down, but it was all too wet.

"Aaaaaaahhhhhhhhhhhhh!!!" I screamed as globs of mud spurted up all over my face.

Just when I thought being at the mercy of jungle sludge was as bad as things could get, I landed and submerged in a pool of soupy muck at the bottom. I popped up immediately and army-crawled onto the marginally firmer ground surrounding it.

"Hey," I heard Nekitys yell, still all wet but without a spot of mud on him. "Ty, over here!"

I stood up, wrung the mud off my hands, wiped more from my face and eyes, and walked towards him.

"Jeez, Nekitys," I protested, "thanks a lot for just disappearing. I about died trying to find you!"

"I fell down the same gulley you did," he explained. "It just kind of sneaks up on you, huh?"

"Yeah!" I said. "Why aren't you muddy?"

"Over there," he said, pointing at a small, clear waterfall. "It's not a reinigen, but it gets the mud off."

I walked over and jumped into a pool at the bottom. The water was wonderfully warm, like taking the most relaxing bath ever. After a few minutes, I climbed out and just wanted to pass out.

"Come on," Nekitys said, "we should keep moving."

I went to stand up and noticed blue paint all over Nekitys' shirt and pants. It looked exactly like the stuff that was dripping off the big branch above.

"What's that all over your clothes?" I asked.

Nekitys glanced down at himself.

"Oh, I don't know," he said flippantly. "I must've rolled in something on the way down the hill. Are you ready? Let's go."

I knew we had to keep moving, but I was so relaxed I didn't think I could get up.

"Hey, how about we bed down here and rest?" I suggested, barely flopping onto my back.

A very deep, very loud, and very menacing grumble suddenly filled the air. It reminded me of when I went to a dinosaur exhibit in Chicago with Aunt Andi and Marcus. As we walked around, an artificial sky overhead changed from day to night and from clear skies to simulated rain. There were at least twenty dinosaur skeletons spread throughout. It was really cool. But what got my heart racing and the hair on the back of my neck standing up were the downright bloodcurdling sound effects. The freakiest one wasn't particularly noisy. It was more of a growl that sounded like it started deep in the throat of a really big meat-eater and rumbled throughout the entire room. It came from everywhere at once and consumed the air. I was hearing that growl again, and it was really close.

"Ty, we need to go," Nekitys said, becoming insistent. "Come on, amicu."

Even though every finely tuned instinct was screaming *it's time to rabbit out of here*, I couldn't keep my eyes open, much less get up and run. All I could do . . . was sleep.

FORTY-ONE

PERSONAL BUSINESS
(MARCUS)

"Come on, man!" I yelled at Kinnard as he stood over the fallen Proditor with the other Atlantean kids. "He just saved our lives! Do something!"

"What do you want me to do?" he hollered back. "I'm no 'rat doctor."

Proditor still wasn't moving or breathing, at least as far as I could tell. I'd been kneeling next to him for probably ten minutes and he hadn't given any indication he was still alive.

I finally stood up and walked away. The others followed at a distance. After getting somewhat back under control, I spun back around and faced them.

"Great," I said, frustrated and saddened by Proditor's loss. "This is great. How do we get into the human area now without setting off every alarm on the settlement? This messes up our whole plan."

"I don't know," Yra answered. "Maybe we go back and think of another plan."

"No!" both Kinnard and I yelled.

"We'll just have to figure out something else," I insisted. "Dang, he was perfect. He was the missing link that brought it all together."

"We still have all of us," Kinnard said, motioning around at everyone. "We still have the transport and all the weapons. This is not a big deal, Marcus! As soon as the fireworks start, you and I will head inside the compound and get everybody out. You do your Guelphic thing and I'll cover you with my rifle. We can still do this. We have to do this!"

"It better me go, human," a gravelly voice announced.

I looked behind the group to see Proditor slowly rolling onto his right side. He coughed a couple times and more green stuff came out of his mouth and nose.

"We keep plan," he said.

I jogged over to him and kneeled down again.

"We thought you were dead," I said. "You weren't even breathing!"

He struggled to his paws and knees.

"For Desrata, breathing much is for weak," he said. "We learn when small to use little air. It painful, but hardened Desrata battler only take air four times every sundown."

"So you're okay?" Kinnard asked. "Can we get you anything?"

"Wait," I said and stepped behind Proditor.

I had to fiddle for a moment but finally got his immobilizer off and tossed it away. No one protested.

"Can you get up?" I asked.

"I stand, human," he answered, obviously drained.

He wiped his nose and mouth with his left paw, slung the green stuff to the ground, and smeared the rest on his leg.

"Now we take food," he said.

He walked over to the head of the beast he'd just killed, grabbed onto where the rest of its body disappeared into the sand, and yanked up to expose more of it. He did the same thing another dozen times until its entire body was above ground. It must have been fifty feet long with ten thousand tentacles hanging limply off it. Proditor tore off a couple handfuls, shoved them into his mouth, sat down, and leaned back against the transport.

The thing's head was shaped like a squid's, long and conical, except it didn't have any eyes. The very tip of its head formed into the shape of an arrow, probably to help it burrow through the sand. Its body was flat on the bottom where the tentacles were but more rounded on top. It must've moved through the sand upside down so the tentacles could grab stuff on the surface. The Atlantean kids and I walked over by Proditor, who was thoroughly enjoying his meal.

"What is this thing?" I asked him.

"Yeah, what is this?" Kinnard joined in. "The entire way from Atlantis, we never saw anything like this."

Proditor swallowed a mouthful and rested his head back against the transport.

"Grimess," he said. "This is grimess. It is Desrata legend we learn when small. Many Desrata stories about battle heroes who save settlement from grimess attack. First Desrata settlers hunt and kill all grimess to live in peace."

"I never would've left Atlantis if I knew these things were out here!" Arianas said.

The others kids eagerly nodded in agreement.

"Have you seen one before?" Anina asked.

"Only on buxxon hides when small," Proditor responded. "Early Desrata make pictures on hides to record stories passed down father to son to preserve Desrata ways so we be strong as they were strong."

"Buxxon?" Kinnard questioned. "There haven't been buxxon in the arduszone for over eight-hundred annos."

"Yes," Proditor added. "Desrata kill them all for hides. Desrata sad when no more buxxon."

"How did you know how to kill this thing?" Naetth asked.

"Stories say only way to kill grimess is grab neck and pinch hard until breaks," Proditor explained.

We all listened intently, entranced by Proditor's knowledge of our would-be subterranean death merchant.

"But must go underground to find neck," he said. "Only ropes come up to pull food down so it eat."

"Are there any more?" Iryni asked nervously.

Everyone's eyes widened as we all apprehensively looked down around our feet. A scared silence hung in the air, as if we were expecting another couple dozen tentacles to burst up at us. Proditor took a deep breath through his nose.

"No more grimess smell," he confirmed. "I know now. No more grimess here. Mmmmmmm, grimess good eat, just like in legend."

He took another big, sloppy mouthful.

"Well, I'm not sleeping anywhere near that thing," Anina said, looking at me and shaking her head.

"No, none of us are," I agreed. "We'll move the transport away from it. We still have time to get some rest."

"You go ahead," Kinnard said. "I'll take watch."

I was really hoping he'd say that.

We moved the transport and heavy weapons a good fifty yards away. Proditor stayed with the grimess carcass. He apparently wasn't worried about sleeping on the ground now that he could identify the strange odor. I got the feeling bagging a grimess was going to be a big deal back at the settlement. It wouldn't surprise me if he came back to claim his trophy and show it off at home once our mission was done. I imagined him hanging out with the guys, embellishing every detail about his heroic encounter.

Not surprisingly, nobody else shared Proditor's sense of security about snoozing outside. I passed out on the floor in the back of the cab while Kinnard stood guard. Everyone else divided up and slept in the water tanks. They weren't exactly roomy or comfortable, but it beat trying to sleep where we'd be easy pickings for supposedly extinct underground monsters.

As tired as I was, I didn't sleep very long, or very well. I woke up and found myself alone in the cab.

"Please tell me everybody didn't get eaten by something again!" I whispered cynically to myself.

I hopped outside and found the rest of our little army still asleep in the water tanks. Proditor was passed out in the distance. He'd gone from using the grimess as a pillow to just sleeping on top of it like it was some oversized stuffed animal.

Kinnard was nowhere to be found. The sun was just starting to break on the horizon, so there was still a little time to sleep. I didn't want to start yelling for him and wake up everyone. I found footsteps leading away from the front of the transport and chased after them. After about five seconds, I saw Kinnard walking back toward our makeshift camp.

"Hey, what's going on?" I asked.

"Nothing," he replied. "I just had some personal business to take care of."

"Personal business?" I asked. "Like what?"

"Like personal business I prefer to take care of without everyone waking up to see me taking care of it," he said, becoming irritated. "That kind of personal business. If you need a more precise explanation, you can follow the rest of my footsteps back to my personal business piled up on the ground back that way."

That was his sarcastic way of saying he was answering nature's call. Still he shouldn't have left us alone without someone keeping watch.

"Sorry," I said. "Guess I'm a little edgy after the whole grimess thing. You should have woken me up."

"Nah," he said with a shrug. "Proditor's going to hear or smell anything strange long before any of us do. You needed the rest."

Kinnard was usually a nice guy. He was a smart guy. I liked Kinnard. But, too often, he came to conclusions on his own and then did stuff without telling anybody until after he'd done it. All by himself, he'd decided that a sleeping Proditor was a good enough lookout while he tromped off into the desert. He'd also taken off and left me alone in the tunnel when the chycrotas attacked. He hadn't really done anything to hurt anybody yet, but this tendency to wander off at key times made me wonder exactly where his head was.

FORTY-TWO

IT'S GOOD TO BE . . . HOME?
(TY)

The roar and clapping of a large crowd rousted me out of my sleep.

"And, of course," a guy standing at a podium with his back to me said, "none of this would be possible without my loving, beautiful, and brilliant wife, Decorias, and our family."

Bright lights made it hard to see anything.

"They are the sun in my sky," he said, gesturing back to where I was sitting, "and my inspiration every single day."

He was speaking to hundreds, if not thousands, of people that cheered so enthusiastically my chair rattled. Where was I? Why was I sitting on a stage behind this guy?

"Thank you, fellow Spartanicans," the man continued. "It is with great pride and personal accountability that I accept this mantle of leadership you've bestowed on me for another ten annos. We have come far and prospered together, and we shall continue to do so going forward."

The crowd erupted again as the man waved and stepped back from the podium. Everyone around me stood up.

Someone tapped my shoulder. A lady with beautiful, long dark hair smiled and gestured for me to stand. She put her hand on my shoulder and gently prodded me forward with her until we were standing next to the man. Everybody was waving, so I started to as well. The lady softly tugged my shirt as we walked off the stage to the left, waving the whole way.

"Congratulations, Commander," the lady said, straightening the man's collar with a big smile on her face.

"Thank you, my love," he said. "Did I sound okay?"

"No," she responded, shaking her head, still smiling. "You sounded perfect!"

The man crouched down.

"What do you think, buddy?" he asked me. "Did Father knock 'em out tonight?"

Father? I was frozen, utterly befuddled by what was going on around me.

"Are you okay, buddy?" the man asked as a flash of concern crossed his face.

I nodded. He smiled and winked at me. Two other kids with us stepped forward from the lady's other side and hugged him.

"You did a great job, Father!" the girl said.

"Yeah, you're the best," the boy said.

"Ho, ho, hey," the man said playfully, hugging them both back. "Don't knock over the commander." He looked at the girl, kissed her on the cheek, and said, "Thank you, my sweetest girl." Then he turned to the boy, kissed his forehead, and said, "Thanks, big man."

He stood back up and looked across the room.

"Sublevos," he yelled, gesturing for a man on the other side of the room to come over. "Sublevos!"

The lady crouched down and looked at me.

"Tymaeus, are you feeling okay?" she asked.

Tymaeus? She looked at me with genuine concern. Her eyes were really dark, warm, and caring. I immediately sensed I needed to stick close to this lady, at least until I could figure out what was going on.

"I knew you should have had more for dinner, silly boy," she said, "and now it's getting late."

She fiddled with my hair for a second and put her hand on my forehead.

"Hmm, you don't feel warm," she said, "but let's get you home."

I nodded, still completely lost.

"He's fine, Mother," the boy said with a smile. "He's just all bent out of shape because I beat him at cruckers today."

"Oh, please," the girl said, rolling her eyes, "Marconis actually won at cruckers. Fazah, he gets lucky for once and has to brag about it all jorno."

"What do you mean 'once'?" the boy said in his own defense. "I can beat you anytime, Bellana."

Marconis? Bellana? They were little kids, like five or six years old. What the heck was going on?

The room we were in was right out of a fairy tale. Thinking about it, the whole thing felt like a fairy tale, so why would the room have been any different?

There were a dozen or more huge, fancy chandeliers hanging down from a ceiling two floors above. The second floor shared the same ceiling and looked down over the first floor on all sides. People were moving between levels as if they were on escalators but nothing was visibly there to hold them up. They were literally floating between floors! I looked real hard and barely saw a semi-transparent slope that was somehow shuttling people up and down.

A lot of people, like the commander, were dressed in all black with suit coats that buttoned at the neck but had no collar. The Spartanica symbol was prominently displayed on a patch on the left shoulder of each suit coat.

The man to which Father had gestured before walked over and shook hands. "Congratulations, Commander," he said. "It is an honor to be here with you tonight. Seriously, Forticus, thank you for the invitation."

The two men walked away, laughing and talking.

That was Forticus! He looked different in person but a lot like Marcus from the side, only older and much bigger. The lady had called me Tymaeus. The other kids were Marconis and Bellana, and Marconis called the lady *Mother*. So she was *my* mother? It suddenly dawned on me Forticus had called her Decorias when he was at the podium. She was *my* mother? So if I was comprehending any of this properly, I was in Spartanica with my family, my *real* family, and none of that other stuff on Earth with Aunt Andi and Marcus ever happened? But how could I be thirteen while Marconis and Bellana were half my age?

"Quaesitor," Decorias, or rather, Mother yelled, trying to get someone's attention. "Quaesitor? Magister!"

Mother pulled me along as the four of us squeezed through the crowd. Several people shook her hand or hugged her along the way, and said congratulations. One really annoying, rather large lady with awful-smelling perfume and the ugliest hat I'd ever seen pinched my cheek and said I was *just precious.* I thought for a moment the whole scene was turning into a nightmare.

We finally reached where Mother wanted to be.

"Magister," she said again, tapping a man on the shoulder, sounding exasperated he hadn't heard her before.

"Oh, yes, oh, uh, hello," the man turned and said. "Yes, hello, Decorias. Oh, excuse me, Madame First Lady of Spartanica, yes?"

He was an inch or so shorter than Mother with long, dark, frizzy hair that was neatly combed straight back and a skinny black and gray goatee that hung off his chin almost down to the top of his pants. I got the impression he didn't eat much because his suit drooped off of him like clothes off a scarecrow.

"Yes, yes, how are you?" he continued. "Oh my, where are my manners? Congratulations, yes, certainly, congratulations!"

He hugged Mother awkwardly.

"Uh, well, so, how are you?" he asked again.

"I'm fine," Mother said with a smile, "and thank you, Magister. Did you see the latest lab results?"

"Lab results?" the Magister said, rubbing his beard between his left thumb and forefinger. "Yes, yes, let me think. Lab results. Hmmmmm."

He was obviously struggling to figure out what Mother was talking about.

"Testing Protocol 88," Mother said, hoping to jog his memory. "Did you see the results? I sent them to you earlier."

"Oh, yes, of course!" the magister finally said, closing his eyes and tapping his temple with his right forefinger. "TP88, yes, yes, yes, dear. Of course. Very encouraging. Very encouraging, indeed. To think we may one day safely travel between central cities in less than a protoka . . . yes, very encouraging. Oh, oh dear."

The magister realized the bottom of his beard was swimming around in his drink.

"Oh, I'm afraid I really must be more careful," he exclaimed with an embarrassed smile. "Perhaps you could arrange a little trim for me one day soon, my dear."

He pulled his whiskers out of his glass and started to dry them on his suit coat. Mother stopped him and gave him her napkin.

"Oh, yes," he said, "thank you, yes, thank you."

He looked down and saw Marconis and Bellana giggling.

"Oh, oh my," he snickered with a whimsical grin. "Is old Professor Otherblood being silly again?"

Professor Otherblood? This was the guy we were looking for! He was right there! Where was Nekitys? He had to see this!

"Eccentric," Bellana said.

"Excuse me, my lady?" the professor replied.

"You're too smart to be silly," Bellana explained with a big smile. "You're just eccentric."

"Oh, yes, yes, of course," the professor responded impishly. "Thank you, my lady."

He looked over at me and kneeled down.

"And how is Spartanica's youngest genius boy today?" he asked.

I smiled and said, "Professor Otherblood?"

"Yes, yes, my boy, go on, what is it?" he urged.

"We've been looking for you!" I blurted. "We're coming to your studium in Petras to find you."

He pulled back and looked up suspiciously at Mother.

"Petras?" the professor said, blushing. "Petras? Oh, uh, hmm, yes. If you'll excuse me, please." He looked at Mother and said, "Madame First Lady," before walking away.

Mother turned to face me, visibly flustered, and crouched down.

"Tymaeus," she asked, "how do you know about Petras? Did you hear Mother speaking about it?"

She was talking to me like I was a little kid.

"Um, no," I said, *sounding* like a little kid. "I don't know."

She stared directly into my eyes.

"Okay, sweetie," she said, smiled again, and hugged me. "Wow! It's been a very busy day, huh? With Father accepting Global Command again and all the people. I know I'm tired! How about we get home and get some rest. Sound good?"

I nodded, and we fought our way through the crowd toward the front door.

Once we got outside, I was completely mesmerized by what I saw. Looking up, the cupola dominated the vertical horizon, undamaged and hovering high above the city. The six white towers met at the center, thousands of feet overhead, just like we'd seen in SMILEy.

"Good evening, Madame First Lady," a man dressed in a military uniform said. "Shall I summon the command charrius?"

"Yes, thank you, centurion," Mother said. "We will be heading to the residence."

"Well, Decorias!" another man said, stepping from the darkness between two buildings. "I suppose congratulations are in order."

He was around the same height as Mother, with similarly tan skin and dark features. He was one of the few men I'd seen not wearing some kind of uniform.

"Of course," he said, "all of Sapertys has lost, again, so you'll excuse me if the excitement I express for my sister is, shall we say, less than heartfelt."

"Wraven," Mother responded, "not even you can ruin a perfect night such as this."

The coolest vehicle ever made pulled up next to us. It looked like a fighter jet in the front, complete with a bubble canopy and aerodynamic nose. It floated almost silently on a cushion of air like the lofters and draiders. The rear was more like a regular car except the door closest to us automatically slid open and there was only one seat.

"Get in, everyone," Mother directed. "I'll be along shortly."

Bellana sat down and the seat slid back into the vehicle. Marconis did the same on another empty seat that slid around after Bellana moved inside.

Wraven grabbed and forcefully jerked Mother's left wrist with a sneer on his face.

"Oh, come now," he said, "you don't want to be rude to your loving big brother, do you?"

"Half-brother," Mother clarified. "Let go of me!"

Mother wrenched her arm away, easily breaking free of his grip.

The centurion grabbed Wraven, twisted both of his arms behind his back, and forcefully pulled him away from Mother. Two other centurions ran over to assist.

"I shall take him to confinement immediately, Madame First Lady," the centurion insisted as Wraven calmly accepted his sudden bondage.

"No," Mother responded. "This one last time, Wraven. Do you understand? I shall afford you this final courtesy, brother. You lost the election. Your shameless power grab has been resoundingly rejected by the people of Sapertys. Any further disturbances or threats from you will be dealt with harshly."

She looked at the centurion restraining Wraven.

"Take him away," she commanded, "and do not allow him to follow us. Give his image and information to the commander's security team and tell them this man is to be incarcerated any time he approaches anyone in the Command Family without prior personal approval from the commander or me."

"Yes, Madame First Lady," the centurion said. "As you wish."

"This isn't over, Decorias," Wraven yelled, becoming almost deranged as the centurions dragged him away. "You've won nothing! You think this is the end, but it's only the beginning. You and your contemptible husband will be sorry you've chosen sides against us. You'll regret every minute of your wretched lives!"

Mother sat down, and her seat slid into the charrius. The door closed as we started moving. Wraven blathered on, writhing furiously to break free of his captors.

Mother struggled to regain her composure in silence for a few moments.

"Why is Uncle Wraven so mean to you, Mother?" Bellana finally asked.

"Your Uncle Wraven is not well," Mother said, wiping her brow with a tissue. "He is consumed by envy. He desperately wants Father's seat on the council, but he doesn't have the proper disposition or support of the people. His failures along with his greed and endless hunger for power are destroying his mind. The good people of Sapertys have made it very clear, once again, that they want Father to be their leader, and your uncle simply must accept it. But enough about that. This has been a wonderful day of celebration and fun, and we should always first remember it as just that."

Bellana and Marconis tried to smile but still looked disturbed by the whole episode as we continued home.

KA-THWARP!

A blinding light followed by an ear-shattering shriek filled the charrius as its back end vaulted up over the top of us, almost flipping completely over. Although we dropped properly back to the ground with a soft bounce, we all had to battle to sit upright again.

Mother looked out the rear window and gasped.

"Oh, no!" she exclaimed. "What's happening?"

Peering out the back, I saw a huge beam of yellow light surging from the ground straight up into the sky from right where we'd just been standing. It was a blazing, sun-like yellow, narrow at the bottom but wider and less intense as it rose, eventually fading well before it reached the cupola. Dark orange pulsing rings wrapped around the outside of the yellow beam and surged up from the ground every second or two.

"Father!" Bellana yelled and started to cry.

As we all sat, staring in horror, Mother turned and pressed a button on the side wall.

"Continue quickly to the residence," she ordered. "Go directly inside using the rear entrance. Contact the Command Guards. Have them search the entire premises for anything unusual. They are to dispatch a fully armed escort to meet up with us as soon as possible. Follow emergency route six until the escort arrives. Only go to the residence once the centurions indicate it's safe."

"Yes, Madame First Lady," a voice responded.

"Listen," Mother said, visibly trying to stay calm. "Everything's going to be okay. We're still going home. The guards will make sure it's ready for us first. Everything will be okay."

Bellana was crying hysterically.

"Mother," she sobbed, "is Father all right?"

Mother, still looking out the back window, had tears rolling down her cheeks. She finally turned to Bellana and took hold of her hands.

"Listen to me!" she said, trying to get Bellana to settle down enough to hear what she was going to say. "Bellana, listen to me! Father is the strongest man I've ever known. I'm sure he's fine. It looks like whatever happened was outside. Father was inside. I'm sure he's fine."

Bellana nodded and relaxed a little, comforted by the thought that Father probably wasn't near the blast.

The streaming light beam flashed brilliantly once again and flamed out.

Marconis was breathing rapidly, still completely spellbound by what had happened behind us.

"What was that?" he said, bewildered and frightened. "Mother? What is going on?"

He finally peeled his gaze away from the rear window and looked at her, desperately hoping for a response he could understand. Mother reached out and put her hand on his cheek.

"Sweetheart," she said, "you need to take deep breaths through your nose and slow down. Come on, breathe with me."

They did as she described and Marconis began to calm down.

"We don't know what that was yet, sweetheart," she continued. "It may have just been an accident, or maybe something else. Right now, we're just going to be extra careful and get home. But I promise you . . ."

Marconis' gaze wandered back to the rear window.

"Marconis!" Mother snapped, pulling his attention back to her. "We will find out exactly what happened."

FORTY-THREE

WHEN YOU LEAST EXPECT IT
(BELLANA)

Crivera had one of her soldiers escort me from the hologram room back to my spot of light. We walked down several hallways until we stopped and the soldier slid open a door. There was nothing but solid black on the other side.

The soldier carefully lowered a super-thin, shiny silver visor connected to his helmet down over his eyes and we stepped through. As soon as we did, the light from the hallway completely disappeared. It was even darker than the darkways I used to get to my room in the coliseum. At least some light shined through the reflectors in there.

The soldier led me blindly by the arm through a maze of twists and turns and stairs until we ended up back in my personal circle of gehanna. Just like with the hallway, I couldn't even see the lit space coming until we stepped into it. Even standing in the light, my hand disappeared when I poked it into the blackness, as if my arm ended where the darkness began.

I assumed I'd be "turned off" again using their little Bellana power switch, what they called the *attenuator,* once he dumped me back in my cell, but I wasn't. Crivera's soldier stopped before stepping out, reached up, and unclicked the shiny visor from his helmet. With his back still to me, he knelt down and set the visor just outside the lit area, at the edge of the darkness, where I couldn't actually see it but could reach it without leaving my circle. He stood back up and slid another silver visor down over his eyes. He must have had two attached to his helmet, one right over the top of the other.

He looked at me and put his right forefinger to his lips as if to say *keep quiet, this is our little secret.* I nodded to let him know I understood, and he disappeared into the gloom, leaving me to ponder exactly what had just happened.

FORTY-FOUR

IF YOU CAN'T WALK AWAY, ALWAYS TAKE THE FIRST SWING

(MARCUS)

"Nekitys?" I yelled, touching the remote talker in my ear, hoping for a response from the other end.

Before I could say his name again, the talker beeped three times.

"What does it mean when it beeps three times?" I asked Kinnard.

"No idea," he replied. "Let me try."

He activated his talker and called out to Nekitys but shook his head to indicate he didn't get a response either.

"Oh well, so much for that," I said.

We'd just arrived at the staging site for the two "escape" lofters. I wasn't sure exactly how long it took to get there, but it felt like forever.

Proditor was out collecting rocks as he'd done every stop along the way. It wasn't as easy as it sounded to find good-size stones in the middle of a wasteland. Naetth and Yra had walked off to "take care of business." The girls went the other direction to do the same. Ty had been kind enough to pack toilet paper for us, something I hadn't thought of. I hoped he was okay. We'd always done things together, as a team. It took me a long time to realize I was better off when he was around, in spite of the annoying stuff.

Kinnard and I heard somebody yell in the distance. We looked around for a few seconds but didn't see anything so we went back to what we were doing. Then we heard it again, coming from the direction Naetth and Yra had gone.

"Run!" we barely heard Yra yell. "Run! They're coming! They're coming!"

"What's their problem?" Kinnard asked, squinting and putting his hands on his forehead to shield his eyes from the sun.

As Naetth and Yra got closer, we could see they were running full speed. Yra tripped, fell down, rolled a couple times, but got right back up and took off.

"They're coming!" Naetth yelled. "Get in the transport! Get in the transport!"

He blew right by us and clambered into the front water tank, obviously terrified.

Kinnard stepped in front of and grabbed Yra before he could do the same.

"What is wrong with you?" Kinnard demanded.

"Behind us!" he insisted, pointing in the direction from which he and Naetth had come. "There's thousands of them! They're coming!"

"What's coming?" Kinnard asked, holding on tightly to Yra's shirt.

"OUTLANDERS!" Yra blurted.

"Outlanders?" Kinnard said. "So what? We stayed with outlanders on our way here."

We started hearing and feeling a low rumble in the ground.

"Yeah!" Yra said, panting heavily. "I know! But these outlanders are running full speed right at us! Thousands of them!"

Yra jerked out of Kinnard's grip and dove into the water tank with Naetth, closing the lid behind him.

We could partially see what Yra was talking about. A massive dust cloud rose up from the desert maybe two football fields away. Running out from under it was a wall of very determined-looking humans with long, dark, gnarly hair, all dressed in animal skins and furs. They were sprinting just as hard as Naetth and Yra had been.

"Get the draiders!" Kinnard yelled.

We hustled over and started untying the weapons.

"What's going on?" Anina asked, coming up behind us.

She startled me and I hit my head on a handle on the side of the transport.

"Ooh, sorry," she said.

"Fazah, why are all those people running at us?" Iryni asked, watching in bewilderment as the horde bore down on us.

"We don't know," Kinnard said. "Just get into the transport. Marcus and I will hold them off with the weapons."

"No!" Anina said. "We have enough draiders. Give me one."

She helped us untie them. Arianas and Iryni joined in until everything was loose. Kinnard quickly fired up and slid the lofters out of the way while the rest of us each activated a draider. The dust cloud was quickly closing in.

Proditor came up from behind.

"What comes?" he asked.

"We don't know," I said. "Can you help us here?"

"Yes," Proditor replied.

He opened a pouch that had been slung over his shoulder and poured out a dozen or more apple-sized rocks, picking up one in each paw.

Kinnard jogged back over and took a draider.

"Give me one of these things," he said, turning it on and sliding it away from the transport. "Let's give 'em a little warning shot."

"Hurry up, Kinnard!" I yelled, the horde so close their screams were starting to rattle my brain.

"I got it!" Kinnard yelled, still fidgeting with the draider controls. "Come on you piece of . . . yes! Here we go!"

Kinnard aimed his draider to the far right of the advancing outlanders and ripped off three pulses, which exploded in the distance with absolutely no effect.

"They're still coming!" Anina yelled.

"Oh, tough guys, are ya?" Kinnard said. "Take this!"

He rotated to his left and fired again, with the resulting explosions landing much closer to the mob. This time, they took the hint and changed direction to our left.

"Yeah, that's right!" Kinnard yelled and turned to the rest of us. "Everybody ready to fire?"

We all nodded and set our sights on the quickly approaching insanity.

"On my mark!" he said.

He lifted his right hand up while keeping his eyes glued to his draider's monitor.

"Wait!" he yelled. "Not yet! Not yet! Okay, get ready! No! No! Wait!"

He pulled up and looked out over the top of his weapon.

"What is it?" I hollered, peering over the top of *my* draider.

The outlanders were no longer running directly at us. They'd changed direction and would pass to our left, maybe fifty yards away. Even at that distance, it was easy to see that they were big people. Not overweight big, but tall and muscular big. There had to be at least a thousand of them. The dust cloud kicked up by their running engulfed us, making my eyes water and everyone else, other than Proditor, cough.

"They're running from something!" Kinnard said, struggling to get the words out while hacking desert out of his lungs. "They weren't chasing the guys. They weren't attacking us. They're afraid of something."

All the grit in the air made us blind to what, if anything, was pursuing the outlanders.

"Everybody stay ready!" Kinnard urged. "We don't know what's coming at us! Don't shoot until we can see what we're dealing with!"

With the outlanders past us in the distance, it got quiet again. If something was, indeed, charging after them, I'd have thought we'd already hear it coming. The dust slowly settled and the sun began to re-emerge far to our left. As our visibility gradually returned, dozens of sand-covered mounds became visible across the wide-open space in front of us. The closest one we could see was at least fifty yards away but looked to be the size of a baby elephant. With the cloud dispersing further to the right, more and more sand mounds became visible, and they were getting closer!

The haze finally rolled completely out of our line of sight, exposing countless additional mounds, including one no more than five feet directly in front of me. I could have literally leaned over and touched it if I wanted to. It was a foot or two taller than me and as long as a car from head to tail.

In the not-too-far distance, one of the mounds slowly disintegrated as a head that resembled a small tyrannosaurus rex with an exaggeratedly thick skull plate and an oversized mouth full of teeth materialized and guardedly surveyed the space around it. It slowly stood up and stepped forward on two short legs that bent backwards at the knees and oversized feet that each had three toes with long, curved claws at the end. Its thick, muscular, compact, gray and brown body sported an abbreviated tail and connected directly to its head with no visible neck. Its eyes, anchored a few inches above its mouth and behind its nostrils, protruded out on each side of its head and swiveled three-hundred-sixty degrees.

The creature leaned back, raised up, and let out several short, but loud, grunts that echoed across the open landscape. Instantly, the other sand mounds dissolved as dozens of additional creatures stood up, including the one right in front of me.

We all stood motionless, desperately wanting to somehow remain unseen, when the thing in front of me swiveled its big round eyes. Sand noisily skittered off its eyelids to the ground. It scouted around without moving its head and sluggishly flicked a swollen, stumpy blue tongue in and out of its mouth, probably to taste the air like a snake. I hadn't noticed on the one further away, but up close I could see these things also had two short, but beefy, arms, each with its own oversized razor-sharp claw.

Although I had my eyes glued to it, it gave no indication of seeing me. Without warning, it shook its entire body like a dog drying off after a bath, and spewed sand all over me. My throat, which was already dry and itchy from the gritty fog that had blanketed us moments before, became downright barren.

The creature fixated its eyes on me and took one small, calculated step forward to get a closer look. It extended its body forward, still tasting the air, until the tip of its tongue almost touched my chin. The rushing of air through its alternately-flaring nostrils with each deep, heavy breath eerily drowned out any background noise and flopped my hair back with each exhale. It stopped flicking its tongue, closed its mouth, and eased its nose right up against mine, emitting a low-pitched growl deep in its larynx.

The sand in my throat finally became too much to hold back and I involuntarily coughed without opening my mouth, startling the creature, causing it to jump back defensively. It opened its huge, dagger-tooth lined white mouth and let out a blood-curdling screech right at me. We all tried to stay still, hoping beyond hope it would just go away, but it didn't look like that was going to happen.

Aunt Andi always said we should walk away from a fight any time we could, but, if we couldn't, we should always take the first swing and go full out until it was over. I loved Aunt Andi.

"Aaaaahhhhhhhhh!!!!" I yelled and ripped off several rounds from my majrifle right into its bony head, sending it flailing over onto its back but leaving it otherwise unharmed.

"Now! Now!" Kinnard yelled, and everyone opened up with the draiders.

I was so focused on the creature in front of me I hadn't noticed that dozens more were running at us poised to strike with their arms extended. I quickly lined up my draider on my little friend and let him have it again before he could fully regain his balance. The blast put a softball-sized hole through its abdomen, knocking it clumsily backward onto its side, where it stopped moving.

Iryni screamed next to me as I looked up to see another one leap, literally airborne with it hind legs elongated in front, aiming to land right on top of her. I inserted myself between Iryni and the attacking beast, ready to try to stop it and somehow throw it back out where it could be blasted. As its right claw swung down to shred me like a piece of paper, a couple draider pulses pegged it on the left side. It squealed in pain, its body contorting awkwardly, and flew sideways, landing violently to the right of my draider. Iryni, who had ducked and covered her head with her hands, looked up and smiled when she saw she was still okay.

"Iryni!" Kinnard yelled. "Get up! Come on!"

Having saved both of us, Kinnard swung his weapon back around and fired into the continuing onslaught as I stepped back behind my draider. Iryni immediately jumped up and started firing, albeit wildly. One at a time, creature corpses started piling up in front of us. Just when it looked like the shooting gallery might ease up, Proditor yelped loudly behind us. I looked back and saw him dazed and pinned down on the ground by a creature trying to open its mouth wide enough to get around his mid-section.

"Kinnard!" I yelled. "Behind you!"

Kinnard glimpsed back but kept shooting targets in front of us.

"Kinnard!" I yelled again, but he totally ignored me.

I tapped Iryni on the shoulder and pointed back to indicate I was going to help Proditor. She nodded, and I leapt over the transport. By the time I got there, the creature had Proditor in its mouth and was ready to run off. I blasted it from behind with my rifle. It fell forward onto its stomach and lost its grip on Proditor, who rolled away but didn't immediately get up. I made sure my rifle was set to kill and squeezed off half a dozen rounds directly into its head and body just as it stood back up to snatch Proditor again. The skin on these things was like armor. Even on kill, the rifle only shoved it further away and made it roll over a few times without inflicting any noticeable damage.

"Kinnard!" I screamed. "Shoot it!"

He paid no attention, even though I knew he'd heard me.

Anina glanced over and quickly figured out what I wanted. She swung her draider around and aimed it at Proditor's attacker between Kinnard and the transport. I dove back out of the way and heard several blasts followed by a loud reptilian scream. When I glimpsed up, Proditor's would-be assassin was dead, bleeding white liquid from its abdomen a good twenty feet away from where it had been. I dragged Proditor behind the transport and hopped back over to my draider, but nothing was coming at us.

"They're running away!" Kinnard yelled. "They're retreating! Take that, you scaly pedicabos!"

Slaughtered creature bodies littered the landscape in front of us. In some places, they were two and three deep. Everyone was still wide-eyed, scouting for more aggressors. Iryni and Arianas were shaking noticeably. Who could blame them? We came out here to fight one enemy and had been attacked by two others before even reaching our impending battle.

"Is anybody hurt?" I yelled, but got no response. "Hey!" I tried again, finally getting everyone to look at me. "Is anyone hurt?"

I didn't see any blood except for what was coming out of Kinnard's mouth.

"What happened to you?" I asked him.

"Nothing," he answered curtly and turned away.

"The shock wave from my draider shoved his face into his range finder when I blasted that one," Anina said, pointing at the creature that tried to carry off Proditor.

I'd forgotten about Proditor! I jumped over the transport and found him sitting up, leaning against the side.

"Hey, how ya doing?" I asked.

"Head hurts," he replied, holding his skull with both hands. He moved them over his ribs and said, "Body hurts." He looked up and said, "But we go now. Attack settlement during umbra."

I couldn't imagine what it had to feel like to almost be eaten by a giant half-dinosaur, half-lizard, but Proditor was seemingly unfazed. Animal or not, big P was one tough dude.

"You were going to let him die!" I heard Anina yell from the other side of the transport.

"So I was just supposed to turn my draider all the way around with those things coming at us ten at a time?" an exasperated Kinnard responded.

"I did!" Anina insisted. "Because I knew you'd cover me until I was done. You don't think I'd do the same for you?"

The lid over the front water tank flipped open. Yra and Naetth poked their heads out and looked out over the massacre in front of us.

"Whoa," they both said.

"And where the gehanna were you two?" Kinnard demanded. "We almost died out here while you were hiding like scared little babies!"

"We thought everybody would pile in the transport and we'd leave," Naetth said. "Then we heard all the shooting and . . . I don't know."

"You heard all the shooting and, let's see, checked out for the day!" Kinnard yelled. "If Arianas, Anina, and Iryni hadn't come back and volunteered to take draiders, we'd all be dead!"

"And Proditor," Anina said.

"What?" Kinnard asked.

"And Proditor!" she repeated emphatically. "He took down at least four of those things. I saw the rocks he threw lodge right in their eyes. It was amazing!"

"Five," Proditor confirmed. "Five dead beasts, not including that."

He gestured at the creature that had tried to carry him off for dinner.

"Whatever!" Kinnard interjected. "My point is everybody else helped while you two did nothing. I think you can just walk back to the city and let the rest of us handle the dirty work."

"No!" Yra yelled, red-faced and sounding upset enough to maybe start crying. "We're staying!"

"Why?" Kinnard continued. "So you can run and hide again when things get hairy?"

"NO!" Yra insisted. "It won't happen again!"

Kinnard walked over, stepped up on the transport, grabbed them both by the front of their shirts at the neck, and pulled his face right up to theirs.

"It better not," he snarled. "Understand?"

Both boys nodded vigorously. Kinnard let them go, stepped down, and walked around the front of the transport to where Proditor was sitting.

"What were those things?" he asked.

Proditor shook his head to indicate he didn't know.

"What?" Kinnard said. "No legends on the buxxon hides about giant lizards that run on two feet and jump through the air to pounce on their prey?"

"No, huuuummmmaaaaaan," Proditor reiterated. If 'rats had an irritated tone, I think he was using it.

Kinnard looked out over the carpet of dead reptiles, shaking his head.

"I don't get it," he puzzled. "The arduszone didn't used to be like this. It wasn't the safest place on the planet, but it wasn't a death trap, either."

He paused a few seconds.

"Arianas," he continued, "please stand in front of the transport and keep watch for anything dangerous, or even just strange. Iryni, please do the same from the back."

Both girls nodded and started walking.

"Okay," he said. "Let's go. We gotta get everything tied up again and head out so we can hit the settlement during umbra."

Yra and Naetth jumped down and hustled ahead of everyone else.

I walked over to Anina.

"Thanks for the help," I said to her. "You saved the day."

A half-grin, half-smirk crossed her face as she looked into my eyes.

"You were brave," she said. "Proditor would be dead without you."

She took hold of my left hand with both of hers and squeezed gently. She was still shaking a little, although I knew she was trying to hide it. She had the prettiest blue eyes. They were a little sad and scared, but strong and determined.

"Come on, you guys!" Yra yelled as he hustled an escape lofter over to its staging location. "Help out a little!"

Anina laughed as I rolled my eyes and grinned. She softly let my hand go and turned away.

This was supposed to be the "simple and easy" part of our expedition. Setup the weapons and get some sleep. Instead, in less than one day, we'd just barely survived two horrific attacks by deadly desert-dwelling behemoths none of us had ever dealt with or even seen before. I hated to think of what lay ahead, but it didn't matter. It was finally time to get my sister back.

FORTY-FIVE

MY BIG TOE

(TY)

"I am so sorry, Forticus," Mother said, crying quietly while Father held her close. "I never imagined Wraven could be capable of something like this. Had I even suspected . . . ."

I heard Father come in a bit ago, so I climbed out of bed to listen to what they were saying. A guard told us earlier he wasn't hurt in the blast but didn't know when he'd be home, so Marcus, Bellana, and I got sent off to bed. Now the two of them were in a big room a couple of floors beneath me. I snuck out of my room and lay on the hallway floor behind the banister looking down on them, just trying to listen and be invisible.

"Is he dead?" Mother asked.

"We didn't actually find his body," Father said, "but, based on the extensive destruction, everyone's assuming so. Personally, I don't believe it, not for a protoka. He killed half a dozen centurions and blew the walls off all the surrounding buildings, not to mention ten or more charriuses on the pathway. Luckily no one in the reception hall was hurt."

"What do you mean you don't believe it?" Mother asked. "How could he still be alive after something like that?"

Father walked away from her and ran his left hand through his hair.

"I find it suspicious," he said, "and hard to accept that Wraven's dead when we can't find a single remnant of his body or clothing anywhere. A finger, a toe, part of a shoe, anything. We know he's been doing intensified majinecity experimentals for annos. What if . . . what if he and his people figured out something . . . a way to directly transport him out of there?"

"That's just not possible without the equipment to do so," Mother said. "He was standing out in public, surrounded by centurions. Quaesitor and I are just now having some initial successes with living matter recomposition, but it's very tricky to control. I can't even theorize how to do it without teleportation equipment at both ends."

"I know," Father conceded. "I know you're probably right, and I can't speak to the science like you can. Something caused a disturbance tonight unlike anything that's ever been seen before. If there's one thing about Wraven, he always comes back, like a bad cold. I refuse to believe he's actually gone unless I witness it for myself. And with two majstices in the next four mensis, I think we should talk about protecting the children, just until we have a better handle on what's going on."

"Tymaeus," a voice from behind me said. I snapped my head around and slid back, startled out of my mind.

Mother was sitting on the floor right in front me. But how? She was still talking with Father below.

"I know this is hard to understand," she said, "but I need my wonderful, silly boy to listen right now. Can you do that for me?"

"Who are you?" I asked.

"I'm your mother," she responded with a pensive grin. "You're my youngest boy. My little genius."

"No," I exclaimed, shaking my head and pointing to the floor below. "My mother is down there, talking to my father. I don't know who you are!"

"Sweetheart," she said, "I'm sure this is all very confusing, but you're reliving a memory. A memory you weren't meant to remember yet. You're in danger, sweetheart. You need to wake up now."

"I am awake!" I said.

"No, you're not," she explained. "You're still in the jungle. Time is running out. You must wake up. Do you understand? Mother loves you, just as I dearly love and miss your brother and sister. It's important you trust me now. Close your eyes and tell yourself to wake up over and over until you do. Be my strong boy now."

All I could do was stare at her. Everything was so messed up, but a distant feeling somewhere in the annals of my mind told me she was who she said she was. She was my mother, and I needed to do as she asked.

"Tymaeus," she said, snapping me out of my daze, "be my strong boy. Say it out loud so Mother can hear you."

I closed my eyes and tried what she said.

"Wake up!" I said out loud. "Wake up! Wake up, Ty! WAKE UP!"

I repeated it a million times and opened my eyes, expecting to still be on the floor outside my room, but I wasn't.

I was back in the jungle. The last thing I remembered was falling asleep after washing the mud off under that wonderfully warm waterfall. I was kind of woozy but pretty sure I still heard the waterfall in the distance. My eyes had trouble focusing. The last time I felt like this was after I got my tonsils out when

I was seven. I woke up in the hospital and felt like I was moving in slow motion for a while. Aunt Andi said it was because of the sedative they gave me to knock me out.

In the distance, an animal walked up and took a drink from the pool where I'd washed off. I thought I'd passed out right next to the waterfall. How did I get so far away? The animal lifted its head and looked around. It wasn't a quagga but looked like a deer or gazelle with a dark brown body, black legs, and ringed horns that zigzagged up from its skull. It walked away from the water, swishing its black tail around, when it suddenly stopped, lowered itself to its knees, and fell over. I guessed it felt like taking a nap, too.

I went to rub the sleep out of my eyes and realized I couldn't move my arms. I couldn't move my legs, either. I was pinned up against an embankment with my entire body, except my head, encased in a thick, super sticky green slime that felt like trying to move through chocolate syrup when it was really cold and didn't want to come out of the bottle. What was this revolting stuff?

As I struggled mightily to free any part of my body, the blood-curdling growl I'd heard before came back, and a loud rustling noise reverberated from somewhere to my left. It sounded like something very big was moving through the trees, like the noise a t-rex made when it was sneaking through the forest, just before it pounced on its prey.

I couldn't turn my head but, with my eyes all the way to the left, I saw an enormous, mostly purple, *cucumber? A purcumber, perhaps?* It extended at least one hundred feet into the air with two columns of prickly spikes running up and down the front of its body and thorns encircling the top and bottom of its cavernous, pink mouth. It must have been anchored to the ground at one end because it slithered through the air like a snake over to the far side of the steep incline from which I was hanging. From its still-open mouth, it coughed up a glob of disgusting dense green sludge that splatted onto an open spot on the embankment. Then it slinked over and nuzzled the dozing animal into its mouth, carried it to the embankment, and flung it into the sludge. The animal stuck to the embankment but slowly started to droop down the incline. The purcumber quickly spewed more green yuck over the top of it until it stopped sliding, completely enshrouding it except for its head. That must have been what it did to me! It swung its mongo head and body around and retreated back into the trees, completely camouflaging itself from sight.

A very scary reality suddenly dawned on me. What if this whole thing . . . the path into the forest, the mud slide down, the pool under the waterfall . . . all of it . . . was all one big, brilliant yet deadly trap? Dumb animals (in this case, uh, me) walked by and drank the nice water, which was spiked with something to make them pass out. Once they were out, the purcumber wrapped them up in one of those disgusting green snot coffins and saved them for a later meal. Saved *me* for a later meal! I had to get out of there!

I tried to break free for a good fifteen minutes and got exactly nowhere. The gunk holding me against the incline hardened like a rock, literally locking me in place.

There were two embankments at right angles to each other. The first one ran across in front of the trees where the purcumber was hiding. The second, the one I was on at the far end, stuck straight out at a right angle from the first. I counted at least twenty-two green globs hanging on the sides, and I couldn't even see the space closest to me.

Where was Nekitys? He had come here with me, hadn't he? In fact, it was his great idea to come through this house of horrors to begin with! He drank the water, too, so he was probably wrapped up the same as me somewhere nearby. I called out his name a couple times but heard nothing back.

The growling noise reanimated the air, and the trees started their ominous dance again as the purcumber reappeared, but instead of rising straight up out of the foliage like last time, it wormed itself out the side of the trees and stretched all the way out until it was less than ten feet in front of me.

Even with my overactive imagination, I'd never envisioned dying as part of some overgrown vegetable's mid-day snack. Nothing could have been worse, except maybe falling into a boiling vat of liquefied liver and onions, but that was a different dream.

After hovering motionless in front of me for a few seconds, the purcumber curved its neck around one-hundred-eighty degrees and quietly slid back to the far embankment. It opened its mouth wide, glommed onto a suspended green glob, and, with a nauseatingly disgusting slurping sound, sucked it right off, leaving nothing but a faint green shadowy outline behind. I'd just witnessed some unsuspecting jungle creature get devoured whole and, sooner or later, it'd be my turn on the menu!

While the outside of my shell was hard, the inside was still a little wet and gummy. My legs and left arm were all jammed up and practically immobile, but I could move my right forearm a little since it was still covered by my rifle. My rifle? Duh! My dang rifle! I could blast my way out!

I angled my wrist to adjust my aim above my right foot and flexed my hand.

KWANG!

The muffled sound of a maj-pulse leaving my rifle was immediately followed by excruciating pain as I realized I'd blown off my big toe.

"Ahhhhhhhh!" I yelled in agony.

Blood instantly spewed down my foot. How was I going to walk without a big right toe? I'd have to use a cane and hobble like an old man for the rest of my life!

Just as I contemplated being permanently disfigured and disabled, I thought I felt my big toe wiggle. It still hurt tremendously, but at least it was still there! I wouldn't need a cane after all!

I must've blown off part of my cocoon because I could actually move my right foot and lower leg a little more, but not enough to break free. Lot of good using my rifle did! I'd probably just bleed to death before being unceremoniously imbibed off the wall.

"Ty?" I heard Nekitys yell.

He came running down through the forest and stopped next to the waterfall, scanning the area for me.

"Shh!" I said, trying to get his attention without rousing the purcumber.

He heard me but couldn't see me.

"Shh!" I tried again.

He narrowed his gaze down to the direction of my voice and started walking toward me.

"Ty?" he said in disbelief, finally seeing me and jogging over. "What happened? I thought I heard a rifle blast."

"I'll tell you later," I said. "Just get me out of this thing."

He grabbed the top edge of my shell and pulled, but it didn't budge. He let go and looked curiously at some of the still-wet gunk on his hands. He reached up, carefully secured a solid grip, and leaned back with his entire body.

"Rrrrrrrrr!" he grunted. "It won't give. I'll have to use this."

He gestured to his rifle.

"What?" I exclaimed in a loud whisper. "You can't shoot me out of here! You'll kill me! I already blew off my big toe!"

"Not the rifle," he said, sliding his left forefinger between his right forearm and the appendage.

I heard a barely audible, high-pitched squeak as a semi-transparent, four-foot-long blade emerged from the top of the appendage above Nekitys' knuckles.

"The cutter," he said.

He stepped back, jabbed it into the underside of my restraint, and used a sawing motion to slice along the length of it. He did the same on top before turning the cutter off.

"I'm going to pull outward from the top," he explained. "Just push out any way you can. Ready?"

I nodded, and we both put everything we had into setting me free. The shell made a gross, gooey, cracking noise but started to peel away. The wet stuff inside smelled like Aunt Andi's compost pile in the backyard after a heavy rain, just a gazillion times stronger. It was all I could do not to hurl all over Nekitys.

"It's moving!" I said hopefully.

"Keep pushing," Nekitys grunted.

The door to my purcumber mucus prison eventually rotated all the way down, but I still levitated on the embankment because of the sticky slime on my back side. Nekitys started leeching out my legs when the growling sound ominously returned and the trees resumed their violent swagger.

"You need to hurry!" I whispered frantically. "It's coming."

"What's coming?" Nekitys asked innocently, placing his hands behind my lower back and pulling.

"The purcumber!" I insisted. "Hurry!"

"What's a purcumber?" he asked.

"Just pull!" I said. "Wait! Do my head first so I don't snap my neck!"

He did as I asked. I grimaced in extreme distress as my hair fought belligerently to remain part of the landscape behind me. I'd probably have a huge bald spot back there, but that was better than waiting for the purcumber to come back.

Finally, just my shoulders were still stuck. Nekitys anchored his hands and pulled. I was almost free when the purcumber's head eased its way above the trees. I gasped loudly before I could stop myself and froze, stunned that I might not get away.

"What?" Nekitys asked and looked back.

Its appearance must've startled him, too, because he suddenly let go of me, but I was far enough along to peel away on my own. I lunged to try to fling myself out beyond the top piece lying on the ground. Everything made it except my feet, which landed ankle-deep in goo again.

"What is that thing?" Nekitys asked, obviously captivated.

"Nekitys!" I yelled. "Get my feet out!"

He snapped out of his trance, spun around, and started prying at my shoes. The purcumber must have realized something was messing with its food supply because it charged right for us.

"Oh, jeez, hurry!" I urged, the panic inside reaching new heights.

"Got it! Go!" Nekitys blurted and took off.

I stood up to run but immediately fell because my pant legs were stuck together with goo. I got back up and hopped as fast as any jackrabbit ever had. I looked back and saw the purcumber heading at me like a heat-seeking missile.

"Don't look back!" Nekitys urged from somewhere in front of me. "Just run, uh, hop!"

SPARTANICA

I finally reached a bunch of fallen trees Nekitys was standing behind and clambered clumsily over.

"What are you waiting for?" I blurted, noticing Nekitys wasn't running anymore.

"It can't reach this far," he replied. "Look!"

I turned around and saw the purcumber straining to extend beyond the front of the trees.

"Ha!" I yelled and bounced closer to Nekitys. "Come and get me now, purcumber mutant! You're not so tough from over there, are ya? Na na na na na na! I hope you choke on that antelope, you pathetic purple prickly freak!"

"Relax," Nekitys said. "We need to clean you up and get moving. I found where the trail starts again up there."

He gestured ahead of where we were standing.

I sat down and struggled to split my legs apart. As the goo dried, it became brittle and easier to peel off. The purcumber hovered in mid-air, scrutinizing our every move. I stood back up and took a few steps toward it.

"What's the matter, tough guy?" I yelled while saluting it. "Feeling lonely? Well, hasta la vista—"

Before I could finish dishing out a perfectly orchestrated verbal thrashing of my perceptibly frustrated jungle playmate, the skin a foot or so below its mouth contorted violently as it launched a final green sputum salvo at me faster than I could react.

SPLAT!

It pelted me square in the chest, knocking me flat on my back. Nekitys walked over and looked down with a sarcastic grin.

"So, can we please go now?" he asked.

I used a couple handfuls of big leaves to clean up again and we climbed up out of the ravine back onto the trail where Nekitys immediately pointed out that we were still lined up with the middle peak. Luckily, I'd only clipped the top of my big toe earlier, but it still bled a lot. The bottom of my sock was mostly red with blood and my toe hurt, but I'd manage to soldier through the pain. We walked for another few hours without tripping into any more booby traps set by humungous carnivorous plants and ultimately reached the edge of the desert.

Nekitys looked back and surveyed the jungle.

"I think we'll go around on the way back," he surmised.

"Gee, Nekitys, you think so?" I responded.

As Marcus had often said about me, Nekitys had a wonderful grasp of the incredibly obvious.

FORTY-SIX

XXENEBRAE
(BELLANA)

I was at the end of the line. Literally.

Once Crivera's soldier had been gone for a while, I felt around in the darkness and found the visor he so cleverly hid for me. I held it up to my eyes and couldn't see anything through it until I poked my head into the gloom. Everything was still totally black except for a thin, barely noticeable orange line on the floor. I started following it when a scary thought hit me. What if this was a test? Crivera talked about trusting me more *once I understood and supported the dream.* For all I knew, this faint breadcrumb trail just led in circles or into the waiting arms of a dozen Desrata battlers.

But if this did turn out to be Crivera's loyalty test, I was going to fail. Desrata battlers or not, I'd been following the orange line for the past thirty protokas right up to where it just stopped. I felt along a wall in front of me, hoping beyond hope that it was actually a door. Looking through the visor, I put my hand over a small, barely visible orange rectangle about waist high. It felt like a hand pull! I tried to move it, and it slid a little to the left. It *was* a door! I slid it open a little more but still couldn't see anything, even through the visor.

I hated how the darkness worked. I'd have to stick my head out into the hallway to see if it was clear. Of course, as soon as I did, I'd get busted if anybody was nearby. But I wasn't going back. If they wanted to torture or kill me for trying to escape, so be it.

Human voices suddenly approached in the distance. I managed to subtly close the door just before they strolled by and faded away without incident. I opened the door again just wide enough to get my eyes into the light but didn't immediately see anyone. I set down the visor just inside the door, stuck my head out a little further, and found the entire hallway clear.

Part of me was waiting for Crivera and her goons to come swooping around the corner. The other part was screaming *get out of here*! I had one big problem, though. As long as Crivera had the attenuator, I could never be myself. I had no idea how far away that thing worked. I might be escaping or even just walking around the armory and *poof!* I'd fall flat on my face, completely helpless. I had to find it before I could even think about getting away.

The route the soldier had taken me to get to the dark room from the hologram room was left, right, right, left, right, right, so I started by turning left and reversed each turn. One short hallway ran along a wall with a window to the outside. I ducked down and peeked my head up slowly to see what, if anything, was out there. Sure enough, the building I was in was surrounded by other buildings, at least on the side I could see. But that wasn't the worst of it. The place was crawling with heavily armed Desrata! There were humans, too, but there were at least ten 'rats for each one. How was I going to get past all of them without getting caught?

"Yes, yes, that's what I said," I heard Crivera say from around a corner. "Don't make me repeat myself, Pediseca."

I hastily tiptoed through an open door into a very elaborate chamber and saw my image in a full-size, ornately framed reflector leaning against the wall. This was perfect! I could hide in the darkways and nobody would ever find me! I ran over to step through and *thunk!* bounced off and fell on my backside. I couldn't even walk the darkways with the attenuator curbing my abilities.

Out of desperation, I hid in a closet full of clothes that reeked of the most hideously awful perfume ever. As I desperately tried to hold my breath for as long as possible, Crivera's voice followed into the same room. Of all the places I could've scurried into, I ended up in *her* office!

"I know the Great One ordered the girl be given over," she said, "but just imagine having the daughter of Forticus at our beck and call. We can give the others away to the animals, but I'm confident I can control this girl. She's already starting to trust me. And when we bring back the citizens from Xxenebrae, they will welcome her as a miraculous survivor of their beloved, wretched Bellator family. As much as that turns my stomach, we will use it to our advantage. She will be everyone's little darling, and we will control her every move, until we no longer need her."

I had no idea what "bring back the citizens from Xxenebrae" meant. What citizens could she be referring to? What exactly was Xxenebrae?

"The Great One will not be pleased, my Nobilis," another voice said.

"Yes, Pediseca, he never is," Crivera said acerbically. "He either hates everything I suggest or turns it around like it's his idea. But no matter. That's why I need your help. Tell me, can you see the genius of my plan? Best case, the Bellator tramp helps us to win over the population and restore the cities. Worst case, we kill her. Certainly that makes sense."

Crivera clearly expected Pediseca to agree with her line of reasoning.

"Yes, my Nobilis," Pediseca responded, clearly uncomfortable with Crivera's proposal. "But I urge you to tell the Great One of your plan immediately."

Crivera's voice had been moving closer and was now right outside my closet.

"Oh relax, Pediseca," she said dismissively. "Honestly, you fret over every little thing. *We* will enlighten the Great One about *our* plan, together, at our next discussion."

"Yes, my Nobilis," Pediseca said.

"Very well, then," she continued. "Now where did I leave my darkviewer?"

She reached into my closet, not more than arms-length away, and shuffled around several items on different shelves.

"It is here, my Nobilis," Pediseca said.

Her hands pulled out of the closet.

"Very well," she said. "Let's go visit our little lady in the shadows, shall we?"

"Yes, my Nobilis," Pediseca replied.

Little lady in the shadows? That was me! As their voices trailed off into the hallway, I stepped out of the closet and frantically searched for the attenuator. If it was in the room, I couldn't find it! What if she'd taken it with her? I'd be trapped forever!

My only hope was that she'd left the attenuator back in the hologram room. I headed toward the door but stopped dead in my tracks as one of Crivera's soldiers suddenly blocked the way. We both froze and stared uneasily at each other.

"Come on," he said, "we need to get you out of here. Hurry!"

I recognized him as the same guy that gave me the visor.

"I can't!" I insisted. "I have to get the attenuator first. Otherwise they'll always be able to control me."

"Where is it?" he demanded.

"I think it's in the room where you took me from last time," I said, "the room with the holo-image of Spartanica. Can you help me get there?"

He looked nervously both ways down the hall.

"Yes, quickly," he finally said, "put your hands behind your back and act like you're my prisoner."

I did as he said and we headed out. We reached the holographic room without incident.

"Go get it and come right back out," he said and opened the door. "I'll wait here and knock if somebody comes. Make sure you hide right away if I do."

I walked into the hologram room and rummaged all around but couldn't find the attenuator. I frantically pilfered through drawers, under chairs, and behind furniture, but it was nowhere to be found! Suddenly, I spotted it resting on a shelf next to the door behind me! I'd walked right past it!

I expected it to be more complicated, but it was just a switch that slid up and down. The indicator was sitting right in the middle. That must've been the setting to keep me at normal human strength. If I was going to have any chance of getting away, I needed a full Varkis infusion.

I slid the switch all the way to the top, and immediately buckled to the floor, utterly powerless. I had adjusted it the wrong way and was completely immobile again! The attenuator was on the floor, right by my nose, but it might as well have been in Lemuria. I couldn't move to reach it.

A moment later, the door opened behind me.

"Hurry!" the soldier beckoned. "Did you find it? Lady Bellator?"

He scanned the room but didn't see me.

"Lady Bellator!" he exclaimed, finally locating me collapsed on the floor. "What happened? Oh, you found it!"

He picked up the attenuator and moved the switch in the other direction. I immediately felt reinvigorated and sat up.

"I adjusted it the wrong way," I said, shaking the cobwebs out of my brain.

"Follow me," he said. "We have to hurry."

He helped me to my feet just as a piercing alarm went off in the hallway.

"They know you've escaped," he said. "You'll never be able to get out now."

"Take me back to the other room, where you found me!" I demanded.

"That's Crivera's personal office," he fired back. "That's the last place you want to be!"

"Trust me," I said. "That's exactly where I want to be, but only if we can get there before her."

He poked his head into the hallway and looked around warily.

"Let's go," he said, gesturing for me to follow him.

I acted like his prisoner again, and we made our way back to Crivera's room with the alarm still blaring.

"I have to go now," he said. "We have specific duties when the alarm sounds. I'll soon be missed. Are you sure you'll be okay?"

"Yes," I whispered. "Thank you!"

He handed me the attenuator and took off. I walked over to the same oversized reflector that had smacked me to the ground before and cautiously stepped through without a glitch. Yes, it was good to be Guelphic!

My plan was to hide in the darkways and wait for a chance to escape. The darkways were a world within a world. The only information in SMILEy referred to them as if they were part of some ancient mythology.

Supposedly, they were infinitely large and used by evil forces to hide and plot against those in our world.

The first time I stepped, or rather, fell into the darkways was a total shock. I went to lean up against the big reflector in the barbery to fix my shoe and plunged right through. It was completely dark except for illumination shining through the reflector from the barbery and several random glimmers of light in the distance. Terrified, I immediately scrambled back out. I went back later and slowly got comfortable passing back and forth. One time, in the coliseum building, I tied a long rope around my waist and anchored it to a heavy chair in the barbery. I stepped through the reflector and headed for the closest visible light, just to see what it was. At first, the glimmer looked way below where I was standing, but by the time I reached it, it was right in front of me. I realized the light I'd seen was shining through another reflector in the atletik on level twelve. I stepped through and looked around. The regular entrance was completely blocked by collapsed building debris. There was literally no other way in or out, so I made it my own little refuge.

What scared me most about the darkways was the potential for getting lost. I'd had terrifying nightmares about vanishing in there and wandering aimlessly, all alone, forever. If I had even the slightest clue about how to reliably navigate them, I'd have already been on my way without a second thought. Unfortunately, my only real option was to sit tight and watch until things looked clear in Crivera's office. Then I'd step back through and head out.

The muffled bellowing of the alarm emanated through the reflector in Crivera's office for another five protokas or so before it stopped. Although I didn't see or hear anyone, I didn't feel alone. Something brushed against my shoulder blades, hard enough to make my hair flop forward into my face. I turned quickly but saw nothing. When I spun back to look into Crivera's room, the reflector actually dimmed for a couple seconds as a shadowy figure passed in front of me.

"So pretty," something said in a loud, echoing, whisper voice that circled me faster than I could follow it.

"Who are you?" I yelled, trying to disguise the absolute terror pulsing through my heart.

"Yes, yes, so pretty," another, deeper, scarier voice said.

The reflector flashed like a strobe light as more and more shadows passed between it and me.

"She must be ours!" multiple voices repeated in unison as dozens of ghostly fingers suddenly danced across my face, hair, arms, and back.

"Ahhh!" I screamed, terrified out of my mind and trying to swat and kick them away as I stumbled backward toward the reflector. "Stop it! Stop touching me!"

"She must stay with us," they chanted as the sinister fingers struggled to clamp down all over me. "Don't let her go! The light. Keep her from the light."

They sounded desperate to keep me in the darkways.

"Let me go!" I shrieked, shaking and jerking with all my strength to keep moving.

As I backed up closer to the reflector, the hands pushing me from behind suddenly let go as several chilling screams rang out.

"Don't leave us!" a voice whispered quietly, but insistently, into my ear. "Help us! Save us! Before he is too strong! Before he rises! He is coming!"

I shrieked again, freaked by how close and relentless the voice was. I ratcheted myself free and fell through the reflector, landing on my back in

Crivera's room. Fingers still pulled at my feet as I realized I hadn't gotten fully out.

"Rrrrrrr!" I growled, yanking the rest of my body through and skittering backwards, away from the reflector.

I was lying on my back on the floor, trembling, breathing in a panic, hoping those things couldn't come through the reflector, which they didn't. I closed my eyes to try to settle down and heard a familiar, albeit unwelcome, voice.

"Hiding in Xxenebrae in my personal room?" Crivera croaked from behind her desk in a much less friendly tone than before. "Now that's original. Utterly offensive, but original."

Half a dozen or more of her soldiers swarmed around me, each targeting me with some kind of weapon.

"If she moves, shoot her," Crivera commanded.

Before they could process what she'd said, I swung my legs around to the left and sent two guards sprawling backwards. I grabbed the legs of two more on my right when I heard a *POP!* and felt excruciating pain in my right shoulder. I screamed and immediately grabbed my wounded joint.

"Stop!" Crivera yelled. "Harm her no further. She is to be turned over to the animals once the others are incarcerated. Keep your distance but shoot her again if she misbehaves in the slightest."

The guards took several steps back.

"Get up, you traitorous wretch," she demanded of me.

I rolled over to stand up but the pain was too intense. I howled again and crumpled back to the floor.

"Get up before I decide you're not worth the trouble of keeping you alive," she said. "Where is the attenuator? I know you must have it if you crossed through the reflector!"

She was wrong. I didn't have it. I must have dropped it in the darkways or, as Crivera just called it, Xxenebrae.

"Give me the attenuator back," she continued, "and tell me how you escaped or my soldiers will take turns shooting you, one joint at a time."

I said nothing and cowered on the floor.

"Very well," she concluded, looking up at a soldier. "Destroy a knee."

The guard instantly pointed his weapon.

"Stop!" I bellowed in agony.

The agony rippling through my shoulder relentlessly compelled me to break down and cry, but I wouldn't dare give them the satisfaction.

"I'll get up!" I yelled. "Don't shoot me again!"

I trudged onto my left hand and knees, grimacing and grunting in pain as blood streamed down my arm onto the floor.

"You have a chance to redeem yourself, my dear," Crivera said. "You've obviously made one fantastically wrong decision today. Tell me where the attenuator is and we'll—"

A loud explosion in the distance interrupted her and shook the building.

"Oh, dear," she said, "your friends are here already." She looked at one of her guards. "Quickly, take her to the cell and await her would-be liberators. Ensure at least two of you walk backwards in front of her at all times. Minimally another two should follow from behind. She's as fast as a quagga and stronger than twenty of you. If she so much as looks up from the floor, shoot her and drag her to the cell, if need be. Once you apprehend her accomplices, bring them all to the animal Great Hall." She turned to me with a sarcastically exuberant grin. "Good news, my dear, your little friends are coming to save you."

Another explosion reverberated in the background.

"If you give us any trouble," she said, "one or more of your chums will have a fatal accident before we give you all to the animals. Do you understand?"

I nodded begrudgingly.

"Now go!" she commanded.

Another far off blast rattled the room as a guard gestured for me to walk toward the door. There were four guards in front of me and another four behind, all with weapons trained on my every move. They didn't take me back to the darkness. Instead, they forced me into my very own standard holding cell. They forced me to the ground, locked the door, and disappeared down the hall, although I got the feeling they hadn't gone far.

I couldn't decide which was worse: Crivera and her goons or those ghostly things in the darkways. Just before I fell back into Crivera's room, it sounded like the voices were asking for help. They said *he is coming*, like they were afraid of something else in there. The whole episode was so creepy I had a hard time believing it had actually taken place. I had no idea what would happen next but, right then, at that moment, I was relieved my cell didn't have a reflector.

FORTY-SEVEN

PETRAS

(TY)

"This is it," Nekitys proudly proclaimed as we stopped outside a range of bright orange rocky cliffs with several passageways in.

"What do you mean?" I said. "There's nothing here but rocks."

"Just wait until you see inside," he said. "It's amazing. Let's go."

We headed for the closest passageway. I was perplexed that Nekitys could be so excited about a place he claimed he'd never been. My fingers were crossed in hopes Petras would be a more positive, less life-threatening experience than the jungle debacle. Thankfully, the trip through the desert since escaping the purcumber had been relatively humdrum.

The cliffs around us extended hundreds of feet into the sky, blocking out most sunlight so that we were walking in shadows. Every sound echoed in all directions. After a minute or so, our pathway opened to a big, clear circular space, also bordered all around by high cliff faces.

While the landscape alone was awe-inspiring, the buildings were unlike anything I'd ever seen. They looked like Greek and Roman architecture with oversized pillars and decorative elevations except, and this was a big except, they were carved right into the sheer stone cliffs at ground level. Imagine the White House or Capitol Building or even the Acropolis carved into the side of a mountain.

"How did they do this?" I asked, quite flabbergasted.

"It took decenniums and hundreds of highly skilled sculptors," Nekitys said as we walked over to a building. "The Petrans were renowned for their artistic and architectural talents. See this?"

He knocked on the front of a building.

"This is granitia," he continued, "the hardest natural material on Sapertys."

The detail was beyond words. Support columns, doorways, steps, window frames, and elaborate symbols adorned each chiseled structure. Some buildings even had chairs and tables carved right onto their patios.

"Come on, this way," Nekitys said.

He led me to the entrance of a building with six columns supporting a patio overhang that had something like a lion's head carved at the center. One animal statue stood on each side of the door. The roofline was straight on the sides but curved in the middle, with fancy, intricate decorations all across.

"Professor Otherblood's studium is in here," Nekitys said.

We stepped into a large, empty rectangular room with an elevated ceiling. Everything was sculpted so precisely it was easy to forget we weren't in a regular building. The walls were naturally decorated with ornately shaded swirls of white, orange, yellow, and brown stone throughout.

We walked to the back of the room and descended a narrow stone stairway, which went totally dark after about twenty steps.

"How far down are we going?" I asked.

"Another protoka or two," Nekitys said. "Put your hand on the triangular guide on the wall on the right side. It's a pathfinder to the bottom."

The guide was right where Nekitys said it would be, and I relaxed a little knowing I could follow it back if we got lost. After walking down a long flight of stairs in one direction, we did a one-eighty and headed down the other direction until a faint light appeared far in the distance.

"See it?" Nekitys asked.

"Yeah," I replied.

"We're almost there," he added, just before ramming into something that stopped him cold as I ambled blindly into the back of him.

"Jeez, Nekitys," I whispered, "you could say something when you're going to stop!"

"I didn't stop," he insisted. "Something stopped me."

Nekitys' hand passed over the distant light as his fingers tapped on it.

"Security field?" I asked.

"No," Nekitys said. "There's a solid wall here. The illumination is a fake image."

Blazingly bright lights suddenly flooded the space we were in, making it impossible to see anything.

"LEAVE NOW OR DIE!" an excruciatingly loud voice proclaimed over a mishmash of blaring noise.

The lights eased off a little, making it easier to see in the direction from which we'd come.

"LEAVE NOW OR DIE!" the voice repeated and erupted in blood-curdling laughter that reverberated off the walls and penetrated my skull like an oversized drill bit.

"Professor!" Nekitys yelled. "Professor! It's me! It's Nekitys!"

The scorching lights immediately softened as the grinding sound of rock sliding against rock echoed from overhead. Grit and dust rained down as an irregular circular opening barely wide enough for a human to navigate slowly revealed itself in the ceiling above us. A shiny black ladder extended down through the breach, and Nekitys, utterly uninhibited, clambered up before I could object.

I watched as he scaled to the top of the ladder, hopped off, and walked away. The lighting immediately went out, immersing me in obscurity again.

"Ahhhhhhhhh hahhhhhhhhhhhhhhhh!" someone screeched from above. "Ahhhhhhhhhhhhhh!"

I immediately bolted back in the direction from which we'd come, using the wall guide to trace my route. The lights came back on, and I heard Nekitys call out behind me.

"Ty!" he yelled. "Don't run! Ty!"

I stopped and turned around, prepared to take off again, but saw Nekitys standing on the ladder, gesturing for me to come back.

"It's him!" he announced jubilantly. "Professor Otherblood! Come on!"

I jogged back to the ladder.

"What was all the yelling?" I asked. "Jeez, it sounded like somebody was dying up there!"

"Sorry about that," Nekitys replied excitedly on his way back up the ladder. "Professor O is really happy to see me!"

I followed him vertically a dozen rungs or so and found a well-lit, very impressive laboratory at the top.

"Father," Nekitys said. "This is Tymaeus of the Order of Bellator."

Father?

"Oh, yes, uh, well, yes, I see, I see," Professor Otherblood said. "Decorias' boy, yes?"

I nodded, still captivated by all the equipment on display .

"I see," he said.

He looked like the guy in my Spartanica dream, only years older with an even longer and whiter beard. His hair was frazzled all over the place, unlike in my dream when it was combed back neatly.

"Oh my," he fretted, "you're not supposed to be here, my boy. No, no, no. Your parents would have a conniption if they . . . ."

He became instantly quiet and changed the subject.

"Well, here you are," he continued. "Well, obviously you are . . . here, that is."

He turned away.

"Nekitys!" the professor announced with his arms out and gave him a heartfelt hug with tears streaming from his eyes. "My boy. My sweet, wonderful boy. You're alive! And you're here! I'm willing to wager you both have many interesting stories to tell the old professor, yes? Nekitys always has interesting stories to tell!"

"Actually, Professor," I said, "we have more questions than stories, and I need your help, but Nekitys will have to explain."

"Why would that be?" the professor asked. "I must say you've riddled me, my boy."

I nodded at Nekitys and walked away so he could tell the professor about my anonymous projecting.

"My boy," the professor yelled across the room after a moment and gestured for me to come back over.

I sat back down with them.

"My boy," he said, "I knew your parents well. I was so blessed as to have worked with your mother. She was a tremendously talented and driven lady and a direct descendant of the Guelphic Varkis, as was your father. When you were very young, your mother and I were working together in the studium outside Spartanica when she quite suddenly took a seat and became very distant. We thought she had taken ill, as she wouldn't respond to anyone or anything.

"A short time later, she blinked her eyes and told us she had just watched you build a working scale model of your father's executive charrius using only children's building cubes. I never did quite understand how you did that."

My gaze stayed locked on him, expecting the story to continue.

"Don't you see, my boy?" he finally said. "You needn't concern yourself. Decorias, your mother, was your projector."

Mother was my projector! *Was* my projector?

"So my mother is dead, right?" I asked, already knowing the answer but, in some twisted way, needing to actually hear it.

The professor closed his eyes, looked down, and nodded his head.

"She was a true gem and loved you children with all her heart," he said, wiping his eyes and nose with a cloth from his back pocket.

So while my exile as an unsuspecting infiltrator for the Desrata was over, I realized I'd never know my mother who, from all accounts, was a quite remarkable person. Still, she'd spoken directly to me in my Spartanica dream so I'd wake up. Maybe, just maybe, the professor was wrong. Maybe Mother was still alive. How else could she have saved me?

"Why don't I remember her or anything about this place?" I asked. "Why didn't I know I had a sister?"

"Oh, yes. I see," the professor replied. "Hmmm, I don't . . . I don't know that it's really my place to discuss this with you, being family business and all."

"Exactly who else should I discuss it with?" I insisted.

He looked at me for a couple of seconds and smiled.

"You have your mother's eyes," he said, "and her persistence. I always admired how she would work at a riddle until it was solved. Yes, you deserve an elucidation of your own history and, indeed, yes, certainly, I am most likely the only one left who can, shall we say, fill in the many blanks."

He explained that highly unusual and dangerous phenomena had been taking place with increasing frequency shortly before and after father accepted his second term as commander.

"While Forticus was very popular and loved by most," the professor explained, "he also had bitter enemies that envied not only his political power, but his Guelphic talents. They believed the abilities should be shared with everyone, not just direct descendants. They claimed to have conceived of a process to metamorphose non-descendants in a way that empowered them with the abilities, but your father insisted they remain exclusive, lest they become a temptation too strong to resist."

"What does that mean?" I asked.

"Your father argued," he explained, "and I agreed, that people would be seduced by Guelphic abilities. Both the mental and physical advantages can become quite intoxicating. Ordinary people given extraordinary capabilities cannot always be trusted to use them responsibly. There are ancient stories of second and third generation Guelph descendants wiping out entire settlements of people that refused to submit to them. I believe the destruction of our world is further proof of that belief."

"You really think someone used Guelphic abilities to destroy the cities?" Nekitys asked.

"Hmmm, well, yes, certainly, but it is merely a hypothesis," the professor said. "I have no direct proof. But it was this same concern, the fear that unbridled use of Guelphic capabilities for personal domination was in the works, which caused your father and mother to send you and your brother through the gateway. Tymaeus, your father feared something evil had arisen but he couldn't find it. He couldn't prove it. We planned to send your sister to the other world at the next majstice, but the cities were decimated before we could."

"We?" I asked. "You were a part of it, too?"

He nodded and said, "Indeed, my boy. Your mother and I dabbled in inter-dimensional travel as a hobby for annos and managed to craft a crude, but reliable, gateway mechanism."

"But it only works on the majstice," I added.

"Well, yes, very well done!" the professor commended. "You always were Spartanica's—"

"Youngest genius," I finished.

That was exactly what he'd called me in my Spartanica dream.

"Yes, youngest genius," he said, obviously startled. "Indeed, my boy. How did you know I was going to say that? Do you have memories of your past life here?"

"Sure, why wouldn't I?" I asked, trying to goad him into explaining how it was I didn't remember anything about my Spartanican life.

"Hmmmm, yes," he said. "You see, before we sent you through the gateway, your father insisted your life here be blocked from recollection so you could live normal lives there. I didn't often disagree with Forticus, but on this I did. He felt any memories of Spartanica could place you in danger should anyone else ever discover a way to go through the gateway."

So Marcus and I had been sent to another world using Mother's science experiment for our own protection. I had a hard time understanding how Father could have been Guelphic Commander of Sapertys yet been powerless to do anything but send us off to another universe.

"Now, please, please, my boy, you must understand," the professor continued, nudging me to look at him. "Your parents loved the three of you more than life itself, but they couldn't come with you. Their absence here would have been immediately

329

noticed, and your father was a man of duty. But, at the same time, his heart insisted he do everything in his power to protect you. Your mother insisted she stay with Bellana, but her sister, Andina, volunteered to go through the gateway first to prepare for your arrival."

Andina? Aunt Andi? Aunt Andi knew about all of this?

"Sending you and your brother was the most difficult decision I've ever seen two people make," the professor said, "but they honestly believed, in their hearts, they might not be able to keep you safe here. And, trust me, if Forticus of the Order of Bellator could not protect you, no one on Sapertys could. He was as strong a man as I've ever known."

A long silence hung in the air as I tried to process everything Professor Otherblood had just said.

"Why doesn't Bellana remember me and Marcus?" I asked. "She never even left Sapertys."

"When you and your brother were sent," the professor explained, "we expunged her memories of you both, lest she question where you were. We planned to selectively restore her memories just before sending her through to Andina, but the apocalypse started shortly before we initiated the process. The gateway became unstable. Your mother and I worked furiously trying to realign and calibrate it, but the equipment became erratic. We feared we'd lose her forever if we tried to use it, so your parents took her to the shelter. That was the last time I saw any of them. It was a terrible, terrible jorno."

"Father," Nekitys said after another long pause, "Ty needs to go home. We were hoping you could help him. The next majstice is in two jornos."

"Yes, indeed," the professor said, turning to me. "But first, how did you get here, my boy? I never expected to see you or your brother again."

I described the humming, the "A" room, the blocks on the wall, and the orb, all of it. The professor looked troubled.

"This is truly disturbing," he finally said. "Your mother and I planned to create a return gateway mechanism, something to be used from the other side to return here. The attack happened before we could start work. But someone else must have developed such an entrance."

"Who else could have done that?" Nekitys asked.

"I have an idea, but no proof, unfortunately," the professor explained. "I worked with many brilliant sciencers over the annos. Not all were true to their commitment to work for the betterment of the people of Spartanica, I'm afraid. A very few, I learned over time, had selfish intentions inconsistent with their promise, and they were immediately dismissed from our team. My boy, when you return, it is imperative you tell Andina to destroy those artifacts. All of them. Permanently. They are dangerous and could lead to the destruction of that world. Do you understand?"

I nodded, getting a little spooked about the whole thing.

"Do you remember where you first entered Sapertys?" he asked.

"Yes, but I don't think I can find it again," I said. "When we left, the door disappeared into a cliff. It was like nothing was ever there."

"Oh, my, my, my," the professor exclaimed and clapped his hands. "This is grand news! The old studium must still be active! You see, my boy, your mother and I set up a location for our riskier experimentals outside the city in case we ever, oh, how to say this properly, blew something up. Tell me, how did you get out?"

"The remote sentry made us leave," I explained. "It was one scary lady. It looked kind of human but—"

"Oh my, oh my!" the professor said, getting progressively louder and more animated. "Do you understand what this means? This is brilliant! Yes, of course! The studium is outside the cupola so it remained intact! Well, first I must repair the hyperporter here . . . ."

"Professor?" I said, struggling to get his attention. "Professor?"

I put my hand on his shoulder as he tried to wander off, engrossed in his own thoughts.

"What exactly is happening?" I asked.

He finally stopped and looked at me.

"Yes? Yes?" he said. "Oh, of course, my boy. Yes, of course. I am so sorry. Please forgive me. My mind starts down a path and I become, as Decorias used to say, *hard to reach*. My boy, you must have come through the gateway using the equipment we originally constructed. It must still function. The apocalypse must have only affected it during that last jorno. My boy, this means we have a way to get you back!"

"Then we need to leave now," Nekitys said. "It'll take two days to walk to Spartanica."

"No, no, no. Come look at this!" the professor insisted, gesturing for us to follow him to the left side of his expansive laboratory. "Fazah!" he shouted and spread his arms as if to unveil something wonderful.

"It's a burned-up closet with no door," I said.

"No, no, no!" he insisted before taking a second look. "Hmm, well, yes, so it is. However, with a little tuning up and refurbishing, this burned-up closet will take you directly to the studium in less than a protoka!"

"Father," Nekitys asked, "you've enabled a hyperporter?"

"Not me," he said, turning to look at me, "Decorias! Your mother invented the hyperporter, and now we're going to use it to get you home, my boy!"

"But why does it look like that," I asked, "like it was on fire?"

"Your mother's testing confirmed the hyperporter to be not only feasible," the professor explicated, "but reliable. When your parents took Bellana away to the shelter on the last jorno, I feared the other studium was no longer safe. I activated the hyperporter and instantly arrived here. The equipment, however, overloaded, and I struggled to repair it expeditiously without your mother's knowledge to guide the way. Then I heard the blast come from the city."

"So you can't fix it?" I asked.

"Ah, but yes!" he countered. "Yes I can! In the days after arriving here, I immediately located and memorized every drawing and note your mother used to document her work. I've left it in disrepair in case those who destroyed the city tried to use it. But now, *we* will use it!"

All the excitement was taking its toll on me. As engrossing as everything was, I was having trouble keeping my eyes open. I hadn't slept well on the journey to Petras, and there wasn't much left in the tank.

"Professor," I said with a yawn, rubbing my eyes, "do you have somewhere I can rest?"

"Of course, my boy," he said. "You can sleep while I repair the hyperporter. Excellent, yes, excellent idea, indeed!"

He led me down a short hall to a room with a couple of beds. I collapsed on the closest one. He started explaining something, but it all quickly faded as consciousness slipped away.

I awoke after who knows how long, feeling reenergized and eager to see whether Professor Otherblood had repaired the hyperporter. I walked back out to the laboratory and saw something that blew my mind.

"Oh, dear," the professor said, clearly startled as he stepped in front of Nekitys, who was sitting in something like a dentist chair. "You're awake. I didn't expect you so soon."

The professor purposefully kept himself between me and Nekitys.

"Is he okay?" I stopped and asked.

"Oh, uh, actually, no," the professor said. "He's been through a tremendous ordeal. He's been tortured, you see, repeatedly. I'm quite amazed he's as well as he is."

I stepped around the professor and found Nekitys with a transparent dome fit snugly over his head, through which an array of tiny, flashing, multi-colored LEDs and circuits could be seen. A large transparent screen behind the professor was lit up with several columns of scrolling data and a rotating image of Nekitys' skull.

"My poor boy," the professor whimpered, clearly upset. "My poor, poor boy. Ah, but the good news is he'll be in tip-top shape after a little retuning."

"Nekitys is a robot?" I asked, clearly flabbergasted by the remarkable technology on display. This was even *better* than *Star Trek.*

"No, my boy," the professor corrected. "Not a robot. Nekitys is a third-generation anthropomimetic person. His thought processes and body motions mimic a human's almost identically. You couldn't tell?"

"No," I replied, shaking my head. "I mean, he's always been a little strange, but a lot of people are strange."

"Yes, indeed," the professor concurred, giggling briefly before his frown quickly returned. "Nekitys has been through an unthinkable tribulation. His activity logs show astronomic levels of majinecity surging through his neural lines, which forced his command processors into self-preservation mode. He may not be human, but his sensors register pain. He felt every bit of the punishment he was dealt. And he's such a good boy."

He gestured weakly at the data streaming across the display behind him.

"Look at what they did to my wonderful boy," he added, turned away, and started crying.

"But he's going to be okay, right?" I asked, growing more and more concerned with the professor's state of mind. If he turned into a basket case, I could have a real problem.

"Oh, yes," he replied, wiping his nose and eyes again. "Thank goodness I designed a very high level of fault tolerance into every neurite. He sustained some minor damage, but that's being restored now."

"How did he know where to find you?" I asked.

"Not long after coming here," the professor explained, "I activated a broadcast message, specifically tuned to a frequency in Nekitys' network. He's the first generation anthropom I did that with. I thought, perhaps, if, by some miracle, he was still alive, it would guide him back to me."

The professor stopped, became very serious, and turned to face me.

"My boy," he said, "you must promise me never to tell him he's not human."

"He doesn't know?" I asked.

"No," he said. "I want him to be a normal boy. Promise me you won't tell him!"

"I promise," I said. "I won't say a word."

"Very well then," the professor replied.

He removed the covering over Nekitys' head and set it down on a table.

"He'll need a few protokas to properly reconfigure but should wake up as if he's been napping. Please step over here. I have something very exciting to show you."

We walked over to the hyperporter. A console next to it was displaying data.

"I made the necessary repairs," he happily announced. "Your mother's machine is charging! It should be ready to go in an ora!"

"Are you pretty sure it'll work?" I asked. "I mean, it's been broken for a long time."

"Yes, certainly," the professor said, "we shall need to test it on something living before we hurtle your electrons through the ether."

He skeptically perused the studium, not looking particularly hopeful about finding any random living beings just lying around.

"I shall go," he said abruptly after a moment. "It makes perfect sense. If there are issues on the other side, I can fix them from there."

"But if this doesn't work," I blurted, exasperated at the thought of losing the professor on a test run, "we won't be able to bring you back. You could even be killed!"

The professor leaned up against a table, deep in thought.

"Yes," he finally said, looking like he was out of answers. "You're quite right."

"I'll go," Nekitys said, just getting up off his chair.

"No," the professor snapped hastily. "It's too dangerous. I never should have brought this up. I'm sorry, Tymaeus, this won't work."

"Father," Nekitys said, "it's our only chance to fulfill the wishes of Forticus and Decorias. You fixed it. I'm confident it will work. I know it will work!"

Professor Otherblood walked over and held Nekitys by both shoulders.

"But what if it doesn't?" he said angrily. "Am I to lose you again? You are my son and I love you! Can't you see that?"

"I have always known that," Nekitys replied. "But you taught me that we are to use our knowledge and gifts to help all Sapertyns. We must help Ty now."

Professor Otherblood looked away, still upset, but nodded.

"Yes, of course," he said, after a deep breath. "You are right, my son. I'm being selfish."

He reached out, hugged Nekitys again, and leaned back to look him in the eyes.

"You are a better man than I will ever be," he said.

A gentle ringing sounded from the hyperporter control panel.

"Oh, well then," the professor said, letting go of Nekitys. "We're ready to go."

He walked over to the panel as Nekitys stepped into the revamped closet. The professor stood motionless for a few seconds, obviously still hesitant about putting Nekitys at risk.

"Father, it's time," Nekitys said.

"Yes, yes, of course," the professor finally ceded. "You won't have to do anything, my son. I will trigger your return from here. Just stay in the hyperporter when you arrive."

Nekitys nodded while the professor fiddled with the controls.

"See you shortly," Nekitys said, looking completely relaxed, which made me wonder whether his programming even allowed him to be nervous.

"Very well then," the professor continued. "Here we go on three, two, one—"

The machine let out a high-pitched whine and the box became incredibly bright for a split second. When it stopped, Nekitys was gone.

"Hey!" I exclaimed. "It worked! It didn't blow up or anything!"

The professor intently watched a countdown timer on the screen in front of him and tapped his finger on the table with each decrement.

"Enabling recapture," he announced after a minute or so and typed a bunch more on the screen. "Oh dear!"

A red warning message flashed on the display. A voice from overhead announced *Condition red! Condition red!*

"The primary controller is failing!" the professor exclaimed in terror, typing even faster. "No! It's completely gone! Switching to backup controller."

The screen reset itself and the audible alarm stopped. The bright light flashed again, forcing us to shield our eyes, but when we looked up, Nekitys had returned.

"See," Nekitys said, "no worries."

The professor exhaled so hard I thought he was going to collapse. Nekitys stepped out of the hyperporter and the professor elatedly welcomed him back with a heartfelt embrace.

The professor insisted on repairing the primary controller before hyperporting me to the complex so we'd have a redundant system again. Nekitys said he couldn't tell there was a problem while he was going back and forth. He beamed into a mostly dark room but saw the Spartanica symbol on the floor. The professor was ecstatic because it confirmed Nekitys had materialized in the right place. What the professor discovered next, however, put an end to the happy times.

"Ghast!" he snorted from behind the control screen. "The backup controller failed when Nekitys came back."

He held up a dark, shiny blue cube.

"Every time someone goes through," the professor explained, "these synchronous bio-containment field generators overload."

"So we're stuck?" I asked, my panic level racing toward new highs. "It won't work?"

"We only have one more intact generator," the professor said. "It'll take me jornos, maybe settimas, to craft a new one that won't fail, and that's assuming I have the proper components."

"So we have one more trip, right?" I asked. "That's all we need to get me there."

Nekitys nodded and looked at his father for confirmation.

"I don't like it, but I suppose it is our only option," the professor said reluctantly. "Very well, then. I'll need several oras to install and verify the new generator. I shall commence forthwith!"

FORTY-EIGHT

GO TIME
(MARCUS)

The remainder of our journey to the Desrata settlement was eerily devoid of further prehistoric surprises. Everyone had been quiet since we left the escape lofters behind.

The human compound was very well lit, which made it easy to spot from afar with the sun down. We circled behind as planned and anchored the last lofter and the draiders at the top of a sand dune per Proditor's recommendation.

Kinnard remotely activated the diversion lofter we'd staged at our first stop. Massive detonations impacted almost immediately in the distance. Dozens, if not hundreds, of Desrata took off running for the fields.

"It is time," Proditor said.

I glanced around at everyone one last time without saying a word. The girls all waved a tiny, comforting wave. Yra and Naetth saluted me. Kinnard gazed intently at the human area Proditor and I would soon be sneaking into.

"Remember, everybody," I said, "give us forty-five protokas to get back here. Then open fire with the draiders and take out everything you can hit before heading out, but don't get caught or hurt."

"But we could end up killing you!" Iryni urged, fretfully uncomfortable.

She'd looked pensive when we'd discussed this part of the plan on the way here but hadn't said anything. With the moment of truth upon us, she couldn't hold her feelings back anymore.

"If we're not back after forty-five protokas . . . ." I said, trailing off because I didn't want to say out loud that we'd likely either be captured or dead.

"We'll take care of things here," Kinnard interjected without turning away from the human area. "Just get back with everybody so we can go home."

As I turned to leave, Anina ran over and hugged me.

"Be careful," she whispered in my ear and gently pulled back, gazing deep into my eyes until she eventually turned away.

I watched her walk back to the others.

"We go now," Proditor urged, snapping my attention back to the task at hand.

I took off my rifle and shirt. Proditor gruffly took hold of the back of my neck and we headed toward the buildings.

As we crossed onto the settlement, it looked as if our diversion had worked. We passed through the outer structures without a problem as Proditor led me to the far side of the center building and in through its main doors.

Two Desrata ran up to us. Proditor slammed my face into a wall and grunted something before they jogged out the exit.

"They say female this way," he said.

We traversed a seemingly endless labyrinth of hallways that felt like being trapped in a big rat maze (no pun intended), hoping to find the proverbial cheese.

Several more Desrata ran by before we came across a series of empty detention cells.

"Bellana!" I whisper-yelled but got no response.

We went around a corner and finally found her locked up alone, sitting on the floor.

"Bellana!" I exclaimed, exuberantly running up to her cell door.

She waved her hands furiously, as if she didn't want us coming any closer. Her right shoulder and arm were covered in blood.

"Jeez, what happened?" I asked. "Are you all right?"

"I'm so sorry, Marcus," she replied. "I tried. I really did, but—"

An onslaught of hurried footsteps raced up behind us from both ends of the hallway. I turned and saw a half dozen or more uniformed human soldiers approaching with weapons aimed squarely at me and Proditor. Two of the soldiers shoved me back away from Bellana's cell.

"Move and you die," one of them said, putting his weapon against my forehead.

Bellana jumped up and aggressively clutched the bars enclosing her. Almost immediately, she winced, doubled over, and grabbed her right shoulder. She slowly straightened back up and grabbed the bars again with both hands, fighting through the pain.

"Sit down, super girl," a soldier said, "or we'll finish off your friends right here where you can watch."

Bellana stood her ground with a vicious scowl.

"Have it your way," the soldier said indifferently and turned back to me, acting as if he was going to pull the trigger.

"No!" Bellana yelled. "Stop!"

She begrudgingly backed away and sat down at the rear of her cell.

"That's a good little girl," the soldier said, lowering his weapon. "Get stupid again, and I won't be so understanding. You two," he commanded, turning back to me and Proditor, "go that way."

The soldiers shoved us down the hall. There were four ahead of us, three behind. They dumped us in a cell at the far end of a hallway around the corner from Bellana.

"Tell Her Nobilis we are ready for the Great Hall," a soldier said.

Another soldier headed off while the remainder hovered outside our cell.

"What's the Great Hall?" I asked Proditor.

"Great Hall of Szenkruyt," he replied. "Desrata building for meeting. Prisoners taken to Great Hall to be killed to make example."

"Great," I snorted. "They knew we were coming. They must have kidnapped Bellana knowing we'd try to rescue her. But it's like they also knew exactly when we'd be here. But how?"

"I no understand human ways," Proditor replied.

"Yeah," I agreed, "me neither. Let's just hope the others are having more luck than we are."

After an hour or so, eight guards escorted Bellana by our cell. They came back a few minutes later and took me and Proditor out of the building. I kept expecting to hear draider blasts and fighting, but we hadn't heard a single pulse or explosion. Once outside, I didn't see any signs that Kinnard and the others had started anything. I just hoped they'd realized our plan failed and were waiting for the right time to attack.

The soldiers walked us out of the well-lit human area onto the ghostly Desrata settlement, which was markedly darker despite numerous torches all around. An odd howling commotion started in the distance and grew louder as we approached a massive circular stone enclosure that looked like a very crude attempt at a miniature Roman gladiator arena. The walls were roughly fifty feet high and constructed by stacking countless long flat orange rocks on top of each other. Ten-foot high, arched entrances, closed-off with makeshift doors that looked like little more than big wood planks wedged into the openings, were visible every twenty feet or so.

As we approached, a 'rat soldier reached through a couple of paw-sized holes in a plank, ripped it from an opening, and leaned it up against the outer wall. The ruckus inside instantly reached an ear-shattering crescendo as we were engulfed by an overpowering wave of stench that flushed forcefully over us through the opening. The odor was so pungent I turned and puked my guts out all over the boots of a human soldier behind me. He showed his appreciation by whacking me across the back of the head with his weapon, knocking me to the ground. Two other guards grabbed my arms and dragged my limp body into the Hall as I tried to focus on the mayhem coming at us.

We emerged in a large, circular open arena surrounded by rows and rows of 'rats starting at roughly five feet above ground-level and rising back to the outer wall. Thousands of slobbering Desrata glared down at us, pumping their paws in the air and howling like wolves celebrating a fresh kill.

I got back to my feet and defiantly shook away the soldiers holding my arms as we approached a U-shaped stage at the far end of the arena. Bellana was standing on the left side of the platform, surrounded by human soldiers and a hideous human woman with a face so red she looked like she was ready to have a heart attack. Half a dozen Desrata in human uniforms sat behind another one dressed in more elaborate human regalia with medals adorning its chest.

Two other humans were already being closely guarded in front of the stage, a guy and a girl, both my age or younger, watching as we approached. The roar of the crowd ramped even louder as everyone's attention turned toward the doors through which we'd come. One by one, the Atlantean kids were shoved into the arena. The crowd threw dirt and stones at them as they were led to where Proditor and I were standing.

"Perdi! Kalahn!" Yra yelled when he saw the two kids that were there before me and Proditor.

The other Atlantean kids gazed over and, for a brief moment, looked relieved to see their old friends still alive.

"They came up from behind!" I barely heard Naetth yell as he walked by with blood trickling out of the left side of his mouth.

"They were on us before we even saw them," Anina added.

A Desrata guard shoved her to the ground and stared menacingly before gesturing for her to stand back up and get in line next to me on my right. Naetth was next to her, followed by Yra, Arianas, and Iryni. Kinnard stood at the far end. Proditor was on my left with Perditus and Kalahn on the other side of him.

It felt like we'd been lined up for a firing squad. How could it have come to this? We had a great plan. We had the weapons. We even had a double-agent Desrata helping us. I just couldn't understand. Nothing added up. How could we have been so easily beaten?

The Desrata on stage with all the medals stood and put his hands in the air to quiet the crowd, which, surprisingly, only took a few seconds. With everyone's attention focused, the red-faced woman walked over and bowed her head to him and the crowd.

"Comrade Desrata," she hollered, gesturing toward Bellana and the rest of us. "It is with great joy and pride that I come to you today."

The crowd exploded in excitement, saliva sloshing through the air and down their faces. The woman held up her hands to quiet them again.

"To my right, we bring you . . . ." she started but paused until they quieted down more. "We bring you the human that so mercilessly killed your defenseless brethren in the city."

The crowd jeered at Bellana angrily. More dirt and stones showered down from the mob. While the soldiers around her ducked to avoid the debris, Bellana stayed upright, unconcerned about anything hitting her.

"Comrades," the red-faced woman yelled, motioning for the crowd to settle down. "Comrades, we also bring you the escapees!"

She arrogantly motioned toward the line of us in front of the stage, as if we weren't even fit to be standing in front of her.

"And . . . ." she started but had to wait again. "And, comrades, comrades . . . ."

The crowd finally settled down enough for her to continue.

"And a TRAITOR!" she pronounced, pointing directly at Proditor, whose eyes were fixed on several specific Desrata on the stage that were visibly less enthusiastic about the proceedings than the others.

"It is with great happiness," the red-faced woman continued, looking at the Desrata with the medals on his chest, "that we turn these enemies of the Desrata Kingdom over to you all and your dear leader, Animarex. Let Desrata justice be served!"

The crowd went insane again and started grunting and howling in unison. Animarex stepped to the front of the stage, waving his clasped hands in front of him as if he'd just won the heavyweight boxing title. He took a long, disparaging look at the group of us and motioned for the crowd to be silent.

"Sttteeeeepppp forward, huuuummmaaaannnnn," Animarex said, gesturing with his paw to the far right of our lineup. "This human help Desrata. He serve Desrata welllllll and get reward."

Kinnard briefly, and without emotion, glanced at the rest of us and strutted toward the stage. The color simultaneously drained out of all of our faces as we scrutinized every shameful step he took to confirm he'd joined leagues with the same dreadful beasts that had inflicted his Atlantean kin with so much pain and hardship. I was shocked to the point of being numb, but couldn't even begin to imagine the rage burning inside each of the Atlantean kids.

"What?" Yra yelled, clearly devastated. "You work for the 'rats?"

"How could you?" Anina yelled angrily, clutching a fist with both hands and fully tensing every muscle in her body. "You just killed all of us!"

Kinnard climbed up on stage and stood next to the red-faced woman, who grinned and patted him on the back as if she was so grateful. Yra finally couldn't contain himself anymore and ran at the stage, but he was quickly intercepted by a Desrata soldier that smacked him hard across the jaw. He flew backward and landed hard on his side.

"I'm gonna kill you, you 'rat lover," Naetth yelled. "You traitor! I hate you!"

Another Desrata soldier came up and whacked him violently from behind, launching him forward until his face planted into the sand.

Kinnard refused to acknowledge any of it as he stood straight and proud, his gaze fixed exclusively on Animarex.

It was suddenly so clear. He'd been a 'rat fink spy all along. The Desrata were waiting for us because he somehow told them when and where we were coming.

We were done before we'd even started. All those times he disappeared, like when the chycrotas attacked and when he wandered off into the desert on the way here, he was probably communicating detailed updates about our every move.

It also explained why he'd so easily given up Nekitys to stay with Ty. It was classic military strategy. Divide and conquer. With two fewer kids on the trip, we'd be easier to capture. Then the humans and Desrata could head to Spartanica, close their trap, and take the city. It was brilliant, and I'd forever hate him for it.

"Quiiiiiieeeeeeettttttt!" Animarex yelled. "We say punishment."

The crowd became instantly silent as Animarex looked to the sky, held his paws up with his palms facing toward him.

"DEEEEEAAAAATH!!!" he yelled.

The mob erupted in hysteria. Desrata soldiers immediately swarmed and forcefully hustled us toward a door when a blindingly bright bolt of light flashed on the stage behind us, casting an instant startled hush over the bedlam. A second flash was followed by a third, but the fourth wasn't just white light. There was something dark and shadowy at its center.

Another burst erupted, followed by a growl, a human growl that reverberated throughout the building. The flashing stopped and revealed a man crouching down on the stage. He stood up slowly, rubbed his eyes, and looked around. His face was stressed and sweating, as if he'd been struggling with all his might.

"Who the gehanna is that?" a flabbergasted Anina gasped as she slid over and took tight hold of my arm.

"Father!" Bellana cried out.

A puzzled buzz slowly permeated the arena as the surrounding throng desperately tried to process the scene playing out on stage.

"Commander Bellator?" Perditus mumbled almost incomprehensibly, clearly uncertain he was actually seeing what his eyes were telling him was there.

I did a double take, then a triple take, my mind expecting each time to see nothing but open space where the flashing had happened. But it didn't matter. There was no doubt. It was Father, Guelphic Commander of Sapertys, staring determinedly across the stage. But how?

"Shoot him!" the human woman demanded with a mixed expression of fear and intense disgust. "Shoot him now!"

Two human soldiers at ground level ran toward Father and opened fire, but their blasts passed harmlessly through him and exploded on the rear wall.

"STOP!" he commanded, and the soldiers backed away, convinced their weapons would do nothing more than further anger him.

Father's laser-sharp gaze zeroed in on the group of Desrata huddled at the middle of the stage.

"Animarex!" he yelled.

The Desrata leader reluctantly stepped forward, clearly confused and intimidated by Father's ghostly arrival.

"Foorrrrrrrticuuuuuuus," he growled with a deep, gruff, animalistic inflection, desperately struggling to portray some shred of composure in front of an immense crowd that considered him to be their leader. "But you are deeeeaaaaad. Your ciiiittttttyyyyy issssss deeeeaaaaad."

"I am not dead," Father responded, wincing as the light flashed briefly around him again. "Animarex, humans and Desrata have never been friends."

"Nooooooooo, huuuuuummmmmmaaaannnn," Animarex agreed.

"But we have been allies," Father continued. "Did not my people come to your father's aid to restore the settlement after the great ground shaking? Did we not work with the Desrata when the Xarnaic hordes attacked?"

"Yes, huuuummmmmaaaaannnnn," Animarex said. "I know old stories. But this is new time, and these new humans will lead us to eternal Elisii!"

Animarex motioned toward the red-faced woman.

"No, they won't!" Father yelled. "They tell you lies to make you their slaves. Your father told me once that eternal Elisii was as simple as a fully restored and safe Desrata settlement, run by Desrata, for Desrata, free of all others. There is no other Elisii! Only you can create it for yourselves. All other promises are tricks!"

Father took off his shirt to reveal a frame as big and muscular as any I'd ever seen, but with deep scars across his abdomen and down his left arm. He turned around, and we saw a scar across his back that resembled a Desrata face with two spears crossed behind it.

"Your Father honored me with this brand after we defeated the Xarnaic," Father explained. "He declared me Consor of the Desrata."

The crowd gasped. Father turned back around and looked at us.

"These children," he said, "these human children, are my people, and I promise you, as your eternal ally, they are no enemy of yours. Animarex, I request that the most honorable Desrata, the Desrata of your father, your father's father, and of all the great warriors before them, release these children under my word they will be no threat to your great empire."

Animarex turned to the red-faced woman.

"Where is eternal Elisii?" he demanded. "Take us now!"

"Animarex," she replied, grinning nervously, "let's not get ahead of ourselves. We agreed to discuss Elisii only after taking the city."

"You say now!" Animarex insisted. "Where is eternal Elisii?"

"I will not be addressed like this by a lowly beast!" she yelled testily, clearly insulted.

She instantly put her hand over her mouth, realizing she'd made a critical gaffe.

"I apologize!" she blurted desperately. "I was confused! You are all valued partners! Please! I apologize!"

A Desrata on the stage behind Animarex stepped forward and put his paw in the air.

"By Desrata, for Desrata!" he chanted.

Several of the other Desrata on stage did the same. Proditor raised his paw and added his voice to the chorus. It gradually spread until the entirety of the crowd joined in unison.

"Aaaahhhh!" Father suddenly yelled through the bedlam, dropping to a knee as the flashing kicked in again.

"Father!" Bellana cried out as a sudden hush fell over the arena.

Father, grimacing in pain, extended his hand toward his distressed daughter, even though she was well out of reach.

"Belly beans!" he hollered.

The light flickered brilliantly several more times until he was gone.

"Nooooo!" Bellana shrieked. "Father! Come back!"

She took a couple steps toward where he had been before a human soldier stepped in front and nuzzled his weapon right up against her forehead to stop her. Bellana defiantly smacked the weapon away with her left hand but ultimately backed off while keeping her gaze locked on where Father once stood.

Several Desrata, including Animarex, huddled closely on stage for a moment before he stepped to the front and started grunting, snorting, and barking.

"He say Forticus good," Proditor translated for me. "Forticus help his father save settlement. Forticus make him remember father say Elisii is strong Desrata settlement, here, now."

Animarex paused, then continued.

"He say new humans trick him," Proditor continued. "He say sorry. Settlement must be by Desrata, for Desrata."

The crowd cheered in resounding agreement.

"All humans leave now," Proditor concluded.

"So we can go?" I asked with tremendous anticipation and relief. "We're free?"

Proditor didn't answer. Animarex had gestured for him to come on stage where they conversed for a short period. Proditor jumped down and motioned for all of us to gather around him.

"Leader say I take you out now, keep you safe," he explained.

"What about Bellana?" I insisted.

"Desrata battlers bring her," he replied.

The Desrata on stage walked toward Bellana, who was still surrounded by human soldiers brandishing weapons. One soldier grabbed her around the neck from behind and put his weapon against her skull. The other soldiers lined up to form an armed barrier between Bellana, Kinnard, the red-faced woman, and the approaching Desrata.

"The Bellator girl comes with us," the woman yelled.

The Desrata stopped in their tracks.

"To think we tried to civilize you mindless brutes," the red-faced woman shouted. "Now step out of our way or we'll kill the girl and every animal that tries to stop us, starting with your disgrace of a leader."

Two of the human soldiers shifted their weapons toward Animarex, who was still standing near the center of the stage.

"Before we go," she said, "here's a little proof that I'm not bluffing."

She nodded at the human soldier closest to her. He fired a round directly into the chest of one of the nearby Desrata, sending it sprawling backward onto the stage. The other Desrata howled and barked in anger but didn't advance.

"We move," the woman said and motioned for the others to follow her.

Before they took a single step, a loud *crack* filled the air. Bellana had reached up and snapped her assailant's right forearm at the wrist, leaving it dangling down at an unnatural angle as he dropped his weapon and screamed in pain. She forced a hard elbow into his ribs, eliciting more cracking sounds as he shot backward and fell off the stage. The other human soldiers, distracted by the turmoil, looked back and were immediately mauled by the waiting Desrata.

Bellana worked her way through the anarchy and jumped down cautiously, cradling her wounded right arm against her body. The red-faced woman, Kinnard, and a couple of human soldiers scampered swiftly off the back of the stage and out of sight.

I ran to Bellana and put her left arm around my shoulder.

"Can you make it out of here?" I asked.

"Yes," she answered, scowling in pain. "Let's go!"

Proditor and the others came over.

"Bellana!" Iryni yelled and hugged her. "Oh no, you're hurt!"

"I'm okay," Bellana insisted, forcing a fake smile. "Let's just go!"

Proditor cleared a path through the crowd, which had scattered in chaotic disarray. We made it out of the arena and headed for the transport. I hadn't realized how long we'd been inside, but the sun was breaking above the horizon. Desrata all around us were tearing off their uniforms, rampaging wildly, and starting fires throughout the human buildings. The ongoing chant of *by Desrata, for Desrata* rang out like a battle cry. Father's words had not only saved our lives, they ignited a real-live revolution!

A couple more Desrata recognized Proditor and helped lead us out until we finally reached the edge of the settlement. The Atlantean kids kept walking while Bellana and I stopped.

"You go now," Proditor said.

I was actually going to miss the big guy.

"Don't forget to bring back your grimess," I said with a smile. "You earned it. Thank you, Proditor."

Bellana just stared up at him, amazed I was talking to him like a friend.

"Gratitude, huuu—" Proditor started to say but cut himself off. "Gratitude, Mmmaaarrrrccccuuusss."

He smiled, I think, and headed back to the melee. All the human buildings were ablaze in one big smoky bonfire.

We hustled to catch up to the others at the transport. The Atlantean kids scrambled into the water tanks while I helped Bellana to a seat in the cab. Her shoulder had stopped bleeding but was still causing her a lot of pain. I had no intention of taking the big weapons. It'd take twenty minutes to tie them up and we needed to take off as quickly as possible. I sat down in the other seat, fired up the transport, and got it moving.

"Are you going to be okay until we get to Spartanica?" I asked Bellana.

"I'll be fine," she replied. "Really. A nice quiet ride home will actually be nice."

She rested her head against the inside of the transport and closed her eyes.

"Thank you for getting me out of there, brother," she said.

I nodded and grinned, feeling relieved for the first time in a long while. *Bellana was back!*

"I have to talk to you about something," I said abruptly.

"What?" she asked. "Did Ty and Anina get married while I was gone?"

"No," I said. "Seriously. When I spoke to Father in a projection, he told me we had to leave here and go back to where Ty and I have been living."

She opened her eyes, lifted her head, and glared at me.

"You're leaving?" she asked in disbelief. "You're going to leave?"

"Father said *we* have to leave," I explained. "He said there's an evil growing here, on Sapertys, and that *we* should *all* leave before it has the chance to kill us. All of us. Ty, me . . . and you."

"*Me?*" she yelled incredulously. "Father said *I* should leave *here?*"

One of the water tank covers slammed open behind us and someone yelled incoherently. Bellana glanced back and gasped.

"Oh, come on," she pleaded. "Will you just leave us ALONE!"

"What?" I asked. "What is it?"

"Sphaeras," she said. "Looks like three of them. Coming right at us."

I looked back and, sure enough, there they were.

"More hamster balls?" I yelled in pure frustration. "You CANNOT be serious!"

"Can this thing go any faster?" she asked.

"Not much!" I yelled back. "Hey, look over there."

I pointed to our left at a rocky area in the distance.

"Let's take 'em in there," I said.

"Have you ever been in there before?" she asked.

"No!" I replied sarcastically. "I didn't *exactly* grow up here!"

"And that's *exactly* my point," she implored. "We don't even know if there's a way out!"

"No," I said, "but we do know the sphaeras will catch us in about thirty seconds unless we do something!"

"Thirty what?" she gasped.

"Ah, jeez," I lamented, "half a protoka!"

I turned the transport hard toward our only hope of losing our pursuers. As we got closer, a narrow valley came into view between two tall, mostly stone hills.

"There!" I pointed.

While our destination was definitely rocky, grassy mounds and trees also dotted the landscape.

"Here we go!" I said as we approached the opening. "Hold on!"

We hit the mouth of the valley going full speed. The very uneven ground bounced the transport around like an airplane in really bad turbulence. I couldn't tell which was louder, the tops of the water tanks flapping all over, or the Atlantean kids flying around and screaming inside.

"Sorry!" I yelled, looking back over my shoulder, doubting they could hear me.

"Watch where you're going!" Bellana urged as the valley curved hard to the left.

I turned to match it, but the transport didn't exactly handle like a Ferrari. The back end swung up on an incline and, for a split second, I thought we were going to flip over, but it slid harmlessly back down. The sphaeras were bouncing all over the place like beach balls, but they hadn't slowed one bit!

"Over there!" Bellana insisted, pointing at a narrow passageway coming up on the right.

Two sphaeras were side by side, right on our tail. I eased the transport ever-so-slightly toward the opening, trying to disguise our plan.

"They're going to hit us!" Bellana said fretfully.

I turned the transport hard and we slid almost sideways through the passageway, then I gunned it as soon as we were clear. The sphaera on our right scraped through the opening but the other one slammed into the orange stony overhang, became visible, and shattered into a million pieces.

"Ha!" I yelled exuberantly, but our victory was short lived.

The other sphaera smacked into our back end as we drove onto a wide-open, grassy clearing.

"Hold on!" I screamed, turning hard to the right and slamming on the brakes. "Aaaaahhhhhhhhh!"

Bellana grabbed onto her seat to keep from flying across the cab. The sphaera went whizzing by, unable to react in time to stay with us but immediately started turning in a big circle to come back. I fired the transport back up to full speed and headed across the clearing. Just when I thought we might put some distance between us, the third sphaera came bouncing into sight. I headed for the only other way out of the clearing, which took us up at a steep grade that slowed the transport to a fast crawl. The slope had a high rocky precipice on the left side but literally dropped off over a cliff on the right. The path forward narrowed as we climbed, to the point where the transport hovered precariously over the edge a little.

"Hey," Bellana cautioned, looking perilously out her door over the ledge. "You know we're hanging over, right? It's a long way down!"

I wanted to stop but both remaining sphaeras hit the bottom of the incline side-by-side at full speed, bouncing off each other, and kept coming right at us. The one on the left scraped up against the rock wall, leaving pieces of it behind as it became fully visible.

Our transport came to a full stop, unable to make any further progress against the incline.

"There's nowhere to go!" I yelled and looked at Bellana. "We're stuck!"

Both sphaeras were about to roll over the top of us when the one on the left stopped cold. The other one kept coming, right up until it ran out of path and launched over the cliff, passing within inches of us on the way down. It landed with a resounding explosion somewhere below.

My door was blocked by the cliff face. We couldn't go forward, and the remaining sphaera, less than twenty feet behind us, blocked the way down. All it had to do was open fire and we'd all be dead. To think we started out with all those rifles, draiders, and lofters, yet there we sat, utterly defenseless.

The tops of the water tanks opened as the Atlantean kids popped up and gazed out the back. Bellana and I sat motionless, waiting for something to happen.

"Maybe they got killed inside," Yra shrugged his shoulders and said.

A loud hissing sound, like air being let out of a dozen high-pressure semi-truck tires at the same time, suddenly erupted from the damaged, yet still glimmering, sphere. A hatch on top slowly flipped up, and a human soldier wearing a glistening silver helmet poked his head out.

"I got this," I said and punched a hole in the cab ceiling, intending to tear open a new door.

"Wait," Bellana said, squinting at the soldier. "I know that guy."

"You know that guy?" I asked in disbelief.

She turned toward the front of the cab and used her left hand to almost effortlessly pop out the windshield. I wished I'd thought of that.

"He helped me earlier," she explained.

She gestured for me to climb out the newly gaping hole in front of her.

"You go first," she said.

I climbed through, up onto the cab roof, and pulled her out by her left hand, but by the time we looked back again, the hatch was closed and the sphaera was rolling slowly down the incline.

"Wait!" Bellana yelled, but it reached level ground and took off.

"That soldier was on our side," Naetth said. "Did you see him run the other one off the ledge? That was amazing!"

We watched in silence as it rolled away through the opening at the other end of the clearing and disappeared.

"Can we please go back to Spartanica now?" an exhausted-looking Anina asked after a few seconds.

Everyone in the tanks plopped back down, looking equally drained. I dropped back into the cab and helped Bellana in. The transport eased back to ground level ever so gently and we headed back to the desert.

FORTY-NINE

PEAK MAJSTICE

(TY)

"You and my mother worked on some really incredible stuff," I said to the professor as he crouched behind the hyperporter controller to repair it.

"What is science, my boy, without creativity?" he exhorted. "Science demands a hunger to seek out and find that which has not yet been found or does not yet exist."

"What's the craziest experiment you ever worked on?" I asked.

"Hmmmm, yes, well, indeed, we were hardly the *crazy* types," he said. "But, yes, now, that's a tough one. Certainly the gateway would have to be the boldest concept we ever made functional. We did dedicate some thought energy to time curling, but never quite reached beyond the hypothesis stage. You see, my boy, when left to its own devices, time always moves in a straight line. We hypothesized that, with sufficient, highly focused majinecity, that straight line could be curled back to a previous time. Your mother fiddled with it from time to time over the annos and even balanced all the equations, but we never took the opportunity to fully realize it. Always some other priority, I'm afraid, not to mention all the implications around altering an existing timeline."

"Mother figured out time travel?" I asked in pure amazement.

"Time curling, actually," he said, standing up, "but yes. Ah, that's it. Some quick testing and we'll get you on your way. Oh, and my boy, you will undoubtedly be accosted again by a sentry once you reach the complex. As soon as one approaches, simply say *override Otherblood activate 110736* to terminate system lock. While they can be pesky, they are also quite obedient. Command it to take you where you were originally found. That's where the gateway will open again. It doesn't matter which sentry you talk to. They're centrally controlled. What one experiences, they all remember."

"Okay, Professor," I said. "You're sure the three of us can go through the gateway at the same time?"

"Oh, yes, yes, yes," he confirmed. "I refined our early assumptions and algorithms quite extensively. Three adults should pass through without an issue during a normal majstice. I wish we would have known back then. We would've sent all three of you kids at the same time. It's still safest to go individually, but in a pinch, do as you must."

"We'll get us all out of here this time, Professor," I said, "thanks to you."

He stopped for a second and smiled gratefully before going back to his testing.

"So you're coming through as soon as possible, right?" I asked Nekitys, who'd been watching Professor Otherblood fix the hyperporter with me. "Marcus, Bellana, and I will probably be gone but the Atlantean kids will need your help."

Nekitys nodded, deep in thought about something.

"And Professor," I continued, "they'll definitely need your help."

"Of course, my boy, of course," he said. "Come now. It's time for you to depart. You'll have roughly two oras until peak majstice. Once activated, the gateway should remain open for ten protokas or so, during which you can step back through to the other world."

"Only two oras?" I protested. "Man . . . I have to get to the city and find Marcus and Bellana first. Then we'll have to get back to the complex. This is going to be really tight."

Nekitys pulled a bandage out of each ear.

"Here, take these," he said.

"Yuck!" I responded, recoiling. "I don't think so!"

"They're remote talkers," he explained. "You can use this one to contact Marcus. This one connects with Kinnard. Put one in each ear. Touch it once to activate it, again to turn it off. We didn't give you one before because of the whole projector thing. They haven't actually worked yet, but I think we've been too far away. You'll be much closer to them once you're there."

"Let me see those," the professor said, scrutinizing them closely. "Yes, yes, these are short-range talkers. They should work splendidly for your purposes there. Now, let's move along, quickly."

I smushed Marcus' talker onto my right ear, Kinnard's onto my left, and reached out to shake the professor's hand.

"Thank you, Professor," I said.

He looked at my hand as if I'd made a rude gesture and placed his hands on my shoulders.

"My boy," he said, "your mother said something to you and your brother when you went through the first time, and now you should hear it again. *Be safe and live a happy life, my sons. Use the gifts you've been given to help make your world a better place. Be creative. Be strong. We love you more than any words*

362

can ever express. We are always with you, and you are always with us."

It took everything I had not to get emotional. There wasn't time for a walk down forgotten memories lane. We needed to get home.

I stepped into the hyperporter, holding back tears. Except for the dream I'd had in the jungle, I didn't remember my parents, but I somehow missed them terribly right at that moment.

The professor did something on the control panel and looked back over at me.

"Bye, Ty," I heard Nekitys say right before a bright light flashed.

I opened my eyes to a mostly dark room with a faint Spartanica symbol outlined on the floor in front of me. It worked! I was back in the complex.

I stepped out of the hyperporter.

"Recognize, Tymaeus of the Order of Bellator," I commanded.

"Recognized," SMILEy responded.

If SMILEy was human, I would've hugged him. It was so reassuring to hear his voice again.

"Illumination on," I said, and the room lit up.

It definitely wasn't the room Marcus and I had first come into. It looked a lot like the professor's place in Petras except there was no equipment other than the hyperporter. A voice came from the doorway behind me.

"Prepare for facial recognition scan," a remote sentry said and immediately shot a bright white light into my eyes.

I stood with my eyes closed until the scan completed.

"Identification confirmed," she said.

"Override Otherblood 110736," I ordered.

"Invalid system lock override command," she responded. "Weapons arming."

She extended her right arm directly at me in what had to be my scariest bout of déjà vu ever!

"Override Otherblood . . . ." I started but paused to think momentarily.

"Override denied," she said. "Weapons armed and locked on. Warning, it is prohibited to initiate system lock override without a valid command. Any further failures will result in severe negative personal consequences."

So I had one more chance to get it right or what? Die?

I knew the number part had to be right because there was a 7-11 store at 1107 Powers Rd. near my house. The middle number between eleven and seven is nine and eleven minus seven equals four. Multiplying nine times four gives 36. The number had to be 110736! What was I doing wrong? I thought long and hard before realizing my mistake.

"Override Otherblood . . . *activate* 110736," I said and waited to be vaporized.

The sentry stood silent for a couple very long seconds and finally lowered her arm.

"Normal complex operations restored," she confirmed.

Alas! I wasn't going to die! The lights in surrounding rooms came on.

"Good day," the sentry said in a very welcoming tone. "How may I be of service?"

With one little command, she had gone from being an unyielding death merchant to my personal butler!

"Um," I said, "take me to the exit I left through last time."

"By your command," she responded. "Follow me, please."

She turned and headed out of the room. We didn't walk very far before the door with the Spartanica symbol came into view.

"Wait," I said, "these walls move, don't they?"

"Yes," the sentry responded. "They are designed to gently encourage an unwelcome visitor to exit the complex expeditiously."

"Yeah, well, let me tell ya from firsthand experience," I said, "they work pretty well."

The sentry obviously didn't get sarcasm. She just stood motionless.

"Please open the door," I requested.

"By your command," she repeated, and the Spartanica symbol dropped to expose the exit we'd gone through last time.

"Okay, leave the door open, please," I said.

"By your command," she responded again.

"Uh, yeah. I guess," I said, chuckling a little.

I walked out of the complex and touched Marcus' talker in my ear. It beeped.

"Marcus?" I said but heard nothing back. "Marcus?"

I totally expected to just turn the talker on and start talking to him.

"Marcus!" I tried again.

Still not a peep. The silence was terrifying. For the first time since they'd left, it dawned on me they might not make it back. What if the 'rats had caught them? What if the 'rats had killed them? I might be the only Sapertyn kid left.

"Marcus!"

At the same time, for all I knew, the talker thing might not even work. The others would never know where to find me. My only choice was to get to the city and find them. I hoped they'd be there. They *had* to be there!

I couldn't go home alone!

I jogged most of the way back toward the city, stopping on top of the sand dune just outside to catch my breath. I'd been trying Marcus' talker every so often but was starting to think it was completely useless. It just beeped at me every time I tried to use it. I decided to give it one last try before heading to the armory.

"Marcus?"

Nothing.

"Marcus?"

"Nekitys?" a faint, distant voice yelled from the other end. "Hey! Where have you guys been? Is Ty okay?"

It was definitely Marcus! They were alive!

"Hey," I yelled, "it's me!"

"What?" Marcus asked. "I know it's you. Who else would it be?"

"No, it's me!" I reiterated. "I mean, it's Ty!"

"Ty!" Marcus replied. "Where's Nekitys?"

"It's a long story," I said, "I'll tell you later. Is everybody okay?"

"Yeah, mostly," he answered.

I didn't like the sound of that.

"Anyway," I continued, "remember the complex? That place we first came into Sapertys? The place by where we first saw the moons? The place where—"

"Yes, Ty," Marcus interrupted, sounding exasperated. "I remember the complex. What about it?"

"That's where you need to go right away," I said. "We have to be at the same spot where we came through when peak majstice starts."

"How are we going to get in?" Marcus asked. "We couldn't even find the door last time!"

"Don't worry," I said, "I figured it all out. The door is already open and a sentry is waiting to show us where to go."

"No way!" Marcus exclaimed. "Seriously? Awesome! So now I just have to find it. Everything out here looks the same. Wait, we're coming back into

Spartanica the same way you and I first came in, by the shortest cupola tower. The complex should be somewhere on the left up ahead. I think I can at least find the cliffs where we first saw the moons. If you can meet us there, we should be close to the entrance."

"How far away are you?" I asked. "I don't know how much time we have, but it's not much."

"I have no idea," Marcus said. "We've been driving forever. I don't think it can be much longer. That or we're totally lost."

"Okay," I said. "Keep this radio on. I have to run back to the complex."

"But I thought you—" he started to say but cut out.

"Marcus?" I said. "Marcus?"

There was no response.

I tried to reactivate the talker but it beeped three times before I could say anything. It wasn't working again. I had to wonder why people smart enough to do all this amazing stuff just with magnetism wouldn't have better walkie-talkies or cell phones or something.

I made it back to the complex entrance and down to where Marcus and I first saw Primus and Beta. The talker still did nothing but beep. I hoped that didn't mean those guys were getting further away. If they were headed in the wrong direction, we'd definitely miss the gateway opening, and I wasn't going home unless we all went.

I slid my rifle off to let my arm breathe a little and looked into the distance on the off chance I'd spot the others heading my way. My legs wobbled a little as I wasn't used to all the running. Being sweaty always made me itchy and smelly, and I hated both. What I hated even more was taking showers, and getting sweaty meant I had to take one more often, although I had to admit the reinigens were pretty cool. I'd probably be more athletic if I lived in Spartanica just because of the reinigens. Heck, I'd even start liking gym class! Well, not really.

A searing pain suddenly bolted through my skull like a freight train, forcing me involuntarily against the cliff face behind me where I slowly slid to the ground. The static and lightning flashes I'd seen before my first projection were back, and I found myself forced to look at the red-faced woman once again.

"It was the animals, my Nobilis," she said. "We turned the prisoners over and they let them go."

"What?" the same man I'd projected through before howled. "Why would the animals just let them go, Crivera?"

"Because, my Nobilis," Crivera answered, "Forticus appeared out of nowhere and convinced them Elisii was nothing but a trick to control them."

"Forticus?" the man bellowed. "That's not possible! Forticus has been locked in the depths of Xxenebrae, alone, for annos! He can't even attempt to escape without destroying himself!"

"My Nobilis," Crivera responded. "I knew Forticus long before his rise to power. We were close. I know it was him."

Crivera's last statement was more horrifying than anything else I'd seen on Sapertys. She and Father had been close? She could have been my mother?

"He was much older than I remember," she continued, "but it was him. He somehow willed his essence into the Great Hall and spoke of the history between Spartanica and the animals. He convinced them Elisii is a fable, a falsehood, and that our alliance was a sham. Then, in the blink of an eye, he was gone, but the damage had been done. Thousands of animals revolted. We barely escaped with our lives."

"So my dear friend Forticus has managed to thwart me again, for the moment," the man said. "You will return here immediately, Crivera."

"By your will, my Nobilis," she responded.

"You may go," he said. "Let me talk to the boy."

Crivera stepped away and a new face appeared. A familiar face. A face I did not expect to see, not like this.

"Kinnard, my liegeman," the man said, "do you agree with Crivera's account?"

KINNARD?

"Yes, my Nobilis," Kinnard said, "it is as she has stated. I led them all back to the settlement, including the Guelphic girl and her brother, so that we could take the city. Everything went as planned until Forticus appeared."

Kinnard was a spy? The whole time? Their escape from the settlement and coming to Spartanica was all part of an elaborate plan to take over the city?

"I understand, my liegeman," the man said, sounding angry. "This is quite a disappointing failure."

"Yes, my Nobilis," Kinnard replied. "I wish I could have done more."

"You still believe in our vision, do you, my liegeman?" the man asked.

"With all my heart and soul, my Nobilis," Kinnard replied.

"Do not despair," the man said. "This is but a minor setback. When you return, we will discuss moving forward with the next phase of our plan. Soon all the cities and their people will be restored under our rule."

"Yes, my Nobilis," Kinnard said.

"There is one request I have of you," the man said.

"By your will, my Nobilis."

"Crivera will depart with you to return here," the man explained. "She shall, however, not survive the journey. Can I count on you to make sure of that?"

He wanted Kinnard to kill Crivera! Kinnard looked as stunned as I felt.

"My liegeman?" the man prompted after a few seconds of silence.

"Of course, my Nobilis," Kinnard responded. "By your will."

Not only was Kinnard a traitor, he was a murderer, too.

"Safe travels, my liegeman," the man said.

My projection went dark. I blinked my eyes and was back outside the complex.

"Ty! Ty!" I heard screaming in my ear.

"Marcus?" I yelled, still fighting the dizziness that always seemed to accompany my projections. "Hey, I'm right here. Stop screaming!"

"I think I see the very top of a cupola tower and rocky cliffs ahead on the left," he said. "I think we're close. Can you see us?"

Looking into the distance, I saw a tiny black dot that I didn't remember being there before.

"I see you! I see you!" I announced ecstatically. "Keep coming to your left!"

It was starting to look like we might actually get home. I waved my hands over my head as the transport approached so Marcus would know where to go. They finally lumbered up and stopped.

"Jeez, what happened to the transport?" I asked. "It looks like you've been driving into rock piles again."

Marcus ignored me, ran to the other side of the transport, and helped Bellana out. Her shirt was all bloody on the right side.

"Bellana!" I gasped. "What the heck happened?"

"It's not as bad as it looks," Bellana said, glancing up at the complex entrance. "What is this place? Are we back in the city?"

The Atlantean kids clambered out of the water tanks.

"Hi, Ty!" Iryni said and ran up to give me a hug.

I hugged her back. It was a tremendous relief to see everybody. Everybody except Kinnard, of course.

"Hi," I said, "I'm so glad you're okay."

"Oh, it was terrible," she explained, "but your father saved us."

"Yeah, I heard," I said.

Marcus looked back at me in disbelief as he helped Bellana into the complex.

"Where's Nekitys?" Marcus asked.

"He'll be here later," I answered. "It's a long story."

"Can we help?" Anina asked.

"No," Marcus yelled from inside. "Just wait here a bit."

I stepped back into the complex and caught up to Marcus and Bellana.

"Did we make it in time?" Marcus asked.

"Sentry, has peak majstice started?" I asked.

"Affirmative," she replied. "Peak majstice was achieved seven protokas prior."

"Shoot!" I yelled. "We only have three minutes! Sentry, take us to where we discussed before!"

"By your command," she replied and started walking.

"What is this place?" Bellana asked, still groggy.

"It's Professor Otherblood's old studium outside the city," I explained.

A brilliantly bright white light and a thunderous hum emanated from a room ahead of us. It had to be the gateway.

"Run!" I blurted, hustling past the sentry down the hall and into the room.

Marcus and Bellana hobbled in behind me. I had to get right up next to Marcus' ear to make sure he'd hear me over the raging commotion coming from the gateway.

"Professor Otherblood said we could go together but it'd be better to go one at a time," I yelled.

"Okay," Marcus shouted back into my ear. "I'll have to help Bellana through. You go first."

Bellana suddenly snapped to, jerked away from Marcus, and took several steps back.

"What is that?" she mouthed, turning slightly with startled trepidation as she hastily raised her hands to shield her eyes.

She had probably said the words but there was no way I could hear her over the roaring gateway.

"Ty, go!" Marcus hollered, motioning frantically at the intensely blazing portal with his left hand. "Go! Go!"

The Atlantean kids suddenly came around the corner and bunched up in the doorway behind Marcus and Bellana. Iryni caught my eye with a perplexed look on her face. I really didn't need to see her right at that moment. I'd read about *heartstrings* before in books, but now I knew the sorrow of having mine tugged.

"Go!" Marcus screamed inaudibly.

I tore my eyes from Iryni's unwavering gaze, turned, and stepped into the gateway.

FIFTY

WHERE DID YOU GET
THOSE CLOTHES?

(TY)

So there I was, back in my nice warm bed. My alarm clock read 1:44 a.m. It had taken six times longer to think through the longest dream of my life than it had to actually dream it. Just recalling all the details wore me out. I pulled up my comforter and drifted off, hoping to actually get some rest.

Per usual, I woke up at 6:50 a.m., right on the nose. I didn't need no stinkin' alarm! It was time to get rolling, and I was famished! I headed downstairs to get breakfast. Soft hues of dawning sunlight gently lit my path to the kitchen. I'd always enjoyed the relative calm of the early morning and rarely turned the lights on until Marcus or Aunt Andi came down. I sat down and helped myself to a generous bowl of cereal in the early morning serenity.

"Ty?" Aunt Andi called from upstairs. "Ty, sweetie?"

"Yeah, Aunt Andi," I responded, "I'm in the kitchen."

"Is Marcus down there?" she asked.

"No," I said. "I think I'm the first one up."

"Well, he's not in bed," she yelled. "Marcus?"

I ran upstairs to see what was going on. Sure enough, Marcus' bed covers were thrown back, but he wasn't there.

"What happened to you?" she asked, her eyes scanning me from head to toe.

Her gaze locked onto the left side of my chest. She gasped, noticeably shaken.

"Where did you get those clothes?" she asked.

I glanced down expecting to be in my pajamas, but I wasn't. Aunt Andi had spotted the Spartanica symbol on the dirty, stinky uniform Nekitys had given me before we left the city in my dream. In my dream? It wasn't a dream? It really happened?

Aunt Andi grabbed me by the shoulders and looked me square in the eyes.

"What is going on?" she asked. "You need to tell me exactly what happened!"

I barely heard what she said. If all that stuff had been real—the gateway, the cupola, SMILEy, majinecity, lofters, draiders, Desrata, the Guelphic Varkis, the Atlantean kids, Professor Otherblood—if all of that was real, there was only one question that needed to be answered. Only one thing mattered.

Where were Marcus . . . *and . . . Bellana?*

###

Now that you've finished Spartanica, please consider writing an online review!

Reviews are the best way for authors to understand what readers liked about a story. They also help other readers discover great new books.

I would truly appreciate your feedback.

So would Ty, Marcus, Bellana, and the other Survivors.

Until next time, fellow Sapertyns . . . .

POWERS MOLINAR

is a project manager by day and sci-fi fanatic by night.
He and his family live under the cupola near Chicago.
Spartanica is Powers' debut novel.

Stay Connected Online:

Website/Blog: http://www.powersmolinar.com

Twitter: http://www.twitter.com/powersmolinar

Facebook: http://www.facebook.com/spartanica

Made in the USA
Lexington, KY
29 July 2014